By Dean Hovey

Amazon Print 9780228612865
LSI/Ingram Print 9780228612872
B&N Print 9780228612889

BWL Publishing Inc.

Books we love to write...
Authors around the world.

http://bwlpublishing.ca

Copyright 2019 by Dean Hovey
Cover Art Michelle Lee

All rights reserved. Without limiting the rights under copyright reserved above, no part of this publication may be reproduced, stored in or introduced into a retrieval system, or transmitted in any form, or by any means (electronic, mechanical, photocopying, recording, or otherwise) without the prior written permission of both the copyright owner and the above publisher of this book.

Acknowledgments and thanks to:

Jude Pittman and Gail Branan at BWL. The book is better because of you.

National Park Service Ranger Steven Rossi who provided background on Walnut Canyon National Monument, the Flagstaff National Park Service office, and a ranger's off-duty life in Flagstaff.

Pat Morris, my friend and fact checker.

Larry Hawes, Dan Fouts, Natalie Lund, and Anne Flagge proofread, commented, and suggested improvements.

Fran Brozo helped with the anthropology, archaeology, natural history, and Arizona culture.

Dennis Arnold made sure the cop stuff is correct. He passed away before this book was completed. I miss him and his input.

Julie, my wife, lets me know when the characters need development and with medical details.

To the many readers of my Minnesota-based mysteries, I promise there will be more Pine County mysteries. Please forgive me for using this new setting. Walnut Canyon is a perfect location for a mystery.

This book is a work of fiction. The people and events are creations of the author's imagination. Most locations are fictional. Actual locations are used fictionally.

"Over 3,000 (migrants) have died in the Arizona desert since January 1999"
humaneborders.org

Prologue

Terry Mahoney's shaved head was covered with a sheen of sweat from the morning Phoenix heat. He walked into Steven Potter's office, closed the door, then slouched in a wooden guest chair across from Potter's antique pine desk.

"We need to talk about our partnership."

"Yes, we do. We can't ship the crap you've been acquiring to my customers. I've spent twenty-five years cultivating a well-respected business. Your stupidity is ruining my reputation and putting my whole business at risk."

"Listen Potter, you're making more money than you've ever seen in your life, and you haven't had to lift a finger. How is that a problem?"

Steve threw his hands up in exasperation. "I've done some research. You've been running scams across the Southwest for years, then ducking out before the house of cards collapses. You don't grasp the value of a long-term business reputation. The only reason your current scam is working is because you're putting my letterhead on your bills. As soon as my customers get wise, you'll be out of here and I'll be sitting with a worthless business, a storeroom full of inventory, and no one to buy it."

"Sell off your inventory now and retire."

"No! I've got a steady cash flow, I've got a mortgage, a business loan, a wife, an employee, and, if you go away, I've got another fifteen or twenty years of business. At the end of that, my loans will be paid off, I'll sell the business then, and I'll have a comfortable retirement."

"I'm not going away," Mahoney sat up in the chair and pulled out a pack of cigarettes.

"If you have to smoke, please take your filthy cigarettes outside."

Mahoney pulled out a lighter and lit the cigarette, blowing the first puff of smoke toward Potter's face. "You seem to think you're calling the shots."

"It's my damned business! Of course, I'm calling the shots!"

"You became the junior partner the day I put the first Potter Antiquities invoice into a box of illegal pottery and shipped it. You might've had a shot at stepping away if you'd torn up the first check I paid you, but you're into this up to your eyeballs and in the eyes of the law you're just as guilty as me." Mahoney pulled an Aztec bowl across Potter's desk and ground out his cigarette.

"Jesus!" Potter snatched the bowl away from Mahoney and carefully wiped the interior with a tissue.

"I guess you've got a couple options." Mahoney reveled in Potter's discomfort as he watched the bowl being set out of his reach. "We can go on as we are, knowing that at some point we'll both have to disappear or face prison time, or you can sell me the business and walk away now. I'll keep it going until I see the handwriting on the wall, and then I'll be gone."

"How will that work?" Potter asked. "What are you offering to pay? Are you going to assume the loans on the building and keep operating?"

"The loans must be in the name of the business, so I'll have my people make the payments."

"Maybe you'll make the payments until you skip town. When you stop paying the loans it all comes back to me because my name is registered as the owner."

"Just go away, Steve. You've got the money I've been paying you. Put a for sale sign on your house and disappear. Maybe you can hang around long enough to collect the equity out of your house, but I wouldn't wait too long. Go to California, outside the reach of the Arizona cops. If you're not comfortable with that, go further, to Chicago or Kansas City. Start a new life. Live off your cash."

"How does that help?" Potter asked. "In addition to the Mexican crap you've been passing off as antiques, I assume you've been buying antiquities recovered from Federal lands and shipping them across the United States and Canada with false papers. Those are Federal crimes!"

"So go to the Caribbean, Argentina, or Panama. Your money will last a long time anywhere in South America. Do your homework. Figure out which countries don't have extradition and get the hell out of here!"

"I can't just pack up like a thief and run." Potter ran his hand through his hair. "I'm an upstanding member of this community."

"You make it sound like you've got options, Steve. You don't. You're complicit in the crimes. You've benefited financially from the sales." Mahoney shook another cigarette from the pack. "My lawyer will have the sale papers ready for your signature in a couple days."

"Get out. Just go away." Potter walked to the door and held it open.

"I've got a couple guys working a new site. I think you should look at it." Mahoney said as he walked past. "They'll pick you up tomorrow morning."

"I'm not going anywhere with 'your guys.'"

"Hey, it's a legal dig on private land near Flagstaff. It'll put your mind at ease about the provenance of the stuff I'll be shipping until we close the sale."

When Mahoney left, Potter closed the door and dialed his wife. A recorder in his drawer started up when the phone started ringing. "Pack a bag. We'll be going away for a few days…"

Mahoney flashed a smile at Potter's assistant as he walked past her desk. He pulled out his cellphone as he walked to his car and pushed a speed dial number. A silky woman's voice answered.

"Tell the Stick Man Potter's not going to play ball. I told him we'd send a couple guys around tomorrow to show him a dig they're working on near Flagstaff. After they take care of Potter, I'll console the widow and make sure the business continues."

Chapter 1

The transaction was swift, hidden by the voices and jostling teens waiting for their burgers and fries. Tom Tsosie palmed the small envelope discreetly handed to him by a man wearing a nondescript gray t-shirt, jeans, cowboy boots, and dark glasses and left through the side door of the Flagstaff fast food emporium. He moved to a trendy coffee shop decorated with Wild West memorabilia further down the street. He sat on a stool at the counter's end under a dusty saddle that probably looked like something off a horse to most people but the broken stirrup and dried leather told Tom it was one of the pieces of junk rescued from his friend Jake's abandoned barn. Jake had told Tom he'd sold it to "decorators" hired by the out-of-town coffee-shop owners, and he'd been almost embarrassed to accept the hundred fifty dollars they'd paid him for the saddle. Spurred on by the saddle money, he'd sold rusty gold-panning pans and kerosene lanterns with cracked chimneys, all dug from the accumulated trash in a ravine behind his barn. The other half of the furnishings were abandoned crap the decorator had pulled out of ghost towns or ranches with collapsed barns.

"Coffee with cream," Tom said to the teenage waitress with black hair and a pierced eyebrow as she tried to move quickly past him. She gave him a look of mild disdain before turning to fill the order. He was unsure if her disdain was due to prejudice toward his Navajo features, or from the fact that his menu choice would only cost two dollars versus a pricier latte or mocha. On the other hand, Tom knew the owner was happy to have "a real Indian" giving the place a bit of Western panache.

When the waitress brought his coffee, he set five dollars on the counter and told her to keep the change. That brought a curious look, but neither a smile nor thanks.

After stirring a dollop of cream and a packet of sugar into his coffee, he casually scanned the room. Satisfied that no one was paying him undue attention, Tom tore open the envelope he'd slipped from his pants pocket. Three items fell onto the scarred wooden countertop: a note, a small black figurine, and a worn brass key.

Tom fingered the figurine for a second— Kokopelli, the symbol of mischief and fertility. Found in ancient Anasazi petroglyphs and in modern Zuni, Hopi, and Navajo art, the hump-backed, flute-playing figure was known throughout Southwest mythology. Modern single women shied away from the figure because of its fertility connection, mythical or not. Others just avoided the symbolism of mischief, which usually meant that someone was about to fall upon bad luck. This figurine particularly was part of someone's bad luck.

The small key was attached to a plastic tag with a logo from one of the many companies offering tourists backcountry Jeep rides. He knew it was for one of the small lockers offered by the outfitter to store purses and other bags, which saved space in the Jeeps for paying riders. The tag was for locker B13 and Tom knew his payoff would be in that locker once the job was completed.

He slipped the key and figurine back into his pocket and read the message. All his jobs were illegal and some troubled him. Others were just busywork that involved minimal risk, usually in the dark, and often many miles away from the nearest human. This message, however, was very direct and very troublesome. "Steven Potter has become a problem. Walnut Canyon is the answer."

Tom tore the note into tiny scraps and stuffed them into the empty sugar packet. He drank the remnants of his coffee and pondered what he'd need for the job. The prime requirement was a car that could be wiped clean and dumped after the job was done. The other was convincing Elmer the reward justified the risk. At least it was summer; not many people would be at Walnut Canyon during the heat of the day. Or so he told himself, anyway.

Chapter 2

We were up at 7:00 a.m., Mountain Standard Time, which meant that my cousin El and her husband Todd had slept in until 9:00 a.m. Central Daylight Time. The state of Arizona doesn't change to Daylight Saving Time, which always makes it difficult for me to figure out how many hours Flagstaff's time is different from everywhere else.

I set a carton of skim milk next to a bag of bulk granola cereal that looked healthy in the bin at Whole Foods. It was my best attempt at impressing my cousins with my new low-fat diet and it meant I had to forgo my usual fried eggs and bacon with a side of toast dripping butter.

By the time my visitors made it to the kitchen, coffee was gurgling into the carafe. Both El and Todd were dressed in jogging clothes and carried their Nikes. Despite repeated encouragement, they couldn't allow themselves to wear their shoes inside my townhouse. They were setting out for a morning run while I was munching on what tasted like honey-covered horse feed with skim milk.

"Do you want to go running with us, Doug?" El asked while tying her shoelaces.

I slid the half-gallon of milk back into the refrigerator. "I haven't run in years. But I'll walk with you down to the trailhead by the golf course."

El gave my slight paunch a furtive glance, a reminder that I had not retained the physique I'd had when I came home from Iraq. But I didn't feel guilty enough to run . . . and wouldn't unless someone wielding a gun was chasing me.

Five minutes later I slipped quarters into the newspaper vending machine as El and Todd jogged down the pine bark covered path. The trail skirted the golf course and was usually inhabited by a few deer and raccoons. I walked the quarter mile back to my townhouse, feeling a bit proud of my half-mile walk, and read the paper over fresh coffee.

They were back, sweaty and hot, in about half an hour.

"Great trail, Doug," El said. "We spooked a deer and saw a couple of jays pecking at a road-kill rabbit. Beautiful golf course too, but there was hardly anyone playing."

I folded the paper and set it on the table. "It's too hot. The locals prefer to golf in the spring and fall. We leave it for the tourists during the summer."

I found two matching SPPD mugs in the cupboard and poured coffee. They were one of the few items left from my years as a St. Paul cop. They'd survived the move so I kept them. El disappeared into the guest bathroom with her cup and Todd plopped down at the table with a towel draped around his neck. He opened the front section of the paper and sipped from the steaming mug.

"It's really nice of you to host us. El said you were the closest of her cousins, like a big brother. Her mother took her to one of your high school football games when she was in grade school. You intercepted a pass and returned it for a touchdown. She was really impressed because the whole stadium stood up and cheered for you. I think she had a crush on you."

"She caught the highlight of my football career. I dropped so many passes that the coach made me carry a deflated football to all my classes one day."

"You gave her the incentive to start running and join the track team. Did you know she still holds the school record for girls' hundred-yard dash?"

"No, I didn't know that. By the time she was in high school I was a cop, and with all the rotating shifts I didn't make it to many family events. Then I went to Iraq, I got married, and drifted even further from the family. I knew she was a runner, but I didn't realize how successful she'd been."

"Didn't you used to run? I mean, all cops have to stay in shape." Todd sipped his coffee and waited for my answer as he flipped through the pages of the paper. Fitness people can't understand the average guy who doesn't like to get sweated up every morning before breakfast, but it was a second reminder about the stomach protruding over my belt.

"I can't anymore. That's why I got a medical pension from the St. Paul Police." I topped off my coffee and sat down. "Do you remember that burglary suspect I ran down about a year before I retired?"

Todd nodded his head. "Vaguely." The expression on his face said he really didn't.

"He kicked me in the knee. At the time I felt something pop. I thought he'd broken my leg. We struggled around on the ground until my partner caught up and pinned him. I couldn't walk, so they took me to the hospital in an ambulance. X-rays showed it wasn't broken, but an MRI showed the posterior cruciate ligament was torn. Three orthopedic surgeons looked at it, but only one had ever done a PCL repair on anyone but a professional athlete, and since the tear wasn't complete and my knee could be kept stable with regular exercise, he recommended against surgery."

Todd frowned. "But they do lots of PCL repairs on football players."

"Yeah, but they only have a twenty-five percent success rate and that's after a year of intensive therapy. The doctor and I discussed my situation and he suggested that if I was willing to give up contact sports plus softball, tennis, skiing, and basketball, I'd be fine as long as I kept my quads in shape to stabilize the knee. The department was nervous about it, and I was going to be steered into a job in IT. I just couldn't see myself as a techie desk jockey, so I met with a tax accountant who convinced me I could live on the medical pension that amounts to sixty percent of my police salary and the investments left after the divorce."

Todd pointed to an article on the front page, a signal that he was bored listening to me talk about me. "This says the border patrol is running intensive patrols in an effort to crack down on illegal aliens. I thought that was more of an issue in California and Texas."

"It's not an issue here in Flagstaff. Most of them get caught in southern Arizona or get a ride north. There may be a few here working as casual laborers, but not many."

"Arizona doesn't have the drug cartels working across the border like Texas?" Todd asked.

"I'm sure drugs are coming across the border here, too. In 2006, the U.S. made it hard to get the raw ingredients for meth by putting the decongestants behind pharmacy counters and limiting the quantity each patient can purchase. Mexican meth has flourished because decongestants aren't regulated there and enforcement of meth operations is lax because the cops are afraid of, or paid off by, the cartels."

El emerged from the bathroom with her hair wrapped in a towel. She was wearing a pair of boxer shorts below her Mickey Mouse t-shirt. She toweled her hair dry and smiled. "I feel just a little queasy and it's hard to catch my breath. What's the altitude here?"

"Flagstaff is about 6,500 feet," I replied. "You're used to a thousand feet in the Twin Cities. It'll take you about a week to fully adjust. Your being in shape helps with the transition. On the other hand, if you keep running here, you'll blow them away in the Twin Cites Marathon." El grinned and flexed her biceps.

"What possessed you guys to come here during the summer anyway? Most Minnesotans come to Arizona to escape from winter."

El cocked her head. "You've been begging us to visit since you left St. Paul. Now you don't want us?" She put on her best fake pout.

"It's not that I don't want you. But people usually avoid Arizona summers."

Todd set aside a newspaper section. "I've always wanted to see the Grand Canyon and it's cold and snowy a lot of times in the winter. We discussed it and decided your offer of hospitality was too good to pass up." He gestured toward the pile of brochures El had stacked on the table.

"We had no clue there was so much to see here," El finished off the carafe of coffee, then spread one of the tri-fold brochures atop the table. "When Mom and Dad hear about all the things there are to do here, I'll bet they make a reservation for your spare bedroom, too."

"How are they doing?"

"They still spend the summers at their lake house and winters in their Fort Myers condo. They're never home and impossible to nail down for events. I guess you'd say they're enjoying retirement."

"I'm happy for them. Your family was like the Cleavers on Leave It To Beaver. Everyone was always smiling and polite." I got up and started another pot of coffee.

"Now that you mention it, there always seemed to be a lot of drama at your house. Your mom and dad used to get into fights over the stupidest things. Like the time Uncle Bob thought he was eating slices of sausage until Aunt Betty told him it was head cheese. He could've quietly spit it into his napkin, but instead he started sputtering and gagging." El's expression softened. "How long has it been since your dad passed away?"

"Over twenty years now. It was really hard on Mom for a couple years, but now she seems to have a new life with new friends and she's on the go all the time. We used to talk Sunday evenings, but that doesn't happen much anymore."

"Say!" Todd put a finger into the air. "Maybe your mother can come down with El's parents when they visit."

I'd just taken a sip of coffee and Todd's comments sent it down my trachea instead of my esophagus. I started coughing and spit coffee all over the newspaper.

"More drama." El shook her head.

"No! I swallowed wrong!"

"You could've just said that you'd prefer to have your mother visit separately so you could have some quality time alone together."

"No, no. That's not it at all. I choked," I said between coughing fits. "I'm just not sure Mom would be happy here."

"She wouldn't be happy here, or you wouldn't be happy with her here?" El asked.

"Some of each. She lost her mental filter when Dad died. Now she likes to critique my life. I've made peace with my decisions and I don't need her dredging up painful old memories or criticizing the path I've chosen."

Todd wisely grabbed the pile of brochures and spread the biggest one on the table. "Here are all the locations we've considered visiting."

"I thought we'd start with Walnut Canyon National Monument," I suggested as I cleaned up coffee spray. "It's spectacular, and it's familiar territory where I can be a knowledgeable tour guide." In fact, I'd taken a job as a seasonal ranger for the Flagstaff area attractions including Walnut Canyon, Sunset Canyon, and the Wupatki Grasslands. The entire contingent of rangers and staff for the Flagstaff Park Service office amounted to nine full-time people. The rangers conducted educational programs and tried to keep the tourists from hurting themselves. In four years, the biggest emergency I'd encountered was a search for a guy when we found his pickup abandoned in the parking lot after closing. We called in every ranger and searched for him half the night thinking he was lying injured on a trail. He showed up the next morning with jumper cables for his dead battery just as we were going to call in helicopters for aerial searches.

Beyond that, my job involved helping overheated people up the 240 steps from the bottom of Walnut Canyon and selling books and trinkets in the gift shop. Occasionally I delivered water and encouragement to hikers. I once helped the EMTs carry a litter to the visitor center at the top of the canyon when a hiker sprained an ankle, but I generally left the heavy lifting to the younger rangers.

* * *

After breakfast I turned my aging Isuzu Rodeo east, toward Walnut Canyon, traversing an old non-public dirt road that took a half hour off the official route. I showed my Park Service ID to the energetic young seasonal ranger in the booth and let Todd pay for two adult admissions. Then we drove the mile-long driveway to the parking lot.

Todd and El looked through the exhibits in the visitor center while I talked to the ranger behind the information desk. I found a postcard showing a nearby archeological excavation and was tempted to send it to Sherry, my ex-wife, who is now an adjunct professor of archeology at the University of Minnesota, with a note saying, "Too bad you divorced me or you could be here." I decided not to poke a sleeping bear.

The visitor center was mostly empty when we started down the long stretch of steps to the canyon housing the Sinagua ruins. I looked back as we turned the first switchback and the only other people on the trail were three guys who'd come in behind us. They looked furtive and something about them made my skin prickle just like when I'd been a St. Paul cop following a carload of kids high on drugs. My prickling skin had preceded dozens of car or foot chases.

I suspected the guys had something to hide. One of the three was gesturing emphatically to the other two. But it was my day off and I wasn't about to hassle visitors just having an argument. They weren't bothering anyone and as long as they weren't throwing punches, I wasn't going to intervene.

Todd, El, and I continued down the rock steps carved into the hillside below the visitor center. A switchback corner had an informational tablet warning, "There are 240 steps from this point to the bottom of the canyon." Unsaid was the intuitive information that there were an equal number of uphill steps on the return trip when the hikers were tired, hot, and often dehydrated.

Todd looked at me. "Are you up to it?" El frowned, not understanding. Todd explained, "Doug's got a torn PCL."

El nodded. In the world of runners, everyone understood the jargon of knee and ankle injuries. All runners suffer through a variety of lower leg injuries from trips, falls, potholes or wear and tear in their efforts to keep their hearts healthy.

"Sure," I replied. "I ride my bike most every day and my knee is stable. Walking stairs is just fine." I started out ahead of them just to reinforce how fine I was, but in my mind I was asking myself if I was being smart or not. The "down" steps were more difficult on my knee than the "up" steps, so I figured if my knee unexpectedly quit while we were going down, I'd wait for them on their return trip. In addition to the long set of steps, the temperature was a concern; it was already over eighty degrees and rising rapidly when we left the visitor center. Each of us had a half-liter of water and I thought that would be enough. The long walk, heat, and low humidity sometimes surprised even experienced hikers.

I went into tour guide mode. "Walnut Canyon, like the Grand Canyon, was carved from the limestone of the Colorado Plateau. Walnut Creek cut through the Permian limestone exposing the Toroweap Formation and the Coconino Sandstone. The Sinagua used the naturally eroded limestone alcoves as living spaces. The canyon floor has several species of walnut trees, for which the canyon is named." I recited the natural history, having read the trail signs a couple hundred times.

We meandered down the stone steps, catching glimpses of open alcoves and walls built into the gaps between the limestone layers across the canyon. At every switchback a plaque gave details about the lifestyle of the Sinagua Indians, their agricultural practices, or highlighted some of the natural history of the canyon. Stops also offered a brief respite from the climb, giving us a chance to study the massive stone spire that loomed in the center of the circular canyon. More houses were carved into the same layers of limestone as the dwellings around the canyon perimeter.

We were standing at a switchback where a 2007 rock slide had cleared an opening in the trees. I yelled to be heard above the howling wind as I continued with my tour guide spiel.

El shot some photos and was changing lenses with the camera bag open at her feet when several small rocks bounced off a ledge next to her. "What the hell?"

A body cartwheeled through the opening above us. It bounced off a rock outcropping ten feet away, making a sickening sound like a melon dropped on the floor. I leaned over the railing, but it was already out of sight. A jacket fluttered past, the arms flailing like a wounded bird in the hot, swirling updraft rising from the canyon floor. It flew over the railing from a switchback above us and tangled itself in a creosote bush at our feet.

I raced up the steps with Todd close behind. He grabbed me at the first switchback. "Why...not . . . down?" He gulped in air through his gasps, pointing in the direction the body had fallen. "He'll need first aid."

I shook my head. "He's already dead." I caught my breath and raced on. At the railing about fifty vertical feet above where we'd stood, the soil and stones next to the trail showed evidence of a struggle. Beyond the railing, near the edge of the cliff, I saw a pair of glasses.

Above us, I caught a glimpse of two of the men I'd seen in the visitor center a few minutes earlier. They were years younger than me, moving fast, and apparently conditioned to the altitude. I glanced down to make sure El was out of danger. She was stuffing gear into her camera bag.

I grabbed Todd's shirt and pushed. "Follow them."

I doubled over with my hands on my knees, the hot air searing the lining of my lungs. The wind roared past, covering the sound of El's approach. She crested the steps as I tried to get my second wind. She was puffing heavily and her huge camera bag was slapping her hip. Her t-shirt clung to her sweaty sports bra in a way that might have been embarrassing, except for the look of terror on her face.

To my surprise, her terror was directed at me, making me wonder just how bad I looked.

"Are you okay?" she asked, gripping my arm as she pulled a pink plastic water bottle from her fanny pack. She flipped up the spout and handed it to me.

"Just catching . . . my breath . . ." I tried to straighten up, to look more in control, but I opted for taking a big drink of her water, and then I bent over again as pain shot into my right side.

She adjusted the camera bag and put her hands on her hips as she took deep, regular breaths. "Where's Todd?" She gestured for me to pass the water back. She squirted a stream into her mouth and put the bottle back in her pack.

I stood up again, having partially recovered, and started for the steps as I pointed up. She was immediately behind me as I bounded up the first few steps, two at a time. As I rounded the next switchback, I heard the distinctive pop of a gun firing. The report echoed off the canyon walls in the screaming desert wind, followed by a ricochet.

"Oh God!" I bounded on, rejuvenated by a shot of adrenaline. "I shouldn't have sent Todd." El's footsteps rang out behind me as I slowed to taking one step at a time. I briefly thought about the pistol locked away inside my townhouse. I hadn't thought about it in months.

After what seemed like an eternity we crested the last switchback and could see the visitor center. I hadn't seen any blood on the trail. I hadn't seen Todd, either. I forged on until the blessed cool of the air-conditioned visitor center swept over me as I pushed the glass doors open.

El reached me just inside the door. "Did I hear a gunshot?" She struggled with her camera bag. "Where's Todd?" She was a picture of panic.

My breath still came in gasps as I forged ahead, ignoring her questions. The center was empty except for a young woman dressed in a gray and green park ranger's uniform with a small gold badge pinned above her left breast pocket. She sat on a stool behind the cash register near the entrance door, quietly reading a Twilight series novel. She had given me a polite nod when I'd been through earlier and now looked up in surprise as I stumbled to the counter covered in sweat. I grimaced as another pain stabbed my side. El's face was still filled with questions as I addressed the ranger. Her name tag identified her as Stacy.

"The two men . . ." I gasped. "Did they run through here?"

Stacy, who had seen me in uniform a couple times, looked at me like I was from Mars. "What?"

"Two men. One muscular with dark hair and jeans. The other kinda scraggly. Did they run through here?"

"About two minutes ago. They seemed to be in a hurry. A guy ran through just after them."

"Dial 911," I said, holding my side. "Tell the dispatcher there's been a murder at Walnut Canyon."

Chapter 3

Todd burst back through the doors. Stacy still hadn't picked up the phone so I reached across the desk and grabbed her arm. She looked at me in surprise, followed quickly by indignation.
"Stacy, call 911. Now."
"To hell with this." El took her cellphone and punched in 911.
Todd flopped his arms on the glass countertop and lay his head on them. Sweat streamed from his face, dripped on the glass, and plastered his shirt to his chest. He raised up and put his hands on his knees. "Light blue Lincoln," he gasped. "License G-R-A-M-P-S."
I caught a breath again, but the stitch of pain in my side made me wonder if I was dying. I hadn't felt anything like it since the first week of high school football practice. "Stacy, listen. My name is Doug, I'm a seasonal ranger and a retired cop. A man's just been murdered in the canyon. The guys who just ran out threw him off the cliff and shot at my cousin." I put my hand on Todd's shoulder. "You need to notify the superintendent in Flagstaff and the sheriff's department."

In the background I heard El, facing away from us, quietly answering questions for the 911 operator.

Stacy finally began to understand the situation. "My supervisor's in the back. I'll get him." She disappeared through a door behind the counter.

She returned with Brad Peck, a young skinny guy in a ranger's uniform. He looked like a thirty-something hippie with a ponytail that hung over his collar. Technically, he was my supervisor, too, but his usual focus was more on the rangers conducting educational programs and he hung out with the seasonal rangers who lived in the Park Service housing just off the entrance road. I wasn't much fun, so the young rangers had little to do with me socially. That was fine with me.

He didn't recognize me and clearly didn't appreciate the disruption to his smoothly flowing day. "What's the matter?"

"Two guys threw a third guy over the cliff," I summarized.

Brad shook his head. "God, I hate that." He turned to Stacy. "Call out the recovery squad." She disappeared into the back.

He turned back to us and put on his best bureaucratic smile. "Where did this guy fall?"

I leaned over the counter so far that Brad backed up to maintain his personal space. "He didn't fall. He was unconscious or dead before he went over the railing."

Brad continued to smile. "The Park Service loses a few folks a year. It's not murder—they're just accidents. It's tragic, but not murder. I'm sure that's the case here."

I slid my police credentials and Park Service badge across the counter. "He's. Dead." I spoke very clearly and succinctly.

Brad picked up my ID and continued to talk as he read it. "Doug Fletcher, right." Now he recognized me. "What makes you believe he's dead?"

"The splat of his body hitting rocks, for one thing. Second, I've seen jumpers. They scream and flail, like they're trying to catch the air. This guy was a rag doll—he didn't make a noise." I snatched my wallet back from Brad and shoved it in my pocket. "He was unconscious when he hit the rocks near us, and his head cracked like a watermelon. There's no way he's alive."

A voice crackled over the radio behind the counter. There was obvious pain in it. "I need . . . ambulance . . . hurt bad."

Brad spun and grabbed a portable radio mounted under the counter. He pressed the transmit button so hard I thought he was going to break the radio. "Ed, what happened?"

There was no response. "Ed . . . Ed!"

"Sonofabitch!" Brad slammed the radio onto the counter, cracking the glass. He grabbed the mike from a different radio from under the counter and switched channels rapidly. "Coconino dispatch, this is Walnut Canyon

Visitor Center." He waited anxiously for someone to answer.

"Dispatch. Go ahead Walnut Canyon."

His face lightened. "This is Ranger Peck at the Walnut Canyon Visitor Center. I've got a ranger down and an injured visitor. Send an ambulance."

I grabbed the mike out of his hand. "Put out an APB, two males, armed and dangerous, blue Lincoln, Arizona plates G-R-A-M-P-S. Updates to follow when available." I handed the mike back to him. He didn't appreciate my initiative and I didn't care, so I figured that made us even.

"Ten-four, Walnut Canyon. We just got a cell call reporting a hiker injury. Deputies and rescue units are already responding."

Stacy came from the back. "I've got Ray and Bill coming with rescue equipment. Anything else?"

Brad reached in his pocket and threw her a ring of keys. "Get to the entrance. Ed's hurt."

She caught the keys and headed to the door.

"There's a first aid kit in the pickup," Peck shouted after her.

"I'll go with you." I yelled back over my shoulder. "Todd, you and El stay here and show them where the guy went over."

Stacy raced the white pickup to the front gate. She didn't have the high-speed driving skills of a cop, but she did a passable job on the winding road.

"What did Ed say? Is he okay?" Stacy asked.

She focused intently on the road, grasping the steering wheel so hard her knuckles were white. Perspiration darkened the armpits of her gray uniform shirt. The speedometer showed eighty-five on a road with a speed limit of twenty-five and the truck tires howled like banshees when she navigated the curves. I guessed she was no more than twenty-one years old and knew for a fact she was scared as hell. My instinct said she was in the throes of the "tunnel vision" cops and military people experience in combat. I needed her to ease back a bit before she did something we'd both regret, like rolling the pickup or hitting a tree.

"Just that he's hurt and to call an ambulance. He's probably okay. He had enough strength to call on the radio." All that was a lie, of course. I knew nothing more than she did, but it seemed to reassure her. Her knuckles went from white to pink on the steering wheel. I hoped her relaxation would increase our chances of arriving at the gate alive. The rangers' hut at the entrance loomed ahead as we rounded a curve.

She slammed on the brakes and skidded to a stop next to the hut. From the passenger's seat I could see blood in the road and splinters of wood spread over thirty yards past the hut, the apparent result of the Lincoln crashing through the gate.

"Sonofabitch. Get the first aid kit."

She pulled the first aid kit from behind the seat as I ran to the hut. Inside, the young ranger lay on the floor clutching his hip. His head rested against a wall of the tiny building. His face was ashen and his eyes were closed. His green uniform pants were soaked with blood and his breath came in short gasps. A piece of pink bone protruded through his pants.

I put a finger on his neck to take a pulse and his eyes popped open. "Who are you?"

"Doug Fletcher. What happened?" He closed his eyes and grimaced. His heart rate was so fast I had a hard time counting the beats. His face told me shock was setting in.

"Light blue Lincoln. They were driving like a hundred miles an hour. I tried to flag 'em, but they didn't slow down . . .clipped my leg." He drew a deep breath and grimaced as a wave of pain swept over him. As I knelt to look at his injury, his breathing stopped and he vomited violently on my foot.

Stacy was standing at the door. It was obvious she had no idea what to do. She disappeared from the door and I heard sounds of retching.

I looked up when she returned. She wiped her mouth on the sleeve of her uniform shirt, her complexion almost as gray as Ed. She needed distraction. "He's going to be okay. He has a broken leg, and he's in shock. It could be a lot worse. Call it in to the ambulance so they know what to expect."

She looked reassured and set the first aid kit down next to my knee. She was happy to have direction and went back to the truck and the radio. Ed's wound was seeping, not spurting, so I knew there wasn't much I could do until Ed got to a hospital with a good trauma surgeon. I wondered if Flagstaff had one on staff.

Chapter 4

The Arizona State Patrol arrived and blocked the driveway past the entrance hut. The trooper checked on me, apparently felt I had the first aid situation under control and returned to his cruiser. It was half an hour later when the Flagstaff paramedics wheeled the gurney carrying Ed into the ambulance. Jill Rickowski, the Flagstaff Park Service Superintendent, arrived in a white Suburban with red and blue lights flashing. After taking in the scene her face looked as gray as Ed's. As the ambulance pulled away she surveyed the guard shack.

"It appears you were the first responder." She took in my bloody hands, pants, and the vomit on my shoes. "So who are you?" She backed up and wrinkled her nose.

I peeled the surgical gloves off my hands and dropped them in the shack, then handed her my wallet with the SPPD I.D. "I'm Doug Fletcher, a retired cop. I work for you as a seasonal ranger but I'm off today, which is why I'm out of uniform."

"What a way to start the day." She looked at my wallet, then pushed back her Smokey Bear hat. I'd seen Jill on two previous occasions and I had been impressed with her professionalism. Anyone who's ever worn a uniform knows there are leaders who command respect due to their appearance, charisma, and demeanor. She was only about five-foot eight-inches tall, but her lean frame, serious expression, spit-polished look, and military bearing made her seem taller. This morning Jill was a deflated version of the confident woman I'd previously seen.

She watched as Stacy turned away a carful of visitors. With surprising assertiveness, Stacy shrugged off the driver's displeasure and directed them to make a U-turn in front of the guard shack. Past the guard shack the Arizona State Patrol's car blocked the driveway.

The roles were perfect. Stacy was a ranger trained to be a helpful guide. The Arizona Highway Patrol is a remnant of the Arizona Rangers, from a time when there was no such thing as a call for backup, when their personal survival often relied on their ability to look like the meanest son of a bitch alive in any situation. The "shoot first, ask questions later" era was long past, but the few highway patrol officers I'd met didn't seem like they'd be concerned about a grand jury indictment if they decided to fire a gun. I thought a jury of their Arizona peers would prefer tough enforcement over the pleas of a lawyer from the ACLU offering arguments about the terrible childhood of the victim and legal nuances of recent federal court decisions.

Jill invited me into the Suburban, slipping my wallet into her pocket. She carefully placed her hat in the backseat. She mopped her brow with her forearm, started the engine, and we waited for the cool air to flow out of the vents.

"No one saw the Lincoln. The Arizona Highway Patrol had a car on I-40 about thirty miles east of us and the Flagstaff P.D. monitored the freeway going west. The sheriff's department had cars on several back roads, but the Lincoln never showed anywhere."

She slipped the Suburban into drive and proceeded slowly to the visitor center, rolling down her window when we got to the Arizona Highway Patrolman. "Thanks, Harry. We're clear here."

The stone-faced ranger cracked a smile and tipped his hat. "Anytime, Jill."

"The Lincoln was stolen from Phoenix." Jill said as she drove to the visitor center. "If they went north or west for a while before turning south, we would've missed them. There are about five hundred miles of dirt roads north of I-40 on the Navajo Reservation and then Utah beyond that. My bet is they went north."

I stared out the front window and thought out loud. "Is there any law enforcement up that way to spot them?"

"If they crossed the Wupatki National Park, there's a chance a ranger may have seen them, but their most likely contact would've been with the Navajo Nation Police. They're spread mighty thin. There are even fewer Navajo Nation Police Officers per square mile than the nine full-time rangers who cover the three

Flagstaff-area national monuments. There's a lot of barren land where you could dump a car . . . and a lot of folks that might see a blue Lincoln as a windfall. They'd strip it and sell off the parts. Someone might find the remnants of the abandoned car a few years from now but chances are they'd never report it."

"You're thinking it was someone from the reservation?"

"Stacy said one of the guys who ran through the visitor center looked Navajo. Have you got another theory?"

"I hadn't given it much thought. I guess it seems odd that someone from the reservation would bring someone inside a national monument to kill them when they've got a reservation covering half of Arizona where there isn't a witness within a hundred miles."

Jill looked perplexed. "Why would they come here?"

"Maybe to send a message." I shrugged. "Someone wanted the body found. Maybe they wanted to prove how bad they are, or maybe it's a reminder to keep their minions in line."

I let that thought dangle as we parked. "Did your crew bring up the body?"

Jill shook her head. "One of my rangers spotted the victim from the trail. I have two guys climbing down to assess the best route for the recovery, but we'll need help from the county rescue squad. It'll be a couple of hours before we get enough people here to make the recovery. It's all bull work to retrieve a body from the bottom and it'll be slow in this heat."

When we parked at the visitor center she left the motor running and turned to me. "Are you really a cop?" She took my laminated SPPD ID out of her pocket and inspected it closely.

"I retired from the St. Paul Police Department. Now I live in Flagstaff and work here as a seasonal ranger." I wondered where she was going with the questions. I suspected I was going to get some kind of reprimand.

We sat in silence for a few seconds before she returned the wallet to me. "This is a Federal case. The U. S. Park Service will have to investigate, but I usually depend on the Coconino Sheriff's Department for assistance. Crimes on Federal lands are often handled by the FBI, but it's their option to choose whether they want to get involved. Their closest office is in Phoenix and they usually don't want to send an agent if we can find local resources to investigate the crime."

She was obviously contemplating something as we sat in silence. "I need to get your address and phone number."

"I'm one of your rangers. You have my life story in a file." My dealings with Federal law enforcement agents was limited, but generally negative. They wanted information and then the accolades. The local cops got the grunt work and weren't mentioned at the press conference after the crime was solved.

She turned off the ignition, retrieved her Smokey Bear hat, and carefully adjusted it on her head. We walked toward the visitor center in silence that I took as anger. "Are you interested in a full-time job?" She asked as she opened the door.

I stopped and stared at her. "What?" I thought I'd misheard her.

She walked into the visitor's center, took off her hat, and spun it nervously in her hands. "Like I said, the Park Service has official jurisdiction in any crimes committed here. We've had the sheriff's department in on a couple of minor things and they're okay to work with. When we've called in the FBI . . ."

I clenched my eyes shut. "Let me guess. When you called the FBI they either declined the case, or ran everything and made you all feel like a bunch of idiots. They probably took all kinds of information and never gave you a clue what was going on. Right?"

She looked surprised. "Right. I mean . . . they apparently do a good job, but it's taken out of our control." She splayed her hands in a show of frustration. "Most of the time our crimes are petty and they rightfully choose not to get involved."

I picked up a scrap of paper from the floor as I considered her question. "I'm retired because I have a bum knee." It was an easy cop-out and didn't really answer the question.

I quickly assessed my interest in doing anything beyond working in the visitor's center a few hours a week, sitting in my house, biking around the golf course, and reading the paper. I'd tried socializing but the park rangers were all too young, and I didn't like the bar flies who were hanging around the few pubs I'd visited. I cancelled the gym membership after I realized I couldn't make myself go there routinely—I didn't want to mindlessly pump away on a piece of equipment—and the women I'd met there were either militant about their exercise routine or unwilling to put up with an overweight guy with a receding hairline.

My stomach started to churn at the thought of taking a full-time job again. Lots of my friends had retired to jobs as security guards at Twin Cities firms like Honeywell or Medtronic. I was sure I didn't want to take that route, although being a part-time park ranger wasn't much of a step away from sitting behind a desk and inspecting corporate IDs all day.

Jill led me to Brad's office and knocked on the door. "Please take Doug's statement, then interview his cousins."

Brad spun his chair and logged onto the computer. After a few seconds a screen popped up with the Park Service Logo. Brad quickly went to a menu and pulled down an icon that opened a form. He filled in the location, date, and time. "Let's start with your full name and birthdate."

"Is this is going to bring down a shitstorm?"

"This goes into the main Park Service database. Every incident in a National Park or Monument gets logged here and there is a hierarchy of notifications. For a death on Park Service property, I think everyone up to, and including, the Secretary of the Interior get notified. I can't imagine that the big guys read the reports, but you can bet they know which parks have the most total incidents and the number of incidents per thousand visitors."

"And they act on that accordingly?"

He shrugged. "I wouldn't know. I'm sure every 'Aw shit' erases a couple hundred 'Attaboys.' Now, let's get this form filled out."

When I was done, I found El and Todd and brought them to Brad's office so he could take their statements. I was sitting on a bench in the lobby with my head in my hands when Jill sat down beside me.

"I just talked with the rangers doing the recovery. The body got hung up on some shrubbery on a near vertical surface and it took them nearly half an hour to get the right gear to climb down. They confirmed that the victim is dead. The Coconino County Rescue Squad is here to help with the recovery." She paused, apparently considering her words. "I'm serious about the job offer."

"I'm collecting a medical pension. I'd never pass an employment physical."

"What was your injury?"

"I tore my right PCL during a burglary arrest."

"You're walking without a limp."

"I bike and do a few exercises. That seems to keep my knee solid enough for the work I do around here."

"The job I'm offering you doesn't involve running, tackling, or wrestling. I need you to run an investigation," Jill paused. "There's a doctor in Flagstaff who'll get you through a physical. We had a Congressman who wanted one of his cronies hired. The guy was a wreck . . . We got him in and he worked here long enough to collect a Federal pension." She looked at me hopefully. When I didn't respond she added, "I've got an opening for a law enforcement ranger that was going to be filled by a college student who just wrapped up her B.A. in criminology. She backed out to take a job with the county sheriff. She was going to replace one of my full-time rangers who took a position in Mississippi last winter. He'd been handling any investigative work that came up."

"I guess I don't understand what you're asking. Are you looking for a seasonal law enforcement ranger or a permanent investigator?"

Her face softened slightly and a hint of a smile appeared at one corner of her mouth. Her face was creased from years of working in the sun, her hair, tied in a ponytail, was more brown than gray. I thought she might've passed 50 but I really couldn't determine her age. Until that moment I'd never seen her with anything but a stiff, professional persona. There was a sudden openness and softness in her body language that made her seem younger.

"There are several categories of rangers," she explained. "I need a law enforcement ranger who can patrol the roads and campgrounds, but I also need that person to be our investigator and liaison with the other law enforcement agencies. You talk like a cop, you step in and take control when it's required. Your St. Paul ID says you were a detective and that you're firing range qualified. Even if you can't run, I'd much rather see you carrying a gun and talking to other agencies than turning this investigation over to someone fresh out of a college criminology program, green as grass, who might be competent to carry a gun, and who's never participated in an investigation, much less led one."

I shook my head. "My cousin and her husband are in town for a week of vacation . . . I promised to play tour guide."

She stared off at Brad's door. Although the words were muffled we could hear El's distinctive voice. "Look, I'm stuck. If I could find a qualified candidate, it'd be at least a month, and probably more, before they could relocate here and start working.

"I'll give you a Park Service vehicle. Let your cousin have your car to run around and you can spend the evenings with them." She looked back at me, her eyes pleading. "In a day I can have pages of applicants and not one person who knows shit about running a criminal investigation. They're all forestry, biology, and environmental science majors. I need somebody who's experienced, knows what questions to ask, and who's not going to get railroaded by the other agencies. You carry yourself like a cop and you take charge. You're what I need."

"Listen, give me a night to think about it. I'll call you in the morning. okay?"

She smiled and we stood and shook hands. "Doug, before you leave I'd like you to fill out an online application so we have something formal showing you were on a list of candidates, just in case you decide to accept."

She set me at a desk with a computer linked to the online Park Service application site. While I entered personal information, still not sure I was interested in the offer, I could hear Jill on the phone around the corner. She was already vetting me with the St. Paul Police. I overheard her say, "Uh huh," a few times, and twice she laughed out loud. Apparently she'd found someone who actually knew me, which meant I was getting verbally roasted, or she may have found someone who thought I'd been an okay guy. With the application entered, I rounded the corner as she was hanging up the phone. She had a smile on her face. "Is it true that the last time you qualified on the pistol range, you shot a smiley face on a silhouette at seven yards?"

I grimaced. "I can explain. I mean, I was already pensioned off and it didn't really matter how I shot, as long as I was putting holes inside the silhouette on the paper. So, I had some fun with it."

"It was a quick-fire test. You had ten seconds to fire seven shots."

I shrugged and she smiled, shaking her head.

"You were a homicide detective. Tell me about some of the cases you were pursuing before you retired."

I gave her a few highlights of my more memorable—to me, at least—cases.

"You blew out a knee after a foot chase. Correct?"

"On a burglary call, yes. It's not much of a problem. I keep it stable by riding my bike a few miles a week."

"I spoke with Captain Baker." Her smile made me nervous because he knew where the skeletons are buried.

"What did Toby have to say?"

"Toby said you were an okay guy. Better than that, he said he'd take you back in a heartbeat if you wanted the job, that you were a hell of a cop and should buy him a beer next time you're in town."

El and Todd came out of Brad's office. Jill handed me a business card. "My personal cell number's written on the back. Use it when you've made your decision."

"Give me until tomorrow morning. I want to think about it."

"Fair enough."

I didn't know if I wanted the job and I felt guilty using Todd and El as an excuse for putting Jill off. I rationalized that it would be easier to call Jill Rickowski in the morning to say no, rather than embarrass her by refusing the job after we'd just shared war stories.

Chapter 5

"All set?" I asked.

"Not selling your guide service short," El said with a smile, "but Brad took us under his wing while you were being interviewed. He has a degree in anthropology and he had some very interesting insights into the life of the Sinagua people. He also took me to a couple of great spots to take pictures."

Neither Todd nor I had the chance to say a word on the drive home. El filled me in on their behind-the-scenes Walnut Canyon tour, Brad's expertise as a tour guide, the upcoming weather, and Northern Arizona natural history. At the townhouse Todd and El dove into supper preparation while I drove to the store to get wine and beer. As I parked my Isuzu, my neighbor walked to the cluster of mailboxes the townhouse complex shared.

"Hi, Doug. Your visitors are real early birds." Sheila was a divorcee who must've been a trust fund baby because I'd never seen her work while raising her two little boys. Day or night her makeup was perfect, she never had a hair out of place, and she wore clothes that were always a little too tight in all the right places. The women in the neighborhood were rather brusque with her and the husbands lingered at the mailboxes when Sheila was there.

"Hi, Sheila." I reached for my own mail. "My guests are runners and they wanted to get their miles in before the heat of the day."

"The woman sure is skinny. You should take her out for a nice steak."

"She's a vegetarian and she's trying to convert me."

"You strike me as a man who likes to see a little meat on a woman's bones."

"She's my cousin, so it's not relevant." I said, trying to stay focused on Sheila's eyes and not the places where her clothes were too tight.

"I've heard of kissing cousins. Maybe there are cousins with benefits, too." Sheila gave me a wicked grin with dimples that made my heart skip a beat, before turning to walk back to her house. She turned back at her doorway to see if I was watching her retreat. Confirming that I was, she smiled and walked inside.

Entering my own house, I smelled something cooking and saw the table was set. A large bowl held an attractive salad garnished with fresh tomato and avocado slices. I removed the screw cap from a bottle of Sauvignon Blanc while Todd brought wine glasses from the kitchen.

"To what do we owe the wine?" he asked as I poured.

"While you two were touring with Brad, I was offered a job." I threw the cap into the garbage, signaling my intention to finish off the bottle before bedtime. "The head ranger offered me a job as a Park Service investigator. I want to bounce some things off you guys before I decide to accept or decline her offer."

"I thought you were happily retired." Todd sat down and sipped the wine.

"For the most part, I am happy. It's just that . . . well, I have to admit I miss the challenge and social interaction." El slipped onto her chair and tucked one foot under herself. "Life is a little lonely sometimes and I don't socialize much."

"Your neighbor seems friendly." El smiled. "Does she find a reason to talk every time you're outside?"

"She's got two little boys and spends way too much time on her appearance. I'm more into low-maintenance, wash-and wear-women."

"Like me!" El said.

"If you weren't a married relative, I'd be standing at your door with flowers and a box of candy."

"Really, Doug, that's so nineteenth century. Now you use a smartphone to send selfies."

"Selfies?" I asked.

"Pictures of yourself," El explained. "If you're really good friends, you text selfies of your naked body. They call it sexting." She raised her eyebrows suggestively.

"Sometimes you don't send selfies of your whole body, just the relevant parts," Todd added.

"Oh no. This beat-up old body doesn't need to be photographed with clothes, much less when it's naked. And the 'relevant parts' are not photogenic. No way. No how."

"Did you like being a cop?" El asked, changing the subject and swirling the wine. She watched as the wine formed legs and ran down the inside of the glass.

"I liked some parts of it. Other parts were pure torture. When the investigation was hot and we were making progress, it was a rush. Making an arrest and taking some brutal gangbanger off the streets was the ultimate adrenaline high."

"But?" Todd prompted me.

"But the paperwork, the lawyers, and the trials were a royal pain. The attorneys don't want to take a case to trial unless they are 99 percent sure they'll get a conviction, and we all knew there was no way the courts could handle all the cases that came through. Felonies were plea bargained down to misdemeanors and too many bad guys walked away without the punishment they deserved."

El sipped the wine and made a yummy sound. "Where did you find this wine? It's wonderful!"

"It's from New Zealand. The guy at the liquor store said Kim Crawford wines are reasonably priced and consistently tasty."

"Back to the question of the day," Todd interjected, obviously irritated by El's change of topic. "Do you want to go back into law enforcement at this point in your life?"

"I don't know. If I can be an investigator and not get caught up in the politics of Federal bureaucracy, I'd take it in a minute. But I committed to guiding you around northern Arizona, so the timing couldn't be worse. It's your first day here and I'm discussing abandoning you."

El reached across the table and put her hand on top of mine. "Doug, we don't expect you to entertain us 24/7. We'd love to have you along, but Todd and I are used to entertaining ourselves."

I looked at Todd and he nodded. "We're driving to the Painted Desert and the Petrified Forest tomorrow. You're welcome to ride along, but I figure we'll be on the road after our sunrise run and we probably won't be back until suppertime."

"You're here for a week, and there are lots of other things to see. I want to show you Sedona and the Grand Canyon."

"That's great, and we'd love to have you ferry us around. But if you really want to take this job, Todd and I will be just as happy to rent a car and show ourselves around. We can spend the evenings with you."

I slid the salad bowl to El and passed her the tongs. "Let's eat." My excuse for refusing the job was slipping away and I wasn't convinced I wanted to lose it.

As we dove into the salads, a timer buzzed in the kitchen. El jumped up and returned with a steaming bowl of black beans and rice. When she sat down, I glanced toward the kitchen, wondering what entrée she'd prepared to go with the beans and rice.

She caught me looking. "There is nothing else. Beans are a great source of protein and they release their carbohydrates slowly so we won't be hungry until breakfast."

I smiled and ladled the mixture onto my plate. Despite my skepticism, El had seasoned the mixture with tomato bits, onions and some green herbs. It was surprisingly tasty. When I took a second ladle, she smiled.

El made small talk as we ate, holding up all three sides of the conversation. Todd and I listened. I came to understand our roles had been cast and my verbal input wasn't required beyond making supportive grunts at appropriate times. El told me about the research she'd done about northern Arizona and recited an impressive list of things they'd planned to see. At some point during supper I realized they weren't just being polite. They really were capable of being tourists without me.

Todd and I cleared the table while El set out soup bowls and tablespoons. I was hopeful they'd snuck a tub of ice cream into the freezer, but I wasn't entirely surprised when El brought out a bowl of mixed fresh fruit topped with a dollop of yogurt. She smiled, guessing my thoughts, but she seemed pleased that I was going along with the menu without complaint.

"If you guys moved in here for a few months, my cholesterol would drop and I'd probably lose a little bit of weight." Todd nodded and smiled. El glowed, taking my comments as a compliment.

After supper El loaded the dishwasher and rattled around in the kitchen while I split the last of the wine among our three glasses. Todd was obviously feeling the alcohol. He leaned close and whispered, "I have burgers and fries for lunch when I'm at work."

El picked up her glass and noted the refill. "Are you trying to get me drunk?" She took a sip and joined us in the living room, snuggling against Todd on the couch. I reached for the television remote, hoping to catch the weather report at the end of the evening news. Like a cat, El snatched it off the coffee table.

"Wait a second. You've been throwing out reasons why you won't take the Park Service job. Todd and I are not a factor in the decision, period. We will entertain ourselves, so that's off the table. Besides, we'll be gone in a week and your decision needs to be made with your future in mind." She paused, then asked, "What are you going to do?"

"Take the job." Todd looked me in the eye. "Everything you've said tells me it's what you really want."

They stared, waiting for me to say something. I shrugged. "I have to sleep on it."

"Let's talk," El jammed the television remote between the couch cushions behind her. "Tell me what happened between you and Sherry. I remember going to your wedding, then

I heard you were divorced. Then you moved to Arizona. Can you fill in the gaps?"

"Hold that thought," I got up and opened another bottle of wine from the refrigerator and topped off our glasses. "I need more alcohol to take on this subject. I was a senior at the University of Minnesota, and Sherry was a freshman with boundless energy and a killer smile. We met at an off-campus party in Dinkytown and there was chemistry."

"Love at first sight?" El asked.

"I thought it was. Really, it was the same old story everyone thinks will never happen to them. Too young, too cocky. She was academia, I was law-enforcement and military. We never should have married in the first place."

El's eyes looked suspiciously moist. "I'm so sorry I scratched open the scab."

I shrugged. "I'm a big boy. And look at me now. New home, new job, an actual new career possibility."

"You're going to take the job, aren't you?" asked Todd.

"I'm going to sleep on it."

Chapter 6

Sleeping on the decision wasn't the best idea. I tossed and turned all night, weighing my self-imposed obligation to El and Todd and my relatively stress-free life against my desire to get back into law enforcement. I was being given the opportunity to restore some meaning and structure to my life, but did I want it? When the alarm went off at 5 A.M. I'd already been awake for two hours.

I showered, shaved, then made a pot of coffee. The absence of running shoes by the door told me Todd and El were already pounding the trail. As we went to bed the night before Todd said they planned to take a sunrise run.

The sun had been up for almost an hour. With coffee percolating, I rummaged through the cupboard and found a box of Lucky Charms. The healthy supper, and the incumbent flatulence from the beans, required an unhealthy breakfast for balance. I tried to remember when I'd purchased the cereal and couldn't remember ever picking something so sweet and childlike. As I poured milk over the cereal I considered how far back in the cupboard the box had been wedged and wondered if it was a legacy left by the previous owners. One bite told me the marshmallows were beyond their expiration date, feeling more crunchy than chewy. I pushed some of them aside and ate the cereal portion, realizing that I'd gone too far to balance the healthy food. The cereal was so sweet it made my teeth hurt.

Halfway through the bowl I dumped the cereal into the disposal and poured myself a cup of coffee. With cup in hand, I went back into the bedroom to find Jill Rickowski's business card. I was dialing her cellphone when Todd and El came through the door, looking flushed and sweaty. They pulled off their shoes as I listened to Jill's phone ring.

El poured a cup of coffee and quietly sat on the arm of my chair. "You've made a decision." Jill answered and I put a finger up to signal her to wait.

"Hi, Jill. This is Doug Fletcher. I'm close to a decision but I'd like clarification of a few points before I give you my answer." El grinned and got up. She knew I was taking the job.

"I'm glad you called, Doug. I'm at Walnut Canyon going through the reports from yesterday. Meet me in the visitor center."

"I'll be there within the hour."

When I hung up I could hear the guest shower running and El was standing at the kitchen counter eating a piece of whole wheat toast that was dripping honey onto a plate. "I'm glad you decided to take the job."

I topped off my coffee and sat down at the table next to her. "I want to make sure I have a

Park Service vehicle at my disposal, so you and Todd can use the Isuzu for your sightseeing."

"With or without your Isuzu, Todd and I will be sightseeing." El downed the last bite of toast and licking the honey from her fingers. The shower shut off and she hopped to her feet. "I'll be out of the shower and ready to roll in fifteen minutes."

* * *

At Walnut Canyon, I got out of the Isuzu and handed the keys to Todd. "Take the Isuzu. I'll get a ride home."

Todd fingered the keys and cocked his head. "I'm not exactly sure how long this drive will take. You might want to make other supper plans."

"I'll wait," I waved goodbye as I walked to the visitor center.

Jill Rickowski was sitting at a desk in the Walnut Canyon office. She looked fresh; her uniform was pressed with crisp, almost military, creases. Only her eyes hinted at the short night she'd had. I imagined the pile of reports she'd filed and the number of calls she'd made to her superiors.

"I spent a lot of time on the phone last night." Jill pointed to a stack of notes with neat handwriting. "About the incident of course, but your old partner called me back."

"Matt Olson?"

"Yes indeed. He told me about the time you waded into an ice-covered pond to pull a toddler out of his car seat after his mom had a seizure and ran off the road."

"It's what any cop would do." I shrugged.

"Not every cop would go back to get the dog and be so hypothermic he had to be taken to the hospital to get his body temperature up before he had a heart attack."

"It was a short-haired terrier. He wouldn't have survived the cold water."

"You coached an inner-city Little League team . . . and bought them uniforms. You're a good cop and you have a heart."

Enough memory lane. Time to move this on. "If I take the job I need access to a vehicle."

"I almost hate to tell you this, but you're already an employee of the Flagstaff office of the National Park Service. After I talked to your Minnesota contacts I went back to my office and changed your job status from seasonal ranger to full-time investigator with an assigned pickup truck."

I opened my mouth to protest, but Jill put up her hand.

"Doug, you're a gift from heaven. I need you."

I was defeated but also pleased about it. "Any words of wisdom before I start this investigation?"

"Don't discharge your firearm. It creates a mountain of paperwork."

I shook her hand. "I always liked being a cop, but this whole thing working with the Park Service is a little strange. Do I have to buy gray shirts and green pants? I burned out on the whole spit-shine business when I was an MP and police cadet."

"The Park Service investigators are Federal law enforcement officers who usually dress in civilian clothes. I suppose I'd describe most of them as wearing business casual apparel that looks okay in an office. When you're out of the office, wear what makes sense for the conditions. Buy a dress uniform for more formal situations."

"Do you issue a gun to me or do I use my own?"

"We'll issue you a Sig after you clear all the background checks and pass the physical. Unofficially, do you have a firearm you can carry until we get through the red tape?"

"I have a Glock .45. It probably doesn't meet Federal standards, but it hits where I aim and I have a concealed carry permit from the St. Paul Police."

"Federal Law Enforcement personnel are required to have access to a firearm 24/7 for personal and citizen protection."

"I'm used to that. All law enforcement is."

"Keep my business card somewhere you can find it. If you ever need me to back up your decisions, or if something about the job is rubbing you the wrong way, call my cellphone, day or night."

She reached under the counter and found a key on a ring with a huge fob. "This is the key for the Ford pickup parked in the lot. If you buy gas, change the oil, or run it through the car wash, keep your receipts. Brad will get you a Park Service charge card so you can buy gas on Uncle Sam's tab."

I spent an hour filling out authorizations for criminal, financial, and medical background checks, then I drove back to Flagstaff to the Park Service's chosen doctor, where I spent twenty minutes filling out more forms.

As soon as my medical forms were completed, I handed them to a receptionist who whisked me into an exam room. Right behind her was a nurse who checked my temperature, blood pressure, and entered my medical history into a computer. Before leaving the room, she handed me a paper gown and directed me to strip and put on the gown with the opening in the back.

Before I was gowned and on the exam table, a balding elderly man wearing a white lab coat and a Littmann stethoscope dangling from his neck, walked into the room, apparently reading my paperwork. He put out his hand and gave me a perfunctory smile. "I'm Doc Heron. It looks like Jill Rickowski thinks you're her new investigator. Open your mouth and say *aah*."

* * *

I passed Doc Heron's muster, though he did tell me a bit of work would get me into the shape of a fifty-year old, which would have been complimentary had I not been closer to forty. I was feeling closer to fifty at the moment, though. After a day of leaving phone messages, I was no closer to knowing what had happened at Walnut Canyon and who, if anyone, was leading the investigation. My cellphone rang and Todd said they were twenty miles from Flagstaff. We agreed to meet at the Christmas Tree Restaurant. It was a little "spendy" for my retirement budget, but in honor of my guests I thought we'd splurge. I had no idea what El could eat that wouldn't set her food alarm ringing. At least with a large menu to choose from, she could make her own healthy selection.

The entire restaurant was decorated in a subdued Christmas motif. Our small alcove had a degree of privacy provided by latticework panels decorated with plastic reindeer and randomly arranged boxes wrapped as Christmas presents. Dinner was fantastic, although the bottle of Stag's Leap Chardonnay we shared may have clouded my judgment. El seemed unusually subdued.

"What's the matter?" I asked as I poured the last of the wine bottle into Todd's glass. El had barely touched hers. "Didn't you guys have a good trip?"

El looked down and rearranged her red napkin. "The trip was fine, but I'm still rattled about yesterday. I've never seen anyone die before. I suppose you're used to it."

I swirled the wine in my glass. "I don't think you ever get used to it. Just more accepting that death is a part of our life experience. Besides, you didn't see anyone die. He was dead when he flew by us." It was a white lie—the guy was at least unconscious, and probably dead when his head hit the rocks next to us. If he had been alive, the impact on the trail would have killed him. I hoped the lie would ease El's anxiety.

Todd was fascinated by the whole experience and was dealing with it from a very analytical angle. El was a soft-hearted, starving photographer who would've protested the harvest of baby carrots.

"You told the ranger he was dead," she stated flatly. "Did you really know?"

I closed my eyes and I was back in uniform, standing on the high bridge in St. Paul.

"I'd been on the force for a year when I had a call about a jumper on the St. Paul high bridge. Just a kid, really, into the Goth thing, thought her life was over. You know teenage angst. I thought I had her talked down, I really did. And then—she was gone. She tried to change her mind, I think, but it was too late.

El stared at me, a tear trickling down her cheek. Todd, the eternal optimist, still hoped for a good ending. "But they picked her up from the water, right?".

I shook my head. "She hit a stone piling and rolled into the Mississippi. She was dead when she hit the water. Just like the guy we saw."

I drained the last of my wine and signaled the waiter for the bill. From the look in their eyes, I probably shouldn't have told them that story. Like most laymen, they had no idea what police work is really like. They watch one-hour CSI-type cop shows and consequently assume there's a definitive, happy ending to every tale. There isn't. It's why cops get cynical and have a high divorce rate. Some crawl into a bottle of booze for comfort. Others are tough enough to handle it or are able to keep it locked away inside.

* * *

As we crested the hill next to the townhouse I saw my neighbor Sheila picking up a Big Wheel tricycle and stowing it in her garage. She smiled at me and waved. When I'd first moved in, Sheila asked me over for a beer after she'd put the boys to bed. While it was a neighborly thing to do, I had the feeling I was being evaluated for the position of husband number two, or maybe three. She was smart, funny, and cute, but I made it clear I was not over my divorce and not interested in an instant family. I left after one beer. She keeps an eye on my place when I'm working, and I help keep an eye on the boys where they're playing in the yard. Sometimes when she smiles, I get the impression I'm still under evaluation. But as I told El, Sheila's a high-maintenance woman and if I ever get into another relationship it'll be with someone who's comfortable in her own skin and doesn't feel the need for all the primping and preening it takes for Sheila to be seen outside her house.

Sheila set a tricycle on the driveway and flagged me down. "Hey Doug." I rolled down the window. She nodded to Todd and carefully examined El. "There's a guy parked across from your place, just sitting in the car. I was thinking about calling the cops to check on him, but the car kinda looks like a cop car. Are you expecting someone?"

A black Dodge Charger with an array of antennae on the trunk sat across the driveway from my entry door. It was the stereotypical unmarked cop car. "Thanks, Sheila. I'll check it out."

As we pulled alongside I smiled and waved to the man in the car. He nodded and shut down his smartphone before opening his car door. As he rounded the back of the Dodge he flashed his FBI credentials at us.

"Doug Fletcher?"

I glanced at the ID long enough to determine it was authentic, then waved him toward the house. "C'mon in."

"I'm Special Agent Snelling." He walked in behind El and Todd and stopped just inside the door. He was dressed like a Fed, in a gray suit with white shirt. The clasp on his bolo tie was a piece of polished turquoise. He looked just like every other FBI agent I'd ever known except for the bolo tie and his cowboy boots.

"Grab a seat and start your questions." I pointed to the overstuffed chair facing the couch as we walked into the living room.

He confirmed our names, then asked, "Which one of you saw the body fall?"

"I . . . I think we all did." El was unable to contain her need to talk. "I mean, we were looking across the canyon and he sort of flew past." She looked at me and asked for a bottle of water.

I took a bottle of water and three cans of beer out of the refrigerator, then set them atop coasters on the coffee table. I sat on a stool at the breakfast bar.

"You told the Park Service Ranger that you thought he was dead before he fell?" Snelling looked at the beer can in front of him but didn't reach for it.

I tipped my can at El, signaling for her to continue. "Well, Doug said he was sure the guy was at least unconscious. His head hit the trail and there's no way he would've survived that impact."

Snelling looked at me. "Is that right?"

"He was certainly dead after he hit the ledge, yes."

"Have you seen many people fall to their deaths?" Snelling reached out and slid the beer and coaster further away on the table, signaling he had no intention of imbibing while on duty. He hesitated a second, then asked, "Just what line of work are you in, Mr. Fletcher?"

"I'm a retired cop."

"Actually," El added, "he was a detective."

"Okay," Snelling sighed. "Detective Fletcher, do you have any ID?" I took the laminated St. Paul credentials out of my wallet and handed them to him. After discerning that they were genuine he handed them back. His demeanor went from skeptic to interested interviewer. He opened the beer and leaned back on the couch. "Tell me the story."

"Not much to tell." I swilled the last of my beer and set the empty can on the counter. "A few pebbles hit the ledge as we were looking at the Indian houses across the canyon. I looked up and saw John Doe flying like a bird. He bounced off the ledge next to us and kept going. His denim jacket fluttered down after him and got caught in a bush."

"That's not the end." Snelling took a sip of beer. "Someone chased after a couple of guys who ran up the steps to the visitor center and someone called 911." He took out a notebook and flipped back a few pages. "Someone reported that two men left in a blue Lincoln with a license plate GRAMPS."

"Todd made the chase, Eleanor called 911, and then Todd came back with a description of the car and the license number."

He looked at his watch. "I'm officially off duty and we're a couple of cops having a beer together. I'd like to be home to put my kids to bed if that's still possible so give me the condensed version of the story."

"I'd noticed three guys on the trail behind us because something wasn't quite right. Two of them seemed nervous and the third guy just looked like he didn't want to be there. We went ahead of them down the trail. When we stopped at the old rock slide, pebbles fell off the ledge above us. Then the body flew by. I knew he was unconscious because he didn't scream or flail, and if he wasn't dead before his head hit the rocks, he was dead after that. We ran up the steps after the two nervous guys. I got winded and sent Todd ahead, thought that made sense since he's a long-distance runner. That was a bad idea. They shot at Todd and ran through the visitor center. When El and I made it to the top, Todd was already out of sight and El dialed 911 while I tried to emphasize the gravity of the situation to the ranger at the desk. The young ranger at the entry shack heard the Lincoln's racing engine and tried to signal them to slow down. They ran him down at the gate. The senior ranger radioed the Arizona Highway Patrol and sheriff's department with a description of the car, but no one saw it on the highway going east or west. They got away. End of story."

Snelling made some notes, then asked, "Todd, they shot at you?"

Todd shrugged. "Not a big deal. The skinny guy swung his arm back and fired off a shot. He didn't even aim and the gun wasn't really pointed at me. I heard the bullet ricochet."

"Where were you when the guy took the shot?"

"Toward the top of the trail, nearing the visitor center."

Snelling thought for a second. "If he was shooting an automatic we might recover a cartridge for forensics. Was he in an area where the ejected cartridge would have stayed on the trail or would it have caromed down the hill?"

"It was like the first straight trail where we could see each other, so we were close to the visitor center, but still a couple switchbacks down from the top. As for the gun, I don't know; I think it looked like those black Glocks on all the cop shows. The way he was facing, I'd say the shell casing ejected over the edge of the trail rather than toward the hill."

"You said, 'skinny guy.' One was bigger than the other?"

"One was huge . . . like a weightlifter or bodybuilder. He had a muscle shirt on . . . blue with red horizontal stripes . . . and dark jeans and dark hair in a ponytail. The other guy was probably Caucasian and smaller. He wore a plaid western-cut shirt and dark pants. His hair was brown."

"I assume you got this same description from the female ranger in the visitor center," I said.

"She remembers some things, but she couldn't remember their clothes, except that they were wearing jeans. She noticed a tattoo on the big guy and a gold necklace on the smaller guy." He addressed Todd. "Did you have the impression the bigger guy was other than Caucasian?"

Todd closed his eyes. "If he was Caucasian, he had a great tan. I think he looked Mexican." He opened his eyes again and shrugged. "I guess I couldn't tell."

"The ranger thought he might have been Navajo," Snelling suggested.

Todd shrugged. "Maybe. He might have been a Native American. I guess I couldn't tell."

Snelling again looked at the three of us. "Anything else to add?" He leaned forward on his knees to rise.

"I don't suppose you have anything to share with us?" I let the comment hang as he rose from the couch.

"You know it's against policy to comment on an ongoing investigation." He got up and walked over to shake my hand. "Thanks for your cooperation."

Snelling opened the door and paused. "I assume you'll all be available for further questions."

El piped up from behind Todd. "We're only here for a week and we expect to do a lot of sightseeing."

Snelling looked at me uneasily. "Leave your home address and number with Detective Fletcher." He closed the door as he left.

"Well, that was interesting." Todd gathered the beer cans and carried them to the sink. "I was hoping he'd share some insight into the case."

I shook my head. "No cop is going to talk with civilians about an investigation. My experience has been that the FBI rarely shares with other agencies. They're very protective of their information and don't want any leaks that might jeopardize a case. It drove me crazy."

Chapter 7

Elmer Swenson was on Tommy Tsosie's heels when they walked into their shared apartment at half past midnight. "Jesus Christ, would you slow down and talk to me?" He grabbed the big man by the biceps, and quickly realized his mistake, recoiling as Tommy turned with fire in his eyes.

"Don't ever touch me," Tommy growled before turning toward the kitchen. Elmer heard the refrigerator open followed by the sound of ice tinkling into a glass.

Elmer took the Glock out of his waistband and set it on the coffee table before he threw himself onto the couch in the cluttered apartment. The furniture was an eclectic mixture of recliners and sofas purchased at garage sales. A seventy-two-inch high-definition television hung on the wall opposite the couch. Beer cans and fast-food wrappers littered the floor, tables, and every other flat surface.

"Tommy, why'd we do this?" Elmer asked, staring at the water-stained spots on the ceiling.

Tommy wandered into the room and threw himself into a chair. He swirled brown liquid, making the ice clink in the glass. He put it to his lips and drained half the bourbon. "We got a chance to make some cash and maybe get some regular business." Tommy rolled the glass against his forehead. Sweat stained his muscle shirt under the arms and down the middle of the chest.

The Jeep Wrangler waiting for them after they ditched the stolen Lincoln hadn't had air conditioning. The howling air inside the open-sided Jeep was no substitute for air conditioning.

"You dumb shit!" Tommy threw his head back and stared at the ceiling. "Why did you shoot at that guy?"

"He was gaining on us. I made sure he slowed down. It's not like I aimed at him."

Tommy pinched his eyes closed. "Without that, the cops might've thought the death was accidental. Shooting at the guy screams it was a murder."

"Bullshit! You said he was supposed to be an example. If everyone thinks it was an accident, there's no message."

"The people who need to know will get it."

Elmer sat on the couch with his eyes closed. "I don't like it."

Tommy took another long drink and drained the glass. "You want out? You'll be the next one to visit Walnut Canyon." Tommy got up and walked to the kitchen. More ice tinkled in the glass. "We'll take it easy and hit the excavation again."

He pinched the bridge of his nose. The headache that had been teasing him in the Jeep now blossomed into a full-blown migraine. He got up and rifled through the medications in the bathroom until he found the bottle of Demerol. The prescription had been filled for a man who'd suffered painfully before he died from lung cancer and one of the man's grandkids figured it shouldn't sit in a drawer if it could bring in some fast cash. He popped two pills into his mouth, threw back his head and washed them down with bourbon.

"Who was the guy who paid us for Walnut Canyon?" Elmer asked.

Tommy's glare was answer enough. "Okay! So I don't need to know a name." Elmer opened the refrigerator. "Is he crazy or something?"

Tommy shook his head. "He's crazy rich. He might have some good paying jobs for us."

Chapter 8

The dawn twilight was glowing pink when I walked home with the newspaper. I'd read that wildfires in California were putting smoke into the upper atmosphere, giving northern Arizona spectacular sunrises and sunsets.

"Morning, neighbor. Are your houseguests already out for their morning run?" Sheila was leaning against her doorframe, wearing a terrycloth robe, her hair damp from the shower, and clutching a steaming cup of coffee.

"They're still on central time so they got up before sunrise, but I don't think they've actually hit the road yet." I stood at the end of her sidewalk, keeping my distance.

"Got time for a cup of coffee? The boys are still asleep and I have one doughnut the boys didn't eat."

"As tempting as that sounds, I'm starting a new job today and I need to shower and be on my way. Thanks anyway."

"Consider it a rain check. I'm up before the roosters crow most mornings and the coffee is always strong and hot." She scratched an itch on her calf with her big toe, exposing way too much thigh through the gap in her robe. The devilish look in her eyes told me she was reveling in my discomfort.

I told El and Todd good morning as they brushed past on their way to the golf course loop. I noticed the dark rings under El's eyes and wasn't surprised. I'd heard someone up and down several times during the night and I wondered if El was having problems getting the Walnut Canyon events out of her head. I hesitated to assess my own feelings . . . had I become so hardened I no longer lost sleep over a violent death? The answer seemed to be yes. Maybe I'd become so good at compartmentalizing things I could shove violent items into pigeonholes and let my mind wander off to some other quadrant while sleep overcame me.

After starting coffee I spread the Phoenix newspaper on the dining room table and sat down. The headline grabbed my gut, "Local Businessman Killed in Fatal Fall." I quickly scanned the article and learned that the man who had flown past us at Walnut Canyon was Steven Potter, a Phoenix antique dealer. Details were sketchy, but an anonymous source had informed the newspaper that Potter had accidentally fallen when hiking at Walnut Canyon. I got up, filled an SPPD coffee mug, and returned to the table to re-read the lead story. The last line said the coroner had determined the death was accidental.

"Bullshit!" I pounded my fist on the table and made the coffee slop on the newspaper. Steve Potter had been murdered. Either the newspaper had misquoted someone or had spoken with someone who wasn't qualified to comment.

One of the tough parts of being a St. Paul detective was having thirty open cases. Once a case was past the first 48 hours, there was never enough time to investigate it fully. This case would be different, I told myself. I'd be working just one case without distractions—it would be a luxury most cops never had. I leaned back and closed my eyes. "What have you gotten into? Is this really what you want to do for the next phase of your life?"

I threw the newspaper on the couch without rereading the full article and poured another cup of coffee. I stood staring out the window, looking at the San Franciso Peaks shadowing Flagstaff. My reflection on the glass showed me how rapidly I was becoming a middle-aged man. I was comfortable. I had my pension. The townhouse was paid for. Nobody told me what to do or when to do it. Gordon Lightfoot's "Carefree Highway" ran through my mind, the lyric about a girl named Ann whose idea of living was "just being satisfied."

Is being satisfied, enough? If nothing else, I wanted to embarrass whoever said Steven Potter had died of a fall while walking the trail. My hunter instinct kicked in and I wanted to solve this murder. I thought about the guy Todd had described as the body builder and I could visualize myself snapping handcuffs on his wrists.

By the time Todd and El returned from their runs and showered, I had a fresh pot of coffee setting on the table along with a plate of dry whole wheat toast. I put a spoon in a jar of strawberry jam and set it next to the toast. As they sat down, I announced the headline story about the "accident" we'd witnessed at Walnut Canyon. They sat dumbfounded.

El was even more upset than she had been the night before. She started reading the article. "The coroner said the fall was the cause of death?" She waved the paper around while Todd tried to grab it from her. She finally handed him the paper and stared at me, awaiting a response.

"Well, I think it's a screw-up or a cover-up. If it's a cover-up, somebody wants the world to think this was an accident. We know better."

Todd scanned the news and looked up. "Holy shit. This isn't at all what happened." He set the paper on the table. "What are you going to do?" He directed the question at me, like I was supposed to have the answers.

"I'm going to ignore the newspaper report and push ahead with the investigation."

Todd looked at me with surprise. "You're serious? You think you can make a difference when a coroner already declared the death an accident?"

"I need to do this. Besides, if the official line is that it was an accident, the county and FBI are not going to do anything. The case is closed." I got up and paced the living room.

"I've got the Park Service pickup, so you guys can continue to roam around in the Isuzu."

* * *

I took the old Walnut Canyon road to the visitor center and grew increasingly irritated about the newspaper account of Steven Potter's death. I found Brad Peck in his austere office. Aside from a picture of the president hanging on the gray-colored back wall, it was devoid of decoration. The furniture was all gray painted metal, which looked like it had been recovered from a battleship.

"Mr. Fletcher!" He looked up from a pile of paper. "It's good to have you back!" He got up from the wooden chair with squeaking castors and offered his hand to me. "I assume you've heard who the accident victim was."

I nodded. "Calling his death an accident will make this doubly difficult from the Park Service standpoint. It puts a black mark on the park's record for having lost a visitor, and no other law enforcement agency will do anything."

Peck had a lost look in his face. "What do you mean, solve the case? It was an accident. The coroner said so."

I shook my head. "Bullshit. Somebody's covering this up."

Peck cocked his head. "Why? I mean, if someone killed the guy, why not say so?"

I sat in his visitor's chair. "I don't know. But I'm going to find out."

Peck shifted uneasily. "So, you're still taking the job?"

"I guess I miss the chase. This is as big a mystery as I've ever pursued." I spun his desk phone around and dialed Jill Rickowski's cell number.

She picked up on the third ring. "This is Jill."

"Hi, Jill, this is Doug Fletcher."

"My caller ID says you're calling from Walnut Canyon."

"I'm sitting at Brad's desk. I'll put you on speakerphone so we're all in the conversation." I punched the button and put down the receiver. "I read the newspaper account of the death and it's not sitting well with me."

Brad leaned back in his chair. "I'm not convinced it was anything but an accident."

I leaned forward and stabbed my finger into his desktop. "First, if it was an accident, why did the two guys shoot at my cousin? Secondly, I know Potter was at least unconscious when he hit the rocks. Thirdly, you've got a ranger in the hospital the assailants tried to run down. At a minimum, those two men are guilty of assaulting a Federal officer."

Rickowski and Peck were silent, apparently weighing my words. Jill spoke first, "The job is still yours. I cleared all the red tape last night. Brad, is there still a Park Service Law Enforcement badge around?"

He pulled open the lap drawer of his desk, sorted through pens, pencils, paper clips, and small, unidentifiable boxes until he found a box and opened it. He unpinned a badge larger than the standard Park Service Ranger's badge. It had "Law Enforcement" embossed across the bottom.

"Got it." He handed the badge to me. I touched the cold brass and felt a rush. I missed being a cop.

"I don't want to delay this. Brad, please swear him in."

Peck stood up and raised his right hand, signaling me to rise also. "Hold up your right hand. Do you promise to enforce the laws of the United States and defend the nation against all foes foreign and domestic, so help you God?"

I looked at him skeptically. "Just so we're clear. I don't have to wear one of those Smokey Bear hats, and I get to use the Park Service pickup?"

"No hat and yes to the pickup," Jill said emphatically over the phone.

"Then I swear." I dropped my hand.

"You can continue to use your current Park Service ID," Jill said. "We'll pull the picture from your current ID and you should have a FedEx package with permanent credentials identifying you as a Park Service Investigator in a few days. Go to the Arrowhead Store website and order a dress uniform. You'll need to wear your gray shirts and green pants while you're on duty inside a Park Service facility or if we've got VIPs around. Any other time, you're free to wear civvies. I've got a conference call with Washington in a minute. Brad, show Doug the information I emailed you this morning and then let him get to work."

I held the badge in my hand and contemplated pinning it on, but that seemed wrong with my faded blue denim shirt, although I'd seen *Walker, Texas Ranger* wear a badge on his denim. I took out my wallet and pinned it to the middle flap. The large badge made my wallet bulky, but it was a secure place to keep it for the time being. I made a mental note to look at badge holders when I ordered the dress uniform.

"It sounds like you and Jill think you should pursue this." Brad handed me a small stack of papers from the corner of his desk. "This in the information Jill got from the Phoenix FBI duty officer. You already know the deceased was Steven Potter. The medical examiner's report says Potter died from blunt force trauma, probably due to his fall. The coroner's file is marked 'Closed.'"

I flipped through the pages and stopped when I got to the autopsy report. "Really? They did the autopsy in Tucson? Why not Flagstaff or Phoenix? In my experience, there's no way to get autopsy results in time for the morning edition of the papers. It usually takes weeks to get the toxicology results."

Peck shrugged. "I guess I didn't question it."

"Why use a county coroner three hundred miles away?" I paused and took a deep breath. "Unless you've got someone on a string and he'll give you the results you want?"

Peck looked embarrassed. "Any chance you were wrong?"

"No way. If this wasn't a murder, why did those two guys run and shoot at Todd when he chased them? Don't forget that they also ran Ed down when they drove out." I was getting frustrated repeating the same words.

"Well, Okay." He went back to his computer and pulled up the autopsy results. "Potter's pockets were empty. The police found his wallet and personal stuff in his car parked in Flagstaff. The coroner found a figurine in his pocket . . . Kokopelli." He showed me a drawing of a stick figure that looked like a hump-backed ant playing a flute. Seeing my confusion, he added, "Kokopelli is a symbol associated with mischief and fertility in Southwest folklore."

"Don't the facts in the report sound strange to you? A businessman leaves his wallet in a car thirty miles away and the only thing in his possession is a figurine. Ignoring the two men shooting at Todd and Ed getting run down, don't you think something doesn't add up?"

Peck shrugged. "The FBI doesn't think so, but Jill is encouraging you to follow your nose."

I looked at the Kokopelli drawing. "I don't mean to sound stupid, but is this what the locals call a fetish?"

"There's a hundred figures that represent different things to the local tribes. A fetish is a small statue of a god-like figure. If you go to the local shops you'll see lots of carved bear and bird figurines. Kokopelli isn't a fetish in the true sense of the word. He's more of a figurine and isn't perceived to have the spiritual powers of a fetish."

I looked up at him. "Maybe someone was trying to leave a message. You said Kokopelli is a fertility symbol. Do you think Potter maybe knocked up someone's sister and this was revenge?"

Brad shrugged. "The press says Potter was a family man. The other thing I'll throw out is that generally the tribal folks don't think of Kokopelli as a symbol of human fertility, they think he's a symbol of the fertility of the earth. But I'll leave you to sort that out."

I smiled. Too many people have opinions about how to approach police work and the powerful ones like to see you follow their lead. I had an old partner who liked to listen to the opinions of folks and then when we walked away he'd say, "I love opinions. They're just like assholes—everyone's got one."

"Did Jill suggest what I should do first?"

"She asked me to set up a meeting for you."

I leaned back in the hard guest chair, took a yellow legal pad off the corner of the desk and put it on my lap. "With whom?" It seemed strange Jill had told me to run without interference when she'd already set a meeting for me.

"An officer from the Navajo Nation Police is going to meet you at the Only Breakfast and Lunch Cafe. The officer is Jamie Ballard. It's about ten miles north of here, across the interstate. Jill figures there's at least a fifty-fifty chance the Lincoln was driven to the reservation after they left here. At a minimum, it's good PR to have them meet our new investigator and to keep them up to speed on what's going on."

I leaned forward and pointed to the map posted on the wall behind his desk. "Show me where the roads run from here."

We stood up and he pointed to a large shaded area of the map. "Here are Walnut Canyon, Sunset Crater, and Wupatki Monuments. All the Park Service lands are brown." He slid his finger up the map from the entrance road on the north edge of Walnut Canyon and traced a red line going beyond the interstate. "Just north of here—you see the border of the light area? That marks the edge of the Navajo reservation. Most people call it the Rez. It covers most all the rest of northern Arizona in a sort of checkerboard, with pieces of private, non-tribal land, and some national forest land in green. The reservation is huge."

He spread his fingers and indicated a massive area that was shaded light green. Compared to the areas to the south of I-17 the tribal lands were devoid of roads. There were only about five towns. I recognized the name

Shiprock as one of the larger towns on the reservation, and I'd heard about a monthly auction in Tuba City.

"I called the Navajo Nation Police station in Shiprock," he continued. "They said it would be around ten before Jamie could make it to the restaurant."

I fished a pen out of my pants pocket and clicked it as I leaned a yellow legal pad against the wall. "What was the name of the restaurant again?"

"The Only Breakfast and Lunch Cafe."

I didn't write, only stared at him. "Really? That's the name?"

Brad shrugged. "I've never been there, but that's what the police dispatcher called it." He pointed his pencil at an unremarkable spot on a thin red line a few miles north of the interstate. "From what I understand, it's about here."

I wrote the name down and made a mental note of the location, then put the pen away. "Any other suggestions?"

Brad looked at me nervously. "Umm . . . have you got a gun?"

I reached back and patted the lump on my hip under the tail of my denim shirt. "Jill suggested I use my personal Glock until she can have a Sig Sauer issued to me."

Having the holster on my belt felt strange. When I retired I had been happy to turn in the Glock I'd been assigned by St. Paul. I still owned personal guns which I kept in a gun safe, but returning the department issued gun made me feel free. This morning, when I pulled my Glock out of the lock box, it had felt like getting reacquainted with an old friend.

Brad nodded. "I hope you never have to use it. I'm sure it takes forever to fill out the reports."

I smiled. "Jill warned me about that. I spent almost twenty years as a St. Paul cop and I never fired my weapon except on the range."

He looked relieved. He took a green credit card from his desk drawer. "Use this card for gas only. We had a couple of seasonal rangers charge candy bars on one, which got them fired and resulted in a week of paperwork for me." From the expression on his face I couldn't tell if he was kidding or not. I promised not to charge any Snickers bars.

Chapter 9

I drove roughly ten miles and found a single-story wood structure that looked like it hadn't seen paint in fifty years. The faded sign in front identified it as the Only Breakfast and Lunch Café, just as Brad had described. The siding had either shrunk or been arranged to allow natural ventilation through gaps between the boards. An older Ford pickup, the only vehicle in sight, was parked near the front door. A saddled sway-backed horse was tied to a post a few feet away from the building.

The interior was much more pleasing than the exterior. A dozen Formica-topped tables were spread around the floor with vinyl-covered chairs at each. The room featured a long counter on one side with eight stools. All the furniture was obviously worn beyond normal restaurant standards but there wasn't a speck of dust or a grease smudge in sight. Someone took pride in this low-budget operation.

A wide man sat on one stool, the gap between his white t-shirt and drooping jeans exposing dark skin and a crack I didn't care to see. He turned just far enough to get a look at me before returning to his newspaper and coffee. I chose a table next to the wall furthest from the door, where I would be able to see the rush of customers. It was almost five minutes before a weathered Navajo woman, wearing a pink tank top and faded jeans, wandered out of the kitchen and noticed me sitting at the table.

She retrieved a coffee pot from a burner and poured a refill for the guy sitting at the counter, who grunted his thanks. She sauntered over to my table and turned my cup over without asking if I wanted coffee. Her jet-black hair was tied in a ponytail, her face creased with tiny wrinkles. She could've been forty, but her weathered face said I might add twenty years to that estimate if not for the lack of gray hair.

"Special's huevos rancheros." She set silverware wrapped in a paper napkin in front of me and looked at me expectantly.

Lacking the offer of a menu, I looked around to see if there was a board listing the chef's offerings. I didn't spot any and the waitress was unmoved by my visual query.

"What else is on the menu?"

Her eyes were almost black and I could see the tiredness in them. My presence and the few bucks I was about to spend were an inconvenience. Maybe she was into a routine and I was somehow breaking the rhythm.

"The usual. Eggs. Toast. Tortillas. Beans." She shrugged as if to say that was about it.

Somehow ranchero sauce and beans didn't light my fire. I'd had "squirrel belly" for weeks after my introduction to real, spicy, Southwestern food. I didn't want to tempt fate now that my system had returned to normal. "Have you got a sweet roll or Danish?"

She shook her head no. I pondered the options as she got uneasy under my stare. "Maybe some toast." That seemed to please her.

I sipped the strong, bitter coffee. Within a minute I could feel the caffeine coursing through my veins. My pulse and blood pressure rose as the level of the cup went down. By the time I could see the white bottom of the cup, the waitress was back with buttered toast on a simple white plate and the coffee pot.

She topped off the coffee and pointed to a little pot of pink sauce in a small bowl. "Prickly pear jam." She walked away before I could request cream for my coffee or peanut butter for my toast.

The toast was made from homemade bread that had a delicious sweetness to it. I was leery of the prickly pear jam but it was sweet and surprisingly tasty.

By the time I finished the toast the early lunch crowd was starting to trickle in. A couple took a table on the opposite side of the room after eyeing me carefully. A guy wearing a cowboy hat and looking like a trucker took a seat next to the wide-backed guy at the counter. I couldn't help but notice the big wallet chained to his belt. The two men grunted back and forth, their words indistinguishable to me, before settling into their coffee cups and newspapers. At eleven-thirty, just as I gave up on my ten o'clock appointment and got up to leave, a hatless young man wearing a badge on a tan uniform shirt, jeans, and weathered cowboy boots, walked in and surveyed the crowd. He was lean to the point of anorexia, with none of the hardness I saw in the faces of most experienced police officers.

When he looked my way, I gave him a nod and sat down. He came to the table and pulled out a chair. He plopped down and leaned heavily on the table. "You Fletcher?"

I pushed the plate away and wadded up the paper napkin. "Yup. You Ballard?"

"Everyone calls me Jamie." He looked around the room and waved a finger at the waitress. "So, what brings a park ranger to the Rez?"

The waitress came to the table and filled his cup before topping off mine. "Huevos rancheros?" she asked.

"Sure. I want the eggs hard . . . no salmonella."

She sputtered an unintelligible response as she wandered off. "The food's good, but . . . I see you already tried it." He nodded toward the empty plate with my napkin.

"I've had plenty of time to eat. I thought we were meeting at ten." I knew sarcasm wasn't going to buy me a friend, but I wanted to set some ground rules.

He didn't seem to care. He continued to survey the locals and nodded greetings as a young woman with a toddler on her hip came in and sat at the counter. "You haven't experienced

Indian time?" His face was stone . . . no hint of mirth.

I took it in stride. "Is that like in Mexico when they tell you *mañana* and you think that means tomorrow, but it actually means some time in the future?"

Jamie raised an eyebrow and asked, "You speak Spanish?"

"*Un poco.* I had a few years of Spanish when I was a kid. Most of it's still stuck in the back of my head somewhere, but it doesn't make me conversational."

Jamie sipped the coffee and nodded. "That's unusual. Most whites don't bother learning another language." Jamie nodded at the two cowboys who sat at the table next to us. "They call a person who speaks two languages bilingual. A person who speaks one language is called American." He waved his empty coffee cup at the waitress and she nodded.

"The Mexicans mean soon, or if I don't get busy. Indian time means I'll be there, but not necessarily by your watch."

The waitress showed up, set a huge plate of food in front of Jamie, and topped off our coffees. His meal was a mountain of eggs covered with salsa with a side plate of tortillas. I watched him sprinkle it liberally with Tabasco sauce before mounding it on a corn tortilla and stretching his mouth wide to take in the load. He broke into a sweat after the first bite. I was relieved I'd chosen toast.

He mopped his face with a paper napkin. "I hear you lost a hiker yesterday." It was a comment, not a question. He finished the first tortilla in one bite without looking up.

"Steve Potter. Two guys shoved him off the ledge. He was dead before he hit bottom."

Ballard swallowed the second load of eggs and washed it down with a swallow of coffee. "Who's Potter and what's it got to do with me?"

"He's a Phoenix antiques dealer. Two guys dumped his body over the railing. They tried to make it look like an accident but there were witnesses. It was murder."

"You're sure it wasn't the fall that killed him?" He piled another load of eggs on the second tortilla.

The more I watched him eat, the more I felt this was a lost meeting. "Maybe I should go and let you eat in peace." I started to push my chair back and stand.

He stuck a finger up as he attempted to swallow the quarter pound of food in his mouth. "Take it easy." He mumbled around the food, catching some dribbles on the napkin in his hand. "I just want to know what's up. I haven't eaten anything but power bars in two days. Been out tracking a guy who beat up his wife and stole the family's jewelry to buy drugs." He wiped the bits of food that had escaped during his comments. "I just want to get some background. Okay?"

I eased back and let my hackles down. I was skeptical about his claim he hadn't eaten in two days. If it was true, his story might explain why he hadn't heard about Potter's death.

"Fair enough. There were two guys with Potter when they arrived at Walnut Canyon. One was a skinny Caucasian. The other was dark . . . maybe Mexican."

"Or Indian," he added.

I nodded. "Or Indian."

He waved a fork at me. "Pretty much the same thing. Most Mexicans are half Indian. It's the same gene pool. Did you know they did a scientific study and determined that all the Indians in the Americas descended from two women? They check the DNA in the mitochondria which is only passed from the mother to her children."

I nodded politely, surprised by his knowledge, and annoyed that he couldn't seem to stay on track. "They pushed Potter over the railing and drove off in a stolen baby blue Lincoln with license plate GRAMPS. The state patrol was coming from the east and didn't see them, and Flagstaff PD didn't see them going west so they either went north or hopped off on a side road. Oh, and they ran down a ranger at the gate who needed surgery for his compound fracture."

He scraped the juice from the plate with the spoon and slurped it down, followed by a wash of coffee. "Big time Federal offense, killing someone at a national park and assaulting a Federal officer." He signaled for a refill of coffee. "What do you want from me?"

"I hope you can help me find the Lincoln, or at least find someone who saw it go by." The waitress refilled our cups and left.

He stared into the cup. "No one's reported an abandoned Lincoln. On the other hand, abandoned cars sometimes have a high vapor pressure." He read the empty look on my face. "Sorry, they evaporate." He made a rising motion with his hands like steam. "The salable parts get stripped and the frame goes to the junkyard for the scrap iron. Someone told me that abandoning a car on the Rez is sometimes like leaving your car on the Chicago expressway—you come back in an hour to a grease spot."

I nodded knowingly. He finished his coffee and threw a twenty-dollar bill on the table. I dug for my wallet but he put up a hand. "I got it. You don't get per diem unless you're out of town overnight. The Council covers all my meals while I'm working."

I shrugged. "Okay."

Outside, he waved me to a dusty Suburban with a star on the door. As I opened the door he picked up a wrinkled uniform shirt off the passenger seat and threw it into the backseat.

"Is it safe to leave my Park Service vehicle here?"

"As long as you lock it up and take the keys," Jamie said as he backed the Suburban away from the hitching rail.

"Did you catch him?"

Jamie pulled out of the lot. "You mean the guy who beat up his wife?"

"Yes. Did you catch him?"

For the first time he smiled, showing the first sign of crow's feet at the corners of his eyes. "He was hiding in an old cave. Seemed pretty surprised to see me."

I nodded. "You spot his car or get a tip?"

Jamie shook his head no. "Tracked him on foot."

I turned and searched his face for a hint he was joking. "You're kidding."

"Two days on foot. It's been dry and we had a full moon. The tracks held up well. Lost him once over some rock, but picked it up again after a couple of hours circling."

We sat in silence for the remainder of the half-hour drive. He slowed as we passed every side road and gulley. Finally, he stopped at a dry gulley and we got out. Jamie stooped low and examined some tire tracks that ran off the road. He grabbed a handful of sand from the bed of the low wash and let it dribble from the bottom of his fist. "It's not the Lincoln, but I think we'd better follow this arroyo for a while. Nobody's got any business down there."

"What's an arroyo?"

"It's a dry wash or a streambed. Sometimes we get enough rain to make it a small stream during the monsoon season. When we get a big rain the arroyos become raging torrents for a day or two. Most of the year they're just meandering low gulches in the desert."

"You're sure it's not the Lincoln?" I climbed back into the Suburban.

He started the engine and we followed the tracks. "The tires are too narrow and too close together—more like a mid-sized car."

He rolled down his window, shut down the air conditioner and the blower fan. I sized up his comments and agreed, although I doubt I would've come up with that analysis on my own. We drove for a few miles across the scrub grass, rock, and sand, the Suburban rolling with the terrain. At each rise he'd slow the Suburban and creep over the edge, listening and getting a slow reveal of the area ahead. After forty minutes we stopped and he turned off the engine just before a rise. Jamie sat still and leaned his head close to the open window. With the air conditioner off the two of us were both sweating like we were melting.

I rolled down my window and listened too. All I could hear was the wind as the gusts swirled sand around the vehicle. From the look of the dusty fender I surmised that the Suburban had spent a lot of time in the desert. The paint looked like it had been sandblasted to a matte finish.

Jamie opened the door and pulled a cowboy hat and a binoculars case out of the backseat. He gave no indication he wanted me along, but I grabbed my Minnesota Twins baseball cap and followed him. As he approached the crest of the hill he crouched and then crawled to the top of the ridge. I followed behind as he fell on his elbows and pulled the Nikon binoculars out of the scarred case. He trained them across the horizon and scanned slowly from left to right.

"Sonofabitch." He pushed the binoculars to me. "Look at the notch in the far ridge, and then follow it down the arroyo."

I finally found the notch and followed it down. Just visible above the nearer ridge was a reflection from glass. As I concentrated on the glint of reflected sunshine, I identified the white top of a car. "What do you think they're doing?"

Jamie stood up and waited for me to rise from my aching knees. "They're probably raiding an archeological site." He stuffed the binoculars into the case as we walked back to the vehicle. "We'll go check."

When we returned to the Suburban he opened the back and took out two plastic bottles of water, handing one to me. "Be careful to stay hydrated."

As Jamie drove a circuitous route toward the distant valley he explained more about the situation. "There's big business in ancient artifacts that are recovered both on and off the reservation. Collectors all over the world are buying them up. Some people are scavenging archaeological sites and others are making fakes. Seems like most of the buyers are private and lots of them aren't smart enough to know a fake from something a thousand years old. Many of the wealthy collectors aren't too concerned about the provenance of the items in their personal collections. As the supply of legal artifacts dried up, those being the ones taken from private land, the prices have gone crazy. As a result, there's more illegal looting of protected sites going on. The looting's pretty well controlled in the national parks and monuments, but on the reservation there just aren't enough Navajo Nation Police officers to keep track of the twenty seven thousand square miles of the reservation spread over Arizona and New Mexico. The Bureau of Land Management and Forest Service do a little better at monitoring Federal lands. They have a few college interns to drive around and make it look like they're paying attention to what's happening."

We rounded a small knob and Jamie shut off the engine and let the Suburban roll down the arroyo behind the knob. When the Suburban stopped he got out, quietly leaving the door open behind him. I followed his lead, trying to be quiet. He opened the back of the Suburban and pulled out an expensive aluminum gun case that looked like it had been dragged behind the Suburban for a hundred miles. He extracted a well-worn Remington 700, a gun I'd seen used by snipers in Iraq. This one was without the sensitive optics that made snipers effective at a thousand yards in the battlefield. Jamie's gun had simple iron sights and the bluing had worn away, making it look like scuffed stainless steel. He worked the bolt to feed a shell into the chamber. After setting the safety and pushing the gun case back into the Suburban, he slung the gun over his shoulder. He opened a small cardboard box and took out a handful of ammo for the rifle, then handed me another bottle of water. He slid a water bottle into his pocket.

"I figured you for a canteen," I was glad that my pants were loose enough to put a bottle in the pocket, too. There didn't seem to be many other options.

"I used to carry a canteen, but the water sometimes sits too long and gets bad. Some of the wells have a lot of sulfur that makes the water stink. It's easier to grab a bottle that I know is fresh and recycle it when I'm done. With plastic bottles there's nothing rattling around either. Canteens slosh or bang against a rock at the most inconvenient times."

"You're not going to call to let anyone know where we are or what we're doing?"

He held the rifle up. "Here's our backup." He slipped his shoulder back into the sling and started down the arroyo. "Looks like you've got a holster on your belt. I hope it's loaded and you know how to use it." He didn't wait for a response.

I had to jog to keep up with his long purposeful strides. I felt like an elephant trying to follow a cat. He carefully chose where he put his feet down, avoiding sticks and rocks, while I stumbled around tripping on stones and kicking rocks loose. To his credit, he tolerated my commotion without comment or accusative glares.

The dry desert wind was non-existent in the arroyo between the two ridges. Jamie's shirt was wet in the small of his back and under his arms. I looked at mine and realized it was soaked. I reached back and felt the damp leather of my holster, then took out the bottle and drank a quarter of it as I loped along.

Jamie started up the slope of a ridge with the skill of a mountain goat. I struggled behind, wishing I were ten years younger and thirty pounds lighter. By the time I approached the ridge top, sounding like a steam train, Jamie was lying flat on a rock, looking through the binoculars. I slid alongside as silently as I could. I looked across a canyon that had a few scrubby bushes along the bottom. It was about a half mile wide and the far slope was layered with stone.

"The car's right below us, but I don't see anyone around." he whispered. I slid up far enough so I could see the car. A Ford Taurus sat in the bottom of the shallow canyon about 150 yards away. The sun had oxidized the car's finish and the sand had worn at a few of the sharp fender's edges but it had escaped the cancerous rust that destroyed cars in the Midwest. The driver's door and trunk were open, but there wasn't a sign of any human activity.

"Can you make out any footprints?" I interjected my one thought, then felt stupid. At that distance I knew he couldn't unless they'd been lighting flares as they walked.

Jamie focused the binoculars on the car. "We're too far away to make out anything on the hardpan. There's an overhang that looks like it might have a cave under it behind the car." He handed the binoculars to me.

It took a few seconds for me to adjust the focus and to find the spot. I was surprised at how much color there was in the layers of rock. Everything looked tan until I looked through the binocular. Then I could make out the greens and rusts in the individual layers that comprised the canyon wall along with dark blue-green of the junipers.

I found the overhanging rock and studied the dark shadow under the edge. As my eyes adjusted I made out a darker spot that might be the mouth of a cave.

Jamie punched my arm. His voice was almost a hiss. "To the left . . . behind the candlewood bush."

I swung the glasses left and studied a group of scrubby leafless bushes with upright spikes. I caught a flash of motion, something white, and watched intently, expecting to see a deer or jackrabbit slink away. A cowboy hat appeared over the top of the bush and bobbed there for a few seconds as if it were on a string. It swung to the side and a very slender man, carrying a roll of toilet paper, emerged walking stiffly along the ridge. The man walked along a seam in the rock where there must've been a trail, I handed the Nikons back to Jamie.

"He went into the hole." Jamie lowered the binoculars. "I wonder if he's got any friends in there." Jamie seemed to be in no hurry to do anything.

I rolled onto my back and flexed my knees. They had both been clicking as we climbed up the hill. Now they ached. The Aleve I'd taken with breakfast had knocked down the pain until now.

"You got a bum wheel?" Jamie asked as he slid back from the ridgeline, leaving the rifle and binoculars where he'd been lying. He took the water bottle out of his pocket and cracked open the plastic lid.

It reminded me about the bottle in my pocket. The water was warm, but tasted good on my parched lips. "Yeah, torn ligament. Remnants of a previous life."

"Hmm." He seemed to understand. "Football?"

"Cop, in St. Paul."

He pushed the brim of his hat up with the lip of the bottle. "You're a long way from Minnesota."

"I'm supposed to be retired."

He cracked a smile. "Are you running to, or from, something?"

His smile hit me wrong and I got a little irritated. "I liked Flagstaff. That's all." I looked for something to lean against among the rocks on the slope and found a sloped flat rock a foot away. I slid my butt over and leaned my back against the hot surface.

"Nobody likes Flagstaff that well. Phoenix, maybe . . . but no one moves to Flag unless they've got a job or family there." He slid around, again peeking back over the top of the ridge.

"How about you, Jamie Ballard? That's not an Indian name." I watched for a reaction out of the corner of my eye. He picked up the binoculars and looked through them toward the car.

"My father was Ballard, a Lutheran missionary sent to save the heathen natives. Dad fell for the pretty Navajo girl and they got married, but she wouldn't leave her people when he was 'called' to a new mission." Jamie's explanation was matter of fact, like he'd given it a million times before. "My mother had to work to pay for groceries and rent, so I was raised by my grandmother. I got a scholarship to a good Lutheran college in Missouri, courtesy of my father's contacts, and then I moved back here. One of the old Navajo Nation Police officers retired and someone remembered I was one of the most well-educated people around, so they appointed me. End of story."

I was a little embarrassed by his simple story and vowed to stay humble. "I ran away from a bad divorce and a bad habit of crying in my whiskey when I talked with old buddies in the cop bars. I kinda like Flagstaff because it has some seasons . . . like Minnesota. It's got clean air and friendly people. Somehow it physically represented the clean start I needed to reset my life."

"They're coming down." His voice changed to a whisper and had a touch of excitement.

I slid up to the break in the ridge and Jamie handed me the binoculars. Two men were walking down the slope from the cave, each wearing a knapsack. The one to the left, seen previously with the toilet paper, was using a shovel like a walking stick. They appeared to be talking but were too far away to be heard over the rushing wind. Their steps appeared stiff, giving me the impression that the men were probably past retirement age.

Jamie slid off the ridgeline and I followed until we were low enough to stand up out of their sight. He handed me the rifle. "Follow the ridge down to the north. I'll grab the Suburban and cut them off." He watched me sling the gun over my shoulder. "You do know how to shoot, don't you?"

I smiled. "Just like a shotgun, isn't it? Point and pull the trigger."

He shook his head.

I watched him disappear behind a hump in the hillside before I pulled the Remington down and checked the round in the chamber. It was a 30-06 with a silvertip bullet. I couldn't tell how heavy the bullet was. Silver tips are deadly . . . intended to penetrate a heavy bone and kill a bear or elk. Anyone shot with this gun was not going to make it to a hospital. I chambered the shell, slipped the safety on, slung the rifle over my shoulder and started down the backside of the ridge.

By the time I got to the bottom of the ridge, I could hear the creaking of the Ford's springs as it bounced over the uneven ground. A second sound, a rattling clatter, came from behind. I found a soft, sandy spot and unslung the rifle. I dropped to my knees and slipped the military sling around my left arm like a sharpshooter, pulling it tight as I slid down to my belly and lined up the sights. Out of the corner of my eye I saw the Suburban bounding over rocks and a small gully before it shot into the bottom of the canyon. It slid to a stop with lights flashing and Jamie jumped out. The car eased slowly to a stop as Jamie waved his arms, carefully maintaining a position behind the Suburban so any gunshots would be absorbed in the mass of the truck's engine.

I watched the two men inside the car over the top of the rifle. I slid my thumb onto the safety as they opened the car doors, my trigger finger carefully outside the trigger guard for safety. The front sight rested uneasily on the driver as he stepped clear of the car. He was about seventy yards away, which wasn't a long shot with a reliable rifle, but I became aware it had been awhile since I had qualified on a range with a rifle. The sights that would once have been locked on a spot on his chest now moved on and off the checkered red shirt. I became aware that the man was waving at Jamie, and the second man was also out of the car.

Both men had white hair, were smiling, and didn't appear to be carrying any weapons. I took a deep breath and watched them approach Jamie, who had moved from behind the Suburban. The driver was talking, his words lost in the wind. Earlier in my life, I would've relaxed when I saw the gray hair of the two men, but experience told me that even old guys carry guns, and a smile is sometimes a ruse prior to a gun being pulled out. Jamie's life might depend on my caution and an accurate shot.

"Hey son, what are you doing out here?" The man's voice was light, almost jovial. I continued to keep the men roughly in the sights, although my adrenaline rush died down.

"Are you lost?" Jamie asked. The men walked up to him until they stood in a cluster. The voices lost volume and I couldn't hear the conversation anymore. After a few seconds, Jamie waved to me as they walked to their car. By the time I rechecked the safety and got the rifle sling back over my shoulder, they had the trunk open and were passing around rocks.

Jamie looked at a chunk of quartz with a streak of purple running through it. "They're prospectors. Looking for gold." He looked back at the two old men. Up close, they appeared to be in their eighties. "You can't prospect here, guys. This is the Navajo reservation. You can't stake a claim here." He set the rock back into the trunk.

The older of the two was the driver, the one in the red-checked shirt, rubbed the gray stubble on his chin. "Well, I can understand, but we don't really want the gold."

"Then why prospect?" I asked. My voice, as I approached from behind, startled the men.

The second man turned toward me. He was thin as a rail and wore a white t-shirt over his blue jeans. He was bow-legged, like he'd been riding horses his entire life. Both of them were caked with red dirt and their shirts were soaked with sweat.

"Because of the chase. Hell, we'll never live long enough to develop a mine and enjoy the riches. We just want to be famous, like the Grosh brothers."

Jamie and I looked at each other, expecting the other to have a spark of recognition. "Who are the Grosh brothers?" I directed the question to the guy in the red shirt.

He gave me a look as if I were from Mars. "They discovered the Comstock Lode, in Nevada." He looked down. "Too bad they were killed before they got the results of their assays. They did discover it, and that's all we want too. It'll be the Benjamin and Frisk Lode."

Jamie shook his head. "I don't want to see you back here until you get a permit from the tribal council."

The man beamed. "Well, I'll tell you, if these rocks assay out as good as their color looks, the tribal council will greet us with open arms."

"How long have you two been prospecting this area?" Jamie asked casually.

"A couple weeks around here. A couple decades across Northern Arizona."

"In our younger days, we used to walk and use a donkey to haul our gear," the t-shirted man explained. "Now we use the Taurus and focus on places with easier access."

I removed the cartridge from the Remington and fed it back into the magazine, then closed the bolt on the empty chamber as Jamie finished getting their names and addresses.

I put the gun back into the case as the Taurus started to lumber over the uneven arroyo floor. After I stowed the rifle, I grabbed another bottle of water and drained it. I opened the driver's door and started the Suburban's engine, turning the air conditioner on high.

By the time Jamie got into the Suburban the temperature inside had dropped to the mid-hundred degrees. I sat in the passenger's seat as he threw his sweat-stained cowboy hat into the backseat.

"Do you run into many prospectors?" I asked as he buckled his seat belt and slipped the transmission into drive.

"I've stopped a couple guys who claimed to be prospectors. I suspect they were artifact hunters and it was easier to say they were unsuccessful prospectors than admit they were grave robbers looting archeological sites."

Chapter 10

The temperature inside the Suburban was starting to feel frosty, maybe eighty degrees, as we neared the road. I took off my Twins cap and set it on the console. My sweat had stained it a darker shade of blue and it had a white ring of salt at the edge of the perspiration. I weighed the wisdom of finding a fully brimmed cap that would protect my face and ears from the intense UV rays at this altitude where the air was thin and the sun unforgiving.

"The old guys saw the Lincoln yesterday. They were further south and it blew by them going north." The words came out with no fanfare and were barely enough to bring me out of the cap discussion running inside my head.

Jamie's voice jarred me back to reality. "What?"

He let out a grunt as we hit a deep ridge at the edge of the pavement. "The prospectors saw the blue Lincoln yesterday. It was headed north." He cranked the wheel and the tires sang on the blacktop as the speed of the Suburban increased.

I stared at him, half in disbelief. "When did they tell you that?"

"I asked them about the car while we were waiting for you to come out of your hiding spot."

"So, what's your plan?"

His eyes stayed riveted on the road. "We go north and check some more spots. Say, you didn't take the safety off when you held the gun on those guys, did you?"

I bristled at the question. "That sounds like a question you'd ask a rookie."

Jamie shrugged, apparently oblivious to my sarcasm. "Naw. It's just that the trigger sear has been honed. If the safety is off, all you have to do is touch the trigger for the gun to fire."

"Thanks for the warning," I paused, waiting for him to catch the sarcasm. "Is there anything else I should know before it kills me or someone else?"

"Nothing that comes to mind, but I'll keep thinking."

I looked at his face, but there was no hint that he was kidding. I reflected back on the old men. I'd put my thumb on the safety and carefully moved it from the "safe" position without putting my finger near the trigger. Those were all the "right" things to do. I smiled inwardly, thinking that my years as a cop were still ingrained in my habits and that I still knew how to be a good cop three years after retirement.

I just wished my body was as prepared as my head. The climb through the hills had one knee aching and my back muscles tight. I wasn't a young man anymore but I had hoped that my experience would offset my physical limitations. I'd had conversations with hundreds of cops over the years and arrests were rarely determined by the fastest sprinter, but rather by the smartest chaser. A guy sprinting away from a stolen car almost always loses when a cop follows in a car and cuts him off at a cross street. Now that the number of candles on my birthday cakes were becoming a fire hazard, I had to rely heavily on smart over speed. It was going to take a while for the cobwebs to clear from the "smart cop" part of my brain as I relearned how to moderate my adrenaline rush.

* * *

After half an hour of silence the Suburban slowed as we approached a small path that wound out of sight behind a low ridge. We followed the rough trail for nearly a quarter mile until we came upon a dwelling that could best be described as a hut. It was constructed from scraps of car hoods, plywood, and corrugated metal siding, all used randomly, apparently as they became available. A variety of windows were cut into the wood portions of the walls. Behind the house an old Ford pickup rested on its brake drums near an outhouse that looked like it had never been painted. Without the ravages of humidity, it was difficult to gauge how long the pickup had been sitting there. Maybe a month. Maybe a decade. I had buddies in St. Paul who spent their weekends scouring salvage yards trying to find an old car or truck to fix up, usually settling on something far less pristine than the old pickup I was looking at.

As we rolled to a stop, I picked up my cap and secured it on my head. As I reached for the door handle Jamie gripped my arm. "Wait."

I looked at his hand, then his face. He was staring at the house and I followed his gaze, expecting to see something. I scanned the house, then the surrounding landscape. I couldn't pick up anything of interest.

"What's up?" I looked beyond the house and nearby bushes, expecting to see someone, or something, lurking in the distance.

"Just wait. She's not ready for us yet." He turned to face me and I gave him a questioning look. "It's impolite to barge into a house. Someone will come out when they're ready for us."

"Do you do this all the time?"

He nodded his head imperceptibly. "Especially with the elders. It's a way of showing respect and it gives them a chance to prepare."

Although it was a little confusing, the more I thought about it, the practice made sense. Who wouldn't appreciate a custom that allows you to throw your shoes under the couch or clear the dishes from the table before visitors knock on your front door? On the other hand, when we'd executed search warrants in St. Paul we burst in and raced through the house before the residents could destroy evidence or flush drugs down the toilet.

While we waited, Jamie commented, "I'm surprised there aren't FBI helicopters buzzing around here like dragonflies."

A smile came to my lips as an elderly person of indecipherable gender opened the door, waiting for us. The stout person had gray hair pulled back in a ponytail and wore a western-cut shirt and jeans. As we got out I explained, "The FBI thinks Potter's death was an accident and they're not looking."

Jamie stopped and looked at me. "What?"

"The FBI thinks it was an accident. They're not looking anymore." I kept walking. Jamie quickly followed but continued to give me a quizzical look. "They declared the death an accident?" he asked again.

We walked up to the elderly person—a woman, I decided. Her face showed no expression and Jamie mumbled something to her before I could get close enough to hear the words. She nodded and led us into her small one-room house without shaking hands or speaking a word. The kitchen was closest to the door and the bed at the farthest recess of the room. The bed was covered with a beautiful wool blanket woven of reds, grays, and yellows. Jamie and I sat on the only two chairs at the kitchen table as she plopped down on the well-worn couch.

"Jamie Ballard, you don't come to visit your aunt often." Her face was lined with deep creases from many years in the sun. A large white scar pocked her neck where she'd probably had skin cancer removed. She sounded disappointed.

"How is your garden, Aunt Mary?" Jamie ignored the admonition.

She shook her head. "It's so dry this year. I spend many hours a day pumping water and carrying it to the squash to keep it from turning to dust and blowing away."

Jamie nodded his head and winked at me. "Yes, it's very bad. Everyone on the reservation is losing their gardens. It will be a difficult winter."

She nodded in agreement. "Almost a waste of the seeds. I'm lucky to have a well that draws. I can't carry as much anymore. The buckets get heavier every year."

Jamie cracked a smile and looked at me. "Aunt Mary carries water about a quarter mile in five-gallon pails." He looked back to her. "So you can only carry them half-full these days?" I did a quick calculation in my head. Even a half-full five-gallon bucket weighed over twenty pounds.

"Oh no, that would waste time. I fill them about six inches from the top, so they don't slop and lose the water." I sized up the woman who couldn't have been five-foot-two and was hauling pairs of forty-pound buckets of water to her garden.

"Tell me, Aunt Mary, did you see a blue car yesterday?" Jamie leaned forward and looked at her intently, signaling this was an important question.

Mary closed her eyes as if she were visualizing the previous day. "Yes, two blue cars. Eddie Passault went to town and back. He has a dark blue car, like lapis. The other was a different shade of blue, like the sky." She opened her eyes.

"Going north?"

She nodded assent. "Yes, north. Short time after Eddie went past."

I gave Jamie a hopeful look. He saw my excitement.

"Aunt Mary, what time did they pass?"

She rocked back and forth a little. "Both were after noon and before sunset."

"Did you see any cars going south after the sky-blue car passed?" I asked.

Aunt Mary looked at me like she'd just realized I was there. Her milky eyes made me wonder how credible she was, looking through thick cataracts.

"A Jeep went by, going south."

"A Jeep Wrangler or Cherokee?" I asked.

"It was an ordinary Jeep with a top."

"Do you remember what color it was?"

"It was very dusty, so it looked brown."

I'm sure Jamie looked at me as I let out a sigh. Jamie made small talk for a few more minutes, then we said goodbye and left Aunt Mary, looking stoic, standing by the door of her home.

"I take it that her definition of, 'very soon after,' falls in the dimension of, 'Indian time'?"

Jamie shrugged as we turned north again on the pavement. "There are so few significant events in her life that she measures them relatively. Two things that happen the same afternoon are a busy day for her." He paused for a second. "Now tell me again why the helicopters aren't flying around here."

"The newspaper said Steven Potter died from an accidental fall at Walnut Canyon. They've apparently decided to ignore the fact that the men shot at a tourist and seriously injured a ranger. In their minds, the case is closed."

Jamie digested that. "So, why are we driving around trying to find a blue Lincoln?"

"Because the official version is not what happened. I told you this morning what happened. We need to find the Lincoln and the two guys."

If Jamie disagreed, he didn't say so. We sat in silence for a while before I got tired of listening to the hum of the tires and road. "Mary looks a little too old to be your mother's sister. Maybe a great aunt?"

Jamie shook his head. "Not a blood relative at all, at least not that you could trace on a family tree. Navajo society is matriarchal and Mary is from the same clan as my mother. That makes her one of my extended family members. I'm considered a bastard child, so all the women in the clan take special care to guide and watch over me. I'm very lucky. I've got a couple dozen 'aunts.'"

I nodded like I understood, although I didn't. We continued to drive north as the sun started to tilt lower in the west. I did a rough calculation that we were at least a two-hour drive from the restaurant where I'd left the Park Service pickup.

"What've you got up your sleeve for the rest of the day?" I threw out the nonchalant question hoping he'd catch the hint and turn south.

"You in a hurry?" Jamie said with a shrug. "There are a couple of dry washes up ahead that we should look at. It'll be too dark to continue searching in an hour or so."

I felt a little so-so about the plan but kept it to myself. In years past, the clock was never an issue. I worked whatever hours it took to follow the investigation. My dedication to that job cost me a marriage and a big chunk of my retirement cash in the form of a divorce settlement. Now that I didn't have a wife who would be irritated by my irregular hours I was unexpectedly worried about getting back. I rationalized that I had to get back to my guests, but realized that was a cop-out. They would fend for themselves. Mostly, I decided I was tired of riding in silence.

"You're pretty quiet. I've had lots of partners over the years and our conversations made the day go faster."

Jamie shrugged. "I guess I don't have anything to say. I've never had anyone ride along since training, so I kinda got out of the habit of talking."

"You married? Divorced? Involved? Gay?"

He smiled. "Not gay. Just unattached at the moment. I had a girl, but it was the usual thing. Her family was upset about her dating someone only half Navajo. On the reservation I'm called an apple—red on the outside, but white inside."

I hadn't considered that people in a minority would be prejudiced too, but it made sense when I thought about it. "Ever think about leaving the reservation?"

Jamie stifled a chuckle. "About three times a day."

"So, if you think about leaving so much, why don't you go?"

He shook his head. "I've got a responsible, respected position here. Out there, who knows?"

I nodded. "Here, you're a big fish in a little pond. Out there is a big ocean and the sharks are immense."

"I guess I never thought about it that way. But that's an okay analogy. I'm kind of nervous about the unknown. This is a sure thing and it's interesting. How about you?" He glanced over at me. "You're a middle-aged guy without a wedding ring. What's your backstory?"

I shrugged. "Divorced. The women I've met since are either drunks or married, with the exception of the young Park Service Rangers, who think of me as a father image." I paused.

"Well, there's an oversexed neighbor with two little boys who drops hints about stopping over after the kids are in bed. I've been avoiding her because she's a little too young and I'm not interested in being an instant dad to two boys."

"So you're still in the hunt but you haven't found someone you'd bring home to meet the family."

"Sort of. I'm not hunting very hard." We rolled to a stop at a dry wash that curved away from the road and got out to look for tire tracks. There weren't any, so we got back in. The sun was easing itself behind the hills and without clouds in the sky it would be a bland sunset. I was continually surprised by how quickly day went into night in the mountains. I was used to the lingering summer twilight in St. Paul. In the Arizona desert, sunset fades more quickly.

We walked back to the Suburban and Jamie started the engine. A blast of stale air from the air conditioner hit me in the face. "You want to head back? It'd be more efficient if you spent the night in Shiprock so we could get a jump on the search tomorrow." By the time he finished the question, cooler air started to flow from the vents.

I pondered his question. How would El and Todd get along without me? That question was quickly replaced by my concern about the Park Service vehicle. "Do you think the pickup will be safe sitting at the restaurant overnight?" I'd heard a rumor that Federal employees were responsible for the equipment allocated to them and had to pay for things they broke or lost.

Jamie shrugged. "It's in the parking lot. It should be okay."

I stared out the window. Given the option of spending a night in Shiprock, the idea of repeating the whole round trip tomorrow seemed ludicrous. "What the hell. Is there a decent motel in Shiprock?"

Jamie smiled. "It's not a Hilton, if that's what you're asking. But it's got clean sheets and air conditioning."

I pulled out my cellphone and was amazed to see two bars of service. I took out Jill Rickowski's card and programmed her phone numbers into my list of contacts, then called her cell number.

"This is Jill." She answered on the second ring.

"Hi, Jill. Fletcher reporting in after day one."

"Have you solved the murder the newspaper says was an accident?"

"I'm with a Navajo Nation Police officer, and we're checking the roads north of the interstate. We've talked to a couple people who may have seen the blue Lincoln going north through the reservation so we're hoping we'll come across a trail leading us to it."

"I'm impressed you've come up with a lead on the Lincoln."

"I'm working with Jamie Ballard of the Navajo Nation Police. The leads we've developed are entirely through his contacts on the reservation."

"Is there anything you need from me?"

"Jamie suggested I spend the night in Shiprock so we can continue the search early tomorrow. The Park Service pickup is going to be in a restaurant parking lot on the reservation overnight and I'll use the Park Service credit card to pay for a room and to buy a toothbrush."

"Parking the pickup overnight at a restaurant isn't a great option, but if that's what makes the most sense, go with it. Use the credit card for the motel charges, but the toothbrush, and maybe a razor, are on your own dime since they're personal toiletries. Save the receipts from your meals and we'll get them reimbursed. On second thought, I'll get you a per diem that should cover your personal expenses and meals."

"That sounds fair." An image of the guard shack with the injured ranger popped into my head. "How's Ed?"

"The surgeons were able to bridge the break with a plate. He'll be out of commission for months between healing and rehab, but he'll be fine. His parents flew in from Texas and they've got a round-the-clock vigil going in his hospital room."

"That's about the best we could hope for."

"Be careful," Jill said, hanging up.

I called El and left an apologetic message on her voicemail and shut down my phone.

* * *

Jamie and I ate supper in a small restaurant that served an eclectic mixture of Navajo and Mexican foods with a few burgers interspersed for less adventurous palates. I'd forgotten I'd only had two pieces of toast at the Only Breakfast and Lunch Restaurant many hours before. The smell of fried onions and cooking peppers caused me to nearly drown in my own saliva as I looked through the menu. I ordered a burger that was too large and came with a huge basket of fries. I didn't have room for the homemade pie.

The conversation was as slow as it had been during the day's drive. Jamie grunted and waved at each person who walked into the restaurant. He seemed to be well recognized if not well liked. An attractive woman came up behind him and gave him a peck on the cheek that caused his face to turn crimson. He offered no introductions or explanation to me, which suited me fine since I probably looked and smelled like a dusty cowpoke who'd been on the trail for a few days. Although it was obvious that a number of the patrons were openly carrying firearms, a lot of stares lingered on the Glock on my hip.

The motel made a Motel Six look fancy. When I requested a wake-up call the proprietor gave me a wind-up alarm clock. He sold me a disposable razor, some shaving gel, a cheap toothbrush, and a tiny tube of Crest toothpaste from a display behind the motel desk. I paid almost as much for the toiletries as I'd paid for supper. I'd turned to leave the office when I saw a stand with electronics, including a variety of cellphone chargers. I paid double what I'd have spent in a Target for a brand of charger I'd never heard of, but my phone was dead, probably from trying to find coverage in the intermittent dead zones throughout the reservation. The room was small but clean. There was an old bulky television I quickly learned had only one channel and a very old black phone. I plugged in the phone and walked into the bathroom.

The face that looked back at me was hardly recognizable and probably explained why I'd garnered so many stares in the restaurant. My sunburned face was caked with dust. Drops of sweat from my scalp had left trails through the dust on my neck. I washed up in the tiny sink, leaving the washcloth looking like I'd wiped the floor with it. I stripped off my boots and pants, and walked into the shower in my shirt and underwear, sending muddy water down the drain for a minute. I wrapped myself in a towel, then wrung out my shirt and undershorts and set them out to dry on hangers over the bathtub.

I had one bar of cell service so I left another message for Todd and El.

My phone chimed, announcing the arrival of a text. El said they were having fun—no worries. I wound the clock, set the alarm, and fell into bed totally exhausted.

Chapter 11

The clanging of the unfamiliar alarm clock fired random neurons telling my brain there was a fire alarm going off. I rolled out of the bed and stared at the unfamiliar room. The morning sun was peeking through the old window, casting shadows on the opposite wall. My second thought, looking at the lattice shadows, was that I was in a jail cell. As the cobwebs cleared my mind, I remembered the aging motel. I had a terrible cottony foul taste in my mouth, like a small animal had slept there.

I looked at my face in the bathroom mirror. One day's growth of beard and the few gray hairs creeping down my temples against the background of my sunburned skin made me look almost as old as I felt. I wet the single washcloth before soaping and scrubbing my face.

The denim shirt had air-dried over the shower curtain rail. It looked like I'd wrung it out by hand, which I had. I hung it over the towel rack while I took a shower, hoping the steam would remove some of the wrinkles. The hot water felt good, washing away the sore muscles from the strange bed and yesterday's trek over uneven ground. I used the deodorant soap on my hair as well as my armpits, since there wasn't any shampoo. The toothbrush bristles were spongy and the toothpaste was wintergreen flavored goo, but they got the foul taste out of my mouth. I used the crappy shave cream and disposable razor, which is when I realized I should have looked for a bottle of aftershave and a stick of deodorant. Jamie would suffer from the lack of deodorant but I decided the heat would overcome any deodorant anyway.

I slipped on socks and shoes that were still damp from the previous day. The leather holster had a white line from the evaporated perspiration. I removed the magazine, ejected the cartridge, and worked the action of the Glock a few times. It behaved as if nothing had happened, which was par for the course for Glocks.

Dressed and with the Glock on my hip, I looked in the mirror once again at the sunburned, rumpled, grizzled mess I'd become and had the terrible thought I was only a retirement check away from being one of the bums we used to roust from the bridges by the Union Gospel Mission. I straightened up and liked what I saw. I had direction and meaning in my life. Family was no longer an abstract concept but people who were interesting and interested in me. I felt proud of the sore muscles I'd earned the day before.

I was watching the network news when Jamie knocked at the door. "Hey old man, you ready to roll?" He wore a freshly pressed shirt and his straight, black hair was still wet from the shower.

"My only problem is that I didn't have deodorant or aftershave,"

"I've got a tube of Right Guard in the Suburban."

"Is that because you spend so much time on the road?" I asked, throwing the motel key on the nightstand next to the alarm clock. I followed him out the door, making sure it locked behind me.

"I spend four out of five nights in my own bed, but the reservation is so spread out that sometimes it just isn't possible to get home. I keep a sleeping bag in the back too . . . just in case."

Sleep had transformed Jamie. He seemed friendlier, almost chipper, as we drove to a small restaurant in Shiprock. He gave me a summary of the weather report for the week, a traditional opening topic whether you lived in Shiprock or St. Paul.

"The television news reported that Potter was in the antiques business and his body was cremated. The memorial service is scheduled for later this week."

"How convenient they could arrange a cremation so quickly," I said, mostly to myself.

"You mean so that no one can second guess the autopsy results?" Jamie asked.

"Yup. Whatever the trumped-up Tucson autopsy results show will be the official version for eternity."

"Doesn't seem to make much difference if no one cares that he was killed."

That comment put my mind in high gear. "Who would care that he was killed?" I asked Jamie. "Do we even know? And who authorized the cremation? Did the news say if he had a wife or children?"

"The news just said that his remains were cremated." Jamie started the engine and pulled onto the street. "If he had life insurance or a huge estate it would point to the beneficiary as the primary suspect, assuming his death wasn't accidental."

"If he had a double indemnity clause for accidental death, the insurance company will have an investigator go over the police reports and death certificates with a fine-toothed comb." I watched the people of Shiprock start their days. A few shop owners were unlocking their doors and a half-dozen people hustled along the sidewalk with backpacks, the briefcase of the new millennium.

Jamie considered that. "It almost sounds like a hit of some kind. I don't see a wife doing that. I'm more inclined to look at his business associates or someone who could stand to make it big if Potter weren't around."

"Like someone who took out a big insurance policy on his business partner?"

Jamie nodded. "Or someone who had a lot to lose if Potter was around."

"Interesting twist." I pondered that angle. "Let's suppose he had a partner in the antiques business and they were selling something illegal. With Potter gone, maybe there's no one to split the profits and no trail to follow."

Jamie nodded as he pulled into a parking space in front of a restaurant. "There are thousands of antiquities stolen from the reservation and public lands every year. Most are just pottery shards, arrowheads, and other small stuff. Occasionally, someone comes up with a real treasure and that's when the heat can really be on the dealers. Most of the dealers are legitimate and call the cops when they see pieces with obvious provenance problems. But there are less scrupulous dealers who have private collectors waiting for special pieces."

Every seat in the restaurant was taken except for a small table near the kitchen. Nearly all the patrons were Native Americans and most gave me a once-over glance before giving Jamie a polite nod. The one Caucasian patron yelled, "Hello," and waved at Jamie from across the room. Jamie gave him a polite nod and kept going toward the open table.

"That's Harold McMurtry," Jamie whispered as he sat down. "He owns a store that sells antiques and items made by local artisans. The locals make stuff and he pays them ten or twenty cents on the dollar. He claims they're getting a deal because he pays them up front, not on consignment, and he has the expense of holding the inventory until it sells. Everyone thinks he screws the artisans over, but they need the money and put up with it."

Jamie settled in his chair and nodded at the young waitress who immediately picked up the coffee pot and a pair of mugs. "There are a few places, like Oak Canyon Vista, on the way to Sedona, where the artisans can set up tables and sell their own items directly. Those are choice spots. So many people who want to sell there that the Forestry Service does a lottery for the days each vendor gets a spot. Obviously, the weekend days are prime."

I nodded my understanding and watched as McMurtry negotiated with a man over a piece of turquoise jewelry. The Navajo man was obviously overwhelmed by McMurtry's fast talking. After a few seconds they nodded and money exchanged hands. The Navajo gripped the cash tightly in his fist but his face said he was unhappy as he walked out the door. I wondered if that was the real world in Shiprock—you feel cheated but life goes on.

"I suggest the pepper omelet with corn tortillas." Jamie's voice jerked me back as the waitress, who acted like she thought Jamie was cute and whose dimpled smile got a smile in return, poured our coffee. The coffee was weak and reminded me of the tinted water my ex-wife used to brew in an effort to reduce her caffeine intake.

"You ready to order?" The waitress set the coffee pot on the Formica tabletop and pulled a pad and pencil from the apron worn over her jeans. She looked about sixteen and skinny, like she hadn't filled out. Her black hair was braided into a long ponytail and there was a silver ring through her left eyebrow.

"Sure." Jamie pushed the plastic covered menu back between the sugar and napkin dispensers. "I'll have the pepper omelet with tortillas."

She looked at me as I studied the menu looking for an option that wouldn't burn a hole in my stomach. "I guess I'll have the same."

She picked up the coffee carafe and walked away. Her jeans hung low on her hips and her shoulder blades protruded under her t-shirt. I noticed that she dragged one leg slightly. Her gait was halting with her boots slightly pigeon toed.

"Does she have MS?" I asked, nodding toward the waitress. I took a sip of coffee. The flavor was as thin as the color.

Jamie cocked his head and gave me a funny look. "Maybe you really are a detective." He sipped his coffee and then leaned close over the table. "Did you notice the guy at the end of the counter when we walked in?"

"The fat guy wearing gold chains and turquoise jewelry?" I asked, knowing exactly who Jamie meant. "Looks like he's trying to impress someone. If he were in the big city, I'd guess him to be a pimp or a drug dealer. The skinny guy next to him looks like his gofer."

"Close. He runs the only Native-owned construction company. He bids high and gets all the state and Federal projects because it's a minority-owned business. Word is he knows what all the bids are before he submits and that way he can get in at exactly five percent over the lowest bidder. The BIA—Bureau of Indian Affairs—and Feds both encourage minority and female-owned businesses by awarding them construction contracts if their bids are no more than five percent higher than the lowest bid. He doesn't have any construction equipment or employees, so he subcontracts all the work, sometimes to the other bidders, and takes his cut off the top."

Out of the corner of my eye I could see a man slapping the big guy on the back. They both looked unnaturally happy. "Hell of a deal if you can work it," I said. "I suppose he pays off someone to get the bidding information, so he probably only nets four percent." The two men stood up and shook hands.

"That's not bad when you're bidding three or four million dollars in projects a year."

I quickly did the math in my head and came up with a quarter-million profit on six-million dollars in projects. I let out a little whistle. "A quarter million a year and he doesn't have any overhead." I watched him for a second and thought he looked self-important.

"Not only doesn't he have any equipment or crews to manage, this is his office. I suppose that end seat costs him five bucks a day in coffee and doughnuts."

The waitress brought our plates, and I noticed the trembling in her hands as she set the plates down. "I'll be right back with more coffee." She limped away.

"Can't you nail him on some sort of a fraud charge?" I dove into the omelet, pushing the peppers aside. I hoped they were mild green peppers, but they turned out to be some variety of green chili peppers. Their mere contact with the eggs set my mouth aflame. I could feel beads of sweat rising on my forehead.

"Why nail him?" Jamie shrugged. "This way a percentage of the money stays on the Rez instead of flowing to the Flag and Phoenix contractors."

I gulped the rest of my coffee just before the waitress refilled the cup with liquid too hot to drink. It didn't put out the flames that were eating my mouth so I took a bite of tortilla, hoping there was enough grease in it to kill the burn.

Jamie sensed my problem. "Smear some sour cream on the tortilla and hold it in your mouth. There's something in dairy products that cuts the burn."

I smeared the mound of sour cream from the edge of my plate onto the tortilla and took a big bite, chewing it slowly. The cool sour cream felt like salve on my tongue and the burning faded to a minor irritation. There must have been a look of relief on my face because Jamie almost laughed.

"So, what are we doing today?" I carefully slid all the peppers aside and trimmed away the egg that had touched any of the peppers or seeds.

Jamie pointed at the pile of peppers with his fork. "It's an old wives tale that the heat in the peppers comes from the seeds. Capsaicin causes the burn and most of that is in the inner membrane of the peppers. Unless you're eating dried peppers, then it all burns."

"Good to know. I'll store that away for future use." I checked to make sure I still had enough sour cream available if needed.

"We'll check the rest of the turnoffs along the road, then stop off at a couple more houses to ask if anyone else saw the Lincoln. Not many people live along the road. They live out of sight, behind the hills." Jamie mopped the last of the juices from the plate with his tortilla scrap. "If we get a lead or find some tracks, we'll follow them."

"Are you okay still pursuing this?" I asked, slathering more sour cream on a tortilla I used to scoop up the last of the egg. "The FBI says it's an accident." I watched for non-verbal responses in Jamie's reply.

He shrugged. "Pay's the same. I don't like guys who try to run down cops, even if it was just a park ranger." His eyes sparkled as he set a five-dollar bill on the table to pay for his breakfast.

I took a ten-dollar bill out of my wallet and set it on the table. I picked up Jamie's five and handed it back to him. "I talked to my boss and she says I'm getting per diem. It's my turn to pay."

"If that's what it takes to make you sleep at night, it's fine with me." He took the five, folded it in half and slipped the corner of it under his plate. He winked at the waitress, who had been watching us, and she gave him a dimpled smile in return.

I held the door for him as we walked into the heat. "Any special reason for over-tipping the waitress?" I expected some vague comment meant to obscure a mutual attraction.

"She's my cousin and, well, she needs a little extra cash sometimes. She takes a lot of medicine and has to drive to the clinic in an old car that sucks gas like a semi."

I looked at Jamie and saw nothing that told me he'd spoken anything but the unvarnished truth. He was a deeper man than I'd thought. He also rose a few notches in my esteem. Without fanfare we were back in the Suburban. At the edge of town we bought gas, bottled water, and energy bars and hit the road.

Chapter 12

Margaret Adams needed closure. She made four calls before she got the number for Walnut Canyon National Monument. The female volunteer who answered put Margaret on hold while she searched for a ranger. Margaret visualized her cellphone statement as a meter running. Since she wasn't sure if she had a job or not, it might be unwise to run up her phone bill.

"This is Ranger Peck. How can I be of assistance?"

Margaret scribbled his name on a piece of scrap paper. "Ranger Peck, my name is Margaret Adams. I am . . . was . . . Steve Potter's personal assistant. I want to know what happened to him. Who can I talk to about the investigation?"

Peck hesitated. The Park Service had warned him about giving information to the press about anything, and reporters often used subterfuge to get their stories. "Miss Adams, I'm not authorized to give out information. Perhaps I could have you contact the Flagstaff Park Service office or the Phoenix FBI office . . ."

Margaret cut him off. "Ranger Peck, I've spoken with the FBI. They claim Steve's death was an accident. Their case is closed." She hesitated. "Do you believe them?"

"I really can't comment. I have no idea who you are."

"I'm Steve Potter's assistant!" Margaret was becoming exasperated. She'd called a dozen people in the FBI and Justice Department without a single tangible result. "I can't show you my ID over the phone. What can I do?"

Peck rummaged in his desk. "Let me give you the phone number for the Flagstaff Park Service office. Perhaps they can verify your credentials and someone can call you back at your office."

Margaret let out a sigh. "Damn it, I don't have an office anymore. Steve's jerk of a partner threw me into the street." She broke into tears.

"I'm sorry, Miss Adams. We have a ranger pursuing the investigation. His name is Fletcher. You can leave a message for him at this Flagstaff phone number . . ."

Chapter 13

The shiny Suburban eased through the narrow alley, doing a careful slalom around the Dumpsters and garbage cans behind the buildings. The vehicle stopped at a door that was unremarkable except for the heavy steel straps riveted to the surface. Based on the bent metal and scrape marks around the lock, it appeared that several attempts had been made to breach it.

The stocky Navajo driver got out, walked to the back of the Suburban and opened the rear doors. His passenger carefully surveyed the area before getting out.

The driver moved to the back of the SUV. "Hey, Elmer, get your ass back here and help."

When the passenger complied, the larger Navajo handed him a Rubbermaid storage container. "Carry this in and quit looking around like you're a burglar. The reason you've been busted so often is because you act guilty even when you're innocent."

"Screw you." The thin man struggled to carry the box into the rear of the store. "In prison you learn to keep an eye on your back all the time."

"If I get busted because you're acting like a five-year-old who got caught with his hand in the cookie jar, prison will be the least of your worries."

Elmer Swenson was smaller in stature and mental capacity than his partner. Sweat beaded his forehead and plastered his blond hair to his head. The armpits and back of his dark blue t-shirt were soaked despite the air conditioning in the Suburban.

"I told you, Tommy, I can't help it. When I get scared, I sweat and act nervous."

The only sign on the back door was a stenciled address. Elmer twisted the knob, pulled the door open, and walked into the poorly lit storage room. A bell jingled in another room, announcing the visitors. Elmer carefully lowered the Rubbermaid container to the floor and deeply breathed in the musty cool air. Tommy set down the second box with a thump that made Elmer jump.

"God, you are the most nervous weasel I've ever seen. If you don't shape up, I'll have to take you to Walnut Canyon."

The smaller man put his hands out and backed away in the narrow storage space. "No, Tommy. I ain't going back to Walnut Canyon with you." Behind them a door creaked and Tommy put a finger to his lips as the bright light from the storefront spilled into the storage room. It quickly faded away when the door creaked shut. The brief sliver of light exposed shelves lined with boxes, pots, and other artifacts. Some items were so coated with dust they looked like they hadn't been moved in years.

The man who walked into the storeroom was grizzled, with wrinkled skin and a face mottled with brown age spots. His dress and demeanor were Western, from the mother of pearl buttons on his western-cut shirt to the bow-legged walk that looked like he'd spent too many years on a horse. In truth, he was a retired lawyer who had moved to Arizona in the '70s after being disbarred in Wisconsin and Illinois. Upon his forced retirement he had taken his nest egg, acquired from mismanaging his client's trust accounts, and invested in the antique store. He'd quickly taken on the persona of a local, picking up the accent, dressing the part, slowing the pace of his walk and talk, even chewing snuff and spitting into a brass spittoon. The tourists were taken in by his "Aw shucks" act, and willingness to haggle over the prices of his overpriced junk.

Tommy greeted him without enthusiasm. "Hey, Joe."

The man offered a bony hand that showed all of his eighty years. His wrinkled smile was wide and displayed his yellowed teeth and receding gums. "Hello to my native friend and his Scandinavian flunky." They shook hands. "So, what've you got today?"

Tommy locked the back door as Elmer Swenson opened the Rubbermaid container he'd carried in. Elmer unwrapped the wool blanket and peeled back the edge, exposing arrowheads and pottery shards, including an unusually large piece with faded blue markings that was four inches wide by six inches long.

"These are older than the pieces from the last site," Tommy said. "The lines are wider and lighter blue and the pot was thicker."

Joe gently picked up the big piece and held it to the dim light provided by a single bulb hanging from the ceiling. "Nice piece. Weathered, but nice." After turning it and examining every surface, he set it on the shelf and examined several smaller pottery pieces that looked like they'd come from the same broken pot. While Joe examined the pottery, Elmer unwrapped an animal bone that had been sharpened into a scraper, along with some other stone tools.

Joe was distracted from the array of Elmer's artifacts by Tommy, who was struggling with something heavy at the bottom of the second Rubbermaid container.

A large gray rock with fluted sides emerged from a blanket. In a depression on top of the rock sat a large egg-shaped, granite stone with rounded ends. The old man tried to hide his excitement, but he was overwhelmed by the sight.

"A fluted metate!" He pushed Elmer aside and lovingly ran his fingers over the cold convex surface of the gray rock. "Beautiful. The Indian equivalent of a mortar and pestle." His fingers examined every nook and cranny as carefully as a blind man dependent on touch.

Tommy watched, at first with pride, then with increasing annoyance as the old man lingered over the metate, finally holding the egg-shaped mano up to the light.

"They're museum pieces," Tommy said. "You hardly ever get a carved metate and mano together. What are you offering?"

Joe set the stones back on the blanket and dug a can of Copenhagen out of his back pocket. The formation of the tobacco plug and the insertion in his lip was a ceremonial way of delaying the announcement of his offer. Tommy watched with disgust as the process exposed Joe's gums and the inside of his lips, blackened by years of chewing tobacco. Joe slipped the can back into his back pocket, where it seated in the round spot worn thin by the can.

"Well, the shards are going to sell for a couple hundred. I'll sell them as a group that can be displayed together." Joe waved his arm across them as he spoke. "But that metate and mano have me perplexed."

He raised his hand to his bristled chin and rubbed it. It was a well-practiced act he'd used for years to give his suppliers the impression that he was trying to discern the true value of the piece. He had, in fact, known what his initial offer would be since they first pulled back the blanket. He was going to make a mint on them. It was just a matter of how much he could take Tommy and Elmer for and the percentage he'd have to pay the middleman who'd identified the remote archaeological sites where Tommy and

Elmer excavated the antiquities. Tommy and Elmer he could easily cheat. There were consequences if the middleman found out Joe had cheated him.

Joe spit a stream of tobacco juice on the worn pine floor as a bell tinkled in the other room. "Hang on. Let me see if I can scalp this one quick and get back to you." Joe looked at Tommy's eyes to see if the mention of scalping had any effect on him. If Tommy was offended it didn't show. Joe eased through the creaking door that separated the storeroom from the retail area of the store.

Tommy watched him disappear. "Fucking thief. The only one he intends to scalp today is me." Tommy wrapped the metate and mano back into the woolen blanket. "Did you see his eyes? He wants these real bad."

Elmer looked at him nervously. "What are you doing? Who else is going to buy this stuff?"

Tommy lifted the blanket into the Rubbermaid container and closed the lid. "I know people who've got contacts in Utah. Maybe they can find a buyer. I'm not going to stand here and let Joe rip me off while he makes a fortune."

Elmer started to wrap up the shards and arrowheads too but Tommy stopped him. "Leave the rest. I know he sells those scraps and arrowheads for a few hundred and he pays us a quarter of that. He can have them. The metate and mano are going with us." Tommy kicked the corner of the Rubbermaid container.

143

They stood in silence for a few seconds until Joe came back. "I got good news boys, I made a call and I think I can get a grand for that mortar and pestle." He looked for the blanket where he'd set them. "What'd you do with them?"

Tommy stood with his arms crossed. "Pay us for the pottery and we'll go."

A look of despair crossed Joe's face. "Tommy, I can't believe you don't want me to have that piece too. What is it? Haven't I been fair with you?" He spread his hands in a dramatic show of supplication

Tommy stood like the wooden cigar store Indian covered with dust standing in the corner of the storage room. "You're fucking us over, old man. I know those are museum pieces. You find the right buyer and you'll get six figures for them." Tommy unfolded his arms and bent over to lift the Rubbermaid container. "Get the door, Elmer."

"Wait, wait!" Joe shuffled up to Tommy and put his hand on top of the Rubbermaid container. "All right. I'll make a couple more calls and see if I can get more for it." He stepped back. "But I can assure you that I won't get a hundred grand for it. Maybe twenty."

Joe dug his hand in his pocket and pulled out a roll of bills the size of a soup can. "I'll give you ten for them right now." He started to count off hundred-dollar bills. "I might get screwed, but what the hell, you guys have been good to me. If I can sell it for more than twenty, I'll give you half of anything over that."

Tommy kept the Rubbermaid container in his hands. "Sure. And how will we know what price you'll get? You don't deal with receipts."

Joe splayed his hands wide and put his hurt expression on. "Tommy, have I ever cheated you?" He counted out the hundreds and held them out to Tommy.

Tommy set the Rubbermaid container down and grabbed the stack of bills from Joe's hand. "Every time I walk in this place I feel like I ought to hand you a condom 'cause I'm gonna get screwed." Tommy grabbed Elmer by the arm and shoved him toward the door. He turned and poked a finger into Joe's bony chest. "If I ever find out for sure that you've cheated me, Joe, I'll cut your nuts off and feed them to you."

Joe tried to look hurt as he watched them disappear, rubbing the spot on his chest where Tommy had poked him. He had no muscle or fat to insulate from the poke. When he heard the Suburban start, he bent down, opened the Rubbermaid container and unfurled the blanket. He held the pestle in his hand, then ran his fingers over the depression in the metate. The depression had been scoured in the granite by hundreds of years of calloused hands grinding corn. He had, in fact, made a call to Rich Hayes, his middleman, who had a buyer who'd pay dearly for the pair. He smiled. Tommy would never know.

Joe pulled out his cellphone and redialed Hayes' number. A woman's voice answered. "Tell the Stick Man I've got the pieces we spoke about."

"And the price?" she asked.

Joe hesitated. He could lie to Tommy and Elmer, and they'd be mad. If Hayes discovered he'd been cheated, Joe knew he'd be dead. "Same as we talked about, Sharon."

"Someone will be there tomorrow to inspect and pick them up," Sharon said. "He'll bring cash."

Chapter 14

I was tired of climbing out of the Suburban to look at dusty tire tracks every few miles. Even with the air conditioning running, the sun beating through the passenger window was hot and my right arm was starting to resemble the shade of Sheila's lipstick. Jamie was talking in spurts that were downright chatty, but there were still long periods of silence

The slowing Suburban pulled me back from a daydream. A young man with tattered jeans and a white t-shirt was walking on the edge of the road ahead of us. The sound of crunching gravel made him turn his head as Jamie edged off the road. The man had a red bandana tied around his jet-black hair. His sweaty shirt said he'd been walking a long time. Jamie stopped a few feet behind him. He got out of the Suburban and left the engine running.

"Joey, where are you going?"

"Home from Shiprock."

"C'mon." Jamie nodded toward the truck.

"Hi," Joey said to me as he climbed into the rear seat. "You a cop, too?"

"I'm a Park Service Ranger."

Jamie climbed in and slipped the Suburban into drive. "Doug's a retired cop."

"Does it show?" I asked, looking over my shoulder.

Joey shrugged. "I don't know. I just figured since you were with Jamie . . ."

"Joey, you seen a blue Lincoln ditched around here?" Jamie accelerated and pulled onto the road.

The response was a beat too slow. "Umm, no. Not lately."

I caught a hint of a smile on Jamie's face. "Where?" He looked back at Joey in the rearview mirror.

"I said no."

Jamie turned his head but kept his eyes on the road. "I know what the words were, but I heard 'yes' in your heart."

Out of the corner of my eye I could see Joey shaking his head.

"Where'd you used to be a cop?" Joey tried to change the topic.

"Up in Minnesota."

"Hmm. Snow and cold weather, kinda like Flagstaff." Joey nodded his head, impressed with his geography. "What's a Minnesota cop doing in Arizona?"

"I live in Flagstaff and work at Walnut Canyon. Where's the Lincoln?"

Joey shifted. "You guys are hung up about the car. What's the deal?"

Jamie didn't offer any comment, but I didn't see any harm in answering. "It was used in a murder."

Joey seemed impressed. "Cool. And you want some prints from it?"

"So where is it?" Jamie asked again.

"Where you been looking?"

"Everywhere from Walnut Canyon to Shiprock." Jamie steered around a jackrabbit smeared on the road. As if it made any difference that one more set of tires had gone over the pizza-flat carcass.

Joey nodded. "Not that I know where it is . . . but, I'd look somewhere they could find a ride after they ditched the car." The Suburban was silent except for the singing of the tires. "I mean, why park it a million miles from anywhere and walk two days to get a ride?"

Jamie nodded. "Is it close to Shiprock?"

Joey shifted uncomfortably. "You know, if I screw up someone's salvage operation, they'd be pissed."

I'd heard informants fishing for money a thousand times and quickly assessed the chances of getting reimbursed by Uncle Sam if I paid for information. The odds of reimbursement were probably nil, but what the hell. I didn't need the paycheck anyway.

"How much, Joey? Five? Ten?" I asked.

I could see Joey squirm again. "I ain't a prostitute. People get mad when you screw up their salvage."

"Twenty?" I pulled out my wallet and fished out a bill. I pushed the wallet back in my pocket and held it over my shoulder. It disappeared with a tug.

"Try behind the Bitterroot Arroyo . . . and you better drop me here before someone sees me with you."

Jamie rolled the Suburban to the shoulder of the road and stopped. Joey stepped out. I rolled down my window and said, "Thanks."

As we drove away Jamie looked in the rearview mirror. "He would've told us for nothing."

"What's twenty bucks? I didn't want to screw around all day."

Jamie smiled. "Like we didn't have all day. I just hope he didn't screw you out of twenty bucks."

* * *

As we continued south I wondered if Todd and El had enjoyed the Painted Desert and what they had planned for today. El was well supplied with maps and Pinterest suggestions but I still felt a little guilty about leaving them to explore on their own.

"You got quiet." Jamie's words snapped me back to the humdrum landscape of browns and tans.

"I thought you liked it quiet."

Jamie shook his head. "Naw, I'm quiet, but I like to have some noise. You were doing a good job of keeping conversation going for both of us. I guess the hardest part of being kinda introverted and in a solitary job is that I can never think of anything to talk about."

I nodded. "I was just thinking about my cousin and her husband. They're in Flagstaff for a week of vacation. I left them with my car to explore. Now I feel guilty I'm not with them as I'd planned."

"I guess I can't relate to that. Everyone on the Rez knows everyone and everything. I go places that I've never been before, but they usually look like someplace I've already been and I always run into someone who's a relative or at least someone I've met. It's not much of an adventure."

I thought about the philosophy behind his comments. "But you went to school off the reservation. Wasn't that an adventure?"

Jamie shrugged. "It wasn't as much an adventure as a trial. Mostly I felt out of my element and I wanted to get back." He slowed the Suburban. "This is the only road around here. We've already checked the washes and turnoffs, so if they really dumped the Lincoln by the Bitterroot Arroyo, it's got to be down this road."

I looked around. "Aren't we only twenty miles north of the I-40?"

Jamie rounded the corner and straightened the wheels. "Yeah, but remember, the car passed my aunt's place, so it has to be this far up. This is a back way to the arroyo. It's not a road someone would usually drive on with a big, boat-like Lincoln."

"That makes it all the better a spot. Who'd look where you think a Lincoln couldn't go?"

The road was rough gravel that hadn't seen a grader in years. There were fresh tire tracks in the sandy spots, and scrape marks that could've been cause by an undercarriage dragging over the high spots in the gravel. The Suburban bucked over the washboard surface, throwing us around like we were riding a mechanical bull. After about fifteen minutes, Jamie slowed as we approached the backside of a ridge.

"We've been following fresh tire tracks since the turn off." He let the engine idle. "It looks like a set of duals, from the rear of a truck, so there may be someone back here. Can you reach the rifle case?"

I unbuckled and crawled between the seats, pulling the scarred aluminum case into the back. I heard the driver's door quietly click open as Jamie stepped out to scout the land ahead. By the time I had the case open and the rifle out, he was back.

"Hang on." Jamie flung himself into the Suburban. "The vultures are feeding." He quietly closed the door and snapped the seat belt buckle. I took that as a sign the ride was about to get wild. I was still struggling with my own seat belt. I kept the rifle clamped between my knees as he gunned the engine and turned on the flashers. The wheels spit gravel and I was pressed back against the seat. As we cleared the ridge, I could see a tow truck backed up to a stripped car frame, probably a quarter-mile away. Two men ran for the truck doors as soon as they saw us on the ridge. I checked for the holster on my hip. Even with the firepower clamped between my knees, the feel of the Glock was familiar and reassuring.

The men climbed into the cab and the tow truck lurched forward, jerking the tow cable attached to the engine. The stripped car frame virtually jumped off the cement blocks that supported it. Clear of the blocks, the frame dragged along behind them, dangling from the steel tow cable. It raised an unholy cloud of dust as it ripped through the dry soil. Jamie steered to cut them off.

"You sure you want to cut them off? I mean . . . they've got you on weight." I held on as the Suburban lurched sideways on the road. I was relieved to see a hundred yards of open land on both sides of any spot he chose to stop. They wouldn't have to ram us to pass.

"They won't win a game of chicken with me."

The car frame bounced along behind the tow truck and stirred up a brown dust cloud in the still desert air as the distance between us narrowed. Suddenly, the engine pulled free of the car frame and slammed into the back of the tow truck. The cable attached to the engine finally pulled free from the motor mounts and drive train. The frame slid sideways and flipped before sliding to a stop. The engine and transmission slapped into the hoist gantry on the back of the truck, causing the truck to shudder.

We were set to converge on the arroyo about 150 yards ahead when Jamie jammed the brakes, pulled the emergency and slammed the gears into neutral. "If they don't look like they're going to stop, take a shot at the radiator." He jumped out the door as the Suburban jerked to a stop.

I threw off the seat belt and jacked a shell into the rifle chamber, reminding myself about the rifle's hair trigger. I cleared the door and leaned my left shoulder against the doorframe as I watched the tow truck barrel down the arroyo toward the Suburban. My heart pounded as I aligned the metal sights on the grille of the truck. The driver showed no sign of slowing so I clicked off the safety and fired.

The rifle bucked with the shot and when it came down from the recoil I could see a cloud of steam billowing from the tow truck's hood and wheel wells. The truck kept bearing down on me, so I ejected the spent cartridge and fired a second shot into the grille. It became a larger target with every second it got closer.

I heard the screech of metal and the clatter of broken engine parts. The truck wasn't going to run long with the engine damage and steaming radiator, but it didn't seem to be slowing as it approached me. I fed the third cartridge into the chamber. I raised the rifle and put the sights on the windshield. Adrenaline coursed through my body. My vision narrowed and all I could see was the driver's round face as the sights aligned with his nose. I knew the moment the driver realized he was staring at the hole in the end of the rifle. He jammed the brakes and the tow truck slid to a stop twenty yards short of the Suburban. I heard antifreeze sizzling as steam billowed from under the hood. The engine emitted a metallic shriek, seized and stopped.

The view down the rifle was jumbled from the uncontrollable shaking of my body. I realized I wasn't going to die and took a deep breath. I slipped the safety on but kept the rifle aimed toward the driver. Jamie jerked open the truck's righthand door and wrestled the passenger to the ground. The driver climbed down and stood next to the truck, glaring at me with his hands in the air.

"You crazy son of a bitch! You was going to shoot me!" The driver yelled at me. He was gray-haired, stout, and his pinstriped shirt was soaked with sweat. A little embroidered name patch was sewn over one pocket. Suspenders kept his pants from sliding off his considerable belly.

"On the ground." I yelled pointing the rifle in his general direction. My voice was strong and more confident than I felt, but years of conditioning took over.

The man fell to his knees and lowered himself to the ground. "Don't shoot." He kept watching like he expected me to put a round through his thick head.

Jamie snapped metal handcuffs on the passenger's wrists, then went to the driver and frisked him. "Fletcher, grab one of the plastic ties out of the glove box."

I laid the rifle across my seat. There were a couple dozen plastic ties, formed like handcuffs, in the glove box, so I grabbed two and carried them to Jamie. I slipped one around the driver's wrists and tightened it. Jamie held a foot on the man's back as he read the Miranda card.

"What's the big deal?" The driver actually sneered. Up close I could see he was Caucasian and weighed more than three hundred pounds. His thinning hair was combed from the top of his head into a small ponytail in an apparent attempt to hide the balding spot on the back of his skull.

Jamie pulled him to his knees and then his feet, not a small task considering the man's weight. "You were stealing parts off that car frame."

Jamie looked at the side of the truck. It was from Blue M Towing Service and had a Flagstaff phone number. "I don't suppose the Flagstaff police would find the fenders and rest of the blue body parts at your yard?"

The big man shrugged. "We're pulling scrap metal off an abandoned vehicle in the middle of the desert." The driver's arrogance, now that the guns were holstered, told me this wasn't his first encounter with law enforcement.

I nodded toward the back of the truck. "I think I'll pull the serial number off the engine and run it. I assume it's from a stolen Lincoln. If it is, you're in possession of stolen car parts."

Jamie's eyes brightened. "Well, gee. If that is indeed a stolen vehicle, and they were moving it, we could press charges for grand theft auto. And that's a felony. I don't suppose either of these fine citizens has ever been in prison?"

"You're dead meat, buddy." I pointed my finger at the driver like it was a pistol and dropped my thumb like the hammer. Jamie pulled out the wallet chained to his belt loop.

"I want a lawyer."

"Lawyers hate the drive to Shiprock. Sometimes they can't get free for days." Jamie fingered through the wallet trying to find an ID.

The truck driver looked at me. "Since when did they start hiring white old farts to ride with the half breed tribal cops?" Not a bad strategy, he was trying to draw a punch to support a police brutality charge.

I looked at Jamie's face for a hint of emotion, but saw nothing other than his constant flat expression. "You think it shouldn't have taken two of us to catch a couple halfwits committing a felony. Is that what you're saying?"

Jamie pushed the fat man past the steaming front of the truck. The handcuffed passenger was laying on the ground. He was slender, with Navajo features in an acne-scarred face and jet-black hair tied in a short ponytail. Like his compatriot, he was wearing a grease-stained, pinstriped short-sleeved shirt over a white t-shirt and jeans that looked like they'd never seen a washing machine. His face was caked with tan dust from lying on the ground and grease was so engrained into his fingers I doubted they'd ever be clean again. His eyes darted back and forth between us and widened like saucers at the word "felony".

Jamie helped him up and made introductions. "Doug, this is Ray Brown. He's visited the jail in Shiprock a number of times and he's spent a few years in the Phoenix Federal prison."

Even though Ray had the look of a lean predatory animal, he seemed too young to have much prison time. Jailhouse tattoos, ragged blue lines made with a pin and ballpoint pen ink, covered his forearms. Rotting teeth and pinpoint pupils screamed meth addict.

"How 'bout it, Ray? You got thoughts about where the rest of the Lincoln went?" Jamie gave Ray a push toward the Suburban. "No, I didn't think so. Time to take a drive, boys."

With our prisoners in handcuffs and seat belted into the rear of the Suburban, we drove to the Only Breakfast and Lunch Restaurant. Neither prisoner said a word during the trip.

Jamie pulled in next to the Park Service pickup and let the engine idle. "You be back tomorrow?"

I nodded toward the hitching rail. We got out and walked over to the pickup together. "We found the Lincoln, which was my primary objective on the reservation, and there doesn't seem to be any evidence left to process. I've got company in Flagstaff. I should probably spend a day with them . . . if my boss will give me a day off." I could see the two prisoners whispering back and forth as we stood next to the pickup.

"They're working on their story." I nodded toward the truck.

Jamie shrugged. "Let 'em. They haven't got enough brains between the two of them to come up with a complete sentence."

I chuckled. "Are you okay taking these guys to Shiprock alone?" I dug in my pocket for the Park Service keys. "I could follow you to Shiprock in the pickup."

Jamie smiled and looked at the Suburban. "You're okay, Doug. Most of the cops I've dealt with are more interested in getting home for supper than they are in my safety." He nodded to the guys in the backseat of the Suburban. "They're in handcuffs and they're pussycats. Don't worry."

I unlocked the pickup and opened the door. Hot air rushed from the interior and the door handle was too hot to hold. "I don't have any police contacts locally, so I'd appreciate it if you could get someone to recover what's left of the Lincoln. Call my cellphone if anything comes up," I waited for the interior to cool enough to even sit on the seat. "I'll check in with the Park Service tonight, just so they know I'm not dead. Then I'll see how my guests are doing. If things are under control in Flagstaff, I might drive to Shiprock to interrogate the prisoners tomorrow."

Jamie shrugged. "We should be okay, I'll get somebody out to go over the car . . . just in case there is a shred of evidence that hasn't been destroyed by the human vultures. Don't bother coming up for interrogation, these two are too seasoned to say anything and they've already asked for a lawyer. The best we might do is to get them to spill some information if a Federal prosecutor offers them a reduced sentence, and that's not going to happen before they sit in the Shiprock jail a couple days and talk to a public defender."

I looked at my watch. It was nearly four. "If I leave now I can make it back to Flagstaff in time to have supper with my cousins." I jumped in the pickup and turned the key. The engine roared to life, blasting my face with hot stale air from the air conditioning system.

Jamie stepped to the door and shook my hand. "If I were you, I wouldn't offer the Park Service too much information about the arrest. The Navajo Nation Police have broad powers to use whatever force is required to make an arrest. You'd have to fill out paperwork for a week if you told the Park Service you fired a borrowed rifle at some suspects, especially since you technically don't have jurisdiction on the Rez."

"It's going to come out when those two talk with their lawyers."

"Who knows exactly what happened? They may, or may not, want to talk about the details. If they have a good public defender, they'll be advised to admit nothing. The whole thing will probably be plea bargained away and the particulars of the arrest won't come out."

Jamie dug out a wallet and handed me a sweat-stained business card. "Stay in touch. My cellphone number works sometimes, but you can always leave a text. I'll get back to you in a day or two."

"I don't have a card yet, sorry."

"Your cell number is already programmed into my phone, If that doesn't work, I'm sure the Park Service would get a message to you."

I shook his hand again. "You're one hell of a cop, Jamie. The Navajo Nation Police are lucky to have you."

He smiled. "Yes, they are. I wish my captain agreed with you."

* * *

The drive to Flagstaff seemed to take forever despite pushing the pickup somewhat over the speed limit. As I drove, I thought about Jamie. He was a strange fellow, but quietly competent. He had warmed up a little and I found myself hoping that we'd have the chance to spend more time together.

I was glad my house was on the east side of Flagstaff. I took the exit and turned up the hill that ran along the edge of the golf course.

There was no sign of the Isuzu in the parking lot when I pulled up. I unlocked the door and threw the mail on the kitchen table. A note in El's scrawl said they'd driven to Sunset Crater, one of the three sites under supervision of the Flagstaff National Park Service office, and would be back by six. My watch showed it was nearly five thirty. I took a hot shower, changed out of the clothes I'd worn for two days, and was back downstairs in fifteen minutes.

The refrigerator still had a few beers, but a huge supply of grapefruit-flavored sparkling water and green, leafy stuff had overtaken the interior. That was a stark contrast to the green moldy stuff that usually resided on the pizza and leftovers I never got around to eating. I pushed around a couple bags of lettuce and broccoli before I found the plastic container of spreadable cheddar cheese hidden in the back corner. I'm sure El didn't approve, but not to the point of throwing it away.

I popped open a beer, removed the cheese lid, and took saltines out of the cupboard before settling at the kitchen table to confront the pile of mail. Bill. Catalog. Bill. Bill. And an envelope with my ex-wife's return address. I opened Sherry's letter first. In her careful looping cursive, she complained about her meager salary from the adjunct professorship. Unwritten was a hint that I should supplement her finances. In the last paragraph she said her divorce lawyer was bugging her for payment and she asked if I would pay her bill. The divorce decree had specified we were each responsible for paying our own legal fees. I crumpled the letter and threw it into the wastebasket.

"Get a real job," I muttered.

Chapter 15

I was finishing the beer, writing checks, and stuffing them into envelopes when Todd and El unlocked the door,

"Hey, look! He does live here." El was carrying a large plastic shopping bag and she swept through the door like the townhouse queen. Todd followed behind and nodded hello without a word.

"We're going to make you supper . . . since you decided to grace us with your presence. I went shopping and picked up a bunch of groceries." She set the bag on the kitchen counter. "I can make a wonderful salad that'll leave you feeling invigorated. Much better than all that animal fat that clogs your arteries." I didn't look up, but assumed she was referring to the empty cheese spread container sitting midst the cracker crumbs.

I gave Todd a pleading look. He grinned wickedly, then sauntered over to the table and sat down next to me while El rattled bowls. He leaned close and whispered, "I ate a piece of jerky while she was shopping. Then I had to buy a pack of gum to cover my jerky breath."

I nodded with understanding. I sealed a couple of checks into envelopes and cleared the papers from the table. Todd set the table for dinner while I put stamps on the envelopes.

"Be back in a second." I waved the envelopes as I went out the door.

When I got back in the house there were three serving bowls on the table with salads large enough to feed a family of rabbits for a month. El was sprinkling something that looked like white worms on top of them as Todd set out cans of fizzy water.

"El, I'll skip the worms, if it's all the same to you."

She stopped and gave me a look of confusion, then looked back at the plastic container in her hand. The revelation swept her. "Oh, you silly. These are bean sprouts. I'm sure you've had them in chow mein." She popped a bunch in her mouth and savored the flavor. "They're excellent raw, too."

"I do appreciate your efforts to improve my health, El, but it's too late to repair forty-plus years of accumulated cholesterol." She finished dressing the salads with a drizzle of balsamic vinegar and a splash of olive oil.

El waved her fork while she finished chewing the sprouts. "I know, but maybe I can make at least a small improvement in your diet. Who knows, you might even discover you like some fiber in your diet.

I nodded, unable to come up with the words to express my enthusiasm. I took my seat at the table and El set a serving bowl of salad in front of me.

"Mmm," El said as she savored a bite of salad. She pointed her fork at me to hold my attention while she swallowed. "I saw your mother at cousin Jeff's wedding. I got the impression she hasn't heard from you much."

I stirred in my greens while I considered my answer. "We don't have much to talk about anymore. Now that I'm on disability she can't nag me about being a cop working crappy hours. She likes to point out I'm not providing her any grandchildren."

Todd nodded. "That's a big deal for her generation. Both our mothers have hinted our biological clocks are ticking and we should start a family. My mother even asked me, in a whisper, if there was something medically wrong with us. She pointed out there're several new infertility treatments."

"Tell me about it. My Mom was the ninth child in a family of eleven and Dad was one of eight kids. Last time I attended a family reunion, and that was a long time ago, Mom lost count when she got to seventy of my first cousins. El was the only cousin who remembered my name. So tell me about Jeff's wedding." I hoped that would redirect the conversation.

"The wedding was one of those fairy tale events," El said between bites of lettuce. "The bride was dressed like a princess and there were fourteen attendants. Two women were needed to carry the train of her dress into the church."

"The only glitch was Uncle Jim." El gave Todd a warning look.

"Did Jim get drunk and throw up on the bride or something?"

El struggled to find politically correct words. Todd jumped in during the silence. "No. He showed up with his nineteen-year-old pregnant girlfriend."

"Enough family drama. I didn't come visiting to talk about family embarrassments."

I couldn't resist. "But El, it's such *juicy* family drama."

She ignored me. "We had such a good time exploring Sunset Crater and its ruins. Doug, is there any place around where we could buy some real Indian pottery and rugs?"

"I've seen some in a couple of Flagstaff shops," I said. "But Prescott's more known for being the antiques shopping mecca. The locals claim the jewelry bargains are in Tuba City and Shiprock."

Todd pushed a piece of curly endive around his bowl, unable to spear it with his fork. "Any chance you could spend a day to show us around a little? I'm getting burned out driving around in strange country. We've been on some roads only fit for mountain goats."

"Why not let El drive?" I smiled. "Or has the male hormone for driving on vacation struck again? Tourists can't drive on unfamiliar roads unless they've got testicles?"

El laughed. "Exactly right! It's right on the 'Y' chromosome next to the gene that won't let men ask directions when they're lost." She pushed aside her empty bowl. "Joking aside, the truth is I just don't like driving your Isuzu. It's too much like a truck." She stood up and took her bowl to the kitchen. End of discussion.

"So, what have you been doing the last two days?" Todd pushed his bowl back, giving up on the last lettuce scrap.

"We found the Lincoln the murderers used." I wiped my mouth and threw my paper napkin in the bowl. "There were a couple of car strippers working on it when we got there."

Todd looked disappointed. "So no evidence?"

"We don't know. The Navajo Nation Police officer is going to have what's left of the chassis gone over. Recovering evidence doesn't look promising at this point. We arrested a couple of hard-looking mechanics who were trying to pull the engine out of the stolen Lincoln. They've been through the criminal justice system before and aren't likely to provide any information. Other than that, I have no leads to pursue."

"So, can you get away for a day, since you don't have any other leads?" El called back over her shoulder as she took the bowls into the kitchen.

"I've only been on the job a couple of days, El. I doubt my boss will give me time off already."

She stuck her head around the corner. "But you will ask her, won't you?"

I rolled my eyes, and Todd smiled. "El's not shy."

I walked to the phone on the end table and took Jill's business card out of my wallet. I picked up the cordless phone and noticed the light blinking, announcing a waiting message. The message could wait until I talked to my boss. Her phone rang and after three buzzes, I expected voicemail. Instead, a breathless voice came on the line.

"Uh, Jill, hi. This is Doug Fletcher."

"Doug, great to hear from you. I heard that you and the Navajo Nation police found the Lincoln. That's super."

"Jamie Ballard's a good cop. He really pulled that off. I was just along for the ride."

"You don't need to play humble, Doug. I already heard how you stared down a tow truck with a rifle." Jill chuckled. "Lucky you didn't have to fire the gun or you'd be filling out forms and answering questions until Christmas." I mentally thanked Jamie for the sanitized version. He'd saved me a lot of paperwork. "Did you talk to Potter's admin assistant, Doug?" I could hear here shuffling papers. "Her name's Margaret Adams."

"Not yet."

"You'll want to. She doesn't think Potter committed suicide or that it was an accident, and she wants to talk to the man who's running the investigation. I gave her both your numbers."

"That explains why my message light is blinking. I'll give her a call as soon as we're through."

"When we spoke, she was really upset. She told me she'd been thrown out of her office by Potter's partner."

"What about the two guys we arrested with the Lincoln frame? Did your source tell you any more about them?"

"The Navajo Nation Police ran their fingerprints. They're both felons with long records who asked to talk with a lawyer. An officer from the Flagstaff PD picked them up from Shiprock this afternoon. I expect you'll get a call from them and the FBI asking for your statement. The Flagstaff police also got a warrant to search their salvage yard and found pieces of several stolen vehicles, including parts from the Lincoln."

I laughed. "The FBI won't call unless they find out there's field work to be done. They don't like to get their shoes dirty." I saw El's stare, which reminded me to ask for the day off. "Say, boss, I've still got visitors. Any reason I can't take tomorrow off to entertain them?"

Jill sounded disappointed. "I thought you were on a roll. Don't you want to run with it while the trail is hot?"

"Well, actually, I'm at a dead end. I hadn't even thought about what's next." Then, I had a lightbulb moment. "Wait a second. Jamie said there's a problem with theft of Indian artifacts from Federal land and the reservation. I'd like to spend a day or two checking out the shops to see if we can find any illegal contraband." El's eyes grew wide and she stifled a laugh.

"That sounds okay to me. First talk to the Adams woman and see if your police sense says you should follow up on anything. Otherwise, as far as I'm concerned, you're on the job and if that means looking for artifacts that may have been taken from national monuments, then you're following the leads you've developed." With that, the line went dead.

I hung up the phone. El was staring at me with a silly grin on her face. "You devil. Is that legitimate?"

I shrugged. "Who's to say it's not?"

Chapter 16

Margaret Adams' voice coming over my voicemail was full of tension. "Mr. Fletcher, my name is Margaret Adams. I spoke with a woman at the Park Service office in Flagstaff who said you're investigating Steven Potter's death. Please give me a call. I think we can help each other." She left a number with a Phoenix area code. I scribbled it down, saved the message, and dialed the number she'd left. "Margaret Adams?"

"Yes."

"This is Doug Fletcher, the Park Service investigator from Walnut Canyon. You left a message for me."

"Mr. Fletcher . . . oh yes. I'm so glad you called." The relief in her voice was palpable. "I understand you're investigating Steve Potter's death. I know his death wasn't an accident."

"Miss Adams, what was your relationship to Mr. Potter?" I hoped she wasn't just a crackpot who'd read about the death in the newspaper.

"I worked for Steve. He called me the night before he died and said he was going to quit. He was fed up with the antiques business and was going to get out."

She sounded credible and tracking me down through the Park Service took perseverance. Her voice in the voicemail was agitated, as though she was genuinely stressed. Still, my years as a cop left me skeptical of unsolicited calls, having been burned by both reporters looking for a story and crackpots.

"Miss Adams, I appreciate your call, but I'm not sure what you want."

There was a pause. "Look, Mr. Fletcher, I got the impression you were the one person who might believe me. If you're not . . ."

"Take it easy." I didn't want to antagonize her, but I wasn't about to give out information to someone I'd never met. "Is there something else that would help me make a case for Potter's murder?"

"I'm scared. If the people behind Steve's death find out I've called the cops I'll be in danger."

"Why would someone kill Potter and why would that put your life in danger?"

"Mr. Fletcher, do you know who Terry Mahoney is?"

"I'm not familiar with that name."

"Mahoney is a Tucson businessman who imports Mexican pottery. He partnered with Steve to expand his business by using our network of dealers. At first it seemed great, we doubled our sales in three months. Steve was making plans for expansion, but something changed last winter when they were working together on a charity project. After the fundraising gala Steve started blocking Mahoney's calls on his cellphone. Mahoney started calling the shop and I made excuses for Steve, but I could tell Mahoney was growing impatient."

"Miss Adams, people aren't killed over fundraising disputes."

"The problem wasn't the fundraising. Steve told me Mahoney had a 'new business model' and Steve refused to be a party to it."

"Business agreements aren't generally murder motives. Besides, if Potter were here, it would be his word against Mahoney's. Without Potter, it's only hearsay unless you've got evidence that Mahoney was doing something illegal."

"Steve was getting paranoid. He was recording phone calls with Mahoney and I have the recordings."

"Have you listened to them?"

"Not all of them, but I got the essence of the most recent conversations. Steve was uncomfortable with the way Mahoney was expanding his business, selling illegal antiquities with falsified provenance. He used Potter's letterhead for customer billing and it was risking Steve's business reputation. Steve said he wouldn't be a part of it. Mahoney told Steve to walk away and Mahoney would take over."

"I'm confused. What was Mahoney supplying you?"

"Our business was primarily wholesale modern Navajo and Hopi pottery and handcrafts. We sometimes got ancient collectables recovered from private land if the sellers could prove the provenance. Steve had a network of retailers who resold our material in their shops and they relied on his reputation, knowing the provenance had been verified when they resold our goods."

"How did Mahoney expand your business?"

"Mahoney had a reputation for importing junky pottery and imitation 'artifacts' from Mexico and selling them in a few tourist shops. At some point he needed a more upscale and expanded market. By falsifying the provenance of the goods and using our letterhead to bill for them, Mahoney was able to sell to an expanding group of retailers who were all taking antiquities with fake papers and reselling them based on Steve's reputation. Mahoney sent Steve a monthly royalty for the use of his name."

"I'm confused. The partnership with Mahoney was selling Mexican goods with fake papers through Potter's network?"

"That's where this all gets hazy. The two businesses aren't compatible. Mahoney was selling stuff that looked like it had been made by Mexican schoolchildren, and we're selling high quality tribal art and a few antiques with proven provenance. Our dealers don't handle the Mexican knock-off stuff Mahoney is importing, but suddenly we're partners. Our retailers were getting shipments and invoices on our letterhead but generated by Mahoney's office. Then we'd get royalty payments from Mahoney for artifacts he was shipping directly to our retailers."

"So, Potter's business was just handling the billing for Mahoney's sales?"

"Not even that. We were getting paid for the use of our business name and reputation."

"Do you know what caused the meltdown at the fundraiser?"

"Mahoney donated something to a charity auction and put Potter's name on it, which implied it had proven provenance, based on Steve's reputation. After the auction, the buyer approached Steve, asking for the paperwork on the piece, but Steve had never seen it before. Mahoney didn't have any papers on the piece, so he and Steve had a huge fight about risking our reputation. The next day Steve asked to see all the invoices for the Mahoney business, but Mahoney refused. He started calling our retailers."

"What did they tell him?" I asked.

"They were getting high quality antiquities from Mahoney and they were satisfied with the documentation that said they'd been found on private land."

"You said Mahoney was importing junky pottery from Mexico. Where were the antiquities coming from?"

"That was Steve's question, too. Mahoney told Steve to stop asking about provenance, take his cut, and shut up."

"How much money are we talking about?"

"Mahoney was billing a million dollars a month on our invoices. We were getting ten percent for using our letterhead."

"Where are the recordings?" My mind whirled as I considered the numbers and the implications of illegal antiquity sales on Potter and his business. "Have you made copies?"

"They're on CDs. I sent the original to a lawyer I trust in Denver with instructions to release them if something happens to me. I have a copy of the last recordings in an envelope. Should I send it to you?"

She didn't sound like a crackpot. If her information was true, Mahoney had millions of dollars at risk and he may have already killed once. If Mahoney thought Margaret Adams understood the nature of his business, or worse yet, knew she had recordings of his conversations with Potter, her life was in danger. I knew the FBI wasn't interested in following up on Potter's death. The information on the recordings could be important but I couldn't think of a way I could use them.

"No, don't send it to me. Call me from a public place with lots of people nearby and I'll give you an address."

"I'll call you back in fifteen minutes."

I hung up the phone and realized that El was standing next to me. "What's up, Doug? You sounded rattled."

"If you had to mail something to someone you could trust implicitly, who would it be?"

El cocked her head and thought for a second. "My mother."

I nodded. "Okay, suppose it was something politically explosive, and it could put the person in danger. Then who?"

Todd had joined us after listening from the living room. "This sounds like Watergate stuff. Are we talking really risky?"

"It may have cost Steve Potter his life." I let the words settle in. "Where would you send it?"

El looked baffled. "The Washington Post or one of the television networks?"

Todd was thinking and he snapped his fingers. "I assume you want it to get out, as opposed to having it hidden or struggling for prioritization against world news, so I think I'd want the information to go to a newspaper, probably a smaller newspaper that isn't owned by a huge conglomerate. It might take a couple days for them to check it out. They won't have the contacts that one of the big newspapers have, but they might put a bulldog on it."

My mind raced. Todd made sense but who would take it seriously and make an earnest effort to track down the details? "I attended a reunion of my old M.P. unit and one of the guys was working for a newspaper. I can't remember where he works."

"I like it!" El exclaimed. "Which newspaper?"

The phone rang and I jumped. "Fletcher."

"Okay. I'm standing next to a mailbox in front of the Phoenix post office with dozens of people walking past, so I'm safe. What address do I put on the envelope?"

"Peter Ward." The details flashing back to me. "*The Santa Fe Journal*, Santa Fe, New Mexico."

"Santa Fe?" She said with obvious skepticism. "Do you know this guy?"

"Yes."

The phone was silent for fifteen seconds before she asked, "Do you know the zip code?"

"Give me one second." I laughed, the tension now broken. "El, pull up the address for *The Santa Fe Journal* for me."

El's fingers flew around her phone screen and within ten seconds she handed it to me. "The address is 202 Mercado Street, Santa Fe, New Mexico, 87501. Add my name to the return address."

I repeated the addresses and waited quietly. After a minute Margaret laughed nervously. "Hang on." Her phone made scraping noises, as if it were being put into a pocket or purse, and then I heard the muffled creaking of the mailbox hinge. "It's gone. Now what?"

"Are you staying somewhere safe, away from your home or apartment?"

"I have a girlfriend with a spare bedroom. I have enough clothes along for a week. Do you think I need to prepare for a longer stay?"

"I'll keep investigating and we'll talk. I think we should have a better idea of the risks and timeframe of the investigation, and then we'll know how much danger you're in."

"What should I do now?"

"Call *The Santa Fe Journal* in a day or two and explain the CD to them."

"Am I really in danger?"

"I don't know. If the contents of the recording were enough to get Steve Potter killed, and if Mahoney knows you have the recording, I think you could be in danger."

"No one else knows I have the recordings." After a few seconds of consideration she added, "I have some relatives in Philadelphia—maybe I'll visit them for a few days."

The more we talked, the more uneasy I felt about her safety. "Skip relatives. They're too easy to trace. Take a vacation somewhere you've always wanted to visit where you've never been and no one knows you. Someplace far away and busy, like Orlando or Myrtle Beach."

"I'm thinking someplace cooler. I'm getting tired of the oppressive Phoenix summer heat. Maybe I'll go to the Rockies."

"Go wherever you want. Just do it soon. Don't tell anyone where you're going, and don't look back until the dust settles on this mess."

After I hung up I realized El and Todd were both staring at me. "I can't tell you right now. But I think we'll read about it in a couple of days."

If Margaret Adams was in danger, was Steve Potter's wife safe? "El, look up the phone number for Steven Potter for me."

"Steve Potter's dead. Why are you calling his number?" She typed away on the screen.

"I need to talk to his wife."

El found the number and handed her phone to me. It rang five times, then rolled over to voicemail. Steve Potter's voice told me they were unavailable and to leave a message after the tone. "Mrs. Potter, my name is Doug Fletcher. I'm an investigator for the Park Service. Please call me as soon as you get this message." I left my cell number.

"What are you going to say to her?" El put her phone in her backpack.

"I'm going to ask her about her husband's business, and then play it by ear. I think she could be in danger when the recordings come out."

Chapter 17

Margaret Adams was past being rattled. She was approaching panic. The conversation with Doug Fletcher had ramped her anxiety level so high she decided that even a trip to her girlfriend's house might put them both in danger. She stepped away from the post office and called for a cab on her cellphone. "Sky Harbor Airport," she said to the cab driver as she slid into the backseat. Leaving her car parked in the Phoenix garage was going to cost her but it couldn't be helped.

"Okay." The cabbie's accent hinted at his recent arrival from somewhere in Latin America. Margaret watched the houses, commercial buildings, and shopping centers fly by as her mind raced through the possible places she could choose. Somehow Salt Lake City sounded interesting. It had to be cooler than Arizona and seemed like a place where her old boss had no contacts. The idea of being among a bunch of peace-loving Mormons was attractive. At the airport she looked at the listing of outbound flights and saw that American Airlines had several non-stop flights to Salt Lake City. She got in a slow-moving line at the counter and started doubting her choice. Utah didn't seem far enough away. She looked at outbound flights and saw Charlotte with connections to Bangor, Maine. *That's about as far from Phoenix as you can get.*

She bought an expensive one-way ticket, went through security carrying only a backpack with a few days of clothing, her wallet, her cellphone, a laptop computer, and a book. She walked to the gate for her flight to Charlotte. She had a three-hour flight and a two-hour layover. She'd have breakfast in Maine. *Maybe I'll have blueberry pancakes with real maple syrup.*

She had a minor panic attack when she realized she was abandoning everything in her life. *My God, I don't even have a tampon! Or conditioner or shampoo or—get a grip, girl! Every town has a Walmart and a Target. All I need to do is find a motel near a mall and do some shopping.* She felt more confident with every step she took toward the departure gate.

Chapter 18

I parked the Isuzu on Cortez Street near the first Flagstaff antique shop I saw. It advertised antiques and Indian artifacts. A man, apparently the owner, was standing guard over a case full of jewelry with a cash register parked on the far end.

"Help you?" The man walked away from the cash register to check me out as I wandered through the pottery section. I gave a quick glance across the store at El and Todd, who were searching through a bunch of rusty antiques. They looked like tourists—I didn't.

"Sure. I'm looking for some antique Indian pottery. All this stuff looks pretty new."

The man picked up one of the pots and turned it over. On the bottom was a small adhesive tag with a price and a couple of initials. He pointed to the tag. "These are consignments. The tag has the initials of the person who made it." He pointed to the tag. "See. E.S. That's Evelyn Sampson. She does a lot of nice stuff and I'd say she's one of the most artistic of my potters."

I nodded. "Well, I'm really more interested in old stuff. Your sign says antiques. Where are the antique Indian bowls?"

He gave me a sly smile. "What agency are you with? BIA?" I wondered how I was giving off cop vibes when I'd had the badge less than a week.

The guy had all the savvy of a pawnbroker. Not much point in playing dumb. "Park Service." I took out my wallet and flashed the badge.

"Hrmph. I've had about every law enforcement agency but the Park Service here at one time or another. What's up?"

"Just doing a little research on antiquities. You got anything in the back?" I tried to look over his shoulder toward a door behind the jewelry counter.

He shrugged. "I got nothin' to hide. Let me take care of my paying customers first."

He started toward El and Todd before I stopped him. "They're with me. Don't worry, they won't steal anything."

He raised an eyebrow. "Now they're good. They don't look like cops." He led me through the door to an area full of shelves cluttered with merchandise, much of it duplicates of what was on display.

"For a small operation, you keep a lot of inventory." I perused the shelves and picked up a pot. It had different initials and a price.

He took it from my hand and set it on the shelf, letting me know I wasn't supposed to handle the stock. "It's easier to keep inventory when I handle consignments. I don't own it. I just hold it and send the artist the money when something sells. I do jewelry and pottery the same way. I sometimes have a few items I own, things that caught my eye at an auction or estate sale."

I pointed at some pots further back that looked older and weathered. "Are those antiques?"

He laughed as he led me down the aisle. "I got one guy who tries to make his pots look like antiques but he doesn't fool many people." He took down one of the pots and rolled it over. The marked price was three hundred dollars. Beneath it were the initials JS. "Joe thinks by weathering his pots a little, and putting on a big price, an amateur archaeologist will jump on them."

He handed me the pot. I rolled it around and looked at all the surfaces. The dark coloring was uneven and there were tiny cracks scarring the surface. "Looks old to me." I handed it back to him.

He held it so I could see the inside. "The inside isn't weathered." He put it back on the shelf. "And the colors are too vivid and the lines too perfect for it to be antique."

"I'm sure you tell the customers who buy his pots that they're not antiquities."

"If they don't ask . . ." he replied with a shrug, He replaced the pot on the shelf. "For a cop investigating illegal antiquities you don't seem to know much."

"It's easier to play dumb than pretend you're an expert." He looked unconvinced.

A bell rang in the rafters and we went back into the showroom. Another couple was working their way to the farm antiques. El and Todd were still looking, but El carried a couple of pots and Todd had a woven "dresser scarf" over his arm.

"So, you never get any antiquities?" I looked at the jewelry in the case.

The man shook his head. "I never said that. Every now and then someone will bring in some arrowheads or an antique pot. But usually they just have just a few shards, not a full pot. Unless they can prove they were recovered on private property, I send them packing. Getting caught with something taken off government land or the Rez is too risky."

I listened to the talk, but the words just didn't fit the character. When I was on the police force, the people with the biggest line of BS were the ones with dirty hands.

"If I came back with a search warrant, we could turn this place and not find a single piece of contraband?"

He held up his right hand, like he was taking an oath. "Scout's honor."

I smiled. "Well, you just keep your operation clean and we won't have any trouble." He knew the rules as well as I did, and without probable cause there was no way a judge would sign a search warrant.

I suspected he wasn't nearly as innocent as the image he tried to project. He'd walked me around the entire storage area, so I suspected he might have been clean on the antiquities, but my cop instinct made me suspect he had some scam running.

El showed up behind me with a stack of pots and some jewelry and laid the items on the counter. "I think that's everything." She dug in her purse for her wallet as the owner gave me a funny look.

"What's the matter? Don't you ever have cops buy stuff?" I watched him peel the label off the bottom of the items and collect them next to the cash register.

"Not often." He rang the tags, one at a time. As he rang up each tag he applied them to sheets of lined paper in a spiral notebook. Some pages were nearly empty and some half full of tags. The earliest tags on each page had an "X" marked on them with a black Sharpie pen.

I watched until he was done. "What's with the notebook?"

He turned so I could see the page where he'd just placed the tag from El's pot. "As I sell stuff, I put the tags on the sheet. At the end of the month I tally up the sales and pay the artists for what I've sold. Once I cut the check I cross the items off the list." He showed me a small, handwritten entry in several places, with the date and sum of sales.

"I send monthly checks to the artisans, less my consignment fee. This keeps all the sales sorted by artisan, and if there is any question, I can show them the tags that sold each month, the total, and what they were paid." He turned to

El. "That'll be one hundred twenty-seven dollars and fifty cents."

She handed him a VISA card and watched him run it through the electronic reader. He handed her the card and carefully wrapped the pottery in bubble-wrap while he waited for the machine to print out the receipt. When he finished wrapping and bagging her pots, he handed the receipt to El for a signature.

As she signed, he commented. "Well, this is a first. I never had two cops come through who acted like a married couple. I can't remember any cop ever buying anything." He handed her the purchases and added, "If any of these break before you get them home, send me a picture of the broken piece, and I'll send a replacement." He took a business card out of a small box on the countertop and dropped it into El's bag.

"That's quite a guarantee," El said as she put the receipt in her purse. I took a business card off the countertop. It said, "Gary Jones, Old and New Antiques," with the e-mail address, phone number and his website.

I slid his card into my shirt pocket. "You even have a website?"

"In this world, you either keep up with the marketplace or you die. I've had orders from Japan and Australia, all from people looking at pictures on my website."

* * *

Todd carried the bag to the Isuzu and loaded it in the back as El got in the front seat with me.

I was watching Gary Jones ring up the other couple as El asked. "Why did that guy think I was a cop?"

Inside, the woman pulled out her wallet and paid cash. "Because I told him you were with me and he knew I was a cop."

Todd got in the backseat as Gary packed the woman's purchases. Gary appeared to set all the stickers from the woman's purchases in a row, on the countertop. I watched as Gary Jones made change for her without ringing the sale on the cash register. After she shook hands with him and walked to the door, Gary peeled the stickers off the countertop and threw them into the wastebasket behind the counter without ever taking out the spiral notebook.

"Why are we sitting here?" Todd asked, buckling his seat belt.

"This is an interesting store. I bet a lot of things get sold here that never show up on any tax forms." I started the engine as the couple exited the store. "It's the nature of the business. It lends itself well to cash exchanges that aren't tallied in the cash register. For instance, you charged your purchase and he thought you were a cop. Gary rang it up on the cash register and put the stickers in a notebook. The last woman paid cash, and it never got rung up. He ran a total on a calculator and then she paid. When she left, he probably put the cash in his pocket and the state won't get sales tax on it, the IRS doesn't get income tax, and it appeared he threw away the price stickers that had the artisan's initials, so I assume they won't get paid for the pieces either."

As I pulled away El gave me a stern look. "You're jaded. He seemed very nice."

I smiled. "If he only reports his credit card sales he makes a tidy margin."

From the back, Todd chimed in. "Worse yet is the impact on the artisans. If they don't get paid for those pieces, Gary just made pure profit on that cash sale."

El shook her head in exasperation. "Why are you guys so cynical? Not everyone in the world is a crook."

Chapter 19

After making her connections, Margaret Adams landed in Bangor, Maine, with a carry-on bag purchased during her layover in Charlotte. She rented a car at the Alamo counter and got directions to the Bangor Motor Inn, not far from the Bangor Mall. She drove from the airport in lingering twilight.

Within five minutes of Margaret Adam's arrival at the Bangor Motor Inn, Rich Hayes' phone rang. "She's dumb. She bought a plane ticket and used her personal VISA card to pay for the ticket and a rental car. The Bangor Motor Inn just put five nights on her VISA bill. I don't think she's going anywhere. Do you want me to make sure?"

Hayes smiled. He loved dealing with professionals. They knew all the investigative tricks and could easily outsmart an average citizen like Margaret Adams. He pondered the possibility of calling her motel and scaring the daylights out of her. It would be fun, but a stupid move that would make her run somewhere else. Her fate was best left to the professional.

"Take your time," Hayes said after pondering the situation. "Make it look like an accident. And, for God's sake, don't tell me about it."

"Are you worried about the envelope she mailed? I couldn't see the address."

Hayes laughed. "Let's hope it was her Last Will and Testament."

"She left before I got the bug on her home phone, but I checked her cellphone records. She called the Flag Park Service, Walnut Canyon, and someone named Fletcher."

"Who's Fletcher?"

"His online records are clean. He's divorced, has no traffic tickets, no bankruptcies, no lawsuits. He moved from St. Paul a couple years ago where his phone number was unlisted."

"Maybe he's a boyfriend," Hayes speculated.

"I don't think so. The only time she ever dialed his number or texted was when she called the day she left Phoenix. He's never called or texted her."

"See if you can find out why she'd call him."

"That may take some time and might be expensive."

"My client said cost was no object," Hayes said with a smile, reflecting on Terry Mahoney's request for help with his "Adams problem."

Chapter 20

El pointed out two antique shops on our drive through Prescott. We locked her shopping bag in the back of the Isuzu and set off down the sidewalk. Living in Flagstaff had exposed me to the mix of cowboys, businessmen, Native Americans, and tourists. Todd sat on a bench watching the menagerie. He was especially intrigued by one middle-aged guy whose face was creased with lines as deep as canyons. He was wearing dusty clothes that looked like he'd just gotten off his horse, which may have been the case.

El and I checked out the first shop. Nothing. The proprietor of the second Prescott antique shop watched us casually from the cash register. He immediately pegged me as a cop while El and Todd roamed the store anonymously. I showed the owner my Park Service badge and we had a friendly conversation. He disavowed any knowledge of illegal antiquities, then explained his system of tracking sales and paying artisans. Apparently, consignments were a way of business in the antique store realm. I meandered through the store as I left and whispered to Todd, "Ask about the availability of 'real' Indian artifacts."

I walked out the front door and stood on the sidewalk where I could see part of the counter and the cash register. Todd made his inquiry and I saw the proprietor shake his head.

After trying for antiquities at two other downtown shops, and getting the same negative response, I wondered if the shopkeepers were honest, or if customers needed a referral to see the real artifacts. I drove the Isuzu northeast, toward Cottonwood. The drive was beautiful, through deep canyons with timbered hills. We hit the outskirts of Sedona where the traffic slowed.

"Can we stop in Sedona, Doug?" El asked from the back seat.

"I think Sedona deserves an afternoon. I've got another place in mind further down the road."

A few miles past Sedona a brown highway sign announced a turn for Oak Canyon, my intended destination.

El pointed to the driveway where dozens of tables were set up in the parking lot. "Oh, turn here, Doug. Let's see what it is."

I wound through a nearly full parking lot and found a parking spot near a maintenance building where a guy in a Bureau of Land Management uniform was cutting up a fallen branch with a chainsaw. We stopped at the brick "outhouse" building and then walked a trail to the edge of the parking lot where a row of native women displayed handiwork, jewelry, and Sedona logo caps that had been made in China.

The arrow on a sign pointed to the scenic view beyond the end of the parking lot. Todd and I walked to a railing overlooking Oak Canyon. Todd searched through El's camera bag trying to find a wide-angle lens.

The view was spectacular. As the walls got steeper, the trees gave way to the layers of red Sedona rock. It was just past noon, and the sun lit the canyon walls brightly. I tried to imagine what it would look like at sunset with deeper red hues and shadows among the trees.

The temperature had been tolerable, but the heat became daunting as we approached afternoon. El looked at the handiwork of each artisan, engaging them in conversation and occasionally buying something. I followed along but was thinking about lunch. I'd seen a Dairy Queen before we turned off the highway and I was looking forward to lunch in their air-conditioned dining area.

Oblivious to my fidgeting, El continued to stop at every table. At one table she talked to the female artisan for several minutes before purchasing a turtle necklace pendant made from a greenish stone I didn't recognize. She stopped at several more booths before buying a silver and turquoise watchband. I looked at pots in the next booth while she tried to find a bracelet that matched the watchband. I casually looked at the bottom of a pitcher and found the tag with the price and the potter's initials, JG.

In the next booth I turned over a pot and found the initials ES. The lady sitting behind the table appeared to be at least seventy years old. Her hands were gnarled and scarred from arthritis and a hard life. I set the pot down and walked to her chair. Her face showed no emotion as she looked up at me.

"Are you Evelyn Sampson?"

A flicker of surprise flashed in the woman's eyes. "Do I know you?"

"No. I looked at some of your pots in Gary Jones' shop."

She nodded, with her whole upper torso. "It's better to buy here."

I thought I knew the answer but had to ask anyway. "Why?" If I bought here, she got one hundred percent of the proceeds. If I bought from Gary Jones, I guessed he probably held back fifty percent.

Her eyes were very sad. Again her upper body rocked. "Gary Jones is not a good friend of the artists. It is better to buy here."

She dodged the question and that made me want to dig further. "But doesn't he sell your pots and give you most of the profit? I mean, if he didn't sell them, they wouldn't get sold at all." It was the typical dilemma of any artisan.

Evelyn Sampson continued to rock on the metal folding chair, not meeting my eyes while we spoke. "He sells, yes. I deliver many pots. He only pays for a few."

My eyes froze on her as the old woman closed her eyes. "He doesn't pay you for all you deliver?"

Her eyes stayed closed as she shook her head. "No."

"Does he tell you why?" I looked around to see if anyone else was listening. The nearest customer was Todd, and he was three tables away and the artists at the adjacent tables were busy rearranging their merchandise.

"There are many reasons. He says children break them and the parents won't pay. Some, he says, are stolen. It is always the nicest ones that break or disappear."

I knelt down, though my knee protested, until our eyes were level. She sensed my gesture and met my eyes. "Have you talked to the police about this?"

Her expression was like stone, never changing. "They cannot help. He is a thief. I know it. They know it. Now you, a stranger knows it. It does not change anything."

"How many pots does he pay for?" I was getting excited. It had nothing to do with my jurisdiction, but sometimes one crime leads to another. I think it was Thomas Jefferson who said, "There is no degree of honesty." Anyone who was in one shady business might be part of another.

"Sometimes he pays for half. Sometimes less." She looked away. Her expression was still stony. All my professional experience told me a person who wouldn't look me in the eye was lying. In this case, though, I believed Evelyn was telling me the truth, but had a cultural aversion to looking a stranger in the eye.

"Then why do you bring him more?"

She looked down the row of tables where El was examining a piece of jewelry. "To make ten pots and sell five is better than to make five pots and sell none." She looked back into my eyes again. "Gary Jones has much business and sends me more checks than anyone else. He also cheats me more than anyone else."

My knee felt like it was locking up, so I slowly got up from my crouch. It screamed in agony while I tried to stay focused on Evelyn Sampson's problem. "Do other artists have this same problem?"

Evelyn looked up and met my eyes again. "Gary is very even. He cheats everyone the same. Are you going to buy a pot?" She had signaled the end of the conversation and I was either to buy or move on. I chose a water pitcher I thought would look nice on top of my refrigerator. I also thought it might be the most expensive piece on the table. The tag said one hundred dollars. I knew that many people got anywhere from ten to twenty-five percent off the sticker price by haggling with the vendors. Our conversation made me sad and I had no interest getting even a dollar off the pitcher's sticker price.

I laid five twenties on the table next to her money box as she wrapped the pitcher in paper and put it in a bag. She handed me the bag and arranged the money, but instead of putting the cash in the box next to her chair she slid it inside her blouse.

"I might be able to make Gary stop cheating you." I said, slipping the bag under my arm.

Her eyes met mine again as she shook her head no. "You cannot make Gary stop. If he goes to jail, we lose money because we don't get anything from him. If he gets mad, he will sell someone else's pots, not mine. Leave Gary alone. Let him cheat me slowly." She spit the word "cheat."

I walked away slowly. *Some things never change.* I'd seen so many similar situations in law enforcement. You can't put a deadbeat dad in jail for not paying his child support because his arrest benefits no one. If he's not earning a salary, he can't pay child support. Using the same logic, you couldn't put Gary Jones in jail because a bunch of artisans, who are living on the edge of poverty, would lose the little he paid them.

El and Todd met me at the Isuzu with their packages. El was surprised to see me with a bag. "What high cholesterol foodstuff were they selling, Doug?"

"I bought a pitcher." I stuck my tongue out at her.

Chapter 21

Margaret Adams hid in her motel room until noon, occasionally peeking through the drapes, half-expecting someone with a gun to knock on the door. It didn't happen. Hungry and slightly less anxious, she walked to a nearby restaurant and had a seafood salad, delighted that it came with real shredded lobster. When she paid her bill, she asked the waitress where she could find a clothing store. The waitress directed her to a boutique a few blocks away where she could shop for reasonably priced clothes. She drove to the boutique and charged two blouses, a six-pack of socks, a pair of jeans, and some underwear. She also tried to find a jacket for Bangor's cooler weather. The racks were full of short-sleeve shirts, shorts, and swimsuits. She looked at the other customers and realized that everyone was in summer clothing, even though she felt chilled. She found a clearance rack in the back of the store and bought two sweaters.

At a sporting goods store she bought a quality backpack, then went to the bookstore next door and spent half an hour perusing the paperbacks before seeing a section of books by local authors. She chose a Sarah Graves mystery with a whimsical cover that looked like it might not cause nightmares. She threw her purchases into the trunk of the rental car with the clothes. At the motel, she took the armload of bags to her second-floor room where she cut off all the tags and changed into the jeans and a t-shirt, then pulled on a sweater. The effect was a transformation from her business power suit. When she tied her hair back in a ponytail and looked at herself in the mirror she felt like a kid again. No job today or tomorrow, no one bugging her about deadlines, but no one to talk to either.

At supper, she got the same waitress, who introduced herself as Connie. There weren't many customers, so they made small talk, eventually coming to the topic of sightseeing. Connie convinced Margaret that she should take a trip to Bar Harbor to see the ocean and eat fresh lobster.

A man sitting at a corner table took it all in while pretending to read a book. Listening, with his back to her, he had considered the options for an attack at the Bangor Motor Inn. He needed some sort of accident that would end Ms. Adams' life, wouldn't draw attention, and wouldn't leave evidence behind. A trip to Bar Harbor might provide the perfect opportunity for Margaret Adams' deadly accident.

Chapter 22

We ate lunch at the Dairy Queen and cooled off. El agonized over the menu which had way too many high-fat options and only three salad options. Todd and I opted for cheeseburger specials that included fries and a sundae. El ate her salad and tried to make us feel guilty by peeling the breading off the chicken and dramatically placing each piece onto a napkin. It didn't work.

As we finished lunch, El said she wanted to check out the bazaar across the parking lot. She crossed the parking lot and struck up a conversation with one of the younger women selling turquoise jewelry. Of course, that meant she was going to buy something. Todd and I sat inside the air-conditioned DQ eating sundaes and watching the haggling process taking place in the heat of the parking lot.

"How'd you like to play cop for a while?" I asked Todd.

He looked at me over the rim of his glasses. "Does it involve getting shot at or chasing bad guys again?"

I shook my head. Apparently one Walnut Canyon type escapade was enough for him. "Since every shop owner looks at me and immediately sees 'cop,' I thought we'd try a different tactic. If you and El go into the shops without me, looking like regular shoppers, maybe you'd be able to get someone to talk to you about antiquity sales."

"So, all you want me to do is let El do what she wants to do anyway—shop? In the course of shopping you want us to try to buy something that's illegal, something no one is going to sell to us anyway. Did I get it right?"

I smiled. "Mostly. Don't act so negative about trying to find someone willing to sell you illegal antiquities. Drugs are illegal and people sell them."

Todd leaned back. "Ah, now I see the catch. Do you think antiquities dealers spend a lot of time killing each other in the course of the dealings, like the Mexican drug cartels?"

"Todd, you watch too much television. Besides, these guys are pussycats. Anyone selling illegal items will do it out the back door to private collectors. They're here every day and can't afford to sell overtly or they lose their suppliers, buyers, and even the store. People who own brick and mortar stores don't hire hit men."

Todd looked skeptical. "Pussycats? Like the two who threw the guy off the cliff and shot at me?" He scraped strawberry topping from the bottom of his sundae and licked the spoon. "You forget. I was with you at Walnut Canyon. I think some of these guys play rough. My greatest hope would be to not catch them."

I pushed my hot fudge sundae aside. "Fine. Don't buy anything. If they offer you something illegal, tell them the price is too high and walk away. Just try it."

Todd ran his hand over his face and made a sour expression. "Okay, we'll ask around. But if someone actually says yes, don't be surprised to see me running like the last striped-ass ape."

We emptied our trash, set the trays on a shelf, and walked outside. The heat was even more oppressive. The armpits of El's blue blouse were dark with sweat when we dragged her away from the bazaar. Todd and I had agreed she shouldn't be a party to the full plan. She'd have a hard time digesting it and might get nervous and screw up the whole thing, or worse yet, just refuse to play along.

I found a public parking lot off Main Street in Sedona and pulled the Isuzu into a shady spot. We said our goodbyes and agreed to meet at five for dinner at a Tex-Mex place across the street from the parking lot. I spent my afternoon looking at antique guns and old law enforcement badges. I kicked myself several times for selling the 1873 Winchester I had owned when I was a rookie cop. It had been an old family bequest, but I was short on cash and really had no use for it. I sold it for a hundred fifty dollars in 1998. In the shops I found four of them. The cheapest was fourteen hundred dollars and looked like it had been stored in a tub of salt water.

I was intrigued by one shop that was selling moose antlers carved into eagles. I tried to envision one on a side table in my dining room, but decided it was too expensive.

A little after five o'clock I sat in the Tex-Mex restaurant and sipped a beer while I waited for El and Todd. Margaret Adams nagged at me—I was having second thoughts about sending her off to who knows where. I considered calling the Phoenix FBI office to share the news about Adams and the tapes, but the FBI had closed the Potter case and it seemed like I'd be better off if I avoided them until I had something solid to present. I thought about Potter's wife, who hadn't responded to the message I'd left. I wondered if she hadn't listened to it, had dismissed it as a crank call, or if she had decided to leave town.

I watched El and Todd wind their way through the restaurant with their shopping bags. El was excited to show me the many trinkets she'd bought friends and relatives for Christmas and birthdays. She pulled two serapes from the large plastic bags and told me about the weavers who'd made them from local wool. Todd just watched with a Cheshire cat grin. They ordered margaritas and I decided to switch to Diet Coke. The beer still tasted good, but a second one might lead to a third and I was driving.

When the margaritas came, El finally ran short of breath and let Todd get a word in. "Best of all, we found a shop that gets some real antique pottery. The owner says most of the time it's just chips and pieces he mounts in frames. But every now and then he gets an entire pot."

Todd handed me a business card from the shop as El chimed in. "He told me to call back in a couple of days, before we head home. He said he was negotiating on a couple things and one might be available in a day or two."

Todd sipped his drink and winked at me where El couldn't see. I pulled out a pen and scribbled the name of the shop and the phone number on the back of a card I'd taken from Gary's. I pushed the other card back to El.

"Any shops you guys missed? We could hang around."

Todd nearly choked on his drink as El answered. "There might be a small one on a side street." She patted Todd on the leg. "But I think Todd's done for the day."

I laughed at the relief on his face, while he nodded agreement faster than a bobblehead. "Yeah, I think so too."

Chapter 23

Tommy Tsosie and Elmer Swenson bounced across the reservation, the Suburban pitching and rolling with the contours of the desert. In daylight, the ride might have been fun, even a great tourist attraction, but in the dark of a new moon and with only parking lights, it was treacherous. At one point the oil pan protector scraped ominously, but it pulled free and they pushed ahead. The trailer hitch hung up briefly on the same rock, giving them a brief jolt.

"Hey, man. Take it easy on the hardware." Tommy rearranged himself on the passenger's seat, only to be jostled sideways as the right wheels dipped into a shallow wash.

"Anytime you want to take over, feel free." Elmer wrestled the steering wheel back after the tires came out of the washed-out creek bed. "I didn't want to drive in the dark and I'll give it up anytime."

A creosote bush loomed ahead of them, forcing Elmer to stop and back up a few feet. He put the transmission back into drive and cramped the wheel to the right. They eased past the bush, its branches scraping down the side of the truck, and then they bounced ahead. On Tommy's lap a glowing Garmin GPS indicated their current location with a blinking blue light.

Their destination, showing up as a red teardrop, was a set of numeric coordinates Tommy had keyed into the machine. There wasn't a road anywhere on the screen.

"You know, Tommy, we're a couple miles off the road. It's probably safe to turn the headlights on. It can't be any worse than me flashing the brake lights to back up and go around stuff." Elmer steered clear of a boulder and bounced down a low wash. "Besides, we're going to have to use the gas lights when we get to the site anyway. They're more visible than the headlights. At least the headlights face away from the road. You know, a candle is visible for a quarter mile—the gas lamps can probably be seen for many miles in any direction."

Tommy kept staring straight out the windshield without responding. Elmer's words had set his mind to work. They'd use a tarp as a shield so someone on the road wouldn't see the lamp, but it'd probably be good to shield the lamp from all sides. As for the headlights . . . that was now a matter of principle. He couldn't let Elmer be right. They'd have to go on without the lights and hope to hell not to hang up the big Suburban on a rock, or worse yet, drop it over the edge of a wash. It'd be a long walk to get help and there hadn't been any cell service since they were a hundred yards from the road.

"What's the GPS say? Are we close?"

Tommy looked down at the LCD display on his lap. He'd walked this land as a kid and knew it like the back of his hand but traveling in the dark disoriented him. The Global Positioning System updated their location, relative to satellites in geosynchronous orbits, every five seconds. "We're about a quarter mile southwest. Turn a little to your left." The terrain was suddenly clear to him. He'd been here a thousand times. Every bush was a friend and every rock a landmark. "Follow this wash."

The truck lurched as it dropped a few inches into the bottom of the wash. The bottom of the arroyo was like driving on a recently graded gravel road. The dryness left the creek bed hard and easy to follow. Tommy had seen it as a raging torrent, but never in the summer when it was too hot to make the long walk from the nearest road. With the dry heat of summer, the streambed hardened like a highway. Tire tracks left from previous trips cut the arroyo. They followed it until the tracks stopped and canyon walls loomed ahead of them.

Elmer was dripping with sweat from the stress of the drive. Tommy reached up and removed the bulb from the overhead light, then jumped out and opened the back as Elmer eased out of the driver's seat and joined him.

"I thought we weren't going to work this place for a couple of days . . . to let the heat die down over Potter getting dumped," Elmer grabbed the shovels and set them on top of a pile of other gear while Tommy set out a tarp.

"We only have a couple more days to work this site. We can't lose a night because of the Potter thing. Now, shut up and get going."

Tommy set a plastic gas lantern case on top of the heap of gear and grabbed the rope lashed to one end of the tarp. "C'mon."

They dragged the tarp over the hard-packed sand like it was a sled. Dodging rocks and small bushes, they stopped near the top of the canyon. The heat of the day had given way to a cool evening. The sand was still hot enough to burn bare feet but the sweat on their shirts was rapidly evaporating in the cooling desert air.

Tommy looked around for any sign of a human. A million twinkling stars supplied the only light. They unloaded the tarp and Tommy used dead branches to prop it up as a wall, while Elmer opened the lantern and attached it to the propane cylinder. By the time Elmer lit the lamp, Tommy had erected a four-sided blind, with one corner tied to a stubby bush. He tied the tarp to the dead branches, forming walls. The lantern light effectively blinded them to the area beyond the walls.

Together they worked their spades to remove dirt. After a few shovels of loose sand, one of the shovels hit plywood with a "thunk." They shoveled the plywood clear, then threw the shovels aside to lift the 4' x 8' plywood sheet. A four-foot hole gaped before them.

It was one of their personal archeological sites, one of dozens Tommy had explored while roaming the reservation as a boy. It had been nothing more than a secret spot to him for two decades. It wasn't until a brief stint in the Federal Correction Institution in Phoenix that he became aware of the economic potential of the unexcavated sites like this. It was ironic that a punch thrown at a BIA agent, followed by prison time, was making him a rich man. Artifacts taken from the reservation provided a modest income for a couple of years. Initially, he'd sold directly to the tourists, at great personal risk. Then he'd found Joe Reber. Everyone on the Rez knew Joe was an equal opportunity crook, cheating both his suppliers and clients. But he had connections and buyers. Tommy sold over one hundred thousand dollars in loot to Joe the first year. It made him hungry for more, but to recover more artifacts he needed help. That led him to Elmer. Elmer wasn't bright, strong, or even good company. But Elmer kept his mouth shut and didn't flash his money. Tommy knew that angry ex-girlfriends, their tongues loosened by alcohol, and crooks openly spending too much money brought more criminals to justice than routine police investigations.

After the first year, Joe's prices started to drop. Following a few days of surly bickering, Tommy suspected Joe could sell only a limited number of illegal pieces to his discreet private collectors. While looking for another dealer to handle his finds, Tommy stumbled across Terry Mahoney, who specialized in importing Mexican pottery he passed off as antiques to unknowing tourists.

After talking with Tommy, Mahoney came up with the perfect business arrangement. He paid Mexican artisans to make fake antiquities, items that any dealer would scoff at. Once the chintzy Mexican items were through customs, they were sold to Joe Reber, with Mahoney making a considerable profit. Reber replaced the Mexican crap with real artifacts, recovered from the reservation by Tommy. As long as Tommy's deliveries matched the flow of Mexican imports, Mahoney had bona fide invoices showing that the relics he was selling had been legally imported. Joe sold a few items to people who walked into his shop, or to private collectors, but his customer base was still limited, creating a growing stock of excess antiquities. Mahoney's other network of retailers were selling Mexican pottery to tourists, but they didn't have customers to buy expensive antiquities. They needed another sales outlet.

They found Steve Potter's business in Phoenix through serendipity. Potter had a reputation for selling artifacts, with legal provenance, to museums and private collectors around the world. Though Potter had a global business, his pipeline of relics recovered from private land, or purchased on the internet, was limited and shrinking.

Mahoney was sipping champagne at a fundraiser when he was introduced to Steve Potter. Within days of their chance encounter, Mahoney arranged to have Joe Reber deliver his excess inventory to Tucson. Through a complicated series of transactions Mahoney used the legitimate business as a front for selling illegal reservation antiquities, without Potter ever seeing the shipments or the documentation that was going to his trusting customers.

The new pipeline seemed to have a never-ending demand, and everyone was making money. The only problem that ever arose was when Tommy dug up something unusual or something of substantial value. Through Potter's contacts, they could sell thousands of pottery shards, but they couldn't handle any big items. No legitimate customer was going to buy an ancient metata with a US Customs declaration saying it was a Mexican pot. Consequently, Tommy was still at Joe Reber's mercy for the big pieces. If a real "museum piece" had the proper provenance, it could go to an auction where the price might soar into the millions of dollars. Because the provenance of those truly valuable items couldn't be easily disguised among the Mexican invoices, Mahoney's contacts sold many of them into private collections where provenance wasn't an issue. Tommy felt, usually quite accurately, that he was getting taken each time Joe paid him for a valuable item.

* * *

Elmer took a shovel, jumped into the hole, and started digging out chunks of packed soil into a bucket. When the pail was nearly full he passed it up to Tommy, who sifted the dirt using a coarse screen. A shard of pottery and some arrowheads emerged from the dirt. Tommy carefully removed the pieces and set them gently in a basket near the canvas wall.

By the third bucketful the sifting was mindless and Tommy's thoughts drifted. It had been easy to club Potter and dump him over the edge, but everything changed when that guy chased them up the steps. Then they hit the ranger when he stepped out of his hut, maybe because someone had called ahead, or maybe because they were just going too fast. Luckily, the Jeep was where they'd left it, and they hadn't encountered a cop either before or after they'd dumped the Lincoln. The whole operation had been strange. According to the guy he'd overheard in the coffee shop, the newspapers were calling the Walnut Canyon death an accident. Did that mean no one was investigating?

The Walnut Canyon job had only interrupted their archeological operation for a day. The money left in the rental locker had been generous, much more than they were making from the illegal archeological dig.

A small turquoise bear and another pottery shard emerged as the dirt sifted through the screen. Again, Tommy gently set them aside in the basket. Tommy noticed that the last shard had a fresh break in it. The bigger they were the more they were worth. "Hey Elmer! Take it easy. You broke that last piece of pottery."

The digging sounds stopped. "You want to trade jobs?" Elmer asked. Tommy didn't answer. It was one thing to sift dirt and another to disturb ancient burial sites. "Then quit bitching."

The relationship between the two men had a quiet tension that kept them both on edge. They each knew their roles and were pushing the limits of what could be said or done before some comment or action would cause permanent damage to their business arrangement. Tommy knew where to dig, so he called the shots and held that over Elmer's head. Elmer took it for a while, then drew a line in the sand. He knew there were things Tommy was unwilling to do. Tommy wouldn't drive in the dark or climb into the hole where his forefathers were buried or the sites where they'd dumped their garbage. They were symbiotic; each benefited from their relationship and neither suffered. But the tension between them was palpable and mounting.

Chapter 24

After their morning run, Todd and El drove off to explore the mining town of Jerome. I called the Flagstaff Police Department and asked to speak with a detective. I was put on hold for a few minutes, which seemed like an eternity, kicking myself when I realized I could have just left a message.

Finally, a male voice came on the phone. "This is Detective McCord."

"Detective, this is Doug Fletcher, from the Park Service." I let that sit for a second, knowing he wouldn't know why he was getting a call from a ranger. "I wanted to follow up on our murder investigation."

"I'm sorry, Fletcher, your name doesn't sound familiar. Have we met?"

"You can check with Superintendent Rickowski in the Flagstaff office. I'm a Park Service investigator. Would you like my badge number?"

There was a pause and I could hear scraping sounds. "Sure. Give me your badge number and a phone number where you'll be for a while. I'll call back in a few minutes." I could hear him scribbling the numbers I gave him. "By the way, you do realize it's a felony to impersonate a Federal officer?"

"I'm well aware of the laws regarding impersonation of officials. If you want to bypass the Park Service phone bank, Jill Rickowski's personal cellphone number is . . ."

My phone rang again in less time than it took me to finish checking the status of my retirement savings account.

"Jill Rickowski verified your employment. How can I help you?"

"I want an update on the Potter murder investigation." I grabbed a pencil and prepared to take notes, knowing the information would be very slim.

"What murder investigation are you talking about?"

I let out a sigh. This wasn't going to be easy. "Steven Potter's murder at Walnut Canyon."

"I'm afraid you're mistaken, Fletcher. Potter died in a tragic accident. I read the autopsy report. There was no murder. There is no investigation. The case is closed."

"Doesn't it bug you that this respected businessman died, but didn't have a bit of ID on him?"

"There's nothing in the autopsy report about that. I assume his personal effects were bagged and given to his next of kin."

"His pockets were almost entirely empty. Are there any leads on the statue in Potter's pocket?"

There was a pause. "What statue?"

I squinted as I tried to remember the name the rangers had used for the figure. "It was a kind of dancing stick figure."

"Kokopelli?" McCord threw the name out.

"That's it. He had a Kokopelli figurine in his pocket. Is that significant?"

McCord snorted. "He was an importer of artifacts and I assume it was some sort of good luck charm or a gift. I'm sure dealers like Potter get gifts all the time."

I was getting frustrated. "A guy shot at a Walnut Canyon tourist and ran down the ranger at the gate. Are you at least investigating that crime?"

I heard papers shuffling. "I don't have any documentation about those incidents. Did someone send a report?" More papers shuffled. "I've got nothing about that, and besides, you're the Park Service investigator. If it happened inside Walnut Canyon, it's your crime, not mine." He left the ending dangle, like it contained a message.

"In other words, it's been closed by someone at a higher level and is now out of your control?"

"It's closed. Let it go, Fletcher. We both have enough work to do."

I rubbed my hand over my face in frustration. Detective McCord didn't give a damn. "Did you get anything out of the guys in the tow truck or from the salvage business?"

"The two guys we arrested at the auto salvage business were small-time punks with a few arrests. We recovered a bunch of stolen car parts. The guy who owns the building lives near Phoenix and claims he doesn't know anything about the day-to-day operation. I doubt there's any way we can tie him to the operation unless a forensic accountant goes through his books and can show he's profiting from the business beyond collecting rent. We don't have the resources to do that."

"The Navajo Nation Police called Jill Rickowski and told her someone for the Flagstaff PD picked up the tow truck guys from Shiprock. I assumed Flagstaff wanted them for the stolen car parts."

"Hmm." I could hear the computer keys clicking. "I checked our logs and there's no record of our officers taking them from Shiprock. Maybe the US Marshal's office got them."

"So the case is dead unless something else comes up?"

"We'll see if the city attorney wants to prosecute the guys from the salvage shop. Beyond that, we don't have any leads to follow right now."

"Well, just in case you find this useful, you might want to follow up with Joe Reber, in Sedona. I've got an informant who says he sells illegal antiquities." It was a little bit of a lie, but not a big one.

"Sedona is split between Yavapai and Coconino Counties, both out of my jurisdiction. You should contact their sheriff's departments."

"That's it, then?" I asked.
"Call me if you find the tow truck guys."

Chapter 25

Margaret Adams had read most of the Sarah Graves book the night before and was pleased there weren't any vivid scenes of terror. If she had been more paranoid, she might have thought the man having breakfast in the next booth looked familiar, but she was relishing the waffles topped with wild Maine blueberries and real maple syrup the waitress put before her.

After breakfast she followed her phone's GPS map to Bar Harbor. She marveled at the landscape, greener and thicker than anything around Phoenix. At one point she had to slow to let a whitetail doe and two fawns cross the road. She didn't notice the black Nissan Altima hanging back a mile behind her.

She drove into Bar Harbor at noon and found a quaint lobster shack along the shore. The breeze off the ocean was cool and fresh. She ordered lobster bisque and an iced tea. She put cash on the table to cover her bill and a five-dollar tip. The young waitress hailed her in the parking lot, thinking she'd made a mistake and left too much money. Margaret assured her she'd intentionally left that much for a tip. The waitress was effusive in her thanks.

The drive up the coast was filled with incredible vistas, including occasional fishing boats and small islands covered with pines. She pulled off and parked at a wide spot along the shoulder of the road. After watching the ocean for a minute, she walked to the huge rocks protecting the shore from the Atlantic surf. It took a bit of effort to carefully climb over the sofa-sized rocks. Once on the shore she picked up flat pebbles and skipped them across the gentle swells.

The Nissan Altima's driver stopped when he saw Margaret's rental car on the side of the road. They were in the middle of nowhere and his first thought was that she'd spotted him. Then he thought her car might have malfunctioned. He drove past. At the next hill he stopped and pulled on a pair of black driving gloves. He sat for a moment to see how much traffic was using the road. No one passed, and there wasn't a vehicle in sight in either direction. He watched for a few minutes as she walked the narrow beach, totally focused on the ocean.

Margaret was mesmerized by the sound of the waves lapping at the rocky shore. She sat on a huge rock with her arms crossed over her knees, her chin resting on her arms. A lazy seagull squawked as it passed overhead. She hadn't been this relaxed since before her move to Phoenix. There, her life had become all business and rushing around in a hot brown world. She was a type A personality and had been willing to sacrifice her personal life to make headway in Potter's small import company, hoping to become his partner one day. Maine was something else. No deadlines. No late shipments. No delays at customs. No heartburn. No sexist assholes who couldn't see past her breasts. No Zantac. The fresh smell of the ocean was invigorating and refreshing. Maybe she'd never return to Phoenix. *There must be jobs in Maine.*

A man walked down the shore toward her. He was looking out to the ocean and seemed in no hurry. People in Maine were so laid back. *They wouldn't last a week in Phoenix.*

He seemed surprised to see another person on the beach. He smiled at her. "Beautiful day, isn't it?"

"I love it." She smiled back. He was a handsome thirtyish man with wavy brown hair. He looked mildly familiar.

"Do you mind if I sit for a while?"

She looked around and realized she was sitting on the only flat rock along the shore. She slid over to make room for him, and something subliminal hit her. Where had she seen him? Was it the restaurant? He twisted as he pulled himself up on the riprap. She noticed something in his hand.

His arm struck out. The long, black rod extending from his fist slashed at her head. She pushed her feet against the rocks to dodge the blow but they shifted, and she fell back. An excruciating pain coursed through her arm. He'd struck her on the elbow, and it felt like it had exploded.

The blow hadn't connected solidly and the momentum carried his torso in a spin that put his feet on a patch of round stones. They spit out from under him. Margaret recoiled in pain and watched him fall. Time stopped and resumed in slow motion. She willed herself to move but her body was frozen. The rod flew from his hand and clattered among the rocks. He fell to his hands and knees on the jagged granite boulders. His right hand slipped into the space between two rocks and his chin struck a sharp granite spire. His mouth snapped shut in a loud crack. His grunt of pain jarred her into action.

She lunched to her feet and stumbled across the boulders, feet slipping and threatening her balance. The adrenaline rushing through her body was a blessing, overriding the pain in her arm. She slipped off the steep side of the last huge rock repeatedly, scraping her shins and ankles. Looking back, she saw he'd gotten to his feet near the bottom edge of the riprap. Blood streamed from his mouth and chin, staining his light-colored jacket. She didn't look back again. Her pocketed cellphone thumped against her leg as she sprinted across the narrow strip of grass toward her rental car. It took two tries to pull it free and twist it so she could read the screen. No Service.

Just as she reached for the door handle, the passenger's window disintegrated into a million crystals. The popping sound of the bullet followed a fraction of a second later. She looked back to see him standing at the edge of the rocks. The black pistol in his hand spit and she heard the bullet hit the car door just before the sound of the shot got to her ears. *Dear God, he's shooting at me!*

* * *

Damn it! The hitman swore, realizing the pain from the dislocated fingers of his shooting hand made it impossible to aim and fire accurately. He switched the gun to his left hand, a move he'd practiced dozens of times, and tried to line up the sights for a shot. His target beyond the effective range of the 9mm, but she'd stopped and stared at him when he fired.

"Stupid bitch." He fired three more quick shots at her as she rounded the car and tried to open the driver's door. After the third shot, she pitched to her left and fell alongside the car. With any luck, she was dead, or at least injured so badly he could get close enough to make the kill shot.

* * *

Ed Adams was driving home from his shift at the sewage treatment plant. He wasn't expecting any excitement nor did he want any, but just as he crested the hill, he saw a woman fall by her car. She tried to stand up and fell again. *Just what I need, a drunk woman stumbling into the road!* Then he noticed movement to the right. A man with a gun in his hand ran toward her. Ed saw a flash from the gun's muzzle. The man's arm bucked from the recoil.

Ed didn't even stop to think. He accelerated the Ford Pickup and veered across the left lane. His eyes fixed on the man whose attention was on the woman. Ed knew the man was firing the gun again and again because he could see his arm bucking as the woman tried to crawl further behind the car. He couldn't hear any shots, though, his heart was pounding too hard for that. Ed aimed his truck straight at the man, engine revving.

* * *

The hitman could smell blood. His field of vision narrowed to his prey, the woman hiding only yards ahead of him. It wouldn't look like an accident, but what the hell, she'd hurt him. He thought at least two of the shots hit her—one while she was standing behind the fender and the second as she scrambled around the front of the rental car. He hoped they hadn't been kill shots. He didn't want her to die fast. She'd caused him excruciating pain and he wanted her to suffer. He stepped behind the trunk and sidled to the left as she opened the driver's door and tried to crawl inside. He hoped she'd hesitate there and he'd be able to pump several shots into her legs and abdomen. That'd hurt like a bitch but she'd live for hours before she bled to death in the trunk of her rental car. Maybe in a few days some local cop would come by and see the bullet holes in the car and the blood on the back bumper. By then, he'd be back in Arizona.

She was there . . . huddled against the driver's door. He took a step onto the roadbed and raised the gun, but a sound distracted him. He turned his head just in time to see the grille of the pickup, traveling seventy miles an hour.

The pickup's fender hit him first and then ripped the door off the rental car as it sped past the woman. The impact shook Ed's teeth and pushed the car away from the woman cringing in the road. The chrome-plated pickup grille carried the hired killer with it until the truck stopped and his dead body fell onto the road.

It took a few seconds for the dust from the jarring crash to settle. Ed stared out his windshield in a stupor, then focused on the woman crumpled on the shoulder of the road.

Ed struggled to open the rusty pickup door and ran back to where she lay in the road. She was bloody and her left arm lay at an unnatural angle.

"Ma'am, are you okay?" Ed knelt down next to her and touched her good arm.

"Are you an angel?" she whispered.

Chapter 26

I flashed my Park Service badge at the dispatcher in the Coconino County Sheriff's office. "Is there a detective I could talk with about an antiques scam?"

The dispatcher was a trim middle-aged woman in a tan police uniform, with short hair and a professional bearing I read as former military. She was tucked behind a barrier of bulletproof glass with phone and radio consoles in front of her. There was a wedding band on her ring finger. She didn't feel the need for social graces such as smiles. She just picked up the phone and dialed a three-digit extension. After a brief exchange, she pushed a button and announced via speaker that Captain Parks would be right down and that I should have a seat. She emphasized that instruction by pointing to a row of red vinyl-covered chairs, most with cracked seats. I decided to stand. God only knew what bodily fluids had seeped into the stuffing under the cracked vinyl.

The electronic door release clicked and a stocky middle-aged man appeared in the doorway. He wore a light blue shirt, open at the collar, and dark pants. A gold badge on his belt indicated he was at least a lieutenant. "You the Park Service guy?"

I flashed my badge again and extended a hand. "Doug Fletcher."

"Greg Parks." He directed me through the door and then led me down a narrow hallway to an office overlooking the parking lot.

He sat down in his desk chair. He didn't invite me to sit. "Are you here to follow up on your discussion with the Flagstaff PD? If you are, the door is still open. Close it on your way out."

"If discussion of the death at Walnut Canyon is off the table, I want to talk about stolen antiquities being sold at an antiques store. Detective McCord made it clear that investigation was outside his jurisdiction."

I noted his desk was clear except for one pen. The only personal touch was a framed photo on the credenza behind him. It showed him in a flowered shirt with his arm around a woman wearing a caftan. They were standing in front of a Pacific island sunset. The office was too neat for a man who did real police work. The guy had to be an administrator.

He leaned back in his chair and visibly relaxed "So what can you tell me about illegal antiquities?"

I chose a vinyl guest chair with chrome-plated arms that matched the ones in the lobby, but in better shape. "What do you know about Gary Jones' and Joe Reber's antique shops?"

Parks picked up the pen from his desktop and spun it between the forefinger and thumb of one hand. He stared at it as he spoke. "I might be curious as to why the Park Service is interested in antique dealers." He looked up at me. "Did you get some bad pots?" A smile crinkled the corners of his mouth.

"Since we're not talking about the Walnut Canyon ranger who was run down or the guy who shot at a tourist, my call is out of professional curiosity." Throwing a bone to a fellow officer sometimes opened a door.

Parks continued to stare at the pen. "Fair enough." He threw the pen on the desk and stared at me. "Gary Jones seems to be fair with his customers. None of them have registered any complaints."

I nodded. "I shopped there. He seems to have some pretty nice stuff. He claims it's on consignment from the artisans."

Parks shrugged. "Could be. I don't think that's any of our concern."

I liked Parks. He was direct and to the point . . . no bullshit. "Have you ever had a complaint from the artists placing consignments?"

Again, there was the hint of a smile. "Nothing formal."

"But informal complaints have been made." I made it a comment, not a question.

Parks squinted his eyes and took a deep breath. "Let's say we have been approached by a couple of the artisans. They have vague complaints but no records or documentation. My detectives have spoken with Gary Jones, but nothing has ever been pressed. He claims they don't understand the realities of doing business. I think he's got a little stink of bad faith on his hands." Parks leaned forward. "There's no way I can take that to the district attorney."

Parks was practical—something that only came after years of experience and some hard knocks. "It's the devil's alternative," I said. "Evelyn Sampson knows that Gary's cheating her, but she's also resigned to the fact that she can't turn him in because even with him cheating, his sales are still her largest chunk of income. She claims he only pays her for half of what she delivers."

He smiled. "Evelyn's been in that very chair and told me the exact same thing. She vented for a while, then she told me to do nothing and left."

I thought for a second. "If it were my call, I'd have a hard time cutting off money for many people living on the edge, even if it meant overlooking a crime."

Parks snorted. "Tell me about it. I'm sworn to uphold the law, but if it hurts little people . . . besides, I don't have any evidence."

I put up a finger. "There I can help. I'm 99 percent sure he's falsifying his records. He doesn't ring up cash purchases, only the ones made with credit cards."

Parks picked up the pen again, twirling it in his fingers. "So, we're looking at what? Tax fraud? The Arizona Revenue Department would definitely like to talk to him about that." The twirling stopped. "But then we're back to shutting him down. That doesn't do people like Evelyn Sampson any good."

"How about a civil case?" Parks stood up and turned to look out the window. "If we get the artisans to put together a civil case, maybe they could get some cash and not cripple the business."

"It isn't going to be easy, but there's a way. It's not exactly within the boundaries of the law."

He turned to face me again. "And that's what we're sworn to uphold." Parks sat back down, indicating the end of that discussion. "Tell me about Joe Reber."

"He told my cousins he didn't have any antiquities when they stopped in his shop, but said he might in a few days. They thought he was serious."

Parks wrinkled his nose. "Reber is a swindler. We had some complaints about items he'd misrepresented as pre-Columbian but were later proven to be modern. We ran a background check on Joe, and his life has been one shady operation after another. For some reason, unknown to me, he's managed to stay out of jail." Parks paused and stared at the desktop for a second, then sighed. "He's a disbarred lawyer and I would expect him to be savvy enough to stay out of jail. I'd like to catch him in a slip-up and throw his ass behind bars, but he's just sly enough to smell a rat and I don't have the resources to mount a large-scale sting." Parks swept the pen into the desk's top drawer. "Tell me about your so-called murder investigation."

The change in direction caught me off guard. "There's not much to tell. Three guys showed up at the park. Two of them threw the third guy over the railing. He died. The other two made a run for the exit. They shot at a tourist who was following them. They hit a ranger as they raced off in their Lincoln, breaking his leg. End of story."

Parks looked at me skeptically. "You're sure the guy didn't die from the fall?"

I chuckled. "You should join the FBI. They were skeptical too. The victim was unconscious, if not dead, when he went over the rail. He didn't scream or flail . . . just fell like a rag doll. The autopsy verified blunt force trauma as the cause of death."

"Who saw him fall and noticed that he didn't struggle?" Parks leaned over the desk and put his elbows on the top.

I looked him straight in the eye. "I did. The body flew right in front of me."

"Not often we get an expert witness to a murder." Parks raised his eyebrows like he was impressed. "The dead guy was an antiques dealer from Phoenix?"

"Steven Potter, a Phoenix antique importer and dealer, yes. Apparently a respected one."

Parks listened, then took out a Post-it note and pen. He wrote Potter's name on a piece of paper and got up from the chair. "Hang on for a second and I'll see if we have anything on him here." He disappeared and was back in a few seconds. "I've got a sergeant running it through the computer. We'll see what he comes up with." He sat back down. "Anything else special about this Potter or the other guys you saw?"

"Potter was Caucasian, and so was one of the others. The third guy was Latino or Navajo and he was big, like a body builder. About the only thing distinctive about the victim was that he had a little Kokopelli statue in his pocket."

Parks perked up. "The victim was found with a Kokopelli figurine?"

I was surprised by his sudden interest. "Is that significant?"

Parks was out of the chair again. "Maybe. Come with me." We walked out of his office and past a row of unoccupied desks to a lone detective who was pounding computer keys.

"Hey, Bernie, this is Doug Fletcher." Bernie was a huge man with rolls of fat straining against his shirt. Several chins filled the space between his jaw and Adam's apple. He acknowledged the introduction with a nod. "Fletcher was telling me about the jumper out at Walnut Canyon. They found a Kokopelli in the dead guy's pocket."

Bernie's eyes glanced between us, and then he punched a few keys on the computer. The screen he was working on disappeared and a new page filled with spaces popped up. Bernie typed "Kokopelli" in one space and ran the cursor over to a command line. He clicked on "Search" and leaned back.

The light on the computer flickered as the computer searched a database of some type.

Bernie looked at me. His face was puffy and tiny ruptured blood vessels crisscrossed the surface of his nose like a roadmap.

"Fletcher. I don't recognize you or the name." He offered his hand. "Bernie Kaiser."

We shook hands. "I'm new at Walnut Canyon."

Bernie was obviously sizing me up. "The Park Service usually doesn't hire anyone older than fifteen." His face was total deadpan.

"I'm younger than I look." I, too, maintained deadpan.

Bernie's mouth crinkled at the corner in a Mona Lisa smile. "I'll bet you are." The computer chirped and Bernie pulled himself back to it. The screen showed a dozen lines. Bernie hit a few keys and the printer rattled to life.

Parks explained as the printed sheets inched into the tray. "We had some crimes a few years ago. At first, the criminals scrawled a Kokopelli drawing at the crime scenes. Later, they started leaving a Kokopelli figurine. We assumed it was some kind of an Indian gang. Turns out, it was some high school kids who thought the Kokopelli was a neat symbol. Kokopelli represents mischief. It fit with their activities."

I must've frowned. "I thought Kokopelli was the symbol of fertility?"

Parks smiled. "He's both. That's why unmarried Indian women avoid Kokopelli. A figurine representing mischief and fertility is a really bad combination."

Bernie pulled the printed sheet from the printer tray and handed it to Parks, who read through the hard copy as Bernie read the computer screen. I read over Bernie's shoulder.

"The last one was eleven years ago. We caught two guys trying to extort money from a restaurant owner. The owner came to us and we set up a sting. We nailed two of them, but the restaurant burned down in a mysterious fire a week before the trial and the owner got amnesia." Kaiser watched to make sure I understood the comment. I smiled and nodded to him.

"The names of the two suspects arrested were at the bottom of the screen. The computer said that one of them, Edward Conklin, was in prison on a subsequent assault conviction. The second, Peter Borgard, had no known address.

I looked up at Parks. "I assume there were more. Do you know who?"

"Oh yeah, there were more. Someone else had to have set the fire because these two were in custody. They never revealed anything, but we were able to find out who they hung with. It was a tight group." He handed me the sheet. It didn't list the names of the other members of the group. "It's a typical pattern. The criminals started with graffiti, then there were a few minor property crimes, then they escalated to extortion and arson."

I looked at the list. The first item on the list was vandalism. It was followed, chronologically, by burglaries and theft. "You didn't have any arrests until the extortion sting?"

Bernie pushed away from the computer and picked up a stained coffee cup. "At first we didn't even see the pattern. There were probably a couple times when there was some kind of Kokopelli image at the scene, but the responding officers didn't note it. After a while, the guys started to compare notes and we tied a bunch of crimes together."

I scanned the list again, then looked up at Parks. "All the crimes stopped after the arson?"

Parks looked at Bernie. "They seemed to. At least we didn't find any more Kokopelli figures at crime scenes. Maybe the guys got smarter, but I think they moved on."

Bernie wiggled his nose. "They outgrew Flagstaff. At least that's my take. We're a pretty small town and people are too close knit for a lot of organized crime to happen without someone catching onto the pattern. It's a lot easier to be invisible in Phoenix or Los Angeles.

"I don't think your guy has anything to do with this burglary ring. It just doesn't hit me right. The kids we caught were Caucasian and they reportedly hung around with a bunch of other white kids. Besides, they've been gone for eleven years now. They wouldn't disappear and then show up again for no apparent reason."

Parks cocked his head. "Unless . . . "

"Unless they hired some new blood." I handed the paper back to Parks. "Your

Kokopelli guys wanted Steven Potter dead and they hired hit men." A bit of a leap.

Bernie stood up. "It's just coincidence." He turned and walked toward a door at the rear of the room. He spoke over his shoulder as he walked. "It ain't right. My cop sense says they're unrelated." He disappeared through the bathroom door.

"What do you think?" I asked Parks.

Parks looked at the list again. "It's the right pattern. A small-time gang works through a progression of crime. They graduate to extortion and arson. No reason they wouldn't progress to murder. But why the eleven-year hiatus?"

I shook my head. "Like Bernie said, there's no hiatus. They weren't in Flagstaff. We have to look somewhere else."

"So, you two give up yet?" Bernie waddled back into the room and threw a paper towel into a wastebasket next to his desk.

I pointed at the computer. "Find out where your crime wave went. It didn't stop. It just moved."

Bernie looked at me blankly. "Say what?"

"Flagstaff lost a crime wave. Someone else inherited it. Let's find it."

Bernie made a face. He didn't make a move toward the keyboard, either. It was obvious I had to sell him. "Look Bernie, how many gangs do you know who quit cold turkey without getting caught and doing time?" Bernie's expression didn't change. "They left, Bernie. They're not in Flagstaff anymore. Let's see where they went. Who got a crime wave when yours stopped?"

Bernie was still unconvinced. "Unreported crimes, Doug. They could still be around. Or they got smarter." He gave me a minor concession. "Maybe they're doing bigger stuff, like drugs, prostitution, or gambling . . . so-called victimless crimes."

Bernie was right. They could be invisible. That's how most organized crime progressed. They started out with petty stuff and grew into crimes that didn't get reported. "Shit. You're right."

Bernie turned back to the computer and tickled the keys. He turned the screen so Parks and I could see it. "Look, Eddie Conklin is back in prison. After his last arrest the biggest criminal lawyer in Phoenix represented him. Considering his history, he should've been broke and represented by the public defender." Bernie leaned back from the screen for emphasis. "He has friends in high places with money."

Parks stared at the wall for a few seconds. "Wasn't Conklin the dummy of the bunch?" He addressed the question to Bernie.

Bernie turned toward us and leaned his head back. "That was a long time ago, before our files were computerized. There were four of them . . . no, five that we looked at, but we couldn't pin anything on the rest. Later there was a drifter in the mix too." He thought for a few seconds. "I'm getting old. I'll go pull the file from the arson investigation." He struggled from the chair and headed toward a row of file cabinets lined against the wall on the far side of the room.

"Doug, I've got an appointment with the chief and mayor in a couple minutes." Parks looked at his watch anxiously. "Call me if you need anything else. Otherwise, I'll leave you in Bernie's capable hands."

I shook his hand. "Is it okay if I chew up a couple hours of Bernie's time?"

Parks laughed. "If you can get him to give you the time, he's yours. Chances are if it involves the computer you could keep him happy for a week. Just don't tell the taxpayers." He spun and nearly jogged for the door.

I looked at the computer screen while I waited for Bernie to find the file, but it was gibberish to me. Bernie set the file on his desktop then rolled his chair to the computer. He pulled up the electronic file of the first person mentioned in the paper file. Edward Conklin was currently a guest of the State of Arizona prison in Yuma. The screen said he'd been convicted of assault with intent to commit murder. His file indicated a dozen other arrests for offenses ranging from car theft to arson. He certainly didn't disappear or get any smarter over the years. Prisons are full of people who were either dumb or unlucky. If you ask any individual prisoner, he'll tell you he was unlucky. If you ask the cops, they'll tell you he was dumb.

Chapter 27

Bernie carried the old arson file to an empty desktop and re-opened the yellowed manila folder. There were a lot of pictures. The first were mugshots of two kids who looked like they might've been high school students with long hair, acne, and sparse whiskers. The rest of the pictures were of the restaurant fire and the resulting mountain of debris piled around charred kitchen appliances.

Bernie flipped through the pages while I glanced at the pictures. "Here are the names of the others we suspected of being Conklin's buddies." He took the stapled stack of papers to the computer without showing it to me. He quickly pulled up a new website.

Within a couple minutes I could tell the search wasn't going nearly fast enough for Bernie. "Damned dinosaur computers. If we had one less than a decade old, I wouldn't be able to keep up with it. Instead we sit here and wait . . ."

When the screen finally loaded he typed in the name Peter Borgard. We waited. The screen flashed, "No listing." Bernie typed a second name. John Rodgers. Again nothing. The third name was Michael Schmitz. Same response.

Buried further in the file we found the final name, Richard Hayes. When Bernie entered it, he looked up at me. "Hayes was the drifter. All the rest were local kids. Hayes lived in an apartment near the train depot."

The computer response was different. "Contact DoD."

I stared at the screen. "The Department of Defense?"

Bernie's fingers were flying over the keys. "I was in the NCIC, the national crime database in Washington. Yah, I suppose the DoD is the Department of Defense."

"Have you ever seen that prompt before?"

"Never." Bernie was intrigued.

The screen changed and displayed an eagle and the DoD logo. Bernie flew through several screens, then re-entered Richard Hayes. The computer displayed several different Richard Hayes, each with a birth date and a couple with the same middle initial.

"Let's see, by their birth dates these are World War II vintage." Bernie worked the cursor down the screen. "Korean war, too old. This one looks hopeful. He's a Gulf War vet, who'd be about the right age." Bernie clicked on the name and waited.

A message appeared on the middle of the screen. "File Sealed. Contact NCIS for further information." It gave a phone number with a Baltimore area code.

Bernie looked up at me from his chair. "Never seen that before, either." He picked up the phone and dialed the number on the screen. When it started to ring he punched the button for the speakerphone. He waited for almost two minutes before a female voice answered. "Naval Criminal Investigative Service, Ensign Palecek speaking. How may I assist you?"

"Hi, this is Sergeant Bernard Kaiser, from the Coconino County Sheriff's Department, in Flagstaff, Arizona. I'm trying to follow up on a suspect in a murder." Bernie looked up at me and winked. "When I queried the NCIC database, it referred me to the DoD. The DoD website referred me to this number."

"Please hold, Sergeant, while I verify your phone number." There was a pause and we could hear the ensign punching keys on her own computer to compare the phone number on her Caller ID with a reverse phonebook. "I have verification, Sergeant. Who are you inquiring about?"

"The name is Richard Benjamin Hayes." Bernie read the birthdate from the computer screen.

Computer keys rattled in the background. They stopped momentarily, and then started again. "Umm, Sergeant Kaiser, that file seems to be sealed. I tried another database and got the same message."

Bernie tapped a pencil on the desk. "Tell me, Ensign, why would a file be sealed?"

"Actually, I've only seen it twice before. In one case I was told there was a pending investigation. In the other, I was told I'd have to be shot if they told me the reason."

I leaned over Bernie's shoulder. "Ensign, this is Douglas Fletcher. I'm an investigator with the Park Service. We have reason to believe Richard Hayes may have been involved in a murder on a Federal reservation. How do I go about getting that file unsealed?"

"Mr. Fletcher, I suggest you approach the Department of Justice. Have them make a formal request to Commander Bitzan." She spelled the name.

"Thank you, Ensign."

Bernie punched the "Off" button on the phone and cleared the computer screen. "Well, so much for that."

I reached for the phone. "Maybe not. I have a friend in the FBI who interviewed me after the murder." I punched in the number for the Phoenix FBI office. Bernie wrinkled his nose. He probably didn't like the FBI any better than most cops. A female voice answered the phone. "Harmon Snelling, please."

Bernie punched the speakerphone again.

"This is Special Agent Snelling," said the next voice.

"Harm, how are you? This is Doug Fletcher."

I could almost feel Snelling cringe over the phone. "What's up, Fletcher?"

"I'm sitting with Sergeant Kaiser in the Coconino County Sheriff's Department."

Snelling broke in. "And, let me guess, you want me to bail you out. Forget it."

"Not right now, Harm," I doubted anyone ever called a Special Agent by his first name, and it irritated him, which, in turn, delighted Bernie.

"Flagstaff had a number of crimes in the early '90's that we've tied together. In every case, the criminals left an Indian figurine that looks like a hump-backed ant playing a flute called a Kokopelli. The crimes stopped eleven years ago. One of the suspects was an ex-Navy guy. We called the DoD but his file is sealed. They also said that the Department of Justice could contact a Commander Bitzan to get the sealed information. Can you make that request for me?"

Snelling's voice showed his irritation. "The case is closed, Fletcher. Let it die."

"This isn't only about Potter's murder. Remember, we have an assault on a park ranger too. Richard Hayes, the guy we're looking at was implicated but never convicted in an extortion and arson ring in Flagstaff. We have every indication this fits his style."

Snelling sighed. "Is this that Kokopelli thing again?" He paused and I didn't offer an answer. I heard a deep sigh over the speakerphone. "Let me see what I can do. But I make no guarantees. Give me your number there."

"Fair enough." I read the number off the phone. "Sergeant Bernard Kaiser is working with me on the case. This is his direct line." The dial tone buzzed before I finished saying thank you.

Bernie punched the button to turn off the speakerphone. "I take it from Snelling's tone that you and he are best buddies." He held up the first two fingers of his right hand and intertwined them to signify the closeness of my relationship to Snelling.

I laughed. "Yeah, that's why I enjoy tugging his tail so much."

Bernie got up from his chair and reached for the sport coat hanging over the back of a guest chair next to the desk. "C'mon Fletcher. We're going to lunch. Anyone who can get under an FBI guy's skin can't be all bad. I'll let you buy."

* * *

We ate in a hamburger joint that served big, greasy, half-pound patties of beef in bakery buns at tables covered by red gingham tablecloths. The waitresses were dressed like '50's carhops. Malts were served in tulip glasses with the metal mixing container alongside. The staff should have been on roller skates.

I ordered a California burger with tomato, lettuce, and onion. I negated whatever positive effects the vegetables provided by ordering it with mayo. I decided to forgo the fries, congratulating myself on my willpower. Bernie ordered a burger combo basket. When our order arrived, he shoved the fries between us, motioning for me to share the mountain of calories heaped in a football-sized plastic basket lined with a paper napkin saturated with oil. So much for my willpower.

He squirted a puddle of ketchup onto his burger wrapper. "So tell me about Douglas Fletcher." He jabbed a pair of long fries into the ketchup and then folded them into his mouth.

"First thing . . . drop the Douglas. I'm Doug to everyone but bill collectors and lawyers." Bernie nodded assent as I spilled my career, divorce, and retirement. We spent half an hour nibbling at burgers and dunking fries while sharing life stories.

We finished up and Bernie worked to remove the remnants of lunch from his teeth with a wooden toothpick as we walked back to the station. "You know, I could make a couple of queries about this Kokopelli business. I'll draft up a note and e-mail an inquiry and send it to a couple dozen departments. Maybe we'll get a hit. I kinda doubt we'll hear back from anyone but what the hell, we've got nothin' to lose."

* * *

When we got back to his desk, Bernie drafted an email requesting information about any crimes in which a Kokopelli figurine was left at the scene. I called the police station in Shiprock. Jamie wasn't there, so I left both my cellphone and landline numbers, hoping he'd call me back before tomorrow. As much as Jamie might deny it, I suspected he ran on "Indian time" when it came to returning phone messages. Some of that was due to the remoteness of his territory, but I suspected he just wasn't as driven by the clock as an urban cop.

I checked my townhouse voicemail from Bernie's phone, hoping Margaret Adams or Potter's wife had left a message. The only message was from my insurance agent.

I called Phoenix and asked for Harmon Snelling. I had no realistic expectation he'd have any new information, but I had nothing else to do and thought I might be able to pull his chain.

"Special Agent Snelling." His voice was well modulated. I would change that.

"Hi, Harm. It's Ranger Doug. You got anything for me on Richard Hayes?"

I could hear papers rustling in his hands. "As a matter of fact, I was just going to give Sergeant Kaiser a call. I got an email from DoD a few minutes ago. It seems you may have hit pay dirt. I suppose even a blind squirrel occasionally finds an acorn." He let the dig settle before going on. "The DoD says Hayes was a Navy Seal. They refused to give me any specific information, other than to say he's a non-com and may have been involved in some covert operations. He's currently AWOL."

I glanced across the room at Bernie, who was feeding a madly beeping copier. I wanted

Bernie to hear this, but I couldn't get his attention. "Hang on for a second, Harm. I want Sergeant Kaiser to hear this." I whistled at Bernie and waved, pointing at the phone. He nodded, cut short the screaming copier by pulling its plug, and walked over.

"This is classified information. I'm only passing it on because it may be integral to your arson investigation . . ."

I punched the button on the speakerphone and hung up the receiver as Bernie got to the desk. "Go ahead, Harm, Bernie's here now."

Snelling let out a sigh. "Richard Hayes was a Navy Seal. He served in covert operations in the Gulf War. He's currently AWOL from the psych ward at the Corpus Christi Naval Hospital. The Navy asked us to take him into custody if we locate him."

Bernie looked at me with awe. "No shit! This guy's a nut case and the Navy wants to lock him up."

"Harm, what type of training did Hayes have? Is he up on explosives and black operations?"

"They were intentionally vague, other than to say we should approach him with caution. Do you guys know where he is?"

"He was in Flagstaff a few years ago, probably before his stint with the Seals. He had loose ties to a couple of high school kids who were involved in the arson case, but he disappeared. We're trying to trace the rest of them, too. We know that one associate's in prison and it looks like the Kokopelli thing may be the link among these guys. I just sent an email to all the nearby agencies asking if any of them had a crime where Kokopelli was left at the scene."

"Refresh my memory on the Kokopelli thing," said Snelling.

"We found the Kokopelli figurine in Potter's pocket at Walnut Canyon which may tie Steve Potter's death to the arson investigation and several other crimes where Coconino County Deputies found Kokopelli figurines or drawings at the crime scene. It all ended here, in Flag, a few years ago, at the same time Hayes and his associates disappeared from the area."

"Give it up, Fletcher. Potter's death was an accident, Kokopelli or not. End of story. End of that investigation."

"I've got orders to investigate the assault on the ranger who was run down. Even if you don't consider it a murder investigation, I know the assault is connected to Potter's death. I've had thinner leads than this pan out." Bernie nodded his assent.

"Okay." I'd never heard so much skepticism in one word. "Keep me posted."

"Right, Harm." I switched the speakerphone off and looked at Bernie. "Don't call us, we'll call you."

Chapter 28

The phone rang in a Paradise Valley house. The blonde resident strolled to the rosewood desk near a window overlooking the valley. "Hello." Her voice was a practiced purr most men found terribly seductive. Her appearance, honed by a few minor surgeries to an imitation of Aphrodite, turned heads when she walked into any room.

"Someone's looking for the Stick Man." The male voice was very nervous and hushed, the effect achieved by holding his hand over the mouthpiece of the phone.

Adrenaline rushed through her system. She saw that the caller ID said the call was from a cellular phone with blocked ID. She clamped the phone to her ear with her shoulder and opened a drawer. She fumbled with the cap of a pen and then pressed it against the top sheet of a pad of Post-it notes. "Give me your number." The satin had left her voice, replaced by a Texas twang.

"Oh, God. Not here. Try me at home . . . after seven." He rattled off the number so quickly she wasn't sure she'd written it correctly, but the caller hung up before she could ask him to repeat it.

She peeled off the note and walked through the house. A man wearing surfer shorts was sunning himself and sipping iced tea on the pool apron. She opened the deck door and walked to the edge of the pool.

"Someone's looking for the Stick Man." She sniffed nervously as she held the note out to him.

He looked up at her without reaching for the note. "You got it wrong again, didn't you? Someone has a job for the Stick Man." He lowered his sunglasses and looked over the rim at her hazel eyes. He ignored the macramé bikini that hid none of her physical assets.

She shook her head. "Someone is looking for the Stick Man. His exact words."

Rich Hayes took the note. He looked at the number for a second and then rolled his eyes. "I hate working with amateurs."

"He said not to call until after seven." The woman tensed, expecting a slap.

Hayes didn't like being told to wait for anyone or anything. He let out a deep sigh and pulled off his sunglasses. He set them on the tabletop before getting up and walking into the house. He scrolled through names in the address file on his laptop, found the one he wanted, and punched the numbers into his cellphone. While it rang, he stared at the brown landscape. Life was good except for putting up with the incompetent idiots who always surrounded him. Life in the Navy had been easier, his Navy Seal brothers were tough, they didn't crumble at the first sign of adversity like the amateur he was calling.

The dispatcher picked up the blinking non-emergency line. "Yavapai County Sheriff's Department."

The male voice was unfamiliar but had authority. "Who's looking for the Stick Man?"

The dispatcher broke into a sweat and spun in his chair to see if anyone was in earshot. "You can't call here!" He muffled his voice, but couldn't hide his anxiety.

"Who's looking?"

"We got an email from Coconino County. They want to know about any agency with any crimes where a Kokopelli figure was left at a crime scene."

"Who else got it?"

"Listen man, we were blind copied on an email, how in hell should I know?"

"Take it easy. Just tell me how wide the distribution might be."

The dispatcher sighed and looked around again. "We do it all the time. The queries usually go to fifteen or twenty departments. Sometimes we blanket Arizona, New Mexico, and southern Utah. It all depends on what they're looking for."

"Shit!" The line went dead, and the dispatcher hung up. He swore to himself he'd never to call the Stick Man again.

Chapter 29

On the way home, I stopped at Safeway and built a sampler from the produce counter—avocados, lettuce, tomatoes, apples, grapes, strawberries, peppers, cilantro, onions, and garlic. In the snack aisle I grabbed a bag of corn chips, baked, not fried.

I heard the phone from outside the door while I was struggling with the keys and grocery bag, I reached the phone just before voicemail picked up.

"Fletcher." I sat the bags of groceries on the kitchen counter.

"Douglas Fletcher?" The voice had a New England accent so deep I could barely understand my own name.

"Yes, this is Douglas Fletcher."

"This is Garrett Evans of the Bar Harbor police department. Are you related to Margaret Adams?" Evans pronounced Bar Harbor as *Bah Habah*.

My mind raced. I'd been so focused on supper prep that the name Margaret Adams didn't immediately register. I was about to say no when I remembered she was Potter's assistant.

"Oh, God. Is she okay?"

Evans spoke slowly. "Well, I need to know your relationship to Miss Adams before I can relay any information to you."

I hadn't written down his name and my mind couldn't dredge it back up from the short-term memory. "Officer, I'm an investigator with the National Park Service. Margaret Adams was working with me on a murder investigation. Did she give you my name?"

"Ah, no sir. We found your name and phone number on a slip of paper in her purse. We hoped you were kin. Do you know her parents or next of kin?"

I let out a deep breath, my heart sinking. She was dead and they're trying to notify the next of kin. "No, I don't. I've only spoken to her about the investigation. She's a material witness in an ongoing murder case. Is she dead?"

"Well, I guess there's no harm in telling you, you being an officer and all. She's hurt, but she is alive."

Bar Harbor? Based on the cop's accent it was somewhere in the Northeast, but where? How did she pick there to hide? A dozen questions raced through my mind and this poor officer wouldn't have any answers to most of them. "What happened to her?"

"Well, sir, somebody tried to kill her. He shot her a couple of times, but a local man came up on them and . . . well, he ran the shooter down with his pickup."

"Somebody tried to kill Margaret Adams? You said the shooter was run down by a pickup. Did you catch him?"

"Well, sir, there wasn't much to catching him. He was killed by the impact of the truck. The coroner is running his fingerprints, but I haven't got much information yet. He didn't have any ID in his wallet, only cash. He had a rental car, but it was rented to Robert Smith. Although that's a common name in these parts, I suspect it probably isn't his real name."

"Margaret Adams was Steven Potter's assistant. He was an Arizona antiques dealer who was murdered a few days ago in Walnut Canyon National Monument. I suggest you contact the nearest FBI office and have them expedite your coroner's fingerprint inquiry."

"Well, Mr. Fletcher, that's a pretty tall tale Ms. Adams already told me. I checked online and the newspapers said Mr. Potter died in an accident. I'd look pretty foolish if I called the FBI and told them I was investigating a lead in Potter's death when he died in an accident."

"You've checked on Steven Potter already?"

There was a pause. "Mr. Fletcher, she had business cards in her purse, and we do have the internet in Maine."

Ah! Maine. That explained the accent. "Do you believe everything you read on the internet?" I paused for effect. "Where is Ms. Adams now?"

"She's in our little hospital. She's banged up but not in critical condition, so we kept her here. Any life-threatening injuries we run up to Bangor."

"Do you have her under guard? There may be more than one person after her."

"That's a little hard, Mr. Fletcher. There are only thirteen of us on the force and one man's down in Boston . . ."

I couldn't put into words the urgency I felt. I had no idea what other resources he might bring to bear. "An attempt has already been made on her life and I suspect there's a criminal organization pursuing her. Isn't there some way to keep her under guard for a couple of days?"

"You're saying organized crime?" Finally I had his attention. I hoped he was one of the traditional New Englanders I'd heard about who didn't trust anyone and found conspiracy under every bush. "I'll see if we can get a couple of officers to work overtime."

It wasn't much . . . a couple of small-town cops on overtime, but it was better than nothing. "All right. You just keep her safe for a couple of days. By then what I'm investigating will all blow up or blow over. Then she'll be out of danger."

"What's going to happen that'll wrap it up?"

"Miss Adams made recordings of some incriminating phone conversations. They're going to a newspaper, which should spur the FBI to reopen the Potter investigation."

"I'll do another internet search for Potter in a couple days. If I don't see anything new, you and I will be talking some more."

The news about Margaret Adams rattled me. An attempt on her life was big and no one else gave a damn. I found the phone number for *The Santa Fe Journal* on the internet. Only after I'd dialed did I realize that it was early evening. The phone rang four times before the Night Desk answered. I told the man on duty to have the editor call me first thing in the morning on either my cell or home phone. After that I put my Glock away and unloaded the groceries. I considered calling Harmon Snelling, but our last conversation made it clear there was little I could say that would spur him to action. I decided to ease myself down by preparing supper.

I made salsa in the food processor and whipped up a fruit salad. When El and Todd walked in, I was sipping a beer and dipping chips in salsa.

"Grab a beer. I've got food. I hope you like it hot."

El clucked her tongue at me. "All that fat with the healthy salsa." She broke a corner off a chip and loaded it with a mound of tomatoes and peppers. "This is sinfully good."

I heard Todd open a beer in the kitchen. "El, you want a beer?"

She broke off part of another chip before answering. "Is there any grapefruit soda left? I'd rather have that." She gobbed salsa on a whole chip as Todd brought her a can of soda water. "This is wonderful. I've got to find out what brand this is. I love it." She looked around for a container.

I puffed up a bit. "It's homemade and the chips are low-fat."

She stopped chewing for a second and then spoke with her mouth full. "You made this? My God, you keep your talents well hidden. I must have the recipe." She pulled another full chip out of the bag and loaded it with salsa while still chewing the first. "Todd, you've got to try this, it's heavenly." As beads of sweat formed on her forehead, she added, "And it has some kick!"

"Part of the secret is the great produce here—no hot-house tomatoes or wimpy peppers. By the way, don't fill up on the chips and salsa, I made a fruit salad and we can have sliced avocado with dressing on the side."

El slid next to me and gave me a hug with one arm. "Todd, we've got a convert."

"This healthy stuff is just to make up for the hamburger and fries I had for lunch." I gave Todd a wink.

We talked through supper about their day's activities and shopping deals. I reported in on the Kokopelli inquiries and said I felt like I was making a little progress. I skipped over Margaret Adam's brush with death, not wanting to send El into another funk. "Until something else breaks, I'm afraid there's not much else to do on the investigation."

El swilled her soda. "How about the Navajo artisan who's getting ripped off by the dealer. Isn't there something you could do for her?"

I leaned back in the chair. "I talked to the sheriff's department. Technically, it's their problem but they haven't got the interest, time, or resources to pursue it. Besides, she hasn't filed a complaint."

El leaned close. "She won't file a complaint because she's afraid he'll cut her off. That's extortion, isn't it?"

"Something like that." I took a sip of beer. "I can't come up with a plan that nails the bastard and leaves her selling through him. It's sort of a Mexican standoff."

El picked up another chip and pointed it at me as she spoke. "What will put the fear of God into the guy? Threats?"

I smiled. "I'm afraid that's extortion. We'd be worse than he is."

"Who else cares that he's ripping off these artists?" El asked. "The local cops have their hands tied. Maybe we should contact the Navajo Nation Police?"

I shook my head. "It's out of their jurisdiction."

Todd held up his beer bottle as if asking permission to speak. I had the impression there were many times when he didn't get a word in edgewise. "The IRS isn't getting a cut. They don't need Evelyn Sampson to investigate a complaint. If someone reports he's cheating on his taxes they can do a taxpayer compliance audit and match the owner's reported revenues with his expenditures. If they don't match, he's got a lot of explaining to do."

El's eyes sparkled. "Isn't Todd smart? Do you think you can leverage that, Doug?"

"I'm sure the IRS isn't seeing a cut of any of the shop's cash business. They'll threaten him with jail time and penalties, but if he has a good lawyer, they'll be happy just to get most of the back taxes. That would leave him free to continue selling Navajo crafts.

"Let me talk to my friend in Flagstaff tomorrow. Maybe there's a way to make him think we're willing to go to the IRS without actually doing it." I got up and walked to the kitchen. "Now let's eat some rabbit food."

Chapter 30

After the conversation with the dispatcher, Rich Hayes made several calls. By ten o'clock he'd convened a conference. The three invitees sat in his house drinking expensive liquor and mulling options.

"Who's pulling this together?" Michael Schmitz paced the floor. By far the most animated of the four, he was also the most casually dressed. He always wore a Hawaiian print shirt over tattered khaki shorts and looked like a beach bum. Nervousness radiated from his slender frame and gaunt face. He never sat still. His sandals slapped on the tile as he paced the length of the room.

Hayes, cool and under control, wore a flowered swim trunks and a gauze shirt to set off his tan and his sun-bleached hair. "I got the first call from Yavapai County and a second from Santa Fe. The Kokopelli queries came from Coconino County."

Schmitz paced. "Shit, Flagstaff is where it all started. It's the seat of Coconino County. Do you think they've put the pieces together?"

Hayes waved him off. "Not yet. If they had, they wouldn't be sending emails asking for more information."

"The Kokopelli thing was cute, but stupid. We'd all be better off if there weren't any mementos left to tie everything together," John Rodgers swirled the ice in his Scotch. His knit golf shirt, complete with embroidered shark logo, and his gaudy pants announced he'd just come off the golf course.

Hayes snapped his fingers, then pointed at Rodgers. "I've told you, that's the key to our reputation. Everyone knows the Stick Man is bad and they don't mess with him. All I have to do is make one call and tell someone the Stick Man doesn't think something should happen, and by God, it doesn't happen!"

Rodgers nodded. "Point taken. But if they crack one of these cases, we all go down like dominoes."

Peter Borgard shook his head. He was the brightest and quietest member of the team, his linen slacks and Columbia golf shirt fit the casual elegance of the room. He sat in a green leather winged-back chair, off to the side of the room. "There's no evidence tying us to any of the scenes. The only way we go down is if someone snitches." He looked around the room at the others. "So, my friends, as long as we all stay quiet, we're all safe. Right?"

The phone rang and Borgard took a step toward it. Hayes stopped him. "Let Sharon get it."

Schmitz stood and started pacing again. "Let's lay low for a while. We can let this blow over and then ease back into business after the heat dies down. The cops have a short attention span. If they can't solve a crime in 48 hours they move on."

"I've got a better idea. Let's franchise. I've been using a couple guys to fill the antiquities pipeline and they did a credible job at Walnut Canyon. We set the two of them up, give them the contracts, and we stay in the background and take half."

"Hayes, have you *lost* your *mind?* You want to use them on the Mexican issue? How low in hell is that better?" Schmitz slammed his glass down on the fireplace mantel. "That's just more people who know what's happening. We've got our necks out a mile and you just added more weak links to the chain."

Hayes saw red, then realized he couldn't afford to alienate these three or let them see any weakness. He composed himself. "Take it easy. I channel all the communications through Sharon so we're invisible. We have fake IDs, we spend laundered money, and we have posh houses. The transactions are handled by an Albuquerque phone number that cuts out before it comes here. Sharon's is the only voice anyone hears and when she puts on her Texas twang, she sounds like half the women south of Kansas."

They nodded their heads. Sharon walked into the room with a cellphone. She handed it to Hayes. "Another call for the Stick Man."

Hayes set his drink down and took the phone. "Yes?"

He listened and then closed his eyes. "Yeah, I got it. Just sit tight and let me call you back, okay?"

Hayes handed the phone back to Sharon, paying no attention to the shimmering green silk dress clinging to her figure like a second skin. She obediently turned the phone off and left, closing the door behind her.

Schmitz shook his head as he watched her leave the room. "Can she handle the communications? She's dropped more pills than a three-fingered pharmacist and she gives me the creeps."

Rogers laughed. "You must be queer, man. All she gives me is a hard on." The rest laughed. The tension broken.

Hayes ushered the partners out the front door. The temperature had dropped when the sun set, but the air was still warm outside. When they were gone Hayes returned to the study, sat on the sofa, and opened his laptop. Sharon cruised in and slid next to him, pressing her hip against him.

"It's late. C'mon upstairs." Slipped her hand inside his open collar and twirled his left nipple between her fingers.

He pushed her away. "I've got work to do." He pulled up a directory and tried to Skype with the name he'd chosen.

Sharon pouted. "Can't it wait?" She shivered and the goose bumps that covered her arms indicated she'd started the early stages of cocaine withdrawal.

Hayes ignored her. Giving up on Skype, he pulled a cellphone from his pocket and punched a number from memory. Sharon watched a few seconds, then started to stand up, but Hayes pulled her back down and pressed the phone into her hand. He whispered directions in her ear.

"Hullo."

"Tommy, there's a man who wants to offer you a job."

Tommy Tsosie didn't recognize the woman's southern accent at first. He'd been in a drunken sleep and had a hard time clearing the cobwebs. "Sharon?"

"Yeah." Hayes listened impatiently as Sharon cooed to Tommy. "Remember, I talked about you getting a few jobs if your last project went well."

The cobwebs cleared and Tommy's brain went into gear. "Oh yeah, I remember. You asked if I would . . ."

"Not over the phone. Can you meet someone tomorrow?"

Tommy closed his eyes and thought. He didn't have many days planned and that made it harder to remember the ones that were committed. Working nights on the dig led to days of sleeping. He couldn't think of anything for the next day, but didn't want to commit to a morning meeting. "Sure. Can we do it in the afternoon? Where?"

Sharon looked at Hayes and shrugged. He thought for a second, trying to come up with someplace crowded, so Tommy wouldn't feel uncomfortable, but would still be a quiet corner with enough privacy for a murder. He cupped his hand and whispered into Sharon's ear.

"A man will meet you at the Visitor Center at the west end of the Grand Canyon. Bring a disposable car that can't be traced back to you and bring your partner. We'll leave the car there and your contact will drive you back."

"That's a long drive," Tommy said. Then he reflected on how well they'd been paid for the Potter job. "But sure, we can be there."

"Can we trust your partner to keep his mouth shut if we meet in person?"

Tommy had dreaded that question. Elmer was a weasel who'd been in jail and would do whatever it took to not return, but he needed him. "Sure, Elmer's tight. What time?"

"Nine at the visitor center."

Tommy moaned. "Are you talking a.m.? Shit. That's only eight hours from now." He realized he was whining to the dial tone.

* * *

Hayes took the phone from Sharon and nodded toward the door. "Go upstairs. I'll be up in a few minutes." He pulled a piece of notepaper from the top desk drawer, then punched the number written on it and waited while the line clicked, routing the call through Albuquerque. It was answered in less than one ring.

"Yeah."

"I talked to my partners. Meet them at the Grand Canyon west end gift shop at eleven. They'll have your money and they'll take care of your problem."

"That's a long drive."

"Tell you what. I'll find someplace close and cozy. Just you and me. No witnesses. Does that better suit you?"

"Uh, no. The Grand Canyon is a good idea. Lots of people around," the dispatcher said, "but I have to work."

Hayes shook his head. "So you want me to deliver your money to the Sheriff's Department? You dumb shit, call in sick."

There was a pause. "I guess . . . yeah, that'll work. You said eleven?"

"Yes, eleven tomorrow morning. There's a Dumpster behind the gift shop. My partners will meet you there."

Next, he dialed a cellphone number he'd programmed into his phone. This man liked to use disposable or stolen cellphones, but only for a few days at a time. This number had only been active for three days. The line rang five times until an automated voice told him the party he was calling was unavailable and offered to let him leave a voice message or numerical page. Rich dialed a different ten-digit number from memory and left a numerical page on the man's "permanent" cellphone, used only in emergencies. He held little hope this call to Maine would be returned since the message two hours earlier hadn't been returned. Maybe there were too many trees and rocks in Maine for cellphone coverage. That was probably the best he could hope for.

Next, he dialed a number from memory and waited seven rings before Terry Mahoney picked up the private line that rang only in his office.

"I haven't heard back from the man I sent east. I assume he's resolved your dangling issue, but I can't confirm it yet."

"What do you mean you can't confirm?" Mahoney asked tersely.

"Just that. I told my man to end his project, but I haven't had a call of confirmation."

"What happens now?"

"I call you back when I get the confirmation. I'm sure there's just a delay of some kind that kept him from ending the project today. There's still tomorrow."

Mahoney didn't like to be treated as anything other than the boss, and Hayes was talking to him as though he were an impatient child. "I'd better get a call tomorrow."

"You'll get a call when I have confirmation."

Hayes hung up and turned off the den lights. He stood in the dark for a moment, thinking about his inability to contact the hitman. If it weren't for the promised wire to an offshore bank once the "contract" was completed, Mahoney would be lying in a gutter with a Kokopelli figurine in his pocket. Hayes fought back his anger and the impulse to hurt Mahoney. He walked through the lower level of the house, turning off the lights as he went, then climbed the stairs that were lit only by the moonlight coming through the windows high in the atrium. He walked down the hallway toward the light spilling through the open bedroom door.

Sharon, still wearing the green dress, was curled on the bed with her legs pulled up and her arms wrapped around her knees. She watched idly as he slipped off his clothes and dropped them on the floor. He sat on the satin sheet and roughly pulled her upright alongside him. "Time to pay for your next fix."

Chapter 31

El and Todd were down to the last days of their vacation, and even though they were having fun, I wanted to enjoy their company for at least for another day. It'd been nice having family visit. I gassed up the Isuzu while they were on their morning run and gathered Grand Canyon brochures from a rack in the gas station. I called *The Santa Fe Journal* and left another message for Peter Ward, the editor. When El and Todd got back, I had filled a cooler with ham sandwiches, soda, juice, and apples.

El opened the door, surprised to see me still at home. "Where are you off to today?" She grabbed a towel out of the guest bathroom and wiped sweat off her face as Todd untied his running shoes by the door.

"I'm taking you to the Grand Canyon. I even made a picnic lunch."

Todd poured himself a glass of orange juice and looked at me skeptically. "We understand you're tied up in the investigation. We're fine with that . . . you don't need to babysit us." He drained the juice in two gulps, rinsed the glass, and set it by the sink.

"It's okay. We're at a dead end until I hear from New Mexico and Maine. A day at the Grand Canyon will do me a lot of good."

El walked into the spare bedroom and Todd protested again. "Really, Doug. We're okay driving ourselves up to the rim. It's not a big deal."

"Listen, Todd. I'm going to the Grand Canyon today. Are you coming with me or not?"

He cracked a smile. "Okay, tough guy. May I take a shower first?"

"Please do. And also, I do need to make one stop on the way."

Todd stopped at the closed bedroom door and looked back at me. "Where?"

"We're going to buy a couple of Evelyn Sampson's pots first."

He raised an eyebrow. "Okay."

* * *

While they showered, I looked up Evelyn Sampson's phone number and called her. She was reluctant to drive to Flagstaff, but I convinced her we had a chance to squeeze money from Gary Jones to pay her for the lost pottery. I told her to park around the corner from his shop and I would get her when the time was right.

Then I called Bernie Kaiser. He agreed to meet me at Gary Jones's shop, too.

Todd and I ate bagels and orange slices for breakfast while El crunched on granola covered with unsweetened yogurt. I explained the plan for the antique shop and they agreed to play along, especially when I told El she'd have an extra couple of pots to take home, my treat. I figured I might be able to bury the costs in an expense voucher somehow.

We parked down the street from Gary Jones's shop and El went in first. I told Todd to wait ten minutes and follow her. Each of them was to buy one of Evelyn's pots and pay cash for it. I went around the corner and found Evelyn sitting in an old Oldsmobile, looking uncomfortable. Both she and the car both looked tired, sun baked, and past their prime.

She rolled down the window and I leaned close to talk to her. "My friends are buying two of your pots. They're going to pay cash. Gary doesn't write down cash purchases so he doesn't pay you for them. I don't think he pays taxes either."

She stared out the windshield and didn't look at me. "Is he going to pay me?"

"We'll see what happens."

A plain blue Ford Taurus rolled to a stop behind Evelyn's car. It was so patently a police car, with antennae bristling on the trunk, it might as well have been marked. Bernie Kaiser walked up to Evelyn's car. I shook his hand.

"This is Evelyn. We're trying to get her some justice."

Bernie nodded to Evelyn, then looked at me. "We doing the good cop, bad cop thing?"

"I think bad cop, bad cop. You got cuffs?"

He smiled. "In the car. They might be rusty." He walked away and came back jingling the handcuffs. "It's been awhile since I used them. I hope I still have a key."

"El and Todd ought to be done. Let's brace him." I leaned down to Evelyn. "You come in the shop in two minutes."

Perfect timing. Todd walked toward the Isuzu with his package. El was already in my Isuzu, a package sitting on her lap. She rolled down the window. "I negotiated him down to thirty-five bucks for mine."

Todd walked up. "He gave me a sob story about the poor native artisans and how they lived in hovels. I gave him the full fifty on the tag."

"Got it. C'mon, Bernie. Let's go." I led Bernie into the shop. Gary Jones looked up when the door opened, ringing a bell. He squinted, like he needed glasses to see us that far away. I flashed a badge at him as I approached the jewelry case. Bernie hung back, looking unhappy.

"What can I do for the Park Service today?" Gary asked, all smiles.

I reached across the counter and pulled out his ledger book. "Gary, tell me, how many native pots have you sold this month?" I flipped through the ledger to the current page and found only five stickers, totaling two hundred ten dollars.

"Slow month. Only five sales so far." He smiled nervously. I didn't think he didn't like the looks of Bernie.

I spun the ledger around so I could see the entries. "The last one was four days ago?"

Gary pulled the ledger back and looked at the entries. "That's right. It was the day you were here last."

He closed the book and started to put it back under the counter. I slammed my hand on it. "This is evidence of tax fraud, Gary."

Bernie moved quickly and pulled Gary's hands behind his back.

"What tax fraud? You guys aren't from the IRS. For God's sake, you're a fucking park ranger."

I smiled at Gary as Bernie clipped the second cuff on him. "Unless something changed, I'm a Federal law enforcement officer and I'm sworn to uphold the laws of the United States. I assume that includes the Tax Code."

Gary sputtered. "This is bogus. You've got no evidence."

I leaned into his face. "You sold two pots this morning, one for thirty-five bucks, and the other for fifty. You also sold one for cash after my cousin left the other day. You didn't put the stickers in the book and the money went into your pocket, not the cash register. You're fucked, Gary. You're going to jail and you're going to owe the IRS a lot of money."

Gary glowered at me. The bell sounded and Evelyn Sampson walked in. Gary looked at her and rolled his eyes.

"Go home, old woman. I got nothing for you today."

"That's not true, Gary." I waved Evelyn in. "You sold two of her pots this morning." I turned to Evelyn. "How many pots have you delivered this year you didn't get paid for?"

Evelyn pulled out a dog-eared index card. "I've given him one hundred and thirty pots. He's paid me for twenty-three of them." She stuffed the card back into her purse.

I smiled at Gary. "That means there must be some of Evelyn's pots on the shelves, right? Like a hundred and seven of them." Gary didn't answer. "Sergeant Kaiser, please read the defendant his rights."

Evelyn and I went over to the shelf where her pots were displayed and counted eighteen pots. She shook her head. "So many lost."

I patted her arm. "We're not done yet."

We walked back over to Bernie, who had Gary Jones bent over the counter, searching him for weapons.

"We'll do the body cavity search when we get to the jail." Bernie straightened Gary up and pushed him toward the door.

Gary stumbled, but caught himself. "What're the charges?"

I looked at Evelyn, and shrugged. "Let's start with fraud. We can move on to tax evasion."

Gary closed his eyes. "Wait a second. I think I get it. This had nothing to do with taxes at all."

I put on my surprised look. "For a bright guy, it took you a long time to catch on.

However, you're only partially right." I poked my knuckle into his solar plexus with a sharp jab I'd learned in a karate course. It hurt like hell and air rushed from his lungs. Tomorrow he'd have a nasty bruise where I'd jabbed and he'd be mighty sore.

"I'd love to turn you over to the IRS. They'll take your store, your house, your car, and every dollar you have in the bank. Then they'll shove you in a cell with Bruno, who'll be your butt buddy for five to ten years." I paused. "But that won't solve the problem."

Gary's face was ashen. "What problem would that be?"

"There're a bunch of Indian artisans who depend on you for the meager money you give them. If you're in prison, they don't get even the few bucks you pay them."

Gary was staring a hole in my forehead. "So what's the answer, asshole?"

Bernie grabbed him by his cuffed hands and lifted until the pressure on Gary's shoulders had him on his toes. "That's Mr. Ranger to you." Gary's feet pattered for a few seconds until Bernie eased the pressure. Bernie gave me a big grin that Gary couldn't see.

"Okay, okay! So what's the answer?" Gary shook his arms.

I spread my hands on the counter. "Two things are going to happen. First, you start keeping straight books—every transaction is recorded—cash, check, or credit. Second, you pay off all the artisans for what's been sold this year and then you pay them monthly for everything you sell in the future."

"That's bullshit. I barely make ends meet out of this rat hole."

Bernie lifted again and Gary howled in pain. Bernie had done some homework too.

"Listen, sucker, driving a Lincoln and living in a stone house on the mountain with six bathrooms is not just 'getting by' in my book." Bernie pushed Jones in front of Evelyn and pushed his head down so that he could look at her. "Mrs. Sampson, how many bathrooms do you have in your house?"

Evelyn looked away. "I have an outhouse."

Bernie was starting to lift higher, getting angrier every second. I put a hand on his arm and he lowered Gary back to the floor.

"Listen, Gary. I think you can handle everything I've suggested and probably more. The choice is yours . . . lower your standard of living and pay the artisans, or the sergeant charges you with fraud and turns you over to the IRS."

"That's fucking extortion!"

Bernie spun Gary around so that he could look him in the eyes. "It's nothing of the sort." He pulled out his badge and stuffed it in Gary's face. "It's poor police procedures. You see, I'm going to take your ledgers, get statements from Mrs. Sampson, and from the two people who bought pots today. Then I'll have to write a report. I hate writing reports. If you do as Ranger Fletcher has suggested, my report will get buried under the more important cases on my desk and it may never find its way to the district attorney or the IRS."

Bernie should've been an actor. He paced back and forth in front of Gary Jones, doing a great ad lib. "As long as the artisans don't complain, I probably won't have any reason to look for it." He spun around and faced Gary. "However, if I hear one complaint from Mrs. Sampson, or any of the other artisans, that lost file will be found and turned over to the district attorney. When he realizes the tax implications, he'll certainly call the IRS."

Bernie stopped right in front of Gary and stared into his face, waiting for a response.

Gary Jones knew he was screwed. "All right. I'll give her a check. Take the fucking cuffs off."

Bernie grabbed Jones by the collar. "Cash. Mrs. Sampson gets cash."

Gary's face turned red. "I don't have that kind of cash laying around."

"Try the box under the counter." I walked over to the counter and opened a cupboard door. Inside sat a flat gray metal cash box. I pulled it out and pushed it toward Gary as Bernie opened the cuffs.

Gary rubbed his wrists and opened the box. He lifted out a black tray and grabbed a stack of hundred-dollar bills that was wrapped with a rubber band. "How much do I owe her?"

I turned to Evelyn. "How much?"

She pulled out the index card and flipped it over a couple of times. "Four thousand six hundred would be good."

Gary grimaced and looked away. Bernie grabbed him by the biceps before he could start negotiating. "Start counting, asshole."

We watched him count out forty-six hundred-dollar bills and push them across the counter to Evelyn. She picked them up and jammed them into her purse. "I will tell the others to come see you, too."

Gary opened his mouth to say something, but the only thing that came out was, "Ouch," as Bernie squeezed his arm.

"You'll pay them, too, or I'll find the file. Don't try anything cute, like closing up and making a run for it. I have a friend in the county treasurer's office and I expect there'll be a lien that will make it very hard to sell your very expensive house for a couple of years."

"Sonofabitch." Gary spat the words out. "Get the hell out of here."

We walked out and stopped at the Isuzu. I gave El and Todd a thumbs-up sign and they smiled.

"Mrs. Sampson, if you have a problem with Gary Jones in the future, go to Sergeant Kaiser and tell him. I think he'll be happy to straighten it out for you."

She looked at Bernie. "Yes, I think he could." She patted her purse. "Now I have many things to do." She turned and left. We followed her outside.

"You'd think she'd have said thanks." Bernie watched her walk down the sidewalk.

"I guess it's a cultural thing. But I can say thanks." I put my hand out and we shook on a job well-done.

He smiled. "It's kinda fun being in the field again, but my computer is less strenuous. I might need a strawberry malt to regain my strength."

He waved as I pulled away.

Chapter 32

We took Highway 180 north from Flagstaff. It went past a closed ski resort and wound through the mountain pass, making it the more scenic, but slightly slower, route than the alternative that went further west. El talked endlessly as I drove past stands of pine interspersed with Alpine meadows. Near the top of the mountain pass was an abandoned church.
"Doug. Stop!" El said.
"What?" I braked and the Isuzu rolled to a stop.
"Back up. I want to get some pictures of that little church."
Todd and I leaned against the Isuzu while El snapped photos of the church. "Does this happen often?" I asked.
"All the time. She has an amazing eye for interesting scenes."
"Does she make any money off her photography?"
"She does a few weddings a year and a couple dozen graduation pictures. She's not making a living off it. She shares lots of her photos on Facebook, but she's also submitted some to magazines. She got quite a rush when The Smithsonian chose one of her Costa Rican pictures for their cover, and a couple of airlines

have used her Caribbean spreads in their in-flight magazines."

"Okay." El packed up her camera. "I'm ready to move on."

The view changed to high desert as we crested the mountain pass, offering a fabulous view of the San Francisco Mountains. We wound through miles of scrub pasture and caught Highway 64 for the final approach to the Grand Canyon.

"So you don't think the murder will ever be solved?" El asked.

"It's hard to say. Unless Margaret Adams' recordings get the FBI's attention, or someone confesses, I don't see what's going to break."

El shifted in the seat and stared out the side window. "You mean a person can kill someone else and walk away? It just doesn't seem fair."

"Life's not fair is an adage that passed around the squad room every time a criminal went free."

El glared at me in the rear view mirror. "How can you be so . . . so calloused about it? A man died."

I took a deep breath and let it out slowly. "El, it's reality." I pondered how to put it best. "There has to be a suspect and a string of evidence that ties the suspect to the crime. We've got a couple of suspects but very little evidence. It's a bitch."

El looked out the side window again. "But we saw them. Isn't that enough?"

"We didn't see him get pushed over the edge. We saw him fall past us, but we really weren't witnesses to a crime."

"But the men ran away."

"It's not Doug's fault, El." Todd reached over the seat and touched her knee. "He's doing everything he can. I was closest to the guys at Walnut Canyon and I doubt I could pick them out of a lineup."

We drove silently through Grand Canyon Village. I slowed to let a family cross the road. I couldn't get El's comments out of my mind.

I flashed my Park Service badge at the young ranger in the Grand Canyon entry booth. "I'll pay for my two guests."

He took the cash and wrote down my name. I knew no one would ever look at the sheet. He handed me a receipt. "It's is good for two days. Go ahead."

I chose the road going east of the main lodge and Visitor Center. We drove in continued silence until we got to a parking area. There was a break in the trees where I parked, but we couldn't see anything until we got out of the car and followed the walkway over a rise. The open expanse between the north and south rims of the canyon rose to greet us. The reds, tans, and purples carved by the Colorado River sprawled before us.

"My God, I had no idea." Todd looked at the huge chasm that spanned the view from horizon to horizon. "There are no way words, or even a picture, can do justice to this view."

El took photos, checked and adjusted the exposure, and then retook the whole panorama. She switched lenses and took another set.

"I heard that if you took everyone who has ever been born and stacked them in the canyon, the pile wouldn't come to the rim." I was quite proud of my one piece of Grand Canyon trivia.

El stopped shooting photos and gave me a disgusted look. "Stacking dead bodies. That's the best way to describe the enormity of this place?"

"Who said they were dead?" I tried to backtrack, but it didn't work. El packed up her camera gear without further comment.

"Let's pop up to the visitor center and find a picnic table," I suggested.

Todd tried to be upbeat. "Great idea, Doug. I'm famished."

Chapter 33

Peter Ward, the editor of *The Santa Fe Journal*, sorted through the mail on his desk. The brown envelope with Doug Fletcher's name on the return address caught his attention. He hesitated briefly, feeling the shape of the enclosed compact disc before opening it. The writing on the CD said "August 13." He thought about giving it to one of his reporters but he remembered Fletcher's name. They'd served together in Iraq and had lost track of each other until a reunion. Fletcher had been a cop in Minnesota. He picked up the envelope and looked at the Phoenix return address, which left him puzzled. He thought it might be something for him personally and decided to check it out himself.

He walked to the picture archives in search of paper's archivist, John Miller. His memories of Doug Fletcher became clearer and clearer. He found his target in a studio, reviewing photos for the next edition.

"Johnnie, you got a CD player?"

Miller pointed to a slot in the bank of electronics in front of him. He took the CD from Ward. "More death threats over the editorial about water rights?" Miller asked.

Ward sat on a well-worn chair next to the desk and watched the CD go into the slot. "I doubt it. Those were all postmarked from New

Mexico. This one was posted by an old acquaintance in Phoenix." Miller punched a key and they both sat back.

At first the conversation didn't mean anything to them. Terry Mahoney's name wasn't at all familiar. Then Ward heard Steven Potter's name and his eyes went wide with recognition. What was it, that article that had come in over the wires? An accidental fall at some national monument, they'd said. It had stuck in his mind because of the strange circumstances. They'd run the story days before, though, near the obituaries. "Stop, Johnnie, and go back to the beginning."

Ward pulled a sheet of paper from the desktop printer and a pencil from his pocket. They listened to the whole conversation as Ward made notes. The conversation ended and Johnnie was reaching to stop it when a new conversation started. It was between Potter and his wife. They listened intently, feeling like intruders on someone's personal life.

"Honey, pack a suitcase for a trip."

"What's up? I thought things were busy."

"They are, but I . . . I have an offer to buy the business."

"That's awfully sudden."

"Yeah. It's just the right time to step away. Maybe it's time for the Panama Canal cruise we talked about."

"Your voice sounds funny. Is everything all right?"

"Everything's fine. I've got a meeting tomorrow morning. After that we can book the cruise and figure out where life's going to take us."

"Is Margaret going to stay on with the new owner?"

"I don't know. Maybe." There was a pause. "I love you."

The recording stopped.

"Pull it out, Johnnie."

Miller removed the CD and handed it to Ward. "What was that all about? The first part sounded like some financial shenanigans."

"Pull up the Associated Press website and type in Steven Potter."

In a few seconds they were reading the wire service article about Steve Potter's accidental fall at Walnut Canyon National Monument on the computer screen.

Ward looked at the date on the CD and then counted back. "This conversation was recorded the day before Steve Potter died."

"Sounds like Potter was being pressured to sell his business and the next day he falls to his death. Sounds fishy."

"A little too much of a coincidence."

Miller nodded. "Potter argues with this Mahoney guy. Mahoney says he's buying him out and Potter falls off a cliff the next day."

Ward got up and tapped the CD on the desk. "Maybe it's no coincidence Potter died the next day." He started for the door. "I've got to make some calls."

Peter Ward closed his office door and pulled up Dexknows.com. There was no Phoenix listing for Doug or Douglas Fletcher, but he found a phone number for M. Adams. He dialed the number and the recorder kicked in.

"I'm sorry you missed me. Leave a message." The female voice was brief and to the point.

"Miss Adams, this is Peter Ward, from *The Santa Fe Journal*. I got your package. Please call me at . . ."

When he hung up he walked into the office area of reporters, copywriters, and junior editors. He walked up to Sarah Hawkins who had been with the paper for close to twenty years. Today, as always, she wore a tailored suit and a sparkling smile. Behind her disarming smile was one of the sharpest and most ruthless campaigners for honesty and government credibility in the entire Southwest.

Ward handed her the CD and the envelope with the return address. "Drop everything and chase this."

Sarah accepted the CD, looked briefly at the date and then looked at the return address on the envelope. "I'm working on a follow-up to the subsidy fraud article right now. It's going to run tomorrow and you know I always finish my own stores. Can't someone else deal with this?"

Ward put a hand on her shoulder and leaned close to her ear. "My gut says this may be a big story and you're the only person I trust to do it justice. Johnnie Miller has a CD player."

Sarah's eyes grew wide. "What is it?"

"Listen to it and be sure to put the original in the vault. Then tell me what you're going to do."

Sarah almost ran to Johnnie Miller, who was studying a photo on a computer screen. She thrust the CD at him. "Play this . . . and make a copy."

He looked at the CD and flipped it over. "I already heard this." He moved to the bank of audio equipment where he put the CD in one bank and inserted a blank disk in the other. He pushed a series of buttons and leaned back. "So the boss decided you're the person to chase this." He pulled up the Associated Press story on his computer and spun the screen so she could read it. "Here's the context you need for this to make sense."

Sarah was hardened from years of tough stories. She felt the butterflies in her stomach that signaled she was onto something big as she read the AP article and heard the voices play back. They listened in silence. Halfway through the first conversation, she started getting angry. When the Mahoney and Potter conversation ended she stood, but Johnnie motioned for her to wait.

"There's more." Sarah's eyes hardened as they listened to the conversation between Potter and his wife.

"The bastards." She motioned for Johnnie to give her the copy of the CD. "Put the original in the safe."

Johnnie smiled. "Sure . . . what are you going to do?"

Sarah was already headed for the door, but she stopped and turned. "I'm going to teach that Phoenix bastard a lesson."

* * *

"Come with me." Sarah motioned to intern Janice Carlson as she walked through the office. "Get me the phone number for the Phoenix office of US Customs. Also get me number of Doug, or Douglas, Fletcher in Phoenix. Then find me an expert in Southwest antiquities."

Janice pushed her glasses up her nose, nodded, and started typing commands into her computer. Sarah rushed to her desk and flipped though her computer contacts file. She dialed the number for *The Phoenix Times* and waited.

"Harold Mitchell, please." The line was quiet as someone tried to locate the newspaper's senior statesman. He came on the line. "Harold, this is Sarah Hawkins, from *The Santa Fe Journal*. I need some information."

Mitchell smiled and leaned back in his office chair. He looked at his office wall, which was covered in pictures of himself with the political leaders of the Southwest. Centered among them was his Pulitzer Prize. He routinely got calls from colleagues across the country and had earned markers by bartering information for early access to breaking stories. He had an encyclopedic memory for names and recalled Sarah from a political fundraising luncheon they'd attended in Albuquerque. "Sure, Sarah, what's up?"

"Harold, I need some background for a story. Have you ever heard of a woman named Margaret Adams?"

Mitchell had just reviewed an Associated Press story they were going to run about Adams' attack in Maine. "You're a little late. We put that story up for this morning's edition. Of course, you folks in fly-over land sometimes don't glean the hot stories off the wire." His tone made the comment more a joke than a jab.

"Give me the bottom line." Sarah initiated a search for Margaret Adams on the Associated Press website.

Mitchell pulled up the early edition of his newspaper. "I'll read it to you. The headline is, 'Dead Antique Dealer's Associate Attacked.' Phoenix resident Margaret Adams, was seriously injured in a shooting near Bar Harbor, Maine, yesterday. Adams suffered multiple gunshot wounds after an assailant attacked her on a highway north of the tourist mecca. A local resident witnessed the attack and struck the assailant with his truck. The assailant died at the scene. He has been identified as Brian Bohnsack, a former Navy Seal reported to be missing from the Corpus Christi Naval Air Station Hospital. No motive has been found for the attack. Ms. Adams' was employed by Phoenix antiquities dealer Steven Potter as his administrative assistant. Steven Potter died last week after falling . . . blah blah and end of story. See, you're too late."

"Is she still alive?"

"At the time this was written she was. Why?" The veteran reporter's interest was piqued by the tone of Sarah's questions.

"There may be more to it."

Mitchell laughed. "Yeah, you think that, along with everyone else in Phoenix. It's too coincidental. Potter falls off a cliff, then his assistant is shot two days later half the country away? Problem is, no one has any evidence. Too bad Adams' attacker didn't live. He might've spilled something." He paused. "What interest does *The Santa Fe Journal* have in Margaret Adams?"

Sarah smiled. "I'll get back to you."

"Wait a second, young lady. If you actually break something, I get it ahead of the wire services."

"You will, Harold. I promise."

* * *

Peter Ward was nearly breathless when he got to Sarah's cubicle. "Here." He handed her two message slips. "These came in last night and were buried on my desk. They're from Doug Fletcher, he's an old Army acquaintance of mine, that's his name on the return address. We were both military police—MPs. He's a former cop who's apparently a park ranger now. He directed Margaret Adams to us, and he wants an update. I just tried his home number but no one answered. His cell rolled over to voicemail."

Sarah turned away and typed quickly. She spun her computer screen so Ward could view it. "Margaret Adams was attacked last night in Maine. *The Phoenix Times* is running an article in their morning edition."

Ward ran his hand over his bald head several times as he scanned the AP article. When he was done he pointed at the message slips. "Call Fletcher to see what he can add to the story, and find out what hospital Margaret Adams is in, then call her too. Whether you talk to them or not, I want a version of the AP article in tomorrow's headlines with a teaser about follow up. Get in front of this story, or you'll get steamrolled."

"Janice!" Sarah yelled over the cubicle wall. "Get over here!"

The intern popped into the cubicle looking harried. "Here's the number you wanted for Immigration and Customs Enforcement. The only Douglas Fletcher I could find in Arizona was in Flagstaff. Here's his number, too."

"A woman named Margaret Adams, from Phoenix, is in a hospital near Bar Harbor, Maine. Find out where and get her on the phone for me." She picked up her own phone and dialed Fletcher's home phone number. She turned to Ward while it rang. "I'll have something to you in twenty minutes. If you leave me alone."

Chapter 34

After our picnic lunch near the south rim of the Grand Canyon, we stopped at every scenic overlook along the westbound road. We saw the Bright Eyes Trail and the site where early entrepreneurs built a lift to take visitors to the bottom of the canyon.

"Do you have a call?" El asked, as my phone chimed for about the tenth time.

"No, it's just my phone telling me we're going in and out of service areas."

The phone chirped again, and I felt it vibrate, indicating I had a voicemail. Given the narrow winding road and Arizona's laws against using a phone while driving, I ignored it.

"Todd could disable that feature. It wouldn't be so annoying."

"I don't even hear it anymore."

"It'd be less annoying for me."

I sighed. "Remind me the next time we park."

The view from anywhere along the south rim was spectacular and the closeness of the road to the rim was sometimes nerve wracking. We stood at a spot that allowed us to see a vertical drop of a mile. I looked along the rim and realized that the road we would soon be driving followed the edge of the precipice. I saw cars that appeared to be nearly hanging a wheel over the rim. I knew they weren't in danger, but the illusion was unnerving—their view wasn't spoiled by a railing.

I pulled out my phone and unlocked it. *The Santa Fe Journal* had left a message, but we were out of service again.

As we approached the gift shop at the western terminus of the road we passed the scary spot I'd seen from the scenic overlook. The road was separated from the rim by a strip of grass about fifteen feet wide and every westbound car was hugging the centerline of the road. Without a guardrail we had a wonderful, unobstructed view across the canyon. El edged away from the door as the cliff passed on her side of the Isuzu. The camera was in her hand, but illusion of being on the very edge of the precipice had her frozen.

I parked in the gift shop parking area and we wandered past a string of people walking toward us. A tour bus idled at the edge of the sidewalk and I caught a few words from the people passing, German or Swedish from the sound. I checked my phone again and still had no service.

The gift shop was a weathered building built out of stones held together with concrete. By appearances, I guessed it to be a Civilian Conservation Corps project, built sometime in the 1930s during the Depression. The interior was full of cluttered shelves displaying a variety of tourist souvenirs, most at outrageous prices. I wandered into a side room, trying not to look like a cop on the lookout for shoplifters as I scanned the faces in the crowd. I kept an eye on Todd and El until a heated conversation between an Indian woman and a young man working behind the counter distracted me. I tried to ignore them as I worked the edges of the room, killing time while El inspected souvenirs, but the argument was escalating.

"Ranger Doug, come here."

The words didn't register at first. When I turned, I realized the Indian woman was Evelyn Sampson. She was waving a wad of currency like she was ready for a Las Vegas craps table. I walked to the counter, built like a safe with a bulletproof glass lid. Inside were silver and turquoise pieces of jewelry that looked out of place with the shoddy items on display in the rest of the store.

"Ranger Doug, tell this man he has to sell me the dead pawn." She waved the money at the clerk. "I have the money to pay."

I looked at the sign built into the counter. It explained that many native artisans pawned their crafts to get cash. When the artisans failed to pay off the pawned items in the prescribed time period, the goods became "dead pawn" and were put up for sale by the pawnbroker. The goods for sale in the counter had been bought in the pawnshops on the reservation.

"What's the problem? Isn't this stuff for sale?" I examined the goods in the display as I pulled out my wallet and showed my Park

Service badge to the clerk. There were finely engraved silver belt buckles, carved stone animals, and turquoise necklaces.

The young man behind the counter was close to six-three and couldn't weigh 130 pounds. His Park Service shirt hung loose on him and his armpits were stained from sweat. He mopped at the perspiration on his forehead with his forearm.

"She wants to buy everything!" He swept his hands over the countertop.

I looked at Evelyn, and then back to the counter. "Doesn't she have enough money?"

The kid swallowed hard. "I guess she does, but that would empty the counter. This stuff is a big tourist draw. Everyone who comes through looks at the genuine Indian pawn goods. I've got to leave some stuff here. I'm pretty sure my boss would be royally pissed if I sold everything." He swallowed and his Adam's apple bobbed like Ichabod Crane in Disney's Sleepy Hollow.

I leaned close to Evelyn and whispered. "Evelyn, why do you want to buy everything? Can't you get a few things and leave the rest?"

She glared at me and then at the kid. She swept her hand over the counter. "These belong to my family. My uncle got drunk and pawned it all for liquor. We never had the money to get it back. Now I have the money and I want to buy back what's left." She stated her case very factually and without emotion, though I could tell she cared . . . a lot.

"Is this stuff all for sale?" I asked again, looking into the case. Each piece had a price tag attached with white string.

"Well, technically yes. We only sell a few pieces a week . . . "

"So you'd sell it to the tourists but you won't sell it to a Native American woman?" The implication of what I said registered on the kid's face. More beads of sweat formed on his forehead and the armpits of his gray shirt got darker as he stood there speechless. I went in for the kill. "I think that's called discrimination." I let that sink in for a moment. "What's the total price of everything in the case?"

He unfolded a slip of paper wadded in his fist and read it to us. "Thirty-three hundred, fifty-eight dollars."

"Evelyn, do you have three thousand three hundred and fifty-eight dollars?" I knew she did, but it added to the drama for the kid.

Evelyn set the wad of currency on the glass countertop. "Three thousand four hundred." She stared at the money on the counter, not wanting to make eye contact.

I pushed the money to the kid. "You owe her forty-two dollars change. Bag the stuff."

He picked up the wad of bills and counted them into the cash register. Then he counted the change and laid it in Evelyn's hand. He took the pieces out of the counter, carefully placed each item in a small white box, and then put the boxes in a plastic bag with a Park Service logo.

Evelyn and I watched every move until he handed her the bag.

I knew better than to expect any thanks from taciturn Evelyn. She clutched the bag to her chest and waddled ahead of me. Outside, she turned and looked past me. "My relatives will be pleased."

I nodded. "They should be proud of you."

She glanced into my eyes for an instant, probably to check my sincerity. "Perhaps."

Chapter 35

Todd flew around the corner of the building and almost ran over me. "I think I saw one of the guys from Walnut Canyon in the restroom. I don't think he recognized me." Anxiety and excitement danced over his face.

I shepherded Todd and Evelyn Sampson away from the building. I studied the faces of people coming around the corner from the restroom entrance on the far side of the building. Two men emerged from the area beyond the building. One was a very large Native American and the other a slender, sandy-haired man. They were talking intently and their faces had the look of predators who were keenly aware of their immediate surroundings. The smaller man was fidgety, his head on a swivel as he scanned the nearby people.

Evelyn almost spat out the name. "Tommy Tsosie. He steals from the ancients." Her words startled me.

I took her by the arm and quietly steered her away with Todd on our heels. "What do you mean?" I whispered as we headed to the parking lot.

"He robs ancient sites and sells the pottery."

I unlocked the Isuzu and motioned Evelyn to get in the passenger side. Todd got in the backseat behind Evelyn. For the first time I looked back, confirming that Tommy and his friend hadn't followed us.

"They must have gone into the gift shop." I relaxed just a bit and took a deep breath. I closed my eyes for a second and tried to remember the second man's face. It was familiar, but I couldn't dredge up the connection.

"Did you recognize the other man, Evelyn?"

She shook her head. "I don't know him."

I tried to remember if I'd seen his face among the mugshots I'd waded through in Flagstaff. There'd been a blond guy's photo in the arson file but this guy was too old to be one of the high school kids accused in those case.

"I didn't think I'd be able to recognize their faces . . . you know, I wasn't that close. But the big guy is one of them." Todd's voice was sure and certain.

My face flushed with fear. I'd left my Glock in the townhouse because this was supposed to be a day of vacation. I heard Jill's voice in my head, telling me that law enforcement rangers were supposed to have a service weapon with them 24/7. Today proved an alternate version of Murphy's Law—the day you don't have a gun is the day you'll need it. I walked around the Isuzu, opened the rear window, and unlatched the panel built into the left fender for the jack. I used it for something else. I pulled out an oily rag and felt the weight of my Smith & Wesson against my palm. It hadn't been my police weapon since the department switched to Glocks but I didn't travel without backup protection. I chambered a round, clicked the safety on, and slid it into the pocket of my Dockers. I fished the spare magazine out of the rag, checked the shells, and put it in the opposite pocket. I briefly considered contacting the Park Service superintendent at the lodge for backup versus dialing 911. Then I remembered there was no cellphone service anyway.

Another busload of tourists pulled into the parking lot, providing me a chance for some camouflage. I stuffed the Isuzu key into Todd's hand. "Here. Head for the main entrance and tell the first ranger you see that I need backup."

Todd's eyes widened and he shook his head at me, but I jabbed my finger toward the driver's door. "Get going . . . and send Evelyn off in her car."

I trotted across the parking lot and joined the end of the string of tourists going to the gift shop. I looked over the crowd and fell in alongside two gray-haired ladies who might have been mistaken for my mother and one of her friends. "It's sure a lot cooler at this elevation, isn't it?" I tried to pretend I was part of the group. They smiled at me politely and joined in the conversation without hesitation.

"Yes, it is. The temperature is just beastly on the bus. There's so much hot air with all us old windbags the air conditioner can't keep up." They giggled as we moved along slowly. The smaller woman dug in her purse. She produced a plastic case and opened it, revealing a pack of Marlboros. I looked ahead and saw no sign of Tommy and his friend or, for that matter, El.

"Where did you ladies stay last night?"

"Oh, we were in Kingman last night."

Seeing the smaller woman struggling to light the cigarette, I took the Bic lighter from her shaking hand and touched the flame to the cigarette. She inhaled deeply.

"Thanks." She blew a cloud of smoke into the air. Her voice had the deep rasp of a life-long smoker. "It's a filthy habit and it's going to kill me. But I might as well go happy." She winked at her friend.

From her lined face I guessed her to be past eighty. "Ma'am, you look like a lady who has lived a long and full life. You should find enjoyment where you can."

She patted my arm. "Amen."

When we reached the gift shop door, I glanced in. The room was jammed with people from the buses. I felt claustrophobic even before entering. The gun weighed heavily in my pocket, forming a lump in my pants pocket I felt was too noticeable, but with summer-weight khakis and a knit golf shirt I had few options to hide it. I crowded up close to my new lady-friends, hoping it wasn't too obvious.

"Be careful. The prices here are outrageous." I whispered to the nearest woman. She was taking deep drags on the last of the cigarette before we walked through the door.

She smiled and blew a stream of smoke skyward. "Honey, it doesn't make any difference. My late husband was a car dealer. He left me more money than I can spend in my lifetime." She threw her cigarette butt in the receptacle next to the door and we stepped inside the shop. "I'm sure as hell not going to leave it for my money-grubbing sons and their pitiful children. Isn't that right, Clara?"

Clara was already digging through a pile of polished stones set in a little display that looked like a wishing well. I saw her palm a few stones and as she looked up they slipped into her purse. "What were you asking?"

I closed my eyes and pretended I hadn't seen it. They probably weren't worth a dime. I'd always heard the shopkeepers dreaded the busloads of little old ladies more than the teenagers.

"I was telling our friend here . . . What's your name anyway?"

"Doug."

"I was telling Doug I don't intend to leave any money to my worthless kids."

Clara nodded. "There's no point. They'll just spend it. We earned it, why shouldn't we spend it?"

I nodded. "It works for me." I spied El coming out of an aisle wearing a Mexican style serape. She found a large enough hole in the crowd to twirl in front of a mirror, checking out the look. It apparently met with her approval because she smiled, then scanned the room. I gave her a discreet wave and she waved back before getting in the queue at the cash register. She was about the fifteenth person in line, and I wanted to get out in case the killers recognized me as a cop like the antique shop owners had. I looked around for Tommy and his friend but didn't see them. I had the sinking feeling they'd driven away while I was digging through the Isuzu or when I followed the ladies on their slow walk to the gift shop.

I told Clara and her friend goodbye and drifted toward El. I tried to be casual as I looked down each aisle in passing, but I knew my actions screamed "Cop!" to anyone who knew what to look for. When I got to El, I saw Tommy, without his blond friend, coming out of the dead pawn jewelry room. He walked toward the door. I looked away from him but saw him surveying the room in my peripheral vision.

"Doug, where's Todd?" El's tone was inquisitive, not alarmed.

"He's in the Isuzu." I concentrated on acting naturally while keeping an eye on Tommy. He kept moving and the shifting crowd of people in the gift shop made watching him nearly impossible.

"Stay in line. I'll be back."

El frowned. "Where else would I be?"

I patted her arm and worked my way through the crowd and up to the counter. Tommy was still near the gift shop door, scanning the crowd for trouble as thoroughly as I'd scanned it for him. I felt the hairs on my neck rise as I watched this predator prepare to ounce on unsuspecting prey.

I pushed my way behind the counter. "Excuse me, sir, only employees are allowed here." The female clerk was barely five feet tall with a pageboy haircut that looked out of place with her forty-something face and well-worn uniform.

I pulled out my wallet, holding it below the counter as I showed the clerk the Park Service badge. "How can I call the Visitor Center?"

"If you're a ranger, why don't you know how to use the phone?" Her look was skeptical.

"Ma'am, I'm an investigator out of Walnut Canyon. I need backup right now. Where's the damned phone and how do I call the Visitor Center?"

She searched my eyes for a hint I was lying or joking. Not finding any, she reached under the counter and pulled out a corded beige phone. She punched three digits and handed me the receiver before returning to her customer.

"Visitor Center."

"This is Douglas Fletcher, a ranger from Walnut Canyon. I'm at the gift shop at the west end of the south rim. I need backup for an arrest."

There was a pause and then I heard the rustle of paper and the click of a ballpoint pen. "What's the nature of assistance you require, Fletcher?"

I searched the sea of heads for Tommy Tsosie. He was talking to a blond, zit-faced guy I didn't recognize. Suddenly there were three guys in a discussion. Their conversation was very animated. "I'm watching two murder suspects in the gift shop and I need backup."

There was another pause. "Fletcher—was that your name?"

"Yes, Douglas Fletcher." I recited my badge number. "You probably heard about the Walnut Canyon death last week. One of the suspects is standing about thirty-five feet from me in the gift shop. I need some law enforcement rangers out here for backup."

"Hang on, Fletcher."

Tommy was waving his arms at the zit-faced man. The body language said, "Emergency!" and I was on hold. I knew if this was a typical government operation, the guy manning the visitor center phones had to tell his boss, who would have to talk to me, and then probably call a bigger boss.

A woman's voice came on the line. "Is this Fletcher?"

"Yes, who are you?" I was getting testy as the exchange with Tommy got even more animated.

"This is Roxanne Chandler, the Park Superintendent. What the hell is going on?"

"I'm Walnut Canyon's investigator. I'm in your west end gift shop and I'm staring at one of the men we want to talk to about a death last week in Walnut Canyon. I need backup."

"Do you know somebody named Todd, driving a red Isuzu?"

I lit up. "Yes! Yes! He's with me."

She let out a deep breath. "He flagged down one of our vehicles and told us a story that had us considering a straitjacket. So he's on the level?"

Tommy was headed for the door, with the blond guy in tow. "Jesus, yes! Will you get some people out here? The guy just walked out the door."

"The cavalry is coming, Fletcher. Are you armed?"

"Yes."

"For Christ's sake, don't shoot anybody!"

I threw the phone down and pushed through the crowd to the door as fast as possible. El was still about three customers back from the counter. I leaned close and said, "Stay in the gift shop until I get back."

"Why?" I didn't answer as I rushed away.

Tommy was nowhere in sight when I finally got outside. I rushed toward the parking lot where a new influx of retirees was walking toward me. The first busload of shoppers were blocking the other half of the sidewalk. Over a sea of gray heads, I spotted Tommy and the blond guy weaving through the parking lot.

I pushed my way through the crowd and ran across the parking lot. I lost sight of Tommy for a few seconds and stepped on a lady's toes as I rushed past the retirees. I excused myself and got past the crowd just as two cars backed out of parking spots. It was impossible to see which car the two guys were in, and I had a hard time even keeping track of them at all because they mingled with a dozen other cars currently cruising the lot looking for parking spaces. I ran toward the exit looking for either of the two vehicles. One had a red roof and the second had a white roof. Luck was on my side. Because of the mass of cars trying to exit and the incoming cars looking for parking spots, I was jogging faster than the cars were moving. Now all I needed was a plan in case I beat them to the exit.

"Ranger Doug." Evelyn Sampson was standing about ten feet away. "Your friend told me to go to my car. Can I leave now?"

She was standing next to her thirty-year-old Oldsmobile. The paint was gone in several spots from the incessant wind-blown sand on the reservation. The remaining paint was all oxidized to a matte finish.

"Evelyn, give me your keys." I raced to the driver's door. Her car was thirty feet from the parking lot exit. I put my hand up and stopped a car approaching her spot, effectively creating a space for me to back out and leaving me an opening to the exit.

"No keys. The ignition's broke. Just turn the silver thing where the key goes." She shuffled to the passenger side.

"You stay here. This could be dangerous." I jerked the door open and threw myself into the seat. A broken spring in the seat stuck me in one butt-cheek, sending a shooting pain up my back.

"My car. I go too."

Evelyn settled into the passenger side before I could say no.

The engine spun over and caught without a hitch, even though the rumbling told me the muffler was full of holes. When I threw the transmission into reverse, the car lurched back with a screech.

"Holy shit! What kind of engine have you got in here?" I slammed the transmission into drive. The car lurched ahead with screaming tires. A white Honda Accord crossed the end of our row, closely followed by a red Cadillac. Tommy was driving the red Caddy.

"It's a Rocket 455. Real gas hog." Evelyn made a face as we lurched ahead, racing to catch up with the Cadillac. "Chews up tires if you're not careful."

The Olds had so much power I had a hard time controlling my urge to just floor it and run Tommy's car down. Every time I accelerated in the stop-and-go traffic the bald tires spun, making the back end fishtail.

"You need new tires," I said, as we finally got to the exit. We were three cars behind the

Cadillac after cutting off a Dodge Intrepid. The Dodge's driver honked and gave me the finger.

"Evelyn snorted. "The tires aren't bald, they're okay." I stole a brief glance at her. She had crossed her arms over her chest. I'd insulted her.

"Buckle your seat belt." I tried to stay focused on the red Cadillac.

"The seat belt's broken." I shuddered as we crept along. Just wonderful. On the bright side, our greatest peril was hurtling over the edge of the Grand Canyon and working seat belts weren't going to save us if that happened.

The traffic sped up, the gap between the Olds and Tommy's Cadillac opened up. The further we got behind, the higher my anxiety rose. As we rounded a curve I saw the oncoming traffic pulling to the narrow shoulder. Behind them, a Park Service pickup, with red and blue lights flashing, threaded its way through the jammed traffic. I pulled the Olds broadside to block both lanes and jumped out to flag the rangers.

Two unarmed rangers stepped out of the vehicle as I ran to them. I pulled out my badge and flashed it. "They're in the red Cadillac just ahead." I pointed ahead and saw the Cadillac accelerate around a curve ahead of us. Tommy knew he was being chased now.

I almost jumped into the rangers' pickup but decided Evelyn's 455 was a better chase vehicle. I ran back to it and smoked the tires as we swerved forward on the empty road. The rangers made a three-point turn and fell in behind us. I could see one ranger on the radio and hoped they could get someone to block the narrow road ahead of the Cadillac without putting park visitors at risk. I flashed back to the young ranger Tommy had creamed at Walnut Canyon. I hoped the responding vehicles ahead of us were law enforcement rangers, prepared to deal with armed suspects. No matter how many scenarios I ran through my head, a roadblock meant a deadly collision, a shooting, or both. "Shit!"

The Olds' rusty shocks bounced over every bump in the road as we slid around corners, scaring the life out of oncoming drivers. The pickup's lights and sirens were doing a good job though, and I was glad to see so many cars eased over to the narrow shoulder.

We flew over a rise and I veered over onto the low grass shoulder to avoid smashing into the back of a white Honda stopped in the travel lane. I continued on the shoulder until we passed several cars and regained the road. The Cadillac was still ahead somewhere, and I accelerated back onto the blacktop. The tires screeched and the back end of the Olds slewed as if it were on ice. I looked in the mirror and saw the Honda pull to the shoulder, letting the rangers pass.

Evelyn's speedometer was broken, so I had no idea how fast we were traveling. Between the roaring engine and narrow road, it felt like at least 100. We flew past a scenic stop and I scanned the parked vehicles for the red Cadillac, the images rushing past in kaleidoscope fashion. Nothing. I pushed the pedal to the floor and the surge of power pushed my left butt-cheek into the broken spring again.

As we rounded a sweeping curve to the left I could see the Cadillac across the open canyon. Tommy was flying too, trying to pass a few cars bottled up ahead of him. By the time we hit the end of the curve, we were only fifty yards behind him but he'd managed to put two cars and a minivan between us.

The oncoming traffic broke as I approached the first car, so I swung into the oncoming lane and kept going. None of the oncoming drivers wanted to play chicken. They swerved off the road and I didn't steer back into the right lane until I'd passed all three vehicles. The Park Service pickup couldn't keep up the pace and lagged about seventy yards behind us, fading in the traffic.

Tommy's Cadillac swerved onto the grassy shoulder to pass a full-sized conversion van, and then it raced on ahead. I did the same but killed a prickly pear cactus. I prayed the thin rubber on Evelyn's tires was thicker than the cactus spines were long.

"You drive like an idiot. Pull over and let me out." Evelyn hadn't said a word until then and her sudden demand disrupted my concentration. I over-corrected my steering and sideswiped an oncoming Ford Taurus. The impact was so slight it didn't break the momentum of the Olds.

"Idiot! You ruin my car."

I grinned. At least she wasn't worried about getting killed. I couldn't say the same for me. "The Park Service will repair it, and probably buy you new tires too."

To my left, the trees opened up and the road looped to the right, then back again. On the left side of the road, the apron of grass narrowed to a sliver. We were going too fast so I backed off the gas and felt the car start to slow. The Cadillac continued to race ahead, but the right-hand lane was blocked by a slow-moving tourist bus.

I maintained speed and tried to figure out my best move. I had to end the pursuit before I put any more civilians at risk. There were rangers ahead of me, best to let them make the traffic stop in an area more controlled than this busy, narrow two-lane road.

The Cadillac slowed. I heard the ranger vehicle behind us approaching. All of us were trapped behind the bus, unable to find an opening in the oncoming traffic. There wasn't enough clearance between the road and the trees to pass it on the right so we followed behind the Cadillac at the bus's pace.

We were moving too fast when I realized the Cadillac was nearly stopped. I stood on the brakes and slid into the Cadillac's back bumper. Three heads spun to look at us and then Tommy amazed me.

Neither of us could see around the bus on a curve, but Tommy got impatient, accelerating as he steered into the oncoming traffic lane. The Cadillac disappeared past the bus. Immediately I heard a huge crash the caddy spun into view, skidding toward the precipice. It teetered there, with the front wheels hanging over the edge.

I jammed on the brakes and watched in horror, time slowing to slow motion. The three dazed occupants realized their peril and scrambled for the doors. The trunk slowly lifted into the air, became vertical, and then slid out of sight, like an ocean liner sinking. When it was gone, there was no one on the edge.

The Olds slid to a stop, bald tires smoking. I jammed it into park and threw the door open. I froze, staring at the edge, expecting someone to climb onto the grass. No one did. I couldn't do anything for Tommy and his passengers, but others needed help. Tommy's blind race around the bus had rammed a full-sized van into the side of the bus. The dazed passengers slowly pulled each other out of the van's passenger doors. The driver remained jammed tightly against the side of the bus, trapped by his seat belt.

I edged up to the break of the precipice but got vertigo when I was still a couple feet from the brink. The angle was wrong and I couldn't see the bottom of the cliff.

From somewhere further down the road I heard a kid yelling. "Wow! It's like in a million pieces." His parents grabbed the kid's shoulders and hauled him back from the railing.

I walked over to check out the angle of that view. I could see red fragments strewn across the rocks several thousand feet below me. No one could've survived.

The Park Service pickup stopped behind the Olds and two rangers raced out. One ran to the van and the other ran to me. He was maybe twenty-something, resplendent in his gray and green uniform with the Smokey Bear hat.

"What happened?" He peered over the edge. "Holy shit! They went over?"

"Yup." I turned and walked away.

Evelyn stood by her Olds, inspecting the damage from our earlier brush with the Taurus. "You're a crazy man. Look what you did to my car."

We stared at the car-length scrape together for a few seconds. "Tommy Tsosie is dead."

Evelyn nodded, then solemnly said, "We don't speak the names of those who pass."

"It's very sad." If I was going to stay in Arizona I had a lot to learn.

Evelyn shook her head. "They were not good people. It's not sad."

Sirens, slightly out of sync, approached from the direction of the Visitor Center. Two Park Service vehicles bypassed the stopped traffic by driving on the shoulder. My Isuzu followed behind them. A matronly woman got out of the first vehicle and raced to the van, followed by several armed rangers. The boss had arrived. One of the junior rangers pointed to me as he spoke. She listened and nodded before making her way to Evelyn's car.

"Fletcher?" She didn't introduce herself or offer her hand. Her brass nameplate said Chandler and her badge identified her as the Park Superintendent.

I decided my best strategy was to look official so I held up my park service badge.

Chandler looked me up and down. "Helluva uniform you got there, Fletcher. What's in your pocket?"

I slid my hand over the fabric of my pants and then remembered the pistol. "My sidearm. I was off duty today and didn't have a holster." I put my hand in my pocket and eased the pistol out with three fingers. I offered the butt to her.

"Did you discharge it?" she asked.

"No."

"Then put it away." She shook her head. "I talked to Jill Rickowski before we drove out. She gave me your description and said you were legit, but maybe a little unorthodox."

I slid the pistol back into my pocket. "The bad guys took a flyer over the rim." I pointed to the skid marks that led to the precipice. "We need to get a recovery team down to the crash site." I led her to the observation point and we peered over the railing.

She rubbed her hand over her face. "We can get rangers down in a little bit. My priority is getting the driver out of the van and taking a couple of the passengers to the hospital."

Chandler leaned over the railing and looked at the strewn pieces of red car. "There's no rush for them. They're not going anywhere."

"I suppose you'll need a statement from me," I said.

She shook her head. "Oh, a statement won't do it. You're going to be typing reports until you get carpal tunnel."

Chapter 36

Sarah Hawkins called the Phoenix Customs Border Patrol office and the Arizona Antiquities Association. It had taken several transfers to find someone in the CBP who recognized Steven Potter's name and even that person wasn't knowledgeable about Potter's business. The Antiquities Association was much more helpful. The second person she spoke with said they had lost a friend when Steve Potter died. Their comments about Mahoney were guarded and less glowing.

After several calls, Janice Carlson located Margaret Adams in the Bar Harbor hospital. She raced to Sarah's office with the phone number.

The hospital receptionist told Sarah Ms. Adams wasn't accepting phone calls so she asked for the nursing station. The nurse also advised her Ms. Adams wasn't taking calls or seeing visitors.

"Please give her this message. Tell her the package arrived in Santa Fe and I would like to talk to her." The nurse was uneasy about the cryptic message but took it anyway.

Sarah was outlining her story when the phone rang. She nearly pounced on it. "*Santa Fe Journal,* Sarah Hawkins."

"I have a collect call from Margaret Adams. Will you accept the charges?"

"Yes!"

"This is Margaret Adams." The voice coming through the lines was very weak. "You left a message."

"Ms. Adams, thank you for calling me back. Are you safe?"

"I'm okay. The doctor said I'm pretty banged up and I'll have to stay in the hospital for a while. There's a Bar Harbor police officer outside my door."

"Do I have your permission to record our conversation?"

"Sure."

Sarah pressed the record button on a small digital recorder. "This is Sarah Hawkins of *The Santa Fe Journal* speaking with Ms. Margaret Adams. Ms. Adams, I have your permission to record this conversation, is that correct?"

"Yes, it is."

"Ms. Adams, I listened to the recorded phone calls you sent to the newspaper. Tell me about Steve Potter."

"Steve was a great guy and totally honest. We had provenance on all of our inventory, and we sold through a network of reputable dealers. His new partner, Mahoney, was importing cheap Mexican pottery, swapping it for illegal antiquities, then shipping the antiques to Steve's customers who were willing to accept the merchandise because the questionable documentation was on our letterhead. Steve eventually realized what Mahoney was doing and confronted him. Steve was being forced to sell the business and Mahoney needed to keep Steve from talking." It took a few seconds for Adams to catch her breath from her quick summary of Potter's situation. "Excuse me, but I get tired fast. Anyway, Steve was going to sell his shop and leave Phoenix, but I think Mahoney killed him before he could get away."

"I read the wire service reports on Potter's death. It says he died in an accidental fall. What makes you think it was anything else?"

"There's a Park Service Ranger who saw it happen. He knows it was murder."

"You're kidding! There was a witness and they still ruled it an accident?" Sarah scribbled a note.

"It's got to be a cover-up." Margaret was nearly gasping for breath. "Someone is really worried about what I might know, or what I've told other people. They had me followed to Maine and a man tried to kill me."

"How did you get the phone recordings?"

"I knew Steve was paranoid about the business with Mahoney and he told me he'd started recording his phone calls. I took the recordings from his office as soon as I heard he was dead."

"Why did you contact the Park Service?"

"I was really paranoid myself by then and afraid to talk to any of the local police. When I heard Steve died in a fall at Walnut Canyon I decided to call the park to see if someone there would listen to me. They gave me the name of a ranger who was investigating Steve's death."

"Was the ranger you contacted Doug Fletcher?" Sarah asked, looking at the return address on the CD envelope.

"Yes, Douglas Fletcher," Adams said. "I'm sorry, but his Flagstaff phone number is in my purse and I'm not sure where it is."

"I have his number and I've already left messages with Fletcher. Please get some rest. I'm sure we'll talk again soon."

Chapter 37

El had been waiting in the area of the gift shop for two hours when Todd and I found her sitting on a bench outside the entrance. The Park Service Rangers had ignored my pleas to get a message to her while taking statements from Evelyn, Todd, and me at the main Visitor Center. Evelyn lodged complaints about my driving and the damage to her car before she left for home. Todd and I drove the Isuzu back to the gift shop parking lot after the rangers ran out of questions. We returned to a very unhappy woman.

"Where do you two get off dumping me here and telling me to stay put?" She teed off on us as soon as she saw us. She tapped her watch. "I've been sitting here for over two hours."

Todd didn't know what I'd told El. He looked at me for a response.

"It was for your own safety. The guys who killed the man at Walnut Canyon were in the gift shop. We . . ." I never got to finish the sentence.

"Is that who you were staring at? Why didn't you tell me?" El, beyond words, threw her hands into the air.

We were becoming quite an attraction outside the gift shop. I put my hand on El's arm, trying to steer our argument further from the door.

"Take me back to Flagstaff." She turned toward the parking lot and walked away.

I heard the warble of an approaching siren as El marched away. The siren died when the Park Service vehicle, its red and blue lights flashing, turned into the parking lot and worked its way through the flow of cars. It parked in a reserved spot next to the gift shop. Roxane Chandler, the park superintendent, ran from the vehicle and almost knocked El over to get to me.

"Fletcher, come." She had two younger rangers in tow. I saw that the two men with her were armed law-enforcement rangers who ran with one hand on their firearms. They disappeared into the crowd outside the gift shop.

El froze when she heard the ranger's command. I trotted after the rangers with Todd and El walking along behind. They turned at the end of the corner of the building. When I got to the corner I saw park service employees standing outside an enclosure with a high chain-link fence.

The rangers stopped to question the two employees and were busily taking notes. I just caught just the end of a conversation. ". . . in the Dumpster and I saw a hand." I used my cop voice to tell El and Todd to stay put. I walked into the enclosure that housed two large, green Dumpsters. The August heat had made the garbage a putrid, smelly mess. The lid was open on the right-hand Dumpster. I slipped behind Chandler and the others and peered over the edge. A hand stuck out of a pile of black plastic bags. I reached in and felt for a pulse. There wasn't one. The skin had already cooled to near ambient temperature. The superintendent looked at me, one eyebrow raised in question.

"I'm not a doctor, but you don't need to rush an ambulance."

I stared at the Dumpster. Tommy Tsosie had been nervous in the gift shop. "I think I know who dumped the body here."

Chandler stared at me for a second before that computed. "You mean the guys that went over the cliff?"

I nodded just as a female voice in the back of the crowd called out. "What guys that went over the cliff?" El. Her voice wasn't easily mistaken, especially her upset voice.

I pushed past the crowd and took her by the arm. "We chased the murderers and their car crashed."

She screwed her face up into a frown. "Are they okay?"

I shook my head. "Their car went over the cliff. They were trapped inside it."

Her eyes went wide. She covered her mouth. "My God, why didn't you tell me?"

"We were having trouble getting a word in while you yelled at us."

"Did you see it?"

"I was right behind them."

She stood dumbfounded and Todd pulled her into an embrace.

It suddenly struck me that I had missed something. I went back to the gaggle of rangers and took the superintendent aside. "I want to look inside the Dumpster."

"I thought we couldn't disturb it until the FBI got here."

I waved her to follow me. "Have you got any gloves?"

"Why would I have gloves?" Chandler asked.

"To handle evidence. Let me borrow your pen."

She handed it to me and I took a deep breath and leaned into the Dumpster. Using the pen, I pushed the bags back from where the hand disappeared under them. There was an anchor tattoo on the forearm. I pushed another bag back. A stone Kokopelli carving sat on the victim's chest. The figurine was jammed between a bag and the victim's blue denim shirt.

I pushed the bag aside and then dropped to the ground, gasping for breath. "Take a look." The superintendent leaned into the Dumpster. "See the Kokopelli figurine?"

She stepped on a box to see over the edge of the Dumpster and then stepped back down. She nodded, her face green.

"It's the killer's calling card."

* * *

It took the Phoenix FBI office nearly three hours to authorize use of a helicopter and make the flight to the Grand Canyon. By the time it arrived, the Park Service had recovered two of the bodies from the bottom of the cliff and delivered them to the visitor center where they were placed in a basement conference area being used as a temporary morgue with the body from the Dumpster.

Special Agent Harmon Snelling was the only passenger in the Park Service vehicle that delivered him from the Grand Canyon airport. I met him halfway up the sidewalk and stuck out my hand. "Welcome to the Grand Canyon."

He brushed my hand aside. "Where are the bodies?"

I knew he wouldn't be pleased unless he was the one in the spotlight. I led him inside and opened a door, where we were greeted by a ranger who reached for his holster. He relaxed when he recognized me and saw the FBI badge on Snelling's belt.

The chairs had been pulled away from the table and pushed against the walls. Snelling glanced at the body bags lying on the floor in front of the conference table. "Where are the other FBI agents?" he asked.

"They're with the Park Service recovery team at the bottom of the canyon."

"I thought there were four bodies."

The ranger clarified. "One body is still inside the car. Our guys are still trying to extricate him."

Snelling clenched his teeth. I could see his jaw muscles flex but he didn't comment further. He took off his suitcoat, folded it, and laid it carefully on a chair. He pulled a pair of purple nitrile gloves from his back pocket, knelt down, and unzipped all of the black body bags. Two of the three faces were badly cut up, misshapen and discolored from the impact. He studied each face with the detachment of a professional before pulling the zippers closed.

"Any ID on them?" He got up from where he knelt next to the Dumpster body. I had to give him credit—he didn't flinch, turn away, or even wrinkle his nose at the garbage odor. Maybe he'd lost his sense of smell.

"The Navajo guy was Tommy Tsosie. According to my sources, he was into smuggling artifacts off the reservation and selling them on the black market. The blond guy was Elmer Swenson. He was with Tsosie at Walnut Canyon when the guy went over the cliff. I've seen his face somewhere else, too, maybe the files at Flagstaff PD. The guy from the Dumpster is unfamiliar to me."

Snelling opened a plastic evidence bag containing a brown leather wallet, a key ring, and some loose change. He slid the contents onto the table. "James Kennedy, of Paradise Valley." He flipped through the contents: charge cards, phone card, driver's license, and over a thousand dollars in cash.

"Interesting." He slipped the wallet back into the plastic bag. "Not many people carry around that kind of cash. He doesn't have anything personal, no pictures, no business cards, nothing. It makes me wonder if the ID and charge cards are fake." He resealed the bag and signed the chain of evidence label.

He picked up the vehicle registration card and examined it through the plastic. It listed a Phoenix address. "It was reported stolen yesterday," I said.

Without opening the bag he examined the items the rangers had taken from the glove compartment: owner's manual, repair receipts, oil change receipts, a tube of lipstick, a broken hand-held Garmin GPS, and a pair of women's panties. "The car is registered to a man. He must have a wife or girlfriend," Snelling said.

"I've never had panties in my glove compartment." I'd never had a romantic interlude in a car resulting in panties being thrown into a glove compartment. My life must be dull. On the other hand, the gymnastics involved in removing a pair of panties inside a car, and the subsequent activities, would probably cripple me. On closer examination, the panties obviously weren't from Victoria's Secret. They were "granny style," white cotton, size large. The car had probably been stolen from one of the ubiquitous Phoenix retirement communities. The owner might be a senior citizen who kept spare underwear in her car for emergencies.

Snelling examined the bag containing a Garmin GPS. The LCD screen was cracked and dark, indicating that it had likely been damaged by the car's impact. The battery cover had been dislodged and lost and there was an empty compartment where the batteries normally fit. Snelling turned it over in his hands, shook his head, then put it on the desktop.

He opened the next bag, which only contained a wallet. "Tommy Tsosie." He sorted through a few credit cards and the driver's license. He held up a business card. "Joe Reber. Antiques. The address is in Sedona."

"Tommy's the big guy we saw at Walnut Canyon, the one we chased after Steve Potter went over the side. My source says he was stealing illegal antiquities from the reservation. Joe Reber told my cousins he might be able to get them some real antiquities if they could wait a few days."

Apparently, the FBI didn't care about stolen antiquities from the reservation because Snelling stuck the contents back into the wallet without comment. He removed several hundred dollars and a business card fell out. It had a Kokopelli figure printed on the front with a hand-written phone number on the back.

"The 520 area code is Tucson and most of southeastern Arizona." He flashed the card at me.

"Kokopelli shows up again. That reminds me, I should call Flagstaff to see if they got any responses to their Kokopelli inquiry."

"That's a hair-brained theory." He put the money and card back in the wallet and signed the evidence log.

He opened the wallet from the last bag and pulled out the driver's license. "Elmer Swenson, with an address in Flagstaff." Inside he found two tens and three ones.

"This guy obviously was the low man on the totem pole." Snelling shoved the money back into the wallet and dropped it into the bag. "I suppose our guys started a search on these names." He resealed the bag and signed the log. After removing the purple gloves he flipped open his cellphone. "No service. I need a phone."

We got directions to the superintendent's office from the ranger guarding the door. She wasn't there. Snelling sat in her chair and picked up her desk phone like he owned the office.

I found an empty office to make a few calls of my own. I asked for Bernie Kaiser when I reached the Flagstaff Police Department and the dispatcher put me on hold. I hoped Todd and El had followed my suggestion and were getting something to eat at the snack bar across from the ranger's offices while they waited on me.

"Sergeant Kaiser." Bernie's voice boomed into my ear, diverting my thoughts from El and Todd.

"Bernie, it's Doug Fletcher. I'm up at the Grand Canyon and there's a new twist to the Kokopelli incidents."

"Grand Canyon. I thought you were working out of Walnut Canyon."

"I took a day off, but it turned sour. We ran into a little trouble."

"You and trouble are first cousins. Did you see another guy thrown off the cliff?"

"Close. We ran into the two murderers from Walnut Canyon and chased them down the south rim."

Kaiser made a low whistling sound. "No shit? Did you catch 'em?"

"Ah, sort of. They're in body bags."

I could hear Bernie shuffling around. "What were their names? I'm at the computer."

I had to spell Tsosie for him. "He has an address in Flagstaff. The second guy was Elmer Swenson with the same Phoenix address. There was a third guy, James Kennedy. His address is in Paradise Valley."

I could hear the keys clicking on Bernie's computer keyboard. I told him about the Kokopelli business card in Tommy Tsosie's wallet with the southern Arizona phone number on the backside.

"There is no James Kennedy in Paradise Valley. Any chance it's a fake ID?"

"It might be. There wasn't anything personal in the wallet other than the driver's license and one charge card. How about the other two?"

"Tommy Tsosie has a rap sheet too many pages long to talk about. It's mostly petty thefts. Most of Elmer Swenson's record is in

Minnesota. He spent a few years in a Minnesota prison for passing stolen payroll checks, then he did a stint in a Federal prison for mail fraud. Other than that, it's all petty stuff and he's been clean for eighteen months." Bernie paused for a second. "Do you have the Paradise Valley phone number handy? I'd like to run it through a reverse phone listing database."

"Hang on." I set the phone down on top of the desk and walked to the superintendent's office. Snelling, wearing purple gloves again, was rifling through the bag of stuff from James Kennedy as he talked on the phone. I donned gloves and picked up the bag with Tommy Tsosie's wallet. I took out the Kokopelli business card with the phone number.

Snelling looked up at me and frowned. He put his hand over the mouthpiece. "Don't take that anywhere."

I peeled a Post-it note from a pad on the desktop and wrote the number down. "James Kennedy is a fake name. Any leads?"

Snelling's eyes narrowed. He didn't seem pleased I already had that nugget of information. "Not yet. How about you?"

I shook my head. "I'll run this number and see who it belongs to." I didn't wait for Snelling to reply.

"Bernie, the number is . . ." I read it off to him. Again, I could hear the computer keys clicking. It didn't take him long.

"The number is for a prepaid cellphone, the kind you buy with a thousand minutes and then throw away when your time is used up. It was purchased at a convenience store south of Phoenix." There was a pause, then more clicking. "The department won't like this because it's going to cost a few bucks, but I'm going to see if the buyer used a credit card."

After a few moments, Bernie was back. "Nope, purchased with cash. These folks are getting too smart."

I could hear him shuffling through papers. "I got a half dozen responses to my Kokopelli inquiries, including three murders, one arson fire, and two burglaries. The responses spread out from Santa Rosa, New Mexico, to St. George, Utah. Every crime was against somebody shady who seemed to be getting out of line with his handlers. All the crimes were very professional, without witnesses or evidence. The only thing linking any of them was the Kokopelli figurine left behind."

"You can add another murder to the list. They knocked off a guy at the south rim gift shop. His body was found in a Dumpster."

"Any idea who it was?" Bernie asked.

"Not yet. The FBI is investigating."

The office door shot open and Superintendent Chandler rushed in, looking haggard. "The body in the Dumpster is a police dispatcher from Yavapai County."

"No shit," I said. "Bernie, did you hear that? The Dumpster body was identified as a Yavapai County dispatcher."

335

Bernie snorted. "I'll lay you odds he wasn't clean. Is he the one found with the Kokopelli?"

"I saw it with my own eyes." I looked up at the superintendent. "I'll call later, Bernie."

"I've got more information," I told her. "Let's go back to your office. Agent Snelling's taken over your desk."

"We'll see about that."

* * *

"There's a reason the chairs in front of my desk are called visitor's chairs, Agent Snelling." Chandler's look could've frozen ice, and I grinned to myself as Snelling hastily vacated his position behind her desk.

I took one of the visitor's chairs and waited for him to take the other before starting. "The phone number written next to the Kokopelli is for a disposable cellphone. Coconino County checked and found it was purchased with cash from a convenience store south of Phoenix."

"What else was your contact in Flagstaff able to determine?" Snelling asked.

"Kokopelli has been busy. There were several responses to the Flagstaff email asking about Kokopelli figurines at crime scenes. They came from Utah to New Mexico, and all of them seem to be connected with shady people."

Snelling looked skeptical. "Why, do you suppose, no one ever caught this connection before?"

"The reports came from multiple, mostly small, jurisdictions across several states with no communications between them. I suspect no single agency has seen Kokopelli more than once or twice, and the law enforcement agencies involved are spread over several thousand square miles in at least three states."

"That's the type of trend VICAP is supposed to pick up." Snelling gave new meaning to the phrase 'Doubting Thomas'.

"How many small departments put that level of detail into the VICAP database?" I asked. "Most small departments don't have computer geeks to enter details into the computer for every crime, nor do they have the luxury of being able to assign a dozen detectives to an investigation like the FBI."

Special Agent Snelling's face turned red. The superintendent looked shocked, but I'd never worshipped at the FBI's shrine and wasn't about to start now.

After taking a deep breath, Snelling said, "Give me the name of your contact in Flagstaff and I'll have someone follow up."

Chapter 38

Sarah Hawkins did another internet search for Steven Potter and wrote down both his home and office numbers. She called the office number first and a recording that said the business was temporarily closed.

Potter's home phone rang three times before a woman picked it up.

"Hello, this is Sarah Hawkins, of *The Santa Fe Journal*. Is this Mrs. Potter?"

"New Mexico?" The woman asked.

"Yes. We were contacted by Steven Potter's assistant, Margaret Adams. Is this Mrs. Potter?" Sarah recognized her voice as the one on the office recording.

"I'm Barbara Potter, Steve's wife."

"I'd like to talk to you about a recording of your husband's phone conversation Ms. Adams sent us."

"Margaret sent you a recording?"

"Yes, before she left for Maine."

"Margaret went to Maine?" Barbara Potter asked. "I'm confused. One day Margaret was helping wrap things up at the store and the next day there was no sign of her. I was beginning to think that she might've been embezzling funds or something because she disappeared without saying a word."

"I really apologize for trying to get into this so soon after your loss, but a lot of suspicious things have come up during my investigation and it's got me questioning the official account of your husband's death."

"I don't understand. Steve fell."

"Do you feel safe?"

"Why wouldn't I feel safe?"

"Margaret Adams is in the hospital, Mrs. Potter. Someone tried to kill her. I think you and Terry Mahoney are the only other people close to Steve's business and it sounds like Terry and your husband had a falling out just before he died."

"I think you're mistaken. Terry contacted me after Margaret disappeared and he's been very helpful. He's been doing an inventory of the store and filling orders. He said Steve's bookkeeping was a mess, so Terry took the computer to his accountant."

Sarah scrawled on a Post-it Note. "What type of partnership did your husband have with Mr. Mahoney?"

"Why don't you call Terry? I'm not really interested in discussing business right now."

"Please bear with me for just a couple questions."

Barbara sighed. "Steve had both a retail antiquities store and a wholesale business. Terry has some sort of import business and I think he's been importing antiquities that Steve's been reselling. I know the business has really picked up since Steve teamed up with Terry."

"I got a sense from the recordings your husband was not happy with the partnership and that he was planning to make a change."

"Terry told me they'd patched up everything. Steve was selling the business to Terry. Steve and I were going to take a Panama Canal cruise."

Sarah felt the first stirrings of panic. Mahoney was manipulating Barbara Potter and he was probably behind Steve's murder and the attempt on Margaret Adams' life.

"Mrs. Potter, can you leave your house right now and find someplace secure to stay for a week or two?"

"Oh, that's unnecessary. Terry has someone watching the store and my house to make sure no one steals any antiques. I'm very secure right here."

"I listened to the recording of the last phone conversation your husband had with Terry Mahoney. They didn't patch things up and threats were made."

"I think you're an alarmist, Ms. Hancock."

"My name's Hawkins. And I think you'd be much safer elsewhere."

"I can ask Terry what he thinks about my safety, but I'm sure I'm secure here."

"Margaret Adams is in the hospital. An attempt was made on her life. Her assailant hasn't been identified, but we know he flew from Phoenix on the same flight as Margaret, using phony identification and credit cards."

"You couldn't think Terry had anything to do with that."

"Who stood to gain the most from your husband's death? If there were shady business dealings, who stood to lose the most if Margaret Adams were to tell the police?"

"I don't know that anyone gained from Steve's death. Terry is contacting Steve's lawyer for me and they're going to go over the partnership papers and Steve's Will."

"Can you give me Steve's lawyer's name?"

"Well, not really. Terry told me Steve changed lawyers a few weeks ago and I don't know who the new person is."

A chill ran over Sarah Hawkins as she wondered if she would be so naïve in the same situation. Her years in the news business made her hope she would be more astute about her spouse's business dealings, but she wasn't sure how gullible a grieving widow might be.

"Barbara, here's a proposal I'd like to offer you. I have a friend, Harold Mitchell, who's been with *The Phoenix Times* for quite a few years. He is trustworthy and intelligent. I'm going to call him when we hang up. You tell your story to Harold, and if he says so, I want you to leave your house with him."

"The Harold Mitchell?" Barbara asked.

"Yes, he's a friend. I'll tell Harold to call you at this number. Promise me you'll lock the doors and stay in your house until you hear from him, and please don't talk to Terry Mahoney or any of his people."

Chapter 39

After calling Harold Mitchell, Sarah Hawkins drafted the Margaret Adams story and sent it to her editor. Ten minutes later Peter Ward stood at her desk with a printed copy in hand.

"You're done already?" Ward asked.

"I spoke with Barbara Potter, Steve Potter's widow, and Margaret Adams, who sent us the recordings. There's the AP story about Adams who was nearly killed by a gunman in Maine."

Ward sat in Sarah's guest chair and motioned for her to continue.

"Margaret Adams expanded on the Potter story we heard on the tape and said there's a conspiracy to cover up illegal trade in artifacts." She let that sink in while Peter reread the opening paragraph of her article. "The Arizona Antiquities Association gave me a lot of background on legal versus illegal artifacts. Barbara Potter told me Terry Mahoney, the supposed partner, took Potter's computer and is 'cleaning up' the bookkeeping with his accountant and 'going over the Will' with Potter's new lawyer. She doesn't know either of those people."

"How about Fletcher, the park ranger?"

"I've left messages on his cellphone, his home voicemail, and at the Flagstaff Park Service office. He'll have to pick up one of them pretty soon."

"We'll run this article about the attack on Margaret Adams now. We'll follow it up with another story tomorrow. Call Fletcher again, and do some research on this Mahoney character."

"Excuse me," Intern Janice stuck her head into Sarah's cubicle. "You asked me to look for background on Douglas Fletcher and Margaret Adams. This just came in from the AP." She handed Sarah a sheet of paper.

"Holy shit! There can't be two Park Service Rangers named Douglas Fletcher," Sarah said as she scanned the opening sentences. She handed the article to Ward. "Fletcher isn't answering my calls because he's been chasing murder suspects in the Grand Canyon."

Sarah dialed Fletcher's cellphone number, which immediately rolled over to voicemail. "Ranger Fletcher, this is Sarah Hawkins from *The Santa Fe Journal*. I just spoke with Margaret Adams. An attempt was made on her life, but she's okay and under police protection. We're at deadline and I'll have to go to press with her story shortly, but I need you to fill in more of the details. Please call as soon as you get this message."

Chapter 40

"From this moment forward, this is an FBI case. Hold the bodies for the Phoenix Medical Examiner, no other facility. Got it?" Snelling walked to the door, looked at me, then at Chandler. I nodded; I'd been expecting it.

Chandler stared at the empty door for a second. "Arrogant sonofabitch."

"He didn't say anything about the items recovered from the bodies and car. I'm signing out the broken Garmin. I'll take responsibility for maintaining the chain of evidence."

"You know he's going to be pissed when he finds out about this." Chandler picked up the evidence bag and set it on her desk. She wrote the Garmin's description, model number, and serial number on a chain of evidence receipt before offering it for my signature.

"Snelling thinks it's destroyed, so I doubt he'll miss it and the evidence techs he's sending don't know it exists. I have a hunch there may still be interesting location data on the memory chip. If I can find the right resource, we may be able to recover data from it and have it back before the FBI knows it's gone."

"Good luck. It looks like it's a total loss."

* * *

I gave a good impression of listening to El on the drive back to Flagstaff, but in fact, I was thinking about the Garmin and what information it might have. I figured the best bet was taking it to the electronics guy at the Flagstaff PD. If any location data survived, it might lead me to Tsosie's associates.

"Earth to Doug, come in, Doug." El's voice filtered through my concentration.

"Sorry, guys, I was thinking about something that can help with this mess."

I dropped El and Todd at my townhouse. Minutes later, I handed the evidence bag with the broken Garmin GPS to Bernie Kaiser.

"This thing is a mess." Bernie turned it around in his hands. He took a penknife out of his desk and slit open the evidence bag. He pried the back off, exposing the electronics inside. "The LCD screen is shot and most of the boards inside are cracked or broken."

"There's no hope of recovering any information?"

Bernie smiled. "I didn't say that." He picked up his phone and made a cryptic call. When he hung up he put the evidence bag with the Garmin into the pocket of his polyester suitcoat and led me to the back door.

"Where are we going?"

"I've got a buddy at the University who's an electronics genius. He's helped me pull data from erased hard drives and programmable controllers. He's pulled GPS software off the internet and used it on a car's computer to tell me where the car had been in the previous twenty-four hours. With a bit of luck, he might be able to recover at least part of the memory on this thing."

Bernie's friend had an office buried in the computer science building on the University of Northern Arizona campus. UNA was much smaller than I'd expected and was quiet except for a few students walking near the library. We found a street parking spot nearly in front of the entrance. Bernie put a "police vehicle" placard on the dashboard, then led me through the maze of twisting hallways. Finally, at the bottom of a long staircase we reached Herman Price's cluttered office.

Herman wasn't tall, but he was huge, with a roll of fat hanging over the arms of his desk chair. He was seated precariously on a chair that looked like it might collapse under the stress of his weight. The office countertops were littered with electronic devices. Most had flashing green LEDs showing they were working on something. Alongside his desk was a large wastebasket overflowing with pizza boxes. I briefly wondered what time span the collection of boxes represented. If his garbage was emptied daily . . . no, there were too many. The pile had to represent at least a weekly accumulation, and even that meant Herman was packing away a lot of pizza.

"Herman, meet my new best friend, Doug Fletcher."

Herman's stood to shake my hand. His hand was hot, sweaty, and soft as a pillow. His plaid cotton shirt was wrinkled and sweat beaded his forehead despite the chilly temperature in the basement lab. He retook his seat, causing the chair to squeak in protest of his weight. He pulled a yellowing towel from a nook in his desk and mopped his forehead.

"Let me see this broken Garmin." Social intercourse wasn't one of Herman's strengths.

Bernie pulled the device from his jacket and handed it to him. Herman took it out of the evidence bag and turned it around, then end for end.

"Phew! Someone did a number on this thing. Did it get run over or what?"

"Actually," I said, "It went over the rim of the Grand Canyon with a guy who may have been raiding antiquities from the Rez."

"No way!"

"Really."

Herman wasn't interested in any details. He opened a desk drawer full of cables and wires that looked like spaghetti noodles. After pulling a few free from the others he selected a cable with small rectangular plugs on each end. He plugged one end into a small port on a broken edge of the Garmin and the other went into the back of his desktop computer. He made a few keystrokes and the device chirped.

"It's not totally dead," Hermann said. Then the computer screen flashed, "NO DATA."

Herman dove back into the drawer and pulled out a few more wires, ones with small alligator clips. After removing the Garmin's back panel and working for three or four minutes, he set it on the desk and typed in a new computer command, then wiped his brow again.

"It would've been almost too easy if we could've just plugged into the cable and pulled the waypoints." Herman entered a dozen keystrokes. Within seconds, short strings of letters and numbers started scrolling down the computer screen.

"What are we looking at?" I tried not to sound as totally ignorant as I was.

Herman wiped his forehead again and pointed to the screen. "Each set of numbers represents a specific geographical location. They were likely entered as waypoints; locations the owner saved for future reference. A year ago I helped the Game and Wildlife folks locate a hunter who was missing after a blizzard. I pulled the waypoints off the Garmin he'd forgotten to take along on his hunt. They found him huddled up in a snow house right where he'd set a waypoint for his hunting camp."

The numbers stopped loading and Herman sent them to a printer. As the printer whirred along on its task, he plugged a memory stick into the computer USB port and typed a little more. A second later he handed the printout to me.

"Here you go. Get yourself another Garmin and you can load all the waypoints onto it." He handed me a small black stick. "The thumb drive is your backup. Keep in mind this may all be trash."

Herman pulled all the wires from the Garmin and slipped it into a silvery bag, then into the plastic evidence bag. "I assume you want to retain the GPS in case you need it for court." He handed me the bag. "That silver anti-static bag will protect the electronics much better than the evidence bag alone."

"Thanks." I took the bag. "One more thing. Can you can tell me where these waypoints are located?"

"Sure. Give me a second to pull up a geological survey map."

Within a minute the computer screen displayed a topographical map of Arizona. After a few keystrokes, small red dots started to show up at apparently random locations across the map. It took nearly three minutes for all the points to display and when the computer was done, the map looked like a shotgun had made a pattern centered on the Navajo Reservation then spread out onto Park Service land.

"It looks like the owner spent a lot of time on the Rez." Herman made a rough outline of the reservation with his finger. "Then there are a couple others. One here in Flag and another in Paradise Valley. I assume one of those is the owner's house." Hermann pointed to Paradise Valley. "That's usually the first waypoint anyone enters when they get a new Garmin."

"Is there a way to know if any of these waypoints have archaeological significance?" I asked.

Herman considered the question for a minute, then dialed the phone on his desk. He put it on speakerphone and waited. A male voice said, "This is Alex."

"Hey, Alex. This is Herman. I've got a Garmin with a bunch of GPS waypoints. I've put them on a topo map, but I want to see if they're sites that might have been raided by guys looking for antiquities."

"I'm afraid I'm not going to be much help. I've got file cabinets full of maps for the locations we know about, but the department's never had the money to digitize them. Back in the '70s a grad student put a lot of it on microfilm, but that's not searchable either. Sorry."

"Alex, this is Doug Fletcher. I'm a Park Service Ranger investigating the theft of antiquities on the National Monuments and the Navajo Reservation. Do you have a physical map marking the sites?"

"Sure, but it's not digital." I heard his chair creak. "I'm looking at a map on the wall. It's got pushpins at all the sites we know about. The yellow pins are sites identified before 1962. The blue pins are sites that were identified after 1962 and put on microfilm, and the red pins are on sites the university has excavated. It's all here, but I don't know how you can correlate it with GPS coordinates."

Herman leaned toward the speaker. "Alex, can you take a digital picture of the map and attach it to an email? I'll download the picture and overlay it on the topographic map."

"I hate to be a killjoy, but the pushpins are approximations of the locations. When you look at the map, each pushpin represents like ten acres."

"That's okay," Bernie said. "If we even get close to matching the coordinates with your pushpins, we've got a winner."

"I'll have the picture attached to an email in a couple minutes."

Herman disconnected and leaned back. "I'll be amazed if this works. If it does, it's going to look like an amateur effort."

I looked at the stack of pizza boxes in Herman's wastebasket. "I really appreciate your help. Can I buy you a pizza as thanks?"

Herman pulled a magnet off a file cabinet and handed it to me. "Tell them to deliver a 'Herman Special.' They'll know what it is and where to deliver it."

I dialed the number for the Pizza Plaza on my cell. The phone was answered on the second ring. "I want a Herman Special delivered. Here's my Visa card number . . ."

"It'll be there in fifteen minutes."

I handed the magnet back to Herman. "What's on a Herman special?"

"You don't want to know."

"I just paid for one. I probably should know when I put it on my expense account."

Herman gave me a you asked for it look. "It has pepperoni, sauerkraut, and anchovies. They deliver it with a liter of Coke."

He was right—I didn't want to know. My stomach churned at the thought of combining sauerkraut and anchovies.

Herman's email chimed. Within seconds he pulled open the picture from Alex and was resizing it to match the scale of the electronic geological survey map. It took a few minutes to get the size and angles to match. When that was done, he reloaded the waypoint file. Almost every waypoint fell on top of a pushpin."

Bernie was smiling. "Bingo!"

"Can you print that for me?" I asked.

"Of course!" Herman punched a few keystrokes and I heard a printer start clattering behind a row of shelving. "The Civil Engineering Department bought a large format printer for blueprints. They had nowhere to put it and no one to babysit it, so I acquired it with the agreement I could use it anytime I needed a big layout of something."

I looked at the map on the computer and mentally noted the waypoints in Flagstaff and the Paradise Valley that didn't correlate with the antiquities sites. They were in residential areas, probably the owner's house and another place the owner wanted to remember.

The printer stopped and Herman hoisted himself from the chair, then slipped behind the shelving. He returned with a map, roughly twenty-four by thirty-six inches. He rolled it into a tube and handed it to me. Bernie beamed.

We were shaking hands to leave when the laboratory door opened and the aroma of hot pizza sauce and anchovies wafted into the lab before the teenage deliveryman entered. Herman took delivery and I handed the guy a five-dollar tip.

"Do you want to try a piece?" Herman opened the pizza box.

"I'll pass," I said. "Sauerkraut/anchovy pizza is not on my diet."

Bernie put his hands up. "The doctor told me to limit my salt intake and I haven't had an anchovy since."

"Had you eaten anchovies before?" I asked.

"Not on purpose."

Herman shrugged. He was jamming the second piece into his mouth as we walked out.

Chapter 41

It was nearly eleven that night by the time I got back to the townhouse. El and Todd were still up. El was sorting her purchases and Todd was carefully packing them into a new suitcase they'd purchased.

"There's leftover Waldorf salad in the refrigerator," El offered.

"I haven't eaten anything since our picnic at the Grand Canyon, so I'm happy with whatever I don't have to fix myself." I found the storage container buried behind bottles of Aquafina water. I took a bottle of water, the salad, and a fork to the living room. I munched on the apple, walnut, grape, and celery concoction while watching El *ooh* and *aah* over every item she rewrapped.

"You catch any bad guys this evening?" Todd tucked another bubble-wrapped package into the suitcase.

"Not really," I said with my mouth full of salad. "We did get a lead on possible places to check out, though."

It hit me suddenly that El and Todd were packing for their departure. I'd been a terrible host most of the time they'd been visiting. "You guys aren't flying back tomorrow, are you?"

Todd shook his head. "We have a couple more days here, but I've declared a moratorium on shopping and we decided it would be good to get all the purchases packaged up before the last minute."

"Yeah," El added. "There might be room for just one more tiny thing once we see how full the carry-on bags are." She flashed a sly smile.

I rinsed my bowl in the sink and went into the bedroom to call Jill Rickowski. I spent half an hour giving her all the details of our busy day at the Grand Canyon and the UNA computer lab. I warned her about the possible flak we were going to get from the FBI when they found out I'd taken the Garmin. She had a few questions, then ended the conversation with a reminder to keep the safety of park visitors paramount in my mind at all times. I said I'd check out the waypoints on the reservation with the Navajo Nation Police. Finally, I told her I still had visitors and planned to spend some time with them before they left, hopefully without a dead body.

Then I located Jamie Ballard's phone number in my wallet and called him, expecting to leave a message. My watch said it was just past midnight.

"This is Jamie," the sleepy voice said.

"I'm really sorry to wake you. This is Doug and I need your help with my murder investigation again."

"Hi, Doug. I was kinda wondering if I'd hear from you again. What's up?"

I updated him about the Grand Canyon chase and the Reservation waypoints recovered from the Garmin. "I was hoping you could find some time where we could check out the GPS locations. A lot of them look like they might be associated with ruins, and I was hoping together we might be able to get a better picture of what Tommie Tsosie was into."

"Sounds good. I had to deliver a prisoner to Flagstaff this afternoon, so I'm in a motel just down the road from you. I can pick you up tomorrow morning at sunrise and we can make a run out to the reservation."

Damn. It would be tomorrow. There goes my day with Todd and El. Just like when I was a St. Paul cop, the job won over family. "I'll let my cousins know that I'll be tied up in the morning.

"I'll swing past your place around six."

El and Todd had the new travel bag zipped shut and stowed in the corner. They were picking up the receipts and shopping bags littering the living room floor. "I've got to beg out of guiding you guys around tomorrow morning," I said. "A cop from the Navajo Nation Police is picking me up. We're going to checkout some things on the Reservation."

"No problem." El said. "We assumed you were going to be busy so we booked a Jeep tour outside of Sedona for the day."

"I really feel bad about dumping you again."

"Don't feel bad, Doug. When El and I are on vacation we entertain ourselves. We've certainly enjoyed having time with you, and we really appreciate the great accommodations you're providing, but we really don't need you to babysit us."

"Really?"

"Absolutely! Dump your guilt. Have a good day on the Reservation and we'll see you for supper." Then she frowned. "Damn. I forgot to tell you there's a message from *The Santa Fe Journal* on your voicemail. I replayed it by accident."

I pulled my cellphone off the charger and saw I'd missed three messages while I'd been running around the Grand Canyon and Flagstaff with a dead battery. Feeling sheepish for not checking sooner, I dialed my home voicemail and listened to Sarah Hawkins introduce herself. She left her office and cellphone numbers and asked me to call her as soon as I could. The messages on my cellphone were much the same. I could hear the rising frustration and urgency in each successive message. I dialed her office number and left an apologetic voicemail and promised I'd call her back in the morning. I looked at my watch and realized it was nearly one in the morning and far too late to call Sarah Hawkins' cellphone. And Jamie Ballard was picking me up in a very few hours.

Chapter 42

The buzzing alarm clock intruded rudely into my restless sleep. I pushed the alarm switch off and rubbed my eyes. It felt like I'd only been in bed a few minutes. My stubble beard resisted the dull razor. I went to the drawer for a new blade but there weren't any. Between my rush to prepare for Jamie's arrival and the dull razor blade, I ended up with some nasty razor burns. I paid for it when I splashed aftershave on the raw skin.

I set up the coffeepot with a double-strength batch of "Fog Breaker" blend and hit the shower. I let hot water pound on my shoulders until the knotted muscles started to relax. I could smell the coffee as I dried myself. I chose a pair of slightly wrinkled khaki slacks and a plaid cotton shirt, then remembered I was supposed to order a dress uniform. I set that thought aside. I probably wouldn't have a job with the Park Service anyway once the investigation was through after all the waves I'd created. Hell, I'd broken Rule Number One: Make sure the tourists don't get hurt. Three people died yesterday and many more were endangered. Their deaths weren't directly related to my actions, but a lawyer could argue that if I hadn't initiated the chase, they'd still be alive. On the other hand, they were murderers, so I didn't feel too bad. I pulled up the Arrowhead store on my computer and selected the uniform. I reluctantly hovered the cursor over the Smokey Bear hat a second before selecting it, then I chose next day delivery, and checked out.

El wandered into the kitchen as I set my cereal bowl into the sink. She yawned, leaning against the door frame as she watched me search the cupboards for the stainless-steel Thermos. It was one of the few things I got in the divorce settlement but only because my ex-wife didn't remember it. I found it under the kitchen sink nestled behind the drain trap. I dusted it off, rinsed it with hot water, then filled it with coffee. I poured a mug of coffee and handed it to El.

"You're a peach of a guy." El slid onto one of the stools at the breakfast bar.

"I'll bet you say that to all the guys who make you coffee at six in the morning."

"That list would be very short."

"I'm on quite a few lists." I chuckled. "But most of them aren't for being a peach of a guy."

"I know you feel bad about leaving us on our own." El took my hands in hers. "But please let yourself off the hook. We're independent, and to be truthful, when you invited us to Flagstaff, we were worried about imposing by staying with you. Like we said last night, it's been great to visit with you, but we enjoy doing a lot of our own exploring. You've given us some great ideas about things to see, and that's really all we needed to make this a fabulous vacation. We'll certainly never forget out trip to the Grand Canyon." She smiled.

I stepped around the end of the breakfast bar and gave her a hug. I don't know if it was her reassurance, the lack of sleep, or the stress of the previous day, but my eyes filled with tears.

"You have no idea how much your visit has meant to me," I said. "I sorta stepped away from the family when I moved and you guys are the first Minnesotans who've made an effort to reopen that door." I fought to control my emotions. "And with that, I think I hear my ride in the parking lot."

I met Jamie at the door with the Thermos and two Styrofoam cups. "Wow. You're right on time."

He smiled, looked over my shoulder, and gave a polite nod to El. "It's easier to keep white-man's time when I'm not chasing back roads all over northern Arizona."

We climbed into the Suburban and drove toward the rising sun.

"Is she the cousin you were talking about?" Jamie asked.

"Yup. She got up early to see me off."

"She's kind of cute, in a skinny sort of way."

"Careful, she's a relative and she's married," I said jokingly.

"No problem. I'm not hitting on her, just making conversation. Not much family resemblance in either weight or looks."

"Are you saying I'm not cute?"

"Well, yes, I guess that's what I'm saying."

I was pleased we'd broken the intercultural ice, and I was also pleased he'd become a little more talkative. The day would go faster and be far less painful than our first day together.

"I need to stop at a sporting goods store to buy a GPS. The computer geek gave me a memory stick to load, but I don't have the hardware."

"In the glove box." Jamie pointed to the right side of the dashboard. "I don't use it much because most of the Rez is already familiar to me, but I keep it around just in case. I hope the batteries aren't dead."

I pushed the power button and waited for the display to light up. It slowly lit up the number of satellites it was using to locate us. After it locked onto the signal from four satellites a numerical code displayed our location and the elevation. I examined the GPS case looking for a port to accept the memory stick.

"There's a protective cover on one end. Pull open the flap and you'll see the ports."

I flipped open the cover and inserted the memory stick into a USB port. The display asked if I wanted to store waypoints. I selected yes, then waited while the screen flashed through a bunch of data. When it was through, I removed the memory stick and stared at the screen.

"Now what?" I asked.

Jamie turned the Suburban onto an exit ramp, stopping at the top with the four-way flashers on. I handed him the GPS and watched him flash through screens more rapidly than I could follow.

"Okay. There are about a dozen points on this part of the reservation. We can go to the one that's closest, or we can go to the one that was entered last. I vote for the most recent entry. There might be more signs of what they've been up to there."

"I can buy that. How far away is it?"

"Eighteen miles as the crow flies. It's probably a little less than an hour away when we snake around the terrain."

We covered many times eighteen miles of deteriorating, narrowing roads until the trail came to an end. Jamie turned off the engine and pulled a pair of binoculars from the console.

"The GPS says we're about two hundred yards from the last waypoint." He looked through the binoculars and scanned the horizon. "I don't see anything." He handed the binoculars to me.

He poured two cups of coffee while I took a turn scanning the ground from horizon to horizon. "I don't see anything either."

Jamie settled into his seat and sipped the strong coffee. "Whew! Who brewed this?"

I took a swallow and agreed it was on the strong side of dark. "I needed an eye opener this morning."

"Eye opener, hell! Aren't you afraid of chipping a tooth?" In spite of his complaints, he eventually drank the whole cup.

Jamie started the engine and shifted the Suburban into four-wheel drive. "Let's see what's out there." We lurched ahead over the uneven ground.

Ten minutes later, Jamie stopped and pointed straight ahead. "Look. There. It looks like the ground has been disturbed. At least, it doesn't look like it's been evenly eroded."

I looked where he pointed, but the ground looked the same to me. He pulled ahead another fifty yards and parked.

I followed him to the back of the Suburban where he handed me a shovel and took out water bottles. We walked to the spot he'd indicated and stopped where a row of flat rocks barely protruded from the dirt.

"Doug, my friend, you are staring at an ancient dwelling. The stone wall represents one side of a building and the area to the left looks like someone has disturbed the dirt. I think your waypoints are from a grave robber's GPS."

Jamie took the shovel and dug at the disturbed earth. After about a dozen shovels of dirt had been moved I heard the distinctive sound of the shovel hitting wood.

"I thought these old settlements were made entirely of stone," I said, as Jamie opened his hole further to the sides.

"I don't know that they were all stone, but wood isn't very plentiful around here. What wood they did use is long gone. This isn't ancient wood. I'm scraping at a piece of plywood."

I helped Jamie pry up the half sheet of plywood, exposing a hole nearly three feet in diameter and about four feet deep. Jamie dropped into the hole and soon emerged with something in his hand.

"Pottery shards." He handed a thumbnail sized piece of pottery to me. On one surface, I could barely make out the faint color.

"So, the owner of the GPS was digging up pottery shards on the reservation, and probably selling them on the internet?" As soon as I'd said the words, Joe Reber's name came to mind. "Or, they're selling them to dealers."

Jamie climbed out of the hole, opened a water bottle, and took a drink. "The pottery shards aren't worth a whole lot but burial sites have animal carvings, jewelry, and arrowheads. If you work a lot of sites over a period of years you probably come across some museum pieces that can pull down a hefty price on the private collectors' market."

"We found waypoints for dozens of sites. How long would it take someone to work that many sites?"

"It depends." Jamie shrugged. "Real archeologists would spend a year or more excavating one site to this depth. They'd use trowels and paintbrushes to gently remove the layers of dirt, In the process they'd catalogue each bead, arrowhead, bone, and pottery shard. But two or three grave robbers might be able to dig up a site like this in a few days—they'd just throw the dirt on a screen to separate the antiquities and wouldn't take the time to record any of the archeological information." Jamie paused, and cocked his head in thought. "Those waypoints are time stamped as they're accessed."

I handed Jamie the Garmin. "You know what you're doing."

"It looks like the oldest waypoint was entered about eighteen months ago." He moved quickly through displays. "If the guys who owned this were really grave robbers, they were only working each site for a week or two."

"I should call my friend at the FBI," I said. "They tend to get hostile when they feel they're not fully aware of our progress on their cases."

"So far, we're looking for grave robbers. They're a Navajo Nation Police issue." Jamie said. "Besides, the guy who owned the GPS is dead, right?"

"The guy who owned the GPS is probably dead, but there's still a bunch of other crimes and criminals involved. I don't know which case the FBI will think this is." I shrugged. My cellphone had no service bars. "Can you get cellphone coverage from here?"

"Cellphone coverage is spotty out here. Let's close this hole and look at another recent waypoint before you call anyone. I don't want to be accused of calling wolf based on one piece of information."

We moved the plywood back into place and put some rocks and soil on top to secure it. Jamie pulled up a new waypoint on the GPS and we rumbled back to the road. We'd traveled about twelve miles when he pulled onto what appeared to be a goat trail leading off a minor road.

"The GPS says that way." He pointed down a narrow trail.

We bumped and ground down the goat track for what seemed like miles before Jamie stopped abruptly on the crest of a hill. He pulled the binoculars out of the console and stared into the sky. I looked high above the horizon in his direction of sight but only saw a few black specks moving slowly through the cloudless sky.

"That's bad." He handed me the binoculars.

"What?" I asked. The specks became soaring birds through the binocular magnification.

"Buzzards." He put the Suburban into gear and eased ahead.

The half-dozen buzzards hopping around on the ground made the next site easy to spot. They watched us closely as we approached, then flew away when we got within thirty yards.

The ground seemed as undisturbed to my eyes as the previous site. I carried the shovel while Jamie walked toward a sunken spot next to a sand hill. As I got closer the distinctive smell of rotting flesh was horrendous. I saw a small funnel-shaped hole in the dirt where the buzzards had been dancing. Jamie stopped a few yards away and stared. I wondered if he was queasy or if he was just uneasy about approaching whatever was rotting in that hole.

"The smell might be a deer carcass or something like that," I suggested.

"Nope. There's a certain odor to rotting human remains."

I stepped ahead with the shovel and walked to the spot the buzzards had opened at the end of an exposed sheet of plywood. The stench was awful. I dug a few shovels of earth away from the plywood edge and some soil spilled into the darkness, releasing a cloud of foul-smelling air. It took my breath away, forcing me to step back. I heard Jamie retching.

We worked at the hole for a few minutes each until the opening was large enough to shine a flashlight into the darkness. We saw a jumble of different colored clothing and a few patches of what looked like black, rotting skin.

"I think there's more than one body in that hole," I said. We stepped back to catch our breath. "I think we should leave it alone and get the FBI on the phone."

"Yeah, I suppose we'll have to call them now," Jamie said as I moved some rocks over the hole to secure it from scavengers.

Jamie drove until we were high enough to catch one service bar on the cell. I called Snelling's direct number and was surprised when he picked the phone up after two rings.

"Special Agent Snelling, how may I help you?"

"This is Doug Fletcher. I have a serious complication to the Walnut Canyon investigation."

"Fletcher? You're breaking up badly. Can you get to a landline?"

"I'll call you in half an hour from a landline. In the meantime, line up a helicopter and a crime scene team."

"It sounded like you said helicopter. Please repeat."

"Yes, get a helicopter." I almost shouted. "And get it prepped for a flight to Shiprock."

"This had better be good."

"Trust me, this justifies a helicopter."

Jamie called his Shiprock office and advised his boss we'd uncovered a murder scene and called the FBI.

"Now what?" he asked.

"Take me to a landline so I can confirm the need for a helicopter with the FBI."

The nearest hard-wired phone was at the Only Breakfast and Lunch Restaurant. It was the lunch rush hour and all the tables were occupied. All five of the tables were too close to the ancient pay phone for anyone to have a private conversation. I hadn't seen a pay phone in years and had no guess what it would cost to call Phoenix. I dialed "0" and was relieved to hear an electronic operator's voice. I entered Snelling's direct number and went through prompts to place a person-to-person collect call. I was pleasantly surprised when Snelling accepted the charges.

"Why do you need a helicopter?" He sounded annoyed.

"Dead bodies. Plural. I checked out the Garmin GPS from the Grand Canyon accident evidence. I've been working with the Navajo Nation Police to identify the waypoints logged into the memory. It seems that we've got a series of crime scenes."

"The GPS was broken."

"My sheriff's department contact found a computer geek at the University who recovered the waypoints stored in the memory."

"You used a civilian to access equipment recovered from a crime scene?" Snelling asked, incredulous.

"I used a trusted police resource when you seemed to take no interest in the electronics. We found multiple crime scenes."

"What kind of crime scenes?"

Every eye in the restaurant was turned to me and all restaurant conversation had ceased. "Hang on, I'm on a pay phone in a restaurant." I addressed the populace. "Okay, this is a private conversation. Go on with your business."

As the conversations restarted I cupped my hand over the receiver, and turned my back to the crowd. "We found several dead bodies buried in the hole on the Navajo Reservation. We left the scene intact for your crime scene people."

"How many is several dead people?"

"I couldn't tell. They're dumped in a hole deep enough to hold half a dozen or more. With the small opening it was impossible to do much other than identify that fresh human remains were there."

"This is on the reservation?"

"Definitely. We also have more than another dozen waypoints from the GPS we haven't checked out. Officer Jamie Ballard, of the Navajo Nation Police, is with me and he's advised his superiors."

"I've requested a helicopter. With this additional information we should be able to put a bird in the air within an hour. Where should we meet you?"

I read the GPS coordinates to him and waited until he read them back to me.

"Snelling, aside from the archaeological sites on the reservation, there are a couple other waypoints that need to be checked out, too. One is in Flagstaff and the other in Paradise Valley. I suspect they belong to Tom Tsosie and the dead passenger with the phony ID." I read the other two coordinates to him, not telling him that Bernie was also checking the two city locations.

After finishing my conversation with Snelling, I walked out of the restaurant and saw I had one bar of service. I called Jill Rickowski, hoping one bar of service would be sufficient for a conversation. Her phone rolled over to voicemail and I paced as I tried to leave a concise message. My phone beeped before I finished, indicating that the call had been cut off. I looked and my one bar of service had become "No service." I walked around the parking lot and listened to the phone beep as the service was connected, then was lost, depending on my location and the direction I was facing.

I realized breakfast had been almost six hours ago and my stomach was growling. I was about to put the phone in my pocket when it beeped again, then buzzed. I assumed Jill had received my message and was calling back.

"Doug Fletcher, you're a hard man to catch." The female voice was unfamiliar and I started to pull the phone away from my ear to check the caller I.D. before I realized that might disconnect the call.

"Who's looking for me?"

"This is Sarah Hawkins, from *The Santa Fe Journal*. Do you have a moment to talk?"

"I have a few seconds, but not much more than that. I assume you've spoken with Margaret Adams."

"Do you know she's in a Maine hospital? Someone tried to kill her."

I closed my eyes and tipped my head back. "How's she doing?"

"She's injured but will survive. We discussed the taped conversations and she said I needed to talk to you. I've been leaving messages at every number I can find, but you've been elusive."

"Things were a little tense yesterday."

"I read the AP article about a fatal incident at the Grand Canyon. It mentioned your name."

"Yeah," I said, letting out a deep breath. "That was part of it. Then I got involved in some follow up. By the time I got home my cellphone was dead and it was too late to call the personal number you left for me."

"Just for the record, it's never too late to call me, especially if I've been leaving urgent messages. I'm working on an article for tomorrow and I want to get your take on Steve Potter's death and what was on the tapes."

"Sarah, is that your name?"

"Yes. Sarah Hawkins."

"Things are happening, and this story will be much bigger in a few hours. Can we talk this evening?"

"Ranger Fletcher, I'm on a deadline for the morning edition of the newspaper. Waiting for your comments until this evening may push this story out another day. Unless you can promise you'll call back early this evening with something that's worth the wait, I'd prefer to get a quick comment from you now to verify information I've gleaned from other sources."

"There's another whole angle to this story that's breaking right now. The FBI has a helicopter on the way, and it's likely I'll have much more information in a few hours."

"The FBI doesn't fly helicopters to crime scenes."

"Not unless there's something really big going on."

"Can you expand on that?"

"Not until tonight. I promise I'll call as soon as I know the rest of the story."

Chapter 43

An hour later, with food in our bellies, Jamie and I watched the buzzards soar lazy circles overhead. They started flapping their wings and flew random directions away from the site where we'd uncovered the bodies and seconds later we heard the thumping of helicopter rotors and the whine of the jet turbine.

Jamie got out of the SUV and gestured the chopper toward a flat area well away from the hole of death, as he had named it. Before the rotors stopped spinning, three men were out of the helicopter, duckwalking toward the Suburban. I recognized Snelling's spit-shined shoes. The other two men were dressed in coveralls and carried black flight bags. The pilot hung back, shutting down the rotating blades.

"Where are the bodies?" Snelling paused, still standing in the swirling sand caused by the slowing helicopter rotors.

"This way!" Jamie took the lead.

The helicopter wash had temporarily blown the smell away. Once the rotors stopped the smell permeated the air once again. Snelling, who hadn't flinched at the Dumpster smell at the Grand Canyon, flinched now. His two associates seemed less affected by it. One of

Snelling's men stood at the edge of the hole with a video camera and started filming the whole site. The second man pulled on a white Tyvek suit, black rubber boots, and full-face respirator. The videographer set the camera down and donned his Tyvek suit while his partner carefully enlarged the hole.

While the crime scene technicians continued their work, Snelling walked over to Jamie's Suburban and I introduced them. "Tell me about the GPS."

I told him about Bernie Kaiser and visiting Herman at the UNA computer lab. I gestured toward the plywood-covered hole. "And the buzzards led us here."

"I don't suppose it ever occurred to you that you removed evidence from an FBI investigation and we might not appreciate it?"

"When you left the GPS at the Grand Canyon, it appeared you were done with it. I'm a Park Service Investigator, and I felt it might relate to a crime in my jurisdiction, I decided I could go on where you'd left off."

Snelling's eyes narrowed. "I don't like park rangers stepping on my toes."

"I don't like FBI agents who close investigations that aren't complete."

"Wow, I can't tell you how refreshing it is to have the FBI as a partner in a Navajo Nation Police investigation." Jamie said sarcastically. "Doug called me and said he had some suspicious sites he wanted to investigate. Since the sites are on the reservation, it seemed entirely reasonable to me and my superiors that we take the lead in the investigation. We usually don't call the FBI in unless we've found evidence of a capital offense and it initially appeared we were investigating grave robbers."

Snelling glared at Jamie. "If you two have screwed this up in any way, heads will roll."

"Were you able to locate the other waypoints I gave you over the phone?" I asked.

"We're checking on them." Snelling didn't look like he wasn't being entirely candid.

"And what are they?"

"Urban Flagstaff and Paradise Valley."

"I already knew the general location. I was hoping you might be able to expand on their possible significance."

"The Flagstaff location appears to be Tom Tsosie's apartment." Sharing information made Snelling look like he had a stomach ache.

"Who owns the Paradise Valley house?" I asked.

"The title is cloudy. We've got it under surveillance and we've got local cops checking on the ownership."

"You don't want to share any more, do you?" I asked.

"Not really. It's all out of your jurisdiction. You don't have the need to know."

"Another great example of interagency cooperation," I said to Jamie.

Snelling shook his head and returned to the crime scene. One of the technicians was lowering himself into the hole.

I heard the clatter of car parts dragging on rocks. A dusty Crown Victoria came bouncing toward us.

"That's the lieutenant," Jamie said.

A tall man with a silver bar on each collar point approached us. He was gaunt and his face was creased with lines. He offered his hand to me.

"You must be Fletcher, the park ranger." His smile accentuated the weathered lines in his face. "I'm Ray Horn."

"Lieutenant Horn," I said, "the good news is we have reinforcements from the FBI. The bad news is we have reinforcements from the FBI."

Ray smiled. "You've worked with the FBI before, I see."

We brought Horn up to speed on the series of crimes since Potter's death while Special Agent Snelling ignored us. We watched the two technicians carefully lift body bags from the hole and set them in a row on the ground. When the second technician climbed from the hole he stripped off purple gloves and stepped over to Snelling, who was holding a handkerchief over his nose and mouth.

Snelling acknowledged Ray Horn with a nod and introduced FBI Senior Crime Scene Analyst Hank Pike.

"There were two badly decomposing bodies in the hole," Pike reported. "Based on a quick look, I'd say they've been dead at least a couple of days, but no more than a week. Both are adult males and both were wearing striped work shirts with name patches."

Jamie spoke before I could. "It could be the tow-truck drivers who were trying to salvage the Lincoln. They were picked up from the Shiprock jail two days ago by two guys with Flagstaff PD badges."

"We have their mugshots and fingerprints at the office," Ray Horn said. "I'm not sure we have their real names, but at least we can verify they're the same characters."

Snelling looked unhappy. "So we have two dead bodies of men who may have been caught trying to salvage a stolen vehicle used in the assault of a Park Service Ranger."

"It doesn't appear we have anything more than questions," Horn said. "Before we let the helicopter go, I'd like to use it to look at a few of the other GPS locations on Jamie's Garmin."

"Sure. I'll leave the crime scene guys here to finish collecting evidence. The rest of us will fit in the helicopter."

Jamie sat in the front with the pilot so they could use the GPS to navigate to the next waypoint. We hadn't been in the air three minutes when Jamie pointed to the horizon. At first I couldn't see any significant topographic landmark. "Buzzards. At least a dozen."

"Please tell me there's a dead cow lying down there." Snelling's voice came over the intercom.

"Looks more like a hole," the pilot replied.

Chapter 44

I spotted a coyote partially hidden behind a bush. He skulked away through the underbrush as the helicopter hovered. Clouds of sand swirled with pieces of cloth and other debris as the helicopter hovered above the coyote's hiding spot.

The sand around the hole was littered with bones. Some small bones had bits of darkened flesh and other larger bones had white tendons attached. They fluttered like frayed strings in the helicopter's wash. A boot tucked under a prickly pear cactus caught my eye. A ragged pair of jeans was tangled in a creosote bush. There was no question these were human remains—possibly many sets of human remains.

"Don't touch anything when we get down there." Snelling retrieved a video camera stowed behind the second row of seats and was already recording the carnage below us. The pilot set the helicopter down gently several yards from the depression at the center of the carnage. No one rushed out the doors. We stepped out and solemnly appraised the ground around us.

I bent down and studied a sturdy medium-sized bone with two small knobs on one end—a tibia, I thought. It had been stripped of all tissue and small grooves showed that a carnivore had gnawed it clean. Nearby, a larger bone with a knob on one end, maybe a humerus, had been broken, apparently to get to the marrow. A hip ball, once set into a pelvis, was striated with teeth marks large and small. Jamie and Ray stood back from the hole, making notes and whispering to each other.

There was a line of stones like the ones we'd seen at the other archeological sites—likely the wall of an ancient dwelling. A half sheet of plywood, probably dislodged from the hole by scavengers and blown aside by the wind, now rested against a cactus.

I peered carefully into the open pit, hoping not to surprise any critters that might react negatively. The smell was pungent, but not as overpowering as the last hole. The flesh was now gone or desiccated by the desert and so no longer a feast for the bacteria that create the stink of rotting flesh. In the dark recesses of the hole, I could make out a skull and more exposed bones. Although my view was imperfect due to the shadows, I had the impression that at least another full set of remains still lay in the hole, in addition to those strewn outside it.

"Let's leave this for the crime scene techs. I'd like to at least fly over another two waypoints before we go back to pick up the body bags." Even Snelling was shaken. His tone of voice would have been appropriate for libraries and churches. Maybe he'd finally recognizing that Jamie and I had uncovered something bigger than the theft of pottery shards. This was something that was going to take a lot of physical work, would generate reams of paperwork, and would consume hundreds, if not thousands, of hours of analysis.

The helicopter covered ground quickly. There were no buzzards at the other three sites, but the grim reality of bone remnants strewn on the ground at each location gave silent testimony.

We flew back to the first site where the techs were finishing up their evidence collection. Snelling talked with the pilot, then took off his headset. He looked worn out when he stepped out of the helicopter. He'd shed his suit coat, pulled off his bolo tie, rolled up his shirt cuffs, and unbuttoned the top button of his shirt. For an FBI Special Agent, he was almost naked.

"This is fucking awful. How many waypoints were on the GPS?"

"I think there were thirteen correlated with known archeological sites on the reservation," I replied, "and another nine or ten on the Wupatki National Monument property."

Snelling did the math in his head. "Even if there were only a couple bodies at each site, we might be talking about dozens more bodies. You said the waypoints have all been loaded in the past eighteen months?"

"Yup. We're talking about two or more missing people a month for the past year and a half." Jamie had already done the math.

"There's no way that many ordinary, law-abiding citizens could go missing without a public outcry," Snelling said.

"Migrants or drug mules," Ray Horn said softly. "No one would report them missing and few in Arizona would know . . . or care."

Snelling motioned for the technicians to join us. "We've got to get out of here. I'll notify the Special Agent in Charge and then we'll get in touch with ICE. They may be able to supply us some leads on the identities. Figure out how to secure these sites until we can get teams out to process them." He pointed a finger at Jamie, Ray, and me. "I don't want this leaked to the media."

Snelling retreated into the helicopter. Ray Horn snorted. "Glory hound. He probably won't even mention us when he calls the news conference to announce that the FBI solved this case."

Chapter 45

Harold Mitchell arrived at Barbara Potter's house within five minutes. He didn't look like her image of a Pulitzer Prize-winning journalist. The man standing on her front step barely resembled the picture that ran alongside his bylines in the newspaper. His suit looked like he'd slept in it and the dinky, faded Mazda in her driveway could use a wash. "Mr. Mitchell, it's so nice to meet you after reading your columns for years." Barbara held the door open for him.

"I'm not here for small talk." He scowled at Barbara. *There's a trophy wife if ever I've seen one.* "I'm here to get you somewhere safe. Do you have a bag packed?"

Barbara fiddled with her necklace. "Well, no. I could throw some things together in half an hour or so."

Mitchell took her hand and led her out the front door. "It's good you haven't raised any suspicions by moping around and packing."

She grabbed her purse as he pulled her outside.

He opened the passenger door and half pushed her into the seat. "Buckle up!" He slammed the door and nearly pinched her foot.

"Hey, take it easy."

Mitchell ignored her and climbed into the driver's seat. He buckled his seat belt and started the engine.

The Mazda spewed smoke and the engine rattled as they left the driveway. Mitchell watched his mirrors to see if he was being followed and made random turns on squealing tires as he raced through several residential Phoenix neighborhoods. Convinced no one was behind him, he slowed to the speed limit. Barbara Potter sat in silence, scared out of her wits by Mitchell's insane driving.

"Well, honey," Harold checked the rearview mirror again. "Your husband's partner is quite a fellow."

Barbara didn't catch the sarcasm. "Yes. He said he's taking care of Steve's legal situation so I wouldn't need to worry about it."

"He's probably very good at it. He used to be a lawyer in Oklahoma. He was disbarred for embezzling money from his clients."

"What?" Barbara snapped her head to look at Mitchell.

"When Mahoney became *persona non-grata* in Oklahoma, he moved to Phoenix and started his Mexican import business. I suspect the IRS and Customs have been keeping a close eye on him, but they apparently haven't got enough yet to indict him."

"That's ludicrous! Steve trusted him with every aspect of their joint business."

"The term 'con man' is short for confidence man. The reason con men are so successful is because they can get the average person to trust them. Just because your husband trusted him doesn't mean he wasn't into some shady business."

"Where are we going? I don't recognize anything."

"We're going to a house the newspaper keeps for special occasions. It's in a crummy part of town, so don't plan on wandering around outside. On the other hand, no one would ever figure this place for a safe house."

The Mazda fit in well with the weathered older cars parked on the streets and in the driveways they passed. Harold slowed his car and darted into a driveway as the garage door eased open in front of them. He pulled into the garage and pushed a button to close the door before the car stopped rolling.

He squeezed his large bulk around the car in the narrow garage. "It ain't much, but it is safe. Juan will whip up anything you'd care to eat, and he's also capable of whipping out a pistol if anything's threatening." He opened a door into a narrow avocado green kitchen. From the floor to the light fixtures, the house was a refugee from the 1960's.

"I see you've been cutting back on the decorating budget." Barbara walked through the kitchen into the harvest gold living room.

A large Hispanic man wearing an ivory guayabera-style shirt over jeans emerged from a hallway and offered his hand to Barbara. "I'm Juan. Don't believe anything Harold tells you.

He's a windbag of the worst variety." His broad friendly face was deeply lined from decades of exposure to the Arizona sun. His thinning black hair was combed straight back.

Juan took Harold's hand next and clamped his left hand on Harold's shoulder. Seeing the quiet camaraderie between the two men put Barbara at ease for the first time since she'd opened the door for Mitchell.

"No wonder they never run a current picture with your byline. You have the ugliest mug in all of Phoenix." Juan grinned.

"I can go home and get insulted. I don't have to take that from you." Harold's smile was genuine.

Juan waved his hand in a dismissive gesture. "I don't insult, only tell the truth. Isn't that so, pretty lady?"

"What? You know, I still don't understand why I'm here."

"Relax." Juan gestured toward the orange couch. "You're as safe here as in Fort Knox. There are multiple deadbolts on the doors. The curtains block out the outside so no one can see in. An electronic security system monitors the surrounding area for intruders, and then there's me, who will lay down my life for you if needed."

"Why in the world do you two think I need all this security? And is that a *gun* under your shirt?"

Juan took a piece of paper from his pocket and handed it to Harold who read it slowly before giving it to Barbara. She read the columns of dates, dollar amounts, and other numbers.

"Sorry, I don't have a clue what all this means."

"Call your friend in New Mexico," Juan said. "Tell her Terry Mahoney's been importing more than antiques. That's a list of the people he's been smuggling across the border with the dates of the border crossings. It tells how many people and how much they paid him. The tragedy is that these people pay Mahoney with blood money to get across the border, but many of their relatives never heard from them again."

"What?" Barbara asked, confused by the New Mexico reference and the list.

Mitchell pulled out his phone and dialed Sarah Hawkins' cellphone number. As he filled Sarah in on Juan's research into Terry Mahoney, Barbara Potter sat listening in stunned disbelief.

Chapter 46

Sarah Hawkins called just as we were clearing the supper dishes. I excused myself and took the portable phone into the bedroom, closing the door.

"Hi, Sarah. What's up?"

"You promised to call this evening. I need a verification source for some information I've received."

"I can't comment on the record." I was unsure of how much I could trust a journalist I'd never met.

"Not a problem. All I need from you is corroboration of things I learned from other sources. Did you hear the Border Patrol stopped a van, one owned by an antiques importer? They arrested the driver and took a dozen illegal aliens into custody."

"I hadn't heard that."

"The van driver was also an illegal, told the Border Patrol agents he made weekly desert pickups and delivered them to a white guy in Flagstaff. That's not unusual except he said that the last few times he's had to wash blood out of the van before he used it for another trip. The illegal aliens were chatting up a storm in the detention facility. A Spanish-speaking agent overheard them say they'd been forced to swallow condoms full of drugs. They were taken to a hospital, where they were x-rayed. The hospital confirmed something was inside their intestines, then put them all under observation until the foreign objects pass."

Suddenly the pieces started to fit together. "You heard about the desert graves?"

"My source at ICE speculated there were probably migrants who didn't survive the trip. I think you just confirmed that."

I took a deep breath and blew it out. "Well, it is a fact that frequently drug mules don't survive the process."

"And can you tell me exactly what you mean by that?"

"When human mules are used, particularly smuggled illegals, the drugs are inside condoms they swallow. From experience I know the 'handlers' feed them laxatives to recover their shipment quickly. If the drug mules are dehydrated, the laxatives cause them to lose more fluids, which can be deadly. If the mule dies during the recovery process, the handlers use . . . surgical techniques to recover the drugs."

There was silence on the line, and then Sarah said, "Hang on a second. I'm writing the headlines of these stories on a piece of paper. So you're saying you've linked drug running, the buried bodies of the drug mules, and the illegal archaeology dig sites?" She paused again. "I'm making a second group with the phone recordings, Steve Potter's death, the attack on

Margaret Adams, and Mahoney taking over Potter's business. "Fletcher, they all look disjointed, but your name comes up in each story. Give me a quote to explain what's going on."

"I can neither confirm nor deny. Talk to your source for the illegal antiquities operation, Jamie Ballard of the Navajo Nation Police, and your contact at ICE. I think they'll connect the dots for you."

"I spoke with Harold earlier this evening. His Phoenix contacts inside the immigrant community had border crossing dates and the number of people in each group. They confirmed some of the people were forced to be drug couriers and a number of them disappeared after they got in the country. Because they're in the country illegally they don't call the cops to report being used as drug mules, nor do they report those missing."

"Can you use his information, or do you have to find someone to corroborate the story?"

"Harold's information is golden. The rest of this is incredible. I'm afraid . . . well my first hurdle will be getting the editor to believe the scope of this operation. This is huge!" I heard the excitement in her voice and I knew she was on board.

"Do you need anything more from me?"

"Hang on, my intern reminded me of an interesting internet link." I heard her keyboard clicking. "I read an unbelievable AP story about a car chase along the south rim of the Grand

Canyon that endangered a bus and several cars full of tourists before ending in a deadly crash. My Park Service contact told me they'd recovered the bodies of three tourists from a black Lincoln at the bottom of the canyon. The AP article says you were involved in the chase."

"It was a red Cadillac, and the three so-called tourists were murderers."

"Murderers?" Sarah asked as her keyboard clicked.

"Have you seen anything about the body found in a Grand Canyon Dumpster behind the west end gift shop?"

"I'll check the AP wire, but I haven't heard anything . . ."

"Sarah, hang on for one second. How many resources are at your disposal to help you flesh out this story?"

"Um, I've got a photographer who is also our electronics tech guy and an intern who's an internet and wire service whiz."

"That's it?"

"Why, is that a problem?"

"Look, if I tell you something's off the record, can I trust you?"

"Ranger Fletcher, if what you're going to tell me is off the record, you're tying one arm behind my back. My editor won't let any story go to press without at least two sources. That's Journalism 101. You've already told me I don't have enough resources, and now you want me to take you off the list of sources."

"Shit," I said, softly. "We need to come up with something that will cover my butt so I'm not fired before I can cash my first Park Service paycheck."

"How about this. You are an unnamed Federal Law Enforcement source who is not authorized to release information," she suggested.

"Unlinking me from the Park Service doesn't put me entirely out of the picture. Can you come up with some words that hint I'm with the Border Patrol or ICE?"

"I'll concoct something that leaves your name and your connection to the Park Service out of this. Spill the story and give me people to call who can corroborate your statements."

"How fast can you type?" I asked.

"Faster than you can talk."

"Okay. The truth is, the Grand Canyon story goes together with Steve Potter's murder, the drugs. the dead migrants, and the stolen antiquities. The FBI is pulling the pieces together for the US Attorney and it's about to explode. You can be ahead of the explosion with the facts, or you can follow the FBI, who will undoubtedly be calling a press conference, today or tomorrow, to announce the success of their long-term investigation into a drug smuggling and a murder-for-hire ring. If your story comes out after the FBI press conference, you're going to sound like a crackpot with a bunch of questionable information that doesn't fit the official story. On the other hand, if you can get the sources and facts lined up and publish them before the FBI puts their spin on the investigation, you can look like a genius and the FBI will be on their heels trying to explain how you knew more about the investigation than they're willing to divulge."

Sarah's keyboard clicked with the speed of a machine gun. "I called the Phoenix FBI office this morning. The switchboard rolled me over to their Public Information Officer, who politely told me they couldn't comment on an ongoing investigation."

I started with Potter going over the Walnut Canyon railing and filled in all the blanks, ending with today's discoveries of the migrant bodies. "Was that too fast?"

"Hell no. I'm working on deadline for the morning edition. I'm not quite clear on the Kokopelli connection, though."

"Call Bernie Kaiser at the Coconino County Sheriff's Department. The Kokopelli link goes back quite a few years to some high school kids who later turned into thugs. I think the guys who were killed in the Grand Canyon car crash may have been connected to that group—at least the one guy who had a fake ID. The other members of the drug smuggling ring have gone into cyberspace. There's a mystery house in Paradise Valley that showed up on the GPS from the crashed Caddy."

"Johnnie!" I heard her yell. "I need some help. Can you drop everything for a few hours?"

Johnnie's response was garbled, like he was outside a door or away from the speakerphone, but he must have answered in the affirmative because she started issuing directions. "Call Bernie Kaiser, he's a Coconino County cop in Arizona. Ask him about the Kokopelli gang and how they were related to the crime spree in Arizona. Then get it back to me."

"I've got a great resource who will be happy to be interviewed on the record. I don't know his last name. Call the Pizza Plaza in Flagstaff and pay them to deliver a "Herman special", they know the address, and have them tape your phone number to the top of the box with a big 'Urgent' written on it."

"What are you talking about?"

"A University of Northern Arizona computer geek, the one who recovered the memory of Garmin GPS device. He was able to pull the waypoints programmed into the memory. He'll be glad to talk to you for the price of that pizza." I paused to think. "When you hear back from Herman, and I promise you will, ask him about his buddy Alex from the archeology department."

"Janice! Drop what you're doing!" I heard her giving Janice instructions and Sarah came back on the line. "Okay. That'll give me a second source on the GPS locations of the archeological sites. Who can back up your story about the buried bodies?"

"That's tougher. The FBI used their own techs to work the crime scenes and took control of the bodies as soon as they were out of the ground. None of their techs is going to risk their careers by talking to you." I did know a couple of other people who didn't have a lot of love for the FBI, though. "Call the Navajo Nation Police and ask for Lieutenant Ray Horn. He's pissed about people raiding antiquities from the reservation and dumping bodies there. He's not too thrilled with the FBI, either. And the Navajo Nation Police are an entity all their own."

The keyboard continued to clatter and abruptly stopped. "This is a ton of stuff. I have to give the story to my editor before the final layout of the morning edition. From the notes I've made, it could take me days to contact all these people and pull this all together. My editor wants a story for tomorrow, but I think this might have to be serialized over a few days."

"Do that and the FBI gets their version of the story out. You'll be second guessed and probably discredited."

Sarah sighed deeply. "Do you know Harold Mitchell? He's a columnist at *The Phoenix Times*?"

"I've seen his byline a few times."

"He's my source for the migrant angle. He has Steve Potter's wife stashed safely away somewhere. To get his cooperation, I had to promise him my story before it went into print or to the wire services. I'm pretty sure I can trust him, and it would be useful to have him tap into his Arizona resources."

"That's your call. Breaking a story is your field of expertise, not mine. But be careful, you called the Phoenix FBI office, so they have your name and phone number, and they know you're stirring around at least the fringes of their case. I predict the evening before their press conference some very nice, polite, ego-inflating person, full of praise for your writing skills and past articles, will call to see how things are going. They'll hope they can schmooze you into giving them the details of your story, your sources, and when the story is going to run."

She laughed. "They can try."

Chapter 47

It was after 11 o'clock and it had been a very long day. I decided to get the grime and smell out of my pores with a hot shower. I was brushing my teeth, wearing only boxers, when my cellphone chirped.

"I think I've got it sewn up. The story will run tomorrow in *The Santa Fe Journal*, and a companion article, with my byline, will be in *The Phoenix Times*. A source told me the FBI is poised to make a raid tomorrow, which should nab some conspirators and records. The raid will be followed by a news conference tomorrow at noon. I'll be at the news conference. Look me up if you're there."

"Thanks, Sarah. I'll read your article and skip the news conference."

"You're welcome. By the way, both Margaret Adams and Barbara Potter are now under the protection of the US Marshals."

Chapter 48

Jill Rickowski sat at her kitchen table with a stack of handwritten notes, her cellphone, and her laptop computer. She'd started a letter of reprimand for Doug Fletcher's file half a dozen times and deleted each of them after a few sentences. She flinched when the phone rang.

"Rickowski."

"Ranger Rickowski, please hold for Secretary Silverman." The line quickly rolled to elevator music as Jill stared at the phone in disbelief. In her entire career she could count on one hand the number of times she'd received a call from Washington D.C. It took a second for her mind to process Silverman's name and realize she was on hold, waiting for the boss of all bosses in the Park Service chain of command, the Secretary of the Interior.

Her mind raced—the only reason the secretary would be calling so late at night was to chew her butt over Fletcher's actions at the Grand Canyon. Roxanne Chandler had already formally complained to her about Fletcher's high-speed chase along the canyon rim which, according to Chandler, had endangered hundreds of visitors and ultimately ended in the deaths of the fleeing subjects. She'd probably formalized her complaint and forwarded it up the chain of command. It was after midnight in Flagstaff and three hours later in D.C. *"No good news comes in the middle of the night.*

"Jill, I apologize for calling so late in the evening. I hope I didn't wake you."

"No, Mr. Secretary. You know the government runs on paper and I was just dealing with more of it when the phone rang."

"If you have a moment, I'd like to talk to you about Ranger Douglas Fletcher. I believe he works for you out of the Flagstaff office."

"Yes sir. I just hired him as my investigator after our unfortunate tourist death and the injury to one of my rangers at Walnut Canyon." She paused. "If this is about the incidents at the Grand Canyon today, I've already had a call from the Grand Canyon Superintendent and I'm trying to decide how best to reprimand Fletcher."

"I have some input on that. I assume you haven't seen the stories on Reuters or AP wire services. I had a call from an attorney at the Department of Justice."

Jill shrank in her chair. Now the FBI and US Attorney were after Fletcher's hide, too. If they took pity on her, maybe early retirement would be an option. But they might fire her outright and her pension would be in question. She steeled herself.

"The DOJ lawyer complained that one of the Park Service Rangers had leaked information about an ongoing FBI investigation. Somehow, AP had a story about an extensive crime syndicate. The story named Ranger Fletcher, working with the Flagstaff Police, the Coconino Sheriff's Department, and the Navajo Nation Police, as the lead investigator who cracked a syndicate terrorizing and murdering people, selling stolen Navajo antiquities, and using migrants to smuggle drugs across the border. The syndicate may have been killing the drug mules and dumping the bodies in the illegal archeological excavations." Silverman paused. "According to the Associated Press, Fletcher identified the criminals, tied them to the crimes, and was following three of them when they tried to pass a busload of tourists and ran off the south rim of the Grand Canyon. With a hand-held GPS device recovered from the wrecked car, Fletcher used Coconino County and University of Northern Arizona resources to find the sites where the antiquities were being stolen, notified the Navajo Nation Police, and together they discovered the looted reservation sites and the bodies of the drug mules."

"I hadn't heard all those details," Jill admitted. "Fletcher is very capable and very independent. He left me a voicemail this afternoon with a short version of the discovery of the bodies. They were awaiting an FBI helicopter to explore more sites. Did something come out of the helicopter search that set them on Fletcher?"

"As I said, I was in the middle of their official spin on Fletcher screwing up their investigation when my assistant raced in with the Associated Press story. I read it while their lackey rambled on about punishment and possible prosecution for leaking details about an active FBI investigation. I stopped him and had my assistant e-mail him a copy of the AP story while I waited on the phone. He huffed and puffed but said he'd get back to me. I called the Attorney General's office, tracked him down at a Dallas conference, and emailed him the same AP story. About that time, my assistant came through with essentially the same story from Reuters."

"I'm sorry sir, but it would be very out of character for Fletcher to even whisper he'd had a major role in busting up this crime ring. I'm having a hard time believing he'd leak this to the press. He's a retired St. Paul cop and he knows the rules. He's the most competent law enforcement asset I've ever had, and he never comes looking for direction. He leverages his twenty years of investigative experience and lets me know what's happening. He's effusive with his praise of the Navajo Nation Police, the county, and the Flagstaff PD. When we talk, he minimizes his role in anything that's accomplished."

"According to the news service articles, Fletcher didn't take credit for any of this. All his praise came from the secondary sources. A Navajo Nation police captain, a Coconino County deputy, and a UNA computer geek all told the reporter it was Fletcher who pulled all the pieces together. Once the evidence was bulletproof, he called his FBI contact with the details."

"I'm confused." Jill shook her head. "What do you want me to do?"

"Forget that letter of reprimand. I'll have my Information Officer draft a letter of commendation for his file. If I could, I'd give him a medal."

Jill's head snapped up. "What about the complaint from Superintendent Chandler at the Grand Canyon?"

"It's gone," Silverman said. "There is no Grand Canyon complaint. A man was murdered outside their gift shop, Fletcher identified the suspects, notified Chandler, asked for backup, and was following them discreetly until the Grand Canyon rangers could isolate their car and make an arrest. The bad guys lost control of their car going around a curve during their escape attempt and went over the rim. The actions of the suspects caused their tragic end."

"Wow! You just made my evening. Thank you, sir."

"You have one more responsibility tonight. At my suggestion, the FBI will have a helicopter at the Flagstaff airport tomorrow morning at nine o'clock to pick up Fletcher. Let him know he's going to stand next to the lead FBI agent at their noon press conference where he'll be personally thanked for his contributions to the investigation by the Phoenix FBI Special Agent in Charge."

"I hate to be negative, but Fletcher doesn't seek the limelight and will probably say no. I think he'd rather not be on the podium or be personally thanked by the FBI."

"Jill, Fletcher's the new face of the National Park Service. It'll give the public a different view of what we look like and what we do, and it will do wonders for recruitment. He doesn't have the option to say no."

"Yes, Mr. Secretary."

Chapter 49

I'd barely fallen sleep when the phone rang. "Fletcher." I tried to stifle a yawn and glanced at the alarm. It was nearly one o'clock.

"Doug, this is Jill. I just got off the phone with the Secretary of the Interior."

"You're kidding me," I sat up and dangled my legs off the side of the bed. "How deep is the shit?"

"The story about the murders, the buried bodies, and antiquities being stolen from the reservation hit the wire services. He's been talking to the Department of Justice and the Secretary has demanded the Park Service be recognized for your role in sorting the antiquities syndicate and the murders on Park Service properties. You'll be picked up by an FBI helicopter at 9 o'clock tomorrow morning at the Flagstaff airport. Wear your Park Service dress uniform and be sure to take the Smokey Bear hat. And remember, you're representing the entire National Park Service at the press conference. Look professional. Make sure your zipper is up and suck in your gut."

No good deed goes unpunished. There were few things I'd hate doing more. Standing in a ring of rattlesnakes, maybe, but even that wasn't much worse than this. "I don't think this is a good idea. I've been all over northern Arizona for two days and I'm dead tired. I have bags under my eyes, I can't suck my gut in far enough, and I'm hardly a model ranger. Why don't you go?"

"Neither you, nor I, were given an option, Doug. You're going under orders. If it's any consolation, I'm pretty sure the FBI is even more unhappy about it than you are."

Chapter 50

I stood at the edge of the Flagstaff airport, resplendent the brand-new dress uniform that FedEx delivered the day before. The Smokey Bear hat was tucked under my arm. The FBI helicopter idled behind us as I handed the Isuzu keys to Todd and El with a promise to be back in time to deliver them to the airport in the morning. A stern looking middle-aged woman, wearing a suitcoat and slacks, introduced herself as FBI Special Agent in Charge, Susan Arcand. Based on the title I assumed she was Snelling's boss, and the head of the Phoenix FBI office. We climbed into the helicopter and buckled in. She handed me a headset with a microphone, gave me a disgusted look, and never said a word. Apparently, being my official escort didn't include making small talk.

The quiet time gave me a chance to think about what to do now that the Walnut Canyon murder was solved. Did I still want to be employed by the Park Service? I'd really missed the thrill of the chase during my retirement. I hadn't realized how much. But would the Park Service want me after all the drama?

Arcand finally spoke. "The evidence team went back to the reservation yesterday and opened up another dig site. They found three more bodies. It appears they were illegal aliens."

"Were they able to identify any of them?"

"None of them had I.D. They were probably just poor drug mules smuggling meth from Mexico."

"Did they die of dehydration in the desert?" I thought that was the most likely cause of their deaths after getting dumped on the reservation without water.

"Dehydration is the preliminary finding for most of the corpses we've recovered. The medical examiner said the dehydration was exacerbated by feeding them laxatives to speed recovery of the drugs. Of course the condoms were harvested from the corpses. Agent Nash said they'd been gutted like fish. Two of the victims died of massive overdoses when the condoms broke in their gut. I'm sure the loss of those batches upset the drug runners."

"I saw some cruel things when I was a cop, but giving laxatives to a dehydrated person is right at the top of the list. I hate to think the survivors had to sit and watch their fellow travelers be cut open, too."

"This reeks of the Mexican drug cartels, of course."

"If not them, we've got local psychopaths—like the Kokopelli group?"

"Hopefully, the evidence techs will come up with something." She turned to face the window. "But there weren't any little figurines with these bodies. The buzzards and coyotes have already eaten most of the victims and then spread their bones and clothing scraps around. There isn't much evidence to examine except the skeletons of the victims and some broken condoms."

"If the bodies were scavenged, how did the medical examiner determine they died from an overdose?"

"We recovered a dead coyote and two dead buzzards at one site and had their carcasses tested. The victims were so full of meth the scavengers died from meth overdose, too."

She didn't say anything more. It wasn't like the FBI to share that type of information with anyone who didn't "need to know." I figured I'd just been fed a big piece of bait, and now they'd wait to see if any of it showed up in the newspaper.

Chapter 51

From the air, Phoenix was row after row of earth-tone roofs and circles of houses surrounding swimming pools, nestled among brown hills. An incongruous emerald golf course threaded through the barren land near the McDowell Mountains. Ahead of us, Camelback Mountain defined the north edge of the city, followed by another grid of earth-tone houses with brown rock yards dotted with Saguaro cacti and citrus trees. Occasional patches of green lawns started showing up around houses within Scottsdale.

The pilot's voice came over the headset. "I was just told to divert to Paradise Valley. Our ETA should put us on the ground a few minutes after the entry team breaches the front door." The helicopter turned and I felt acceleration push me against the seat.

"What happened to the news conference?" I asked Arcand as we sped south, passing west of downtown Phoenix to avoid the airspace around Sky Harbor Airport.

"The US Attorney was waiting for a judge to sign a search warrant for the Paradise Valley house when I left Phoenix. It looks like we're invited along for the bust. I assume they'll get us in and out with time to spare."

We dropped down and flew over a guard shack for the gated community. I saw a Maricopa County Sheriff's Deputy waving at us. A half-dozen police cars and Suburbans were parked on the driveway or on the front lawn.

A wrought iron gate set into a cement block wall was open. We landed on the white rock driveway between two sections of grass worthy of a golf course in the middle of the desert. The water bill must be higher than my mortgage payments.

The house itself was a tan two-story Spanish-style structure with a red tile roof that would probably appraise at two million plus. The government would be the new owner as soon as the paperwork was filed. Arcand grabbed my elbow when we stepped out of the helicopter. She directed me toward a woman standing next to the nearest car. "Fletcher, this is the US Attorney for Arizona, Mary Fish."

I pegged her at around thirty-five, very young for this job, which meant she was a go-getter and on the fast track in the Department of Justice. Her smooth forehead made me wonder if she just never smiled or frowned or if she used Botox. She shook my hand with authority.

"I heard you had quite a hair-raising experience on the south rim."

I definitely wasn't taking that bait. "I don't like to see justice meted out like that. They should've had their day in court."

She rolled her eyes. "Oh, of course you'd say that for the benefit of the prosecutor." She turned to Arcand. "The primary entry team has the warrant and they should be done clearing the first floor. The secondary team is clearing the second floor, securing the rear of the house, and checking the other outbuildings on the property."

We stopped behind an entry team wearing body armor and carrying assault weapons. They chatted without urgency as they walked up the front steps, so I assumed the house had been cleared of threats. Other agents walked around the garages and various outbuildings, some carrying evidence boxes to a box truck. The action was long over before Arcand, Fish, and I came in.

A beautiful blonde was standing on the steps near the front door. She was trim, tanned, and wearing a gauzy beach cover over a skimpy white bikini that did little to cover her physical assets. I assumed no one had searched her since there wasn't enough fabric in her bikini to hide a toothpick. She wandered the house aimlessly, dabbing a tissue at her nose as she sniffled. I expected hysteria, but she acted more as if she were in shock. She held a copy of the search warrant loosely in her hand and watched the agents searching throughout the first floor of the house. She looked down at the warrant and crumpled it in her hand. She dabbed her nose with it and threw it to the floor. I heard someone calling for Arcand.

"Keep an eye on her." Arcand nodded toward the blonde as she walked away.

I knew I was excess baggage but I stood by the door trying to look professional. I tried not stare at the blonde's nearly naked body and wondered what she was thinking. The agents and police were all occupied elsewhere. The blonde seemed perplexed by the disappearance of her keepers. She cocked her head, appraised me quizzically, then broke for the stairs like a sprinter, her bare feet slapping on the marble steps. Her form was fluid, and it mesmerized me too long before I remembered I was in charge of her. I sprinted after her, feeling like a hippo chasing a gazelle.

She took the steps two at a time and didn't slow as she hit the top and turned left. My knees screamed as I tried to race up the steps. I looked around for help, but everyone was still occupied elsewhere.

I followed her into a room partway down the hall. She pulled something from a small drawer in a bedside table just as I stepped through the door. She lunged through another door. I pulled the gun from my new holster, thinking she'd either grabbed a weapon or something she could use to hurt herself. I rushed through the bathroom door just as she threw a plastic bag into the toilet and pushed the flush handle.

I lunged into the bathroom, knocking her to the floor. I reached into the swirling water with my left hand and snatched out the plastic bag spinning on the surface of the whirlpool. Her bare foot connected with my bad knee.

My leg buckled. I grunted in pain and fell to the cold tile. She pushed herself up and took a step toward the door so I reached out and slapped the butt of the Glock across the arch of her bare foot. Bone cracked. She let out a shriek that rattled the glass in the shower doors.

It probably took a full minute to pull myself to my feet and shake the toilet water from the plastic packet of white powder. The blonde rolled on the bedroom floor, clutching her foot and swearing like a trucker. She had nowhere to conceal a weapon and she wasn't trying to find one, so I slipped the pistol back into my holster and pulled a pair of handcuffs out of the leather case attached to my new uniform belt. My left knee screamed with pain. When I stood it wobbled but held my weight.

I grabbed her left arm and snapped the cuffs on her wrist. She was too quick and I was too injured to cuff her other wrist, so I dragged her by the single cuff across the carpeting to the edge of the bed. She sat on the floor with her knees pulled up to her chest, keening while she held her foot in her free hand.

"You're under arrest. You have the right . . ."

That got her attention. "No, don't do that. I can't go back to jail." She nodded to the bathroom. "Dump the coke. I'll make it worth your while."

"It's a crime to bribe a Federal officer." The adrenaline rush faded and my knee pain intensified. "Add that to assaulting a Federal officer and I imagine you'll be in prison until your roots grow out and turn gray."

She wiped her nose with her free wrist and sniffled. She closed her eyes. "God, I hate this." She took a deep breath and the smooth voice became a sharp Texas twang. "I can't go down again. What'll it take? I've got money."

I shook my head in disgust and lifted her by the arm. With her free hand she untied the small knots that held the front of the beach cover, exposing her deep cleavage and the tiny bikini top. Her breasts looked unnaturally large.

"Sorry, it won't work. C'mon, we're going downstairs to talk to the prosecutor."

"You either play along or I scream rape."

I grabbed her other hand and slapped the other cuff around her wrist. Mary Fish spoke from the doorframe. "Are you two through negotiating yet?"

The blonde moaned "Look, he ripped my clothes and raped me." She tried to put on a credible pout.

Fish looked at her with disgust. "Can it, sister. I've been watching your whole performance."

The blonde grimaced and put her head down. She pulled the bikini straps back up on her shoulders. She did a good job of it, considering her hands were cuffed. "Sonofabitch broke my foot."

I hobbled to the door. "I rescued this for you." I handed the packet of powder to Mary Fish. "She pulled it from the drawer by the bed and threw it into the toilet. She's all yours." I limped away.

I made it down the stairs by stepping down with my bad leg and letting the good one do all the work. It seemed to take half an hour to reach the first floor. By the time I reached the bottom, I was sweating from the pain.

Mary Fish and a male agent stood at the top of the stairs talking with the blonde. I watched them walk down the stairs while I sat on the massive coffee table. The male agent had to help the blonde because she couldn't put weight on her broken foot. He didn't seem to mind, probably because helping gave him a full view down the front of her bikini.

She stopped for a second as they walked past me and spoke. "You know I'll never go to jail."

I sighed. "No, I'm sure you won't. This time."

Fish walked over and stood beside me, watching them walk out the door. "She has a lot of information. The drugs are nothing compared to clearing a dozen interstate crimes. She's going to a secure treatment facility, then into hiding."

"Yes, I know. But she'll probably get herself back on the radar in a year or two."

"Probably. We'll get her then."

I shrugged. "Nothing else to be done about her right now. You know about Kokopelli?"

"You really are clueless, aren't you?" She turned and looked at me. "There were FBI agents at the Grand Canyon before your deadly chase. I thought you'd catch on when they showed up so quickly at the gift shop murder scene."

"Catch on to what?"

"You've been rooting around in the middle of an undercover operation. You almost ruined a three-year investigation by pursuing Potter's death. We tried to discreetly push you off the trail, but you're a damned bulldog."

"I don't suppose anyone in the Department of Justice ever considered filling us in on the investigation?"

"You didn't have a need to know."

"One phone call to the Park Service would've cleared this up, but you didn't trust us to keep your operation confidential." I sighed, flashing back to my FBI dealing in Minnesota and the one-way flow of information.

"Leaving the figurine was stupid. Without the Kokopelli figurines it would've been difficult to tie the string of crimes together. Sharon Paget, the blonde with the broken foot, is going to tie everything together and throw her partners under the bus. All the records are on the computer in the study and she knows the passwords and the codes."

"Agent Arcand told me about the additional bodies her people are recovering on the reservation. Do you think Paget knows where the skeletons are buried, so to speak?"

"We know she can shed light on a number of operations that were controlled from here. Some ruthless people are going to be very upset when she starts naming names and places. The US Marshals are going to have their hands full keeping her alive before and after the trials. If we'd been able to wrap up the investigation at our own pace, we probably could've had a tighter case. Your meddling rushed everything, and that damned reporter in New Mexico was absolutely unwilling to sit on her story for a week, so we had to move the raid up. Hope you're happy."

Actually, I was. If not for my work with the Navajo Nation Police, the FBI might not have found the bodies at the dig sites. The DOJ might have had to rush this case, but the result was the same, maybe better.

"Madam Prosecutor, there's one other thing that might seem rather insignificant now. Can you follow up on an antique dealer named Joe Reber in Sedona? He's selling antiquities that are being removed illegally from the reservation. I think he's the middleman who identified the dig sites to the smugglers for use in their body disposal operation. I'd like to see him busted."

She nodded. "Agent Snelling said something about that. He was skeptical about getting enough evidence for a conviction because the supply of illegal antiquities will dry up now. I'm pretty sure the guys who drove off the Grand Canyon were his suppliers. They're not digging any more holes on the reservation and they're not going to testify against him."

"He offered to sell my cousin antiquities. The folks on the reservation know his supplier was stealing them from the digs where we found the bodies. That ought to be probable cause."

"Give me a name to contact." She pulled a notepad from her purse.

"Jamie Ballard, of the Navajo Nation Police, Shiprock office."

"I'll see what I can do."

Chapter 52

The FBI insisted I go to the emergency room, where a harried ER doctor diagnosed a torn exterior collateral ligament based on the pitch of my swearing as he flexed and twisted my knee. I was close to punching him when he finally decided he'd determined every twist or bend that made my knee scream in pain. He wanted to send me off for an MRI but Arcand said something to him and suddenly I was being discharged. A physical therapist strapped me into a brace with half a dozen Velcro closures that immobilized my knee. I refused narcotics, so a nurse fed me 800 mg of Ibuprofen mixed in a cup of applesauce.

* * *

I verified my fly was zipped before hobbling up the steps to the podium at the Press Conference. Agent Arcand actually smiled when she turned and thanked me, the National Park Service, and the Navajo Nation Police for our assistance in closing the case. There were several embarrassing questions for the FBI posed by the local Phoenix media, seeded by Harold Mitchell, and based on the morning's newspaper article by Sarah Hawkins. Most of the questions related to the delay in the Potter investigation, the recordings of Potter's conversation with his partner, the bogus coroner's report, and Potter's quick cremation.

I was enjoying Arcand's discomfort as she stumbled through her answers when someone shouted from the back. "Ranger Fletcher, I'm Sarah Hawkins from *The Santa Fe Journal*. Did you injure your knee during the investigation?"

I searched the crowd for the questioner and finally made eye contact with a dark-haired woman fighting to maintain her balance in the crowd of news people. Mary Fish looked at me and shook her head almost imperceptibly. I was a bit offended she'd even think I might name her star witness.

"I aggravated an old football injury." I drew laughs from the crowd with that and Sarah gave me a thumb's up.

Within moments of the end of the press conference, all the FBI people on the platform were swamped by reporters asking for special quotes, all hoping for some slip of the tongue no other station or newspaper would have. I hobbled down the steps and walked behind the podium, relieved to be able to slip away without someone sticking a microphone in my face. I was almost away from the crowd when a bristly-haired older man wearing a crumpled suit cut me off and took my elbow. I wasn't sure what he had in mind, but his smug smile didn't seem anything I needed to be afraid of. Sarah Hawkins spotted us edging away and ran to catch up. Once we were out of earshot of the gaggle of reporters, the man shook my hand.

"I'm Harold Mitchell, from *The Phoenix Times*, and it appears you've already figured out who Sarah is. You did one hell of a job with this investigation, despite the FBI's best efforts to sideline you." Harold nodded his head toward Sarah. "I was happy to be able to pull a couple pieces together for her. All bullshit aside though, and off the record, did the FBI do anything to solve this case?"

"They flew crime scene techs up to exhume the bodies we'd found at the dig sites and I assume they've got an army of people sifting through evidence. Neither the Park Service, nor the Navajo Nation Police have the resources to handle the volume of evidence that's been found."

Sue Arcand extricated herself from the crowd and headed toward us. She wasn't at all happy I was talking to Harold Mitchell and *The Santa Fe Journal* reporter. While she was still out of earshot, Harold asked, "Did the Arcand woman contribute anything?"

I hesitated too long, searching for something politically correct I could say while not lying. By the time I had an answer, Sue Arcand was standing next to us. "All set for your return to Flagstaff?"

"Any time."

Sue put her hand out to Sarah. "I'm FBI Special Agent in Charge Arcand. I don't think we've met."

"Sarah Hawkins." Sarah shook Arcand's hand.

"Ah, the woman who reported all the inside information about our investigation. I'd love to know your sources." Arcand gave me an accusing look. I shook my head.

"The helicopter isn't available, so we arranged for a State Trooper to drive you home."

"You're not coming along? I thought you'd ride along just for the witty repartee."

Arcand gently took my elbow and steered me away from Harold and Sarah, toward the trooper who was standing next to his idling patrol car. We stopped at the open passenger door and she leaned close.

"If you ever interfere in an FBI investigation again, I'll cut off your nuts with a rusty butter knife." She was good. No one else could hear a thing and the smile visible to Sarah and Harold gave them no clue to her words.

I smiled back, equally friendly. "The next time you cut us out of an investigation, Harold will get the rest of the story of this botched FBI investigation and you'll be lucky to get a posting in the Aleutian Islands."

I used my good leg to step up into the car and pulled myself into the seat. Arcand pushed the door closed and gave me a glare that could've melted steel. Although I couldn't hear her through the glass, I wasn't bad at lip reading. "You wouldn't dare."

"Try me," I mouthed back as she stepped away from the patrol car. She stood near Harold and Sarah as we pulled away. I waved and nodded.

* * *

The townhouse lights were off when the state trooper dropped me at my door. He got out of the car and offered to help me up the sidewalk when saw how badly I limped after the two-hour drive, but my dignity demanded that I walk under my own power. El and Todd's bags were stacked inside the door. Someone had set out a pad and pen. They were apparently preparing to leave me a note for the morning, assuming I wouldn't show up in time to run them to the airport.

I scribbled a note that I'd returned late but wanted them to wake me when they left for their morning run. I stood and saw the message light blinking on the phone. I really wanted to blow it off, but it might be from Jamie in response to the message I'd left for him.

When I emptied my pockets, I remembered that I'd turned off my cellphone before the news conference. I turned it on and played back two messages. "Ranger Fletcher, this is Sarah Hawkins. I'll be back in Santa Fe by the time you get this message and will be sitting at my desk until you call. It concerns a follow-up article about Steve Potter's death." She sounded excited and I wondered how long ago she'd left the message. She rattled off the phone number.

The second message was from Brad Peck, the Walnut Canyon ranger and peer. "I heard about your football injury while I was watching the news conference. Let me know if you're not able to work tomorrow."

I dialed the number Sarah left, expecting it to roll over to voicemail. She picked up on the first ring.

"Fletcher?"

"The one and only."

"Did you see the story about Margaret Adams in this morning's papers?"

I hadn't seen anything this morning because of my early flight to Phoenix. "No. What did it say?"

"She's now under US Marshal's protection. She called me this morning and told me the guy who tried to kill her was run down by a passing pickup during the attack. He didn't have any ID, and when the Bar Harbor PD ran his prints all kinds of bells went off in the NCIC computer and they were referred to the Navy. They finally learned he'd escaped from a naval hospital psych ward."

I threw my head back. "Make those keys hum, Sarah. The guys who knocked off Potter went over the rim of the Grand Canyon yesterday, one of them was also a sailor AWOL from a Navy hospital. Sounds like you can make a few more calls and tie them together."

The keys were clicking. "No time. That's tomorrow's follow-up story I'll write it in the morning. This one's going to press right now."

"Great! I'll see it in my morning paper." When I paused, another thought came to me. "I can give you one more lead that absolutely cannot be attributed to me in any way, shape, or form. You might not get a straight answer immediately, but if you contact the Phoenix Medical Examiner, he may be able to tell you something about the illegal aliens he's been examining."

"How does that tie in with . . ."

"I've already said too much," I said, cutting her off. "If the M.E. won't talk, get Harold Mitchell in the loop. I bet he's got a buddy in the M.E.'s office."

"Okay. This is an exclusive for *The Santa Fe Journal* with a byline story going to *The Phoenix Times* and the wire services. You'll see it in *The Phoenix Times* tomorrow, and everywhere else later. I'd guess that CNN will pull the story off the wire overnight and they'll run some commentary before the networks pick it up on their morning news shows." I could hear the pride in her voice and I smiled. My old buddy Peter Ward had been a lucky shot in the dark and Sarah Hawkins turned out to be the bulldog required to pull the story together.

"Good job." I was too tired for anything more effusive.

I shed my clothes and climbed into the bed. No matter how I turned, the stupid brace twisted or jabbed into my thigh. On top of that, my mind was still racing from the events of the day and talking to Sarah made sleep impossible. After an hour of tossing and turning, I gave up and released the brace's Velcro closures. I felt the blood rush to my leg. Initially it felt good but after a few seconds the invigorated blood oxygen made the knee start to hurt. I shuffled to the medicine cabinet and pulled out a bottle of expired narcotic pain killers, left over from the torn PCL injury in St. Paul. I hoped they were still effective. I climbed back into bed and waited for the pain to subside. The last thing I remember was a heavenly flush of codeine that quickly made me drift off to sleep. The last time I looked, it was one o'clock.

The knock on my bedroom door jarred me to consciousness. My head was ready to split open. I'd forgotten codeine gave me a screaming headache. "Yeah?"

Todd stuck his head in the door. "We stayed up to watch you on the late news, but decided to go to bed since we didn't have any idea what time you'd get back."

I shoved myself up so I was resting on the pillows. "Yeah, it was after midnight, and I should've called." I rubbed my face and felt the bristle of a day's growth of beard. Millennials thought that was macho. I thought it was grubby. "Are you guys going for a run now?"

"El's already stretching. We'll see you in forty-five minutes." And he was gone.

I walked to the bathroom without the brace. My knee was stiff but the movement didn't seem to cause any additional pain. I took a couple of Motrin tablets and showered. Getting my leg in and out of the bathtub/shower was dicey at best since I had to put weight on each leg in the process. The hot water made my knee ache but it brought me back to consciousness.

Lathering and shaving had me standing too long. Rushing the shave, I took off a layer of skin along my jaw, which started seeping blood. I stuck a piece of toilet paper on it to staunch the bleeding. I hobbled out of the bathroom and into the kitchen, dressed only in boxers, and was relieved to find the coffee pot filled with hot, fresh brew. I poured a cup before my toast popped up. I buttered the toast and set it on top of a paper towel as I hobbled to the couch.

The Weather Channel predicted a chance of storms in the late afternoon and evening. I switched to CNN, hoping they'd report Sarah Hawkins' story at the top of the hour. I finished off the toast and decided to call Jill Rickowski with an update, something I'd intended to do when I got home late last night, but I just didn't have the energy after talking with Sarah Hawkins.

Jill answered her cellphone, sounding wide awake.

"Fletcher with your update."

"Hi Doug, I was wondering how the bust at Paradise Valley and the news conference had gone. From what I saw on the television, it seemed like everyone was happy and playing well together."

"Special Agent in Charge Arcand told me she'd cut my nuts off if I ever messed up an FBI investigation again. So in return I told her if she ever left the Park Service hanging in the dark again I'd give Harold Mitchell all the details of their screw-ups during this investigation and she'd be lucky to find a posting in the Aleutian Islands."

"You're the only person I've ever known who stood up to the FBI like that."

"I'm sure part of it was the pain. But I've been burned by the FBI so many times over the years I'd finally had my fill."

"Speaking of your pain, I got a call from the Phoenix ER requesting your insurance information. You must've told the hospital your injury is a worker's comp issue. I'll start the paperwork, but you'll have to fill in some of the details when you come into the office."

"Okay." I dreaded the next part of our conversation. "Um, Jill. We should discuss where I go from here."

There was a pause. "What do you mean? Did the doctor tell you how long you should be off work?"

"Not specifically. I'm supposed to keep it iced and wrapped until the swelling goes down. He suggested I see an orthopedic surgeon in the next couple of days. I'll probably need an MRI to determine the extent of the injury if the swelling doesn't resolve on its own." I hesitated.

"But I'm more interested in what you think my long-term job situation will be."

"What do you want it to be, Doug?"

My thoughts from the past two days raced through my head. "I don't know. I miss being a cop. Not so much being a cop as being busy and interacting with people. I've been kinda lonely for awhile, although I didn't realize it." I couldn't believe that I was pouring my heart out to a woman I barely knew as if she was my psychotherapist.

"Then come back. We can use you."

My heart swelled, then fell. "What about my knee? I don't know . . ."

"You can continue as our investigator, although I hope we never have another crime worthy of this type of investigation. But no matter what, I need a Law Enforcement Ranger. I also need an experienced officer to train some of the green off the kids we hire fresh out of college. I know you'd be good at that."

"I don't need charity."

"Take it easy. There's no charity involved. My budget includes at least one Law Enforcement Ranger. The young college grads would rather be walking the trails, guiding tours, and answering nature questions." She paused. "And I like having you around."

"Would I have to wear the stupid hat?"

"If you're officially representing the Park Service, yes. If you're investigating, no. Either way, you have to keep the dress uniform and hat you bought for Phoenix."

I cracked a smile. "I guess I can deal with that. I'll give you a call after I see the doctor. I'd better see how that goes first."

"Fair enough. I do need you to come out here and fill out the workers' comp forms within 48 hours of the injury. If you're not up for the drive, I can bring them to your place."

"I'm sure I can drive. I've got to deliver my cousins to the airport this morning." A light flashed in my head. "There are two things I need you to do." I heard the door open behind me as El and Todd came back from their run.

"Okay, what are they?"

"Please send a letter of commendation to the Coconino Sheriff. Sergeant Bernard Kaiser was instrumental in solving the crimes and capturing the bad guys. He's a computer jock who pulled the Kokopelli and GPS things together for me."

"No problem. I'll jazz it up a bit, make it sound really good. What's the other thing?"

"Call Shiprock and give Jamie Ballard an update and thank him. The personal thanks coming from you will mean more to him than a letter in his file."

"Consider it done."

"Great! My cousins just came in. I'll see you this afternoon."

I hung up and stared at El, who was red-faced and sweaty from the run. She was standing at the breakfast bar with her hands on her hips.

"We saw the news conference. What else happened?" El wiped the sweat from her face.

I gave them a run-down of all the developments, at least those I could share, and El was suitably impressed.

Chapter 53

Terry Mahoney left a message for his attorney while he sat on the bed in a trendy Tucson hotel room. He flipped between the news channels while lighting new cigarettes from the butts of the previous ones. He'd heard several versions of the bodies recovered from the Navajo reservation. Most of the reports had only focused on the bodies, but CNN reported Sarah Hawkins' more detailed wire service story and had a reporter broadcasting live from the steps of the Phoenix FBI office. By mid-morning, all the local stations were broadcasting from Santa Fe, shoving microphones in Sarah Hawkins' face as she repeated the wire service story, condensed to fit into sound bites used as teases for their evening news broadcast.

Mahoney jumped when his cellphone vibrated on the desk. The caller I.D. showed it was from his attorney's office. "It took you long enough."

"Terry, I got your message, but I wanted to speak to the US Attorney before I returned your call. She's been in court all morning and I was lucky she called during a break in the trial. If you give her some names, you might be able to get a life sentence in a Federal prison. If we go to court in Arizona, they'll go for the death penalty. You'll be in the Buckeye Supermax Prison on death row until your appeals run out."

"The news coverage of bodies being found in the desert is everywhere. I won't last a day if I'm put in the Arizona prison—the Mexican gangs will kill me before I'm put in a cell."

"Like I said, if you have something to offer the Feds, we might be able to stipulate that your time be served in a quiet Federal prison, somewhere far from Arizona. You might finish your life quietly reading books and watching television."

Mahoney clenched his eyes shut and considered his lawyer's words for a moment, thinking. *There has to be another option. I've got money in the bank and there are countries that don't have extradition treaties with the US. Is Algeria one? But would life there be any better than sitting in a Federal prison?*

"The problem is I really don't know enough to dangle a carrot in front of any prosecutor. All my dealings were by cellphone and I have no idea who was on the other end of the line. I talked to a woman most of the time, but there were a couple men whose voices I might recognize. The only deal we can make is to plead guilty to avoid a trial. Do you think that's enough to offer the Feds?"

"Like I said, the US Attorney will only deal if you're willing to implicate some more important people. Right now she feels you're not worth the effort it would take to put the

Federal case together and she'll let the state have you."

"I'm sure the names I have are fake. The phone numbers I called were probably untraceable disposable cellphones." Mahoney paused. "I'm screwed."

"Turn yourself in to the Feds. You won't be accidentally injured during the arrest and maybe we can find a tidbit that'll interest the US Attorney."

"Let me think about it."

"Call me as soon as you come to a decision. I can meet you on the steps of the Federal courthouse with a Deputy Marshal who will quietly cuff you, then get you processed into the system."

Mahoney set the phone down and closed his eyes. His career, his freedom, and maybe his life, were over. His name would be synonymous with the murder of Steven Potter after the recording of their conversation played in court. Even if the government agreed not to go for the death penalty, prisons were full of people who'd enjoy sticking a shiv in his heart because he'd ratted out his partners. Inmates hated rats. Mahoney buried his face in his hands.

There was a knock on the door. "Now what?" As soon as the words were out of his mouth he froze. It was too soon for the Feds to be there. He heard a key card slide through the lock and the door opened.

"How'd you get in? Who the hell *are* you?" Mahoney demanded.

A clean-cut man stepped in. "*Shhhhh.* I need five minutes," he whispered. The voice was very familiar. Mahoney searched for a connection between the face and voice. The face was angular, with a severely short, nearly military haircut. The man's linen suit was neatly pressed, his white shirt open at the collar. He moved like an athlete as he closed the door and stepped into the room.

Mahoney finally remembered where he'd heard the voice. It belonged to one of the men who'd called, offering to solve his business problems. The great news was this man was in as deep as Mahoney and now he had a face to go with the name. Better than that, maybe he had an ally!

Rich Hayes knew the moment Mahoney made the connection. He saw it in his eyes. He walked to the hotel room desk with a friendly smile on his face. The room wasn't spacious, but was upscale with beautiful cherry furniture, and carpeting so plush it engulfed your feet.

"Sit down. I figured our way out of this mess."

Mahoney sat in the swivel chair behind the small desk. "Great! Fill me in."

Hayes reached into his pocket and his hand came out holding something dark. Before Mahoney could utter a sound, Hayes leaned close and pushed the muzzle of a small pistol against Mahoney's lips. "Don't make a sound. This'll be over quickly." The gun barked once, smashing through Mahoney's teeth, leaving powder burns tattooed on his lips. The small caliber, low velocity bullet didn't have the power to exit Mahoney's skull, so it ricocheted through his brain.

As Mahoney slumped, Hayes pulled a suicide note out of his pocket. The note had been composed on Mahoney's own computer and printed on his office printer during the night. Hayes carefully pressed Mahoney's dead fingers to the paper, then threw it carelessly on the desk. Next, he took the unregistered gun and wrapped Mahoney's fingers around it in a position so as to appear he'd put the gun to his own mouth. Then he threw the gun on the desk. It skittered across the surface and onto the carpet, as if the recoil had thrown it from Mahoney's own hand. The police would be suspicious if there wasn't powder residue on his hand, so Hayes carefully wiped his gloved hand on Mahoney's. It wouldn't be a lot of powder residue, but when they checked, there would be some.

Hayes carefully stripped off the surgeon's gloves, turning them inside out as he removed them. He slipped them into a plastic bag and slid the bag into his pocket. They'd be dropped in a sidewalk wastebasket many blocks from the hotel. He smoothed the fabric of his pants and brushed at the gray powder residue on the cuff of his coat.

Hayes used his coat sleeve to open the door, then he peeked down the hallway. Seeing it was clear he used the fire exit stairway to walk up two floors. From there he took the elevator to the lobby where he fell in step with a group of business people who exited with him. As he walked away he felt pangs of regret. There were still other loose ends, but it was better to leave the last issues dangling than to wrap them all up and expose himself to the increased risk of discovery. With Mahoney and the idiots who drove off the rim of the Grand Canyon gone, the few remaining links to him would be nearly impossible to find, much less prosecute.

A self-satisfied smile crossed his face as he turned right and walked away from the hotel. The Navy had diagnosed him as a pathological killer, but he wasn't crazy, not at all.

Chapter 54

"You don't need to take us to the airport," Todd watched me limp around the kitchen pouring coffee and making toast. "I'll use my Uber app."

"No, I'm driving you to the airport, but I'll let you load the luggage." I tossed the Isuzu keys to him and he loaded the suitcases while I wolfed down the toast. El carried two overstuffed carry-on bags to the Isuzu and I wondered if they'd fit in the overhead bins.

The drive to Flagstaff airport took only fifteen minutes. Todd insisted we say goodbye at the passenger drop rather than parking and walking together to the security gate. I didn't argue. He unloaded the bags and set them on the curb while El pulled me close and kissed me on the cheek. The tears in her eyes made me mist up, too.

"Thank you so much. We had such a good time."

Todd jammed his hand in mine and shook it vigorously. "You should start a business for people seeking unusual travel experiences. This has been exciting, interesting, and bizarre."

El gave me another hug. "Call your mother," she whispered in my ear as she squeezed me.

Chapter 55

The phone was ringing when I returned to the townhouse but rolled over to voicemail before I could get the door unlocked. I hobbled to the kitchen and listened as the recorder directed the caller to leave a message. My ex-wife's voice came over the speaker. It grated against my nerve endings like fingernails on a chalkboard.

"Doug, I can't believe it! You're all over the news and the Archeology Department here is buzzing about you busting the ring looting antiquities. My department chairman remembers you. He does peer reviews for technical journals and he suggested I interview you and write an article about the theft of antiquities from the Navajo reservation for Archeology Today. He can almost guarantee it would be accepted. Call my cellphone when you get this message. I moved in with a friend and my old home phone has been disconnected."

Two contacts from my ex-wife in one week. A letter begging me to pay off her divorce lawyer and the next playing suck up to gain academic prestige. I shook my head.

I stripped off my clothes and climbed back in bed. My mind and conscience must've been clear because I dropped off to sleep immediately.

Chapter 56

It was nearly five o'clock when I woke. My knee hurt and I was famished. After surveying the variety of green and yellow healthy foods in my refrigerator I decided to rebel. I was leaning on a Safeway shopping cart trying to decide between a T-bone and a ribeye when my cellphone rang. "Fletcher."

"Ranger Doug, you promised to pay for the damage to my car," Evelyn Sampson said.

"Yes, I did." I sighed. "I'll see what forms you need to fill out and call you tomorrow."

"I did not damage the car. You damaged the car. You will fill out the forms."

"I'll take care of it tomorrow." I looked at the phone number on the screen of my smartphone. "Is this a good number to call you?"

"It's my cellphone. If I have service, and if it's charged, this is the best number."

"If I don't get through to you on this number, what number should I call?"

"Call back on this one later." I heard the dial tone before I could ask for her mailing address.

I heard a familiar voice at my shoulder. "Hi, Doug," I turned to see my boss, wearing a green tank top, tan cargo shorts, and sandals. Her arms and legs were tanned, and her muscles toned. Her hair, which I'd only seen in a ponytail, now hung loose over her shoulders.

"I've never seen you out of uniform. I hardly recognized you."

"I do get out of the office occasionally. Let me guess. You're thinking about having steak for dinner. C'mon. I'll treat you to a steak dinner. I don't feel like cooking and I haven't had a good steak in months."

"That sounds great. By the way, I just had a call from Evelyn Sampson. She needs to be reimbursed for the car damage from the chase along the rim."

Jill laughed. "You'll have to fill out a CM22 and submit it to the DSC. If you remind me tomorrow, I'll help you get started."

"I don't suppose you could handle that?"

"It has to be filled out by the person involved in the accident."

My neighbor on the prowl Sheila rounded the corner with her two boys and stopped behind my cart. Her smiling face turned inquisitive when she saw me talking with Jill. Seeing a solution to my Sheila problem, I perked up.

"Sheila, this is Jill Rickowski. Sheila is my neighbor," I explained to Jill. "Jill and I were just trying to decide where to go for a good steak. Do you have a suggestion?"

Sheila sized up Jill and shook her head. "I usually just grill mine on the patio. I guess you're on your own." She herded the boys toward the checkout line.

"Grab my arm and help me to my truck," I said to Jill. "Please. And for more reasons than one." I left the empty shopping cart behind and limped to the parking lot, making a big show of Jill's help. As I unlocked the Isuzu, Sheila walked by. "You can do better," she mouthed while Jill's back was turned.

"I'll meet you at Black Bart's," Jill said.

* * *

We ordered ribeye steaks with salads and baked potatoes. Jill handed me the wine list and I found a bottle of Argentine Malbec that was about halfway between the cheapest and most expensive red wines. When the wine came, we toasted the successful conclusion of the investigation.

"What happens now?" I asked.

"The head of the Park Service suggested your name for the Federal Law Enforcement Training Center."

"What's that?" I asked.

"FLETC is where the Feds send all their senior law enforcement people for advanced training. At the end of the course you'll have your choice of any opening in the Park Service, if that's what you'd like to do."

I swirled my wine and stared into the glass while I thought.

"My ex-wife has moved on with her life and wants to interview me for a journal article," I took a sip of wine while I considered my next words. "I've been marking time in Flagstaff and I guess it's time for me to pack up my emotional baggage and take a leap. I'm not sure where this FLETC experience will lead me, but the timing is right."

"I'll put your name on the roster in the morning." She stabbed a crouton with her fork. "I almost hate to admit this, because I'd really like to have you stay in Flagstaff, but your notoriety will open the door to almost any law enforcement post in the Park Service."

"That's interesting. Having lived in Minnesota, I can guarantee you'll never find me north of the Mason-Dixon line."

"Flagstaff is south of Minnesota," Jill said, looking hopeful as our salads were delivered.

"Flagstaff would be on the list. I like Northern Arizona and the change of seasons. But, as you said, it might be very quiet here and I don't get off handing out speeding tickets on the entrance road. The thought of having a choice of parks sounds tempting. I'll have time to do a little internet search to assess my options."

"I have a canned speech for the departure of every ranger. I'll save you the official boilerplate." She ate a piece of lettuce. "I'm no good at sentimental stuff, but I'll miss your evening briefings and . . . well, it's been nice talking to someone I considered a peer. I was pleased to have a ranger who came to me with solutions rather than problems and who doesn't treat me like their mother. You were the right person at the right time. I wish there was a bigger job here, but there just isn't. If you want more from life than Flagstaff can offer, go with my blessing."

"Thanks." Our steaks and potatoes arrived and we handed our salad plates to the waitress.

Jill asked about Sheila, and laughed as I told some of the funnier attempts to lure me in. I asked Jill if she was a native Arizonan, and she shared some of her history with me. All in all, a very pleasant end. And a very pleasant celebration of the end of a case. When we were done, we walked out to the parking lot together and I watched her back out of the parking spot. I waved as she pulled away and then pulled out after her.

I pulled in at the townhouse. I could see the bluish glow of the television dancing on Sheila's drapes. I got my mail and limped into the house. After a quick sort, I threw all the junk mail into the recycling bin and set the one bill on the breakfast bar to be dealt with later. I stared at the phone, then dialed a number imbedded in my memory. "Hi, Mom. It's Doug .

The End.

Dean Hovey books also published by BWL Publishing Inc.

Stolen Past, Doug Fletcher Book1
Washed Away, Doug Fletcher Book 2
Dead in the Water, Doug Fletcher Book 3

Dean Hovey was the 2018 Northeastern Minnesota Book Award winner for best fiction. He splits his time between Minnesota and Arizona looking for new locations, stories, and interesting characters. His travel and background in science and engineering add depth to his stories.

Made in the USA
Monee, IL
08 January 2024